国外电子信息精品著作（影印版）

Computer Aided Simulations

计算机辅助建模技术

Lanka Udawatta
Buddhika Jayasekara

科学出版社

北京

图字：01-2011-2238

内 容 简 介

　　计算机辅助建模技术一书从概念到程序上阐述了从基础系统到高级复杂系统中基于 Matlab 语言的仿真模拟技术。本书包含计算机辅助建模的设计介绍、物理系统建模仿真、计算机仿真建模实例、高级仿真以及仿真结果的方法性描述等内容，使用了大量的 Matlab 实例。本书对从事系统仿真领域的相关人员有很好的参考价值。

Lanka Udawatta, Buddhika Jayasekara
COMPUTER AIDED SIMULATIONS
Originally published by
© 2010 Narosa Publishing House，New Delhi-110 002
All Rights Reserved
Not for sale outside of China. Export or sale of this book outside China is illegal.

图书在版编目(CIP)数据

计算机辅助建模技术＝Computer Aided Simulations：英文/（印）乌达瓦塔（Lanka Udawatta）等著. —影印版. —北京：科学出版社，2011.5
（国外电子信息精品著作）
ISBN 978-7-03-030757-6

Ⅰ. 计… Ⅱ. 乌… Ⅲ. 系统建模-计算机辅助技术-英文 Ⅳ. TP391.9

中国版本图书馆 CIP 数据核字（2011）第 064652 号

责任编辑：孙伯元/责任印制：赵　博/封面设计：陈　敬

科 学 出 版 社 出版
北京东黄城根北街 16 号
邮政编码：100717
http://www.sciencep.com

源海印刷有限责任公司 印刷
科学出版社发行　各地新华书店经销

*

2011 年 5 月第 一 版　　开本：B5(720×1000)
2011 年 5 月第一次印刷　　印张：18 1/4
印数：1—2 500　　　　　　字数：400 000

定价：55.00 元
（如有印装质量问题，我社负责调换）

《国外电子信息精品著作》序

20世纪90年代以来，信息科学技术成为世界经济的中坚力量。随着经济全球化的进一步发展，以微电子、计算机、通信和网络技术为代表的信息技术，成为人类社会进步过程中发展最快、渗透性最强、应用面最广的关键技术。信息技术的发展带动了微电子、计算机、通信、网络、超导等产业的发展，促进了生命科学、新材料、能源、航空航天等高新技术产业的成长。信息产业的发展水平不仅是社会物质生产、文化进步的基本要素和必备条件，也是衡量一个国家的综合国力、国际竞争力和发展水平的重要标志。在中国，信息产业在国民经济发展中占有举足轻重的地位，成为国民经济重要支柱产业。然而，中国的信息科学支持技术发展的力度不够，信息技术还处于比较落后的水平，因此，快速发展信息科学技术成为我国迫在眉睫的大事。

要使我国的信息技术更好地发展起来，需要科学工作者和工程技术人员付出艰辛的努力。此外，我们要从客观上为科学工作者和工程技术人员创造更有利于发展的环境，加强对信息技术的支持与投资力度，其中也包括与信息技术相关的图书出版工作。

从出版的角度考虑，除了较好较快地出版具有自主知识产权的成果外，引进国外的优秀出版物是大有裨益的。洋为中用，将国外的优秀著作引进到国内，促进最新的科技成就迅速转化为我们自己的智力成果，无疑是值得高度重视的。科学出版社引进一批国外知名出版社的优秀著作，使我国从事信息技术的广大科学工作者和工程技术人员能以较低的价格购买，对于推动我国信息技术领域的科研与教学是十分有益的事。

此次科学出版社在广泛征求专家意见的基础上，经过反复论证、仔细遴选，共引进了接近30本外版书，大体上可以分为两类，第一类是基础理论著作，第二类是工程应用方面的著作。所有的著作都涉及信息领域的最新成果，大多数是2005年后出版的，力求"层次高、内容新、参考性强"。在内容和形式上都体现了科学出版社一贯奉行的严谨作风。

当然,这批书只能涵盖信息科学技术的一部分,所以这项工作还应该继续下去。对于一些读者面较广、观点新颖、国内缺乏的好书还应该翻译成中文出版,这有利于知识更好更快地传播。同时,我也希望广大读者提出好的建议,以改进和完善丛书的出版工作。

总之,我对科学出版社引进外版书这一举措表示热烈的支持,并盼望这一工作取得更大的成绩。

中国科学院院士
中国工程院院士
2006 年 12 月

Preface

The purpose of this book is to introduce basic concepts of computer simulations and provide necessary knowledge on simulation developments. This book is primarily intended to be used in undergraduate courses in the universities, especially electrical engineering, electronics engineering, communication engineering, computer engineering, and mechanical engineering students who need the knowledge on computer simulations. In addition, given the comprehensive coverage and large number of detailed examples, this book should be useful as a primary reference to electrical, electronic and mechanical graduate students and professionals wishing to start research projects focusing on simulations. On the other hand, research scientist who would like to switch on to advanced simulations, starting from basic level simulations, would also reap benefits from this book.

Starting from introduction to system simulations in Chapter 1, it will cover the basic concepts on systems and system modeling. Chapter 2 will cover the details of software & hardware for your own simulations and some computing basics. You will get the background preparation on data visualization through Chapter 3. Chapter 4 and Chapter 5 will introduce different systems and system modeling principles respectively. System integration with different components will be discussed in Chapter 6. While advanced simulations and modeling of complex systems with few examples will cover in Chapter 7 and Chapter 8 respectively. Chapter 9 will bring one example focusing on an application. Chapter 10 presents some examples for getting experience on basic simulations.

Lanka Udawatta
Buddhika Jayasekara

Contents

8. Modeling of Complex Systems — 196

9. Selecting The Right Software Tool — 221

10. Exercises 249

Chapter 1

Introduction to System Simulations

Computer Aided Simulation (CAS) is the discipline of designing a model of an actual or theoretical system and executing that model on a digital computer for analyzing its behavior.

1.1 INTRODUCTION

1.1.1 Model Design

In today's highly competitive environment, different systems are being developed by engineers and scientists at a faster growth rate. These systems are catering various groups in the society at different levels. Technically, we can define the term system as "Pre-defined assembly of resources (A collection of personnel, equipment, or methods) in order to accomplish a set of specific functions or goals, via executing a clearly defined set of instructions". In certain situations, the system under consideration may consist of several sub-systems, which can be analyzed independently or as a single entity, presently referring as "system of systems". After the initial investigation, the first step is to specify a model of a given system mathematically, which will help us to understand and analyze the system behavior. To simulate something physical, we will first need to create this mathematical model, which represents that physical system. In fact, theoretically derived models or empirical models are also analyzed and simulated in certain situations. Model may consist of several variables which are going to decide the system behavior.

Models can take many forms including declarative, functional, constraint, spatial or multi-model. For an example, these mathematical models can be derived using Newton's laws of motion, if the system consists of moving masses and so on. If the system is an electrical one, you may apply Kirchhoff's circuit laws in obtaining a mathematical model. Most of the times, this will lead to a set of differential equations (DE) and these differential equations can be further deduced to different forms as required by the designer. Further more, these dynamic representations of systems attempt to capture and describe the behavior of the system over time under different operating conditions. Finally, the dynamic model consists of system variables and other parameters to be investigated. However, there may be situations where it is difficult to derive a model, which represents the actual behavior of the system.

Theoretical models are derived from the first principles whereas empirical models are derived using observations of system variables. Mathematical models can be also synthesized for certain systems based on measured data. Fundamentally, you should have a scientific background to develop these models, may be in the fields of engineering, medicine, physics, biology, chemistry, finance, etc. The background information will help you to define the variables, identify the constraints, approximate the values, estimate the time frame of interest and make the necessary assumptions [1]-[3].

1.1.2 Model Execution

Once the mathematical model has been developed, you are supposed to execute the model on a digital computer. Here, you need to create a computer program, which steps through the time while updating the state and event variables in your mathematical model. Furthermore, now-a-days it is a practice that you store the output on computer memory or visualize it on the computer screen. In any case, you need some insight measure in order to have a proper analysis of the system.

As the first step, you can develop a flow chart or an algorithm that gives you an idea of the data flow of the system through the time line. In large programs, you have to manage the computer memory where you may go for dynamic memory allocations. For an example, if you are going to use a genetic algorithm (GA) program for a large dynamic system, it is necessary to optimize the memory consumption through a dynamic memory allocation. Once you completed the coding; now you are ready to execute your program and get the results. The coding can be done by a conventional computer language like C or C++. For engineering and scientific research works, MATLAB (MATrix LABoratory) provides a better environment with powerful matrix manipulating capabilities [5],[6]. In fact present day scientific calculations need the capability of manipulating matrices when it comes to higher order system analysis. Nevertheless, FORTRAN, Visual Basic, Pascal, Pro-engineer, Autocad, PSCad or any scientific computer software may help you to execute your codes of the algorithm of that particular model. In this book, Matlab codes are used in order to illustrate most of the examples. However, you are free to use any computer language or software in executing your algorithm.

During the development time of the computer simulations, researcher should plan for better approaches where it brings several outcomes simultaneously that make your computer simulation a great success. For an example, program might provide data storing, data visualizing, performance analyzing, mathematical computing, and other aspects of the simulation. This will save your time in many ways. When you need graphs or numerical results of the computer simulation for writing your reports, just running your program can bring all these. In fact, you may write several programs and get the same thing done consuming more time.

In general, dynamic systems are complex and nonlinear. Systems are simplified under certain assumptions in order to have flexible computer models. In fact, we have to make sure that the desired features of the original system remains unchanged in the synthesized computer model. For an example, the sampling time for a computing model can be selected at different rates; data handling capability of the program can be greatly affected according to the selection. On the other hand, in an electrical or electronic circuit simulation, you might change the values of the devices, which are under the consideration.

1.1.3 Model Analysis through Outputs

After executing your program, you will obtain certain results under different conditions or under different assumptions. As an example, if you can graphically visualize the state variables of a dynamic system through the time line, you are in a position to comment on the stability of it. Sometimes, it is necessary that the model output is to be visualized in a 3D computer animation. Once the simulation is completed under a selected software environment, in order to analyze the output further, you might switch on to a completely different software environment. The output data can be stored in data files, which can be used later.

The system response describes how the output changes over time. For an example, when it comes to systems control, by looking at the output, we might be able to infer additional properties of the system. Typically, we will observe the settling time, transient stability, maximum overshoot, steady-state error and so on. Once you created the simulation model you are in a position to do all these sensitivity analysis or changes without putting much effort compared to the original work. A good computer simulation can bring all these aspects through an innovative thinking. However, there are several discussions in the incoming chapters on developing background knowledge for a better simulation in order to obtain the desired outputs.

Assume that you want to develop a forecasting model using some past data. There are various techniques and methodologies that can be employed in order to derive a forecasting model. As examples, linear, quadratic or double exponential models can be used in order to model your past data set. As the first step, you may select a simple linear forecasting model which might fit to the given data set and desired coefficients are computed. In fact, it will be convenient if you visualize the model graphically. Furthermore, you can visualize the predicted outputs for different time frames which will give you an overall idea of the future behavior. In the same time, programmer can get the exact numerical values of the predictions through that model as outputs. In this particular example, you can compute the modeling error or fitting accuracy that will give you an idea about the model. These three outputs will give you an insight to the model and you may then decide whether it is necessary to develop another model or not for that data set. Once you develop your program in a systematic manner as explained in the above sub-section, your program has the flexibility of including all other possible models. In the same program, you can visualize different models and get the predicted values. Moreover, you can compare accuracy of fitting for these different models and select the best one. When you design the program for these outputs for different models it leads to a better computer simulation.

In certain situations, it may be difficult to obtain all these aspects through a single program. You might need to run software and switch on to another completely different program in order to complete your simulation. Finally, you should be able to analyze your model through this computer simulation and obtain the desired results of the model. For different systems, you have to find the desired software or programming environment in order to obtain the outputs. For an example, if you analyze a biological system that may require a completely different simulation environment compared to an engineering simulation. In these situations, it may require different interfacing or linking to other devices and programs where you run your main simulation program for getting the final outputs of the model.

1.2 DYNAMIC SYSTEM MODELING

Physical systems that we find in our day-to-day life have different dynamic features and dynamic models according to the application. These systems are designed and optimized after analyzing their dynamic models. Figure 1.1 shows four different physical systems and they have different dynamic properties or dynamic models. Most physical systems available are continuous and they can be described using differential equations (DE). On the other hand, discrete systems can be described using difference equations dealing with discrete time signals. In fact, some continuous systems are transformed into discrete systems according to the requirement. As an example, if we consider the electric motor in Figure 1.1(A), for a given input power amount there will be a corresponding output, i.e., the torque generated on the motor shaft.

How to control the angular speed and the desired torque can be investigated using a dynamic model. Once you develop the dynamic model, modifications and different analysis can be easily done through a computer simulation.

The mobile robot in Figure 1.1(B) is a test bed for experimenting different research and development works on mobile platforms. Two independently controllable wheels are located on right-hand and left-hand sides and it is further supported by another two small wheels. To control a mobile robot Position, a dynamic model is necessary and it can be used to employ different control algorithms. This mobile robot needs different navigation algorithms for different situations [4]. These algorithms can be tested in simulation environments before going into the actual practice. In some cases, artificial intelligence concepts are employed in order to have the desired behaviors of the robot whereas in some cases classical control theory based mathematical models are used.

Up thrust generated through gas firing of a hot air balloon is the main controlling force in the dynamic system in Figure 1.1(C). The amount of gas required to fire in a given time depends the factors like number of people carried, wind speed, surface of the balloon, and outside air temperature. Including all these parameters, you can have a dynamic model for the hot air balloon.

In recent years, enormous progress has been made in the development of wind turbines for electricity generation ranging from small scale wind turbines to large scale turbines. Wind power is the conversion of wind energy into more useful forms, usually electricity using wind turbines. Wind wane measures wind direction and communicates with the yaw drive to orient the wind turbine with respect to the wind direction. Wind turbine in Figure 1.1(D) converts energy available in the wind into electrical energy. The power output depends on the wind velocity and rotor swept area. These parameters can be modeled to a dynamic system and analyzed. The power in wind is proportional to the third power of the momentary wind speed and the dynamic model consists of several other parameters. However, once you developed the model you can simulate various scenarios on wind energy, varying from economic analysis to technical analysis.

A. Electric motor

B. Mobile robot

C. Hot air balloon

D. Wind turbine

Figure 1.1: Different Physical Systems

Above explained four systems are examples for different dynamic systems and let us try to understand the basic modeling concepts behind them in the next few chapters. You can use your engineering, scientific, and general knowledge in developing these models. In particularly, theoretical background on Newton's laws of motion, Kirchhoff's circuit laws, Maxwell equations, laws of thermodynamics, differential equations, numerical methods, Euler and Lagrangian equations, kinematics and dynamics, nonlinear systems, and transformation techniques might be useful in modeling physical systems. In certain situations, it is necessary to start with a very basic model and develop an advanced version when you progress. This is basically due to the lack of information or knowledge about the system under investigation at the initial stage. After several experiments or simulations, you are in a position to validate the developed model and test the accuracy of it. In fact one can make a case that greater dependence on pure mathematical approach has sometimes led to neglect of other approaches which might give you a better solution. There is little communication between people in quantitative fields and those in other fields. However, greater cooperation between different fields likes engineering and medicine will lead to a better know-how in system modeling [7]-[10].

1.2.1 Classification of Dynamic Systems

Considering inherent properties and characteristics, different systems or different dynamic models are grouped into several classes. Mathematical techniques are identified and applied to these classes of problems [2]. There are various ways of categorizing dynamic systems. In particular, we define them according to five characteristics as below:

1. Linear or Nonlinear
2. Constant or Variable Coefficients
3. Forced or Unforced
4. Lumped or Distributed Parameter
5. Deterministic or Stochastic

1. Linear or Nonlinear Systems

In linear systems, dependent variables and their derivatives are risen only to the first power (products of dependent variables are not allowed). When it comes to nonlinear systems, the system must be described by dependent variables or their derivatives risen to powers other than the first. Systems, which contain products of dependent variables and/or derivatives, are also nonlinear. Moreover, if you analyze these systems further, you will observe the inherent features of that particular system.

2. Constant or Variable Coefficients

In constant coefficient systems, coefficients are not functions of the independent variables whereas in variable coefficient systems coefficients are functions of the independent variables.

3. Forced or Unforced

Forced systems that contain non-homogeneous terms (*i.e.*, terms that do not contain the dependent variable) are coming under this category. In an unforced system, it is described by homogeneous equations (*i.e.*, all terms contain the dependent variable). In practice, to control a physical system, it is needed to have a controlled force or an input in order to keep the system states at desired conditions.

4. Lumped or Distributed Parameter

Lumped parameter system can be described with ordinary difference or differential equations with time as the independent variable. In distributed parameter systems, it is described by partial differential equations with space and time dependence.

5. Deterministic or Stochastic

Deterministic systems are driven by a forcing function which can be described explicitly (*i.e.,* step or sinusoidal changes etc.). For stochastic systems, forcing function is random and a probabilistic treatment is required. Table 1.1 shows a few examples for different dynamic models of the system under investigation. For an example, in chaotic systems you will see both random and deterministic features.

Table 1.1: Mathematical Examples for Different Physical Systems

Classification of System	Example
Linear, constant coefficient, unforced, lumped	$\dfrac{dx(t)}{dt} = 10x(t)$
Nonlinear, constant coefficient, unforced, lumped	$\dfrac{dx(t)}{dt} = 10x(t) - 12x^3(t)$
Linear, constant coefficient, forced, lumped	$\dfrac{dx(t)}{dt} = 12x(t) - 18t$
Nonlinear, variable coefficient, forced, lumped	$\dfrac{dx(t)}{dt} = [12 + 6t - 8t^3]x(t) + 5t$
Nonlinear, constant coefficient, forced, lumped	$\dfrac{dx(t)}{dt} = 10x(t) + \exp[-x(t)^2] + 5P(t)$
Linear, constant coefficient, unforced, distributed	$\dfrac{\partial x(z,t)}{\partial t} = 15\dfrac{\partial^2 x(z,t)}{\partial^2 z} + 12x(z,t)$
Linear, constant coefficient, unforced, lumped	$\dfrac{dx(t)}{dt} + \dfrac{dy(t)}{dt} = 10x(t) + 15y(t)$

In the fourth chapter, we will investigate a few examples and analyze their dynamic features in various ways in order to observe the characteristics. These systems in Table 1.1 are continuous-time systems (CS) and we have discrete-time systems (DS) as well. Note here that sometimes we transform continuous-time systems into discrete-time systems for the analysis. Moreover, there are various techniques of analyzing above systems. For an example, nonlinear systems will be linearized around an equilibrium point in order to analyze whereas variable coefficient systems will be treated numerically. Distributed parameter systems will be converted to lumped systems (via finite difference methods, thermal network models, etc.), and the study of stochastic systems will be treated as a separate topic. Furthermore, some systems are defined under different sub-classes and analyzed separately. Let us take an attractor where an attractor is defined as the smallest unit, which cannot be itself decomposed into two or more attractors with distinct basins of attraction [2], [3].

A continuous-time physical system can be defined as

$$\dot{x} = f(x,t) \tag{1.1}$$

Where, x is the state vector and $f(x,t)$ is the n–dimensional vector whose elements are functions of $x_1, x_2, ... x_n$ and t.

Similarly, discrete-time system can be defined as

$$x(t+1) = f(x).$$

We assume that the system of equation has a unique solution starting at the given initial condition. We shall denote the solution of equation as

$$\phi(t; x_0, t_0) \tag{1.2}$$

Here, $x = x_0$ at $t = t_0$ and t is the observed time over a given period. Equilibrium states are defined for the above system as given below:

$$f(x_e, t) = 0 \tag{1.3}$$

From a given set of linear differential equations, with an input vector u, linear continuous-time systems can be represented in the form of

$$\dot{x}(t) = Ax(t) + Bu(t)$$
$$y(t) = Cx(t) + Du(t) \tag{1.4}$$

Where, $x \in \mathfrak{R}^n$ and $u \in \mathfrak{R}^m$.

Physical systems that you are going to analyze may or may not consist of an input vector. You can introduce an input vector to the system under investigation whereas some may not need. And also you have to fine-tune or control it.

y = Output Vector
u = Input Vector
A = System Matrix
B = Input Matrix
C = Output Matrix
D = Feedforward Matrix

Similarly, a linear discrete system can be represented in the form of

$$
\begin{aligned}
x(k+1) &= Ax(k)+Bu(k)\\
y(k+1) &= Cx(k)+Du(k)
\end{aligned}
\tag{1.5}
$$

Let us take the systems which must be described by dependent variables or their derivatives risen to powers other than the first. Note here that some systems may contain nonlinear terms like sine or cosine and still they can be expressed in terms of higher order terms (risen to powers other than the first). Nonlinear systems will be linearized around some equilibrium points or the full nonlinear behavior will be modeled with numerical methods [3]. Nonlinear system can be represented with two functions, F and G as below:

$$
\begin{aligned}
\dot{x}_1 &= F_1(x)+G_1(u)\\
\dot{x}_2 &= F_2(x)+G_2(u)\\
&\;\;\vdots\\
\dot{x}_n &= F_n(x)+G_n(u)
\end{aligned}
\tag{1.6}
$$

Equilibrium points of the continuous system can be obtained as below:

$$
\varepsilon = \left\{ (x,u)\in \Re^{n+m}\,\middle|\, f(\overline{x},\overline{u})=0 \right\}
\tag{1.7}
$$

Equilibrium points of the discrete system can be obtained as below:

$$
\varepsilon = \left\{ (x,u)\in \Re^{n+m}\,\middle|\, \overline{x}=f(\overline{x},\overline{u}) \right\}
\tag{1.8}
$$

Linearization of the nonlinear system around an equilibrium point can be obtained using the Jacobian matrix as below:

$$
\dot{x} = \frac{\partial F}{\partial x}x + \frac{\partial G}{\partial u}u
\tag{1.9}
$$

Where the terms $\dfrac{\partial F}{\partial x}$ and $\dfrac{\partial G}{\partial u}$ can be computed using the following expression:

$$
\frac{\partial F}{\partial x} =
\begin{pmatrix}
\dfrac{\partial F_1}{\partial x_1} & \dfrac{\partial F_1}{\partial x_2} & \cdots & \dfrac{\partial F_1}{\partial x_{n-1}} & \dfrac{\partial F_1}{\partial x_n}\\[2ex]
\dfrac{\partial F_2}{\partial x_1} & \dfrac{\partial F_2}{\partial x_2} & \cdots & \dfrac{\partial F_2}{\partial x_{n-1}} & \dfrac{\partial F_2}{\partial x_n}\\[2ex]
\vdots & \vdots & \ddots & \vdots & \vdots\\[2ex]
\dfrac{\partial F_{n-1}}{\partial x_1} & \dfrac{\partial F_{n-1}}{\partial x_2} & \cdots & \dfrac{\partial F_{n-1}}{\partial x_{n-1}} & \dfrac{\partial F_{n-1}}{\partial x_n}\\[2ex]
\dfrac{\partial F_n}{\partial x_1} & \dfrac{\partial F_n}{\partial x_2} & \cdots & \dfrac{\partial F_n}{\partial x_{n-1}} & \dfrac{\partial F_n}{\partial x_n}
\end{pmatrix}
\tag{1.10}
$$

$$\frac{\partial G}{\partial u} = \begin{pmatrix} \dfrac{\partial G_1}{\partial u_1} & \dfrac{\partial G_1}{\partial u_2} & \cdots & \dfrac{\partial G_1}{\partial u_{m-1}} & \dfrac{\partial G_1}{\partial u_m} \\ \dfrac{\partial G_2}{\partial u_1} & \dfrac{\partial G_2}{\partial u_2} & \cdots & \dfrac{\partial G_2}{\partial u_{m-1}} & \dfrac{\partial G_2}{\partial u_m} \\ \vdots & \vdots & \ddots & \vdots & \vdots \\ \dfrac{\partial G_{n-1}}{\partial u_1} & \dfrac{\partial G_{n-1}}{\partial u_2} & \cdots & \dfrac{\partial G_{n-1}}{\partial u_{m-1}} & \dfrac{\partial G_{n-1}}{\partial u_m} \\ \dfrac{\partial G_n}{\partial u_1} & \dfrac{\partial G_n}{\partial u_2} & \cdots & \dfrac{\partial G_n}{\partial u_{m-1}} & \dfrac{\partial G_n}{\partial u_m} \end{pmatrix}.$$

Neglecting higher order terms, we obtain a linearized model around any arbitrary point (x_0, u_0) as follows:

$$\dot{x} = A_0(x - x_0) + B_0(u - u_0) + F(x_0, u_0)$$

$$x(t+1) = A_0(x - x_0) + B_0(u - u_0) + F(x_0, u_0)$$

(1.11)

We can obtain the above two terms A and B as follows:

$$A_0 = \frac{\partial F}{\partial x}(x_0, u_0); \quad B_0 = \frac{\partial F}{\partial u}(x_0, u_0)$$

(1.12)

Equilibrium points of the system can be defined as

$$\dot{x} = A_0 x + B_0 u + d_0$$

$$x(t+1) = A_0 x + B_0 u + d_0$$

(1.13)

Where

$$d_0 = F(x_0, u_0) - A_0 x_0 - B_0 u_0$$

(1.14)

In fact, we know that nonlinear dynamic continuous-time systems (CS) can be described by nonlinear differential equations whereas difference equations for discrete-time systems (DS).

1.3 BASIC SYSTEM ELEMENTS

Understanding of basic engineering and science practices with fundamentals will lay the foundation to system development. In this section, we will look into the basic elements that are commonly used in system modeling. Electrical, mechanical, chemical, and other elements are acting as the basic building blocks for developing various systems [10]-[15]. When you want to model these systems it is necessary to understand the fundamentals behind these elements. For an example, if you consider a temperature variation of a system, you need to study the fundamentals on thermodynamics.

1.3.1 Elements in Electrical Systems

First, we introduce the basic electrical elements, which are going to be the building blocks of electrical circuits. Electrical and electronics systems that you find in many simulations will consist of these basic elements.

1.3.2 Resistor

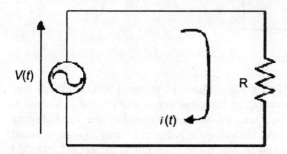

Figure 1.2: Current through a Resistor

We apply a voltage across a resistor as shown Figure 1.2. The voltage across the resistor is changing with time, so the current through the resistor (R) must also be time varying. The voltage and the current are in phase. Transfer of electrical energy is associated with the motion of charges. Due to this motion, there will be an electric current and it produces heat [11]. Note that as the voltage changes sign, the current changes direction. They peak at the same time and see the equations below:

$$v(t) = Ri(t) \tag{1.15}$$

$$i(t) = \frac{1}{R}v(t) \tag{1.16}$$

$$v(t) = R\frac{dq(t)}{dt} \tag{1.17}$$

When you apply a voltage across a resistor, power dissipation (P) of the heating element can be proved as v^2 / R.

$$p = vi = i^2 R = \frac{v^2}{R} \tag{1.18}$$

Where $v(t)$, $i(t)$, and $q(t)$ represent voltage, current and charge respectively. Once you understand the basic concepts behind computer simulations, you will easily employ all these concepts in developing complex systems.

1.3.3 Capacitor

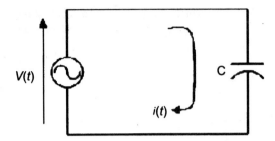

Figure 1.3: Current through a Capacitor

Here, a voltage is applied across the capacitor shown in Figure 1.3. The voltage lags behind the current by 90°. The "resistance" of the capacitor (C) to current is known as capacitive reactance. This two terminal energy storage device has the capability of charging and discharging of electrons. As the voltage is reduced to zero all energy stored in the capacitor is returned to the circuit in which the capacitor is connected (external circuit).

$$v(t) = \frac{1}{C} \int_0^t i(t)dt \qquad (1.19)$$

$$i(t) = C\frac{dv(t)}{dt} \qquad (1.20)$$

$$v(t) = \frac{1}{C}q(t) \qquad (1.21)$$

Where $v(t)$, $i(t)$ and $q(t)$ represent voltage, current and charge respectively.

If we consider the power P and the stored energy E in the two plates, following relationship can be obtained based on above equations,

$$E = \int Pdt = C\int v\frac{dv}{dt} = \frac{1}{2}Cv^2 \qquad (1.22)$$

1.3.4 Inductor

In an inductor, energy is stored in the magnetic field. The inductor in Figure 1.4 changes its magnetic field according to the current across the inductive element. For an example, if you model an electrical transformer starting from the first principles you will introduce these inductive elements into the system with the resistive elements that we already discussed in the earlier sub-section.

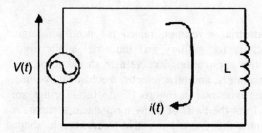

Figure 1.4: Current through an Inductor

The "resistance" of the inductor to current in the circuit is known as inductive reactance. The voltage leads the current by 90°. Here, $v(t)$, $i(t)$ and $q(t)$ represent voltage, current and charge respectively. L is the inductance. The voltage and current relationship can be obtained as below:

$$v(t) = L\frac{di(t)}{dt} \tag{1.23}$$

$$i(t) = \frac{1}{L}\int_0^t v(t)dt \tag{1.24}$$

$$v(t) = L\frac{d^2q(t)}{dt^2} \tag{1.25}$$

Note here that current through the inductor cannot change instantaneously. The energy stored in an inductor depends upon the instantaneous current and independent of the history of the current [1]. If we consider the power P and the stored energy (E) in the inductor, following relationship can be obtained based on above equations,

$$E = \int Pdt = L\int idi = \frac{1}{2}Li^2 \tag{1.26}$$

1.4 ELEMENTS IN MECHANICAL SYSTEMS

Dynamics is a branch of mechanics that deals with forces and their relationship to the motion. However, sometimes it also deals with equilibrium of bodies or branch of physical science and subdivision of mechanics that is concerned with the motion of material objects in relation to the physical factors that affect them: force, mass, momentum, energy etc. When it comes to dynamics, it always depends on the systems kinematics. If you are planning to do a simulation, it can be purely kinematics or purely dynamics based. Dynamic simulators require the knowledge of the dynamic equations and their parameters. In order to implement the simulation equations, the geometrical and inertial parameters of the dynamic equations must be known [13]-[15].

1.4.1 Springs

The eighteenth century dawn of the industrial revolution raised the need for large, accurate, and inexpensive springs, especially for military and industrial applications. Mechanical springs can be found in various applications like vehicle shock absorbers, spring valves, locking devices, shock transmitters, and other electro-mechanical systems. Schematic diagram of a mechanical spring is shown in Figure 1.5. In fact, springs are fundamental mechanical components that form the basis of many mechanical systems. A spring can be defined to be an elastic member that exerts a resistive force when its shape is changed. Most springs are assumed to be linear and obey the Hooke's Law, at least to a defined range. Moreover, for a non-linear spring, the resisting force is not linearly proportional to its displacement.

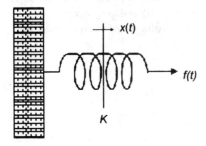

Figure 1.5: Mechanical Spring

If we define the spring constant as K, the force-velocity relationship of a mechanical spring can be obtained as below:

$$f(t) = K \int_0^t v(\tau) d\tau \tag{1.27}$$

The force $f(t)$ on the spring moves the system in the direction of X causing the displacement x.

Force-displacement relationship is given by the following equation

$$f(t) = Kx(t) \tag{1.28}$$

Here, the impedance or the spring constant represents K and it depends on the property of that particular spring used. If space is limited, such as with automotive valve springs, square cross section springs can be employed. If space is extremely limited and the load is high, Belleville washer springs might be the option.

1.4.2 Viscous Damper

Damping elements are generally used to reduce the amplitude of an oscillation in an oscillatory system. A dashpot is a mechanical device which is having damping properties in order to resist the motion via viscous friction. Consider the viscous damper in Figure 1.6.

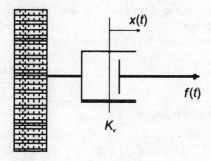

Figure 1.6: Viscous Damper

Let us define the viscous damping constant as K_v. The force-velocity relationship of a viscous damping system can be obtained as below:

$$f(t) = K_v v(t) \qquad (1.29)$$

Force-displacement relationship is given by the following equation,

$$f(t) = K_v \frac{dx(t)}{dt} \qquad (1.30)$$

Here, the impedance or the viscous damping constant is denoted by K_v and it depends on the property of that particular damping medium used.

Note that this basic damping concept will apply under different situations in practical situations. For an example, if you model a robot manipulator you will find different damping coefficients. In fact, the concept behind this modeling is to include a kind of resistive force against the moving object.

1.4.3 Mass

Mass is a fundamental concept which measures the amount of matter in the object. All mechanical quantities can be defined in terms of mass, length, and time which are having the base units. Consider the mass in Figure 1.7 experiencing a force f. Here, you will apply Newton's Second Law of motion, which is the most powerful of Newton's three Laws as it allows us to calculate dynamics quantitatively, i.e., how the velocities change when forces are applied.

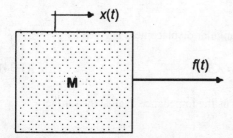

Figure 1.7: Linear Force on a Mass

If you apply Newton's Second Law of motion in the direction of X the force will results the displacement x in the direction of X as below:

$$f(t) = M \frac{d^2 x(t)}{dt^2} \tag{1.31}$$

Force-velocity relationship is given by the following equation,

$$f(t) = M \frac{dv(t)}{dt} \tag{1.32}$$

Assume that the masses slide on a frictionless surface and no change in the weight of the system, *i.e.*, M is a constant. In certain modeling, you will have masses that will vary with time. For an example, in a rocket, mass may vary with time due to the consumption of fuel by the rocket itself. In most of the application, you will have masses connected to other elements like springs, cams, dampers, gear trains and so on.

1.4.4 Torque-Angular Velocity on a Spring

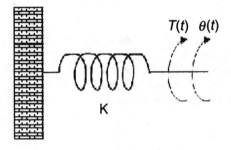

Figure 1.8: Torque on a Spring

If you apply the law of motion in the direction of θ the torque will result the angular velocity ω in the direction of θ (see Figure 1.8). Torque-angular velocity can be obtained as below:

$$T(t) = K \int_0^t \omega(\tau) d\tau \tag{1.33}$$

The relationship between the torque and the angular displacement is given by

$$T(t) = K\theta(t) \tag{1.34}$$

Note here that the constant K will be referred as the impedance against the torque.

1.4.5 Viscous Damper

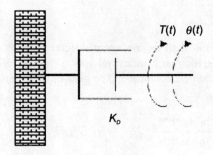

Figure 1.9: Viscous Damper

A torque-angular velocity relationship in a viscous medium is given by the following equation (see Figure 1.9):

$$T(t) = K_D \omega(t) \tag{1.35}$$

Torque and angular displacement relationship is given by the following equation,

$$T(t) = K_D \frac{d\theta(t)}{dt} \tag{1.36}$$

Note here that the constant K_D will be referred as the impedance against the torque in the viscous environment.

1.4.6 Inertia

Inertia of a rotating body can be described as the resistance to change its state around a given axis when it experiences a torque. Consider Figure 1.10 and the mass is rotating when the torque is applied.

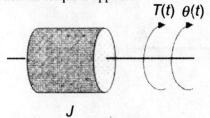

Figure 1.10: Inertia Effect on a Rotating Mass

Torque-angular velocity relationship is given by the following:

$$T(t) = J \frac{d\omega(t)}{dt} \tag{1.37}$$

The relationship between the torque and the angular displacement is given by

$$T(t) = J \frac{d^2\theta}{dt^2} \tag{1.38}$$

1.4.7 Gear Train

Gear trains are used in transferring power from one shaft to another at different speeds. For an example, common electric drive systems for many industrial robots consist of electrical motors and gearboxes in order to provide desired torque. The gear ratio η can be defined as below (refer Figure 1.11):

$$\eta = \frac{\text{Number of teeth in shaft } N_2}{\text{Number of teeth in shaft } N_1}$$

Note here that for a speed reduction application the value η is greater than 1 and you are transferring power from gear 1 to gear 2.

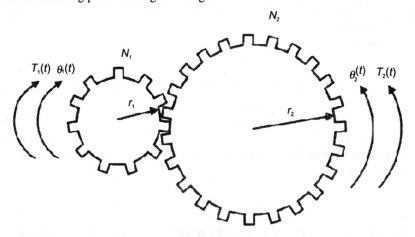

Figure 1.11: Gear Train

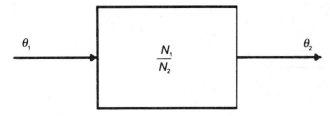

Figure 1.12: Input-output in Terms of Angle

$$\theta_2 = \frac{N_1}{N_2} \theta_1 \tag{1.39}$$

Figure 1.12 shows the relationship between the gear ratio and the input-output in terms of angle.

Moreover, Figure 1.13 shows the relationship between the gear ratio and the input-output in terms of torque.

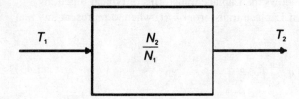

Figure 1.13: Input-output in Terms of Torque

$$T_2 = \frac{N_1}{N_2} T_1 \tag{1.40}$$

1.5 LAPLACE TRANSFORM

The Laplace transform is a standard tool associated with the analysis of signals, models, and control systems. The Laplace transform of $f(t)$ can be defined as follows:

$$F(S) = L\{f(t)\} = \int_0^\infty f(t)e^{-St}\,dt \tag{1.41}$$

Where $S = \sigma + j\omega$ and S is the complex frequency variable.

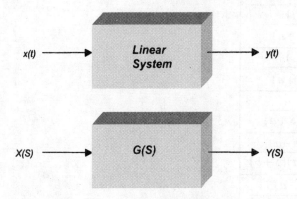

Figure 1.14: Transfer Function of a System

If we can obtain the system transfer function $G(S)$ of a given system, input-output relationship can be written as follows:

$$Y(S) = G(S)X(S) \tag{1.42}$$

Note here that the input $X(S)$ can be obtained through a Laplace transform for a given $x(t)$. Once you get the $Y(S)$ as shown in (1.42) you can get the $y(t)$ through the inverse Laplace transform. This is one of the techniques available to simulate the basic systems explained in this chapter. Table 1.2 shows the Laplace transforms of typical functions.

The condition for the existence of Laplace transform of $f(t)$ when σ represent any real number is given by

$$\int_0^\infty |f(t)| e^{-\sigma t} dt < \infty \tag{1.43}$$

Table 1.3 shows the properties of Laplace transform when we want to simplify the derivations or expressions.

Table 1.2: Laplace Transforms

f(t)	F(S)
$\delta(t)$	1
$u_s(t)$	$\dfrac{1}{S}$
t	$\dfrac{1}{S^2}$
t^n	$\dfrac{n!}{S^{n+1}}$
e^{-at}	$\dfrac{1}{(S+a)}$
te^{-at}	$\dfrac{1}{(S+a)^2}$
$\dfrac{1}{(n-1)!}t^{n-1}e^{-at}$	$\dfrac{1}{(S+a)^n}$
$1-e^{-at}$	$\dfrac{a}{S(S+a)}$
$e^{-at}-e^{-bt}$	$\dfrac{b-a}{(S+a)(S+b)}$
$be^{-bt}-ae^{-at}$	$\dfrac{(b-a)S}{(S+a)(S+b)}$
$\sin at$	$\dfrac{a}{S^2+a^2}$
$\cos at$	$\dfrac{S}{S^2+a^2}$

(Contd.)

f(t)	F(S)
$e^{-at}\cos bt$	$\dfrac{S+a}{(S+a)^2+b^2}$
$e^{-at}\sin bt$	$\dfrac{b}{(S+a)^2+b^2}$

Table 1.3: Properties of Laplace Transform

Property	Time domain Function	Laplace transform
Superposition	$af_1(t)+bf_2(t)$	$aF_1(S)+bF_2(S)$
Time Scaling	$f(at)$	$\dfrac{1}{a}F\left(\dfrac{S}{a}\right)$
Shift in frequency	$e^{-at}f(t)$	$F(S+a)$
First order differentiation	$\dfrac{df(t)}{dt}$	$SF(S)-f(0)$
n-th order differentiation	$f^n(t)$	$S^nF(S)-S^{n-1}f(0)-S^{n-2}f^{(1)}(0)-...$ $-f^{(n-1)}(0)$
Integration	$\displaystyle\int_0^t f(\tau)d\tau$	$\dfrac{1}{S}F(S)$

Let us take one example based on the equation (1.42) referring the Figure 1.14. Consider the following transfer function,

$$Y(S) = \left[\frac{2(s+3)}{S^2+6S+8}\right]X(S)$$

For a unit input, the $X(S)$ will be as follows:

$$X(S) = \frac{1}{S}$$

Then the output in the S-domain will have the following partial fractions,

$$Y(S) = \left[\frac{2(s+3)}{S^2+6S+8}\right]\frac{1}{S}$$

$$= \left[\frac{2(S+3)}{S(S+2)(S+4)} \right]$$

$$= -\frac{1}{2(S+2)} + \frac{1}{4(S+4)} + \frac{3}{4S}$$

This will give the time domain output (see below) and you can write a simple program to see the output in the time domain.

$$y(t) = -\frac{1}{2}e^{-2t} - \frac{1}{4}e^{-4t} + \frac{3}{4}$$

You can easily plot the output with your available knowledge on graphing. See the following code and the Figure 1.15.

```
>> t=0:0.01:4;
>> y=-0.5*exp(-2*t)+0.25*exp(-4*t)+0.75;
>> plot(t,y);
>> xlabel('Time');
>> ylabel('Y');
>> grid on
```

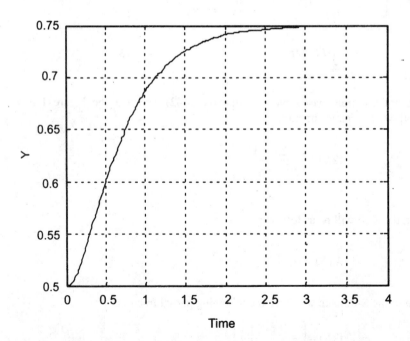

Figure 1.15: System Output to a Unit Input

1.6 COMBINED ELEMENTS

Here, we will investigate how to analyze results when you combine several elements in order to have the desired circuits. First, let us see the electrical circuits when you have different combinations.

1.6.1 Example 1: RLC Circuit

First, we will arrange RLC elements in series and get the transfer function to observe the behavior. Consider the circuits in Figure 1.16 and Figure 1.17.

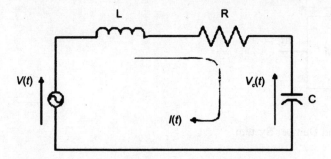

Figure 1.16: Block diagram of series RLC electrical network

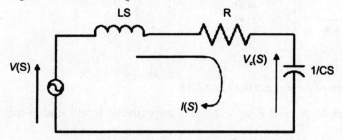

Figure 1.17: Laplace transformed RLC network

From the first principles, we can obtain the following relationship

$$v(t) = Z\, i(t) \qquad (1.44)$$

Laplace transforming

$$V(S) = Z(S)\, I(S)$$

$$= \left[LS + R + \frac{1}{CS} \right] I(S) \qquad (1.45)$$

$$= \left[\frac{LCS^2 + RCS + 1}{CS} \right] I(S)$$

Finally, it will lead to the following relationship between the current and the voltage:

$$I(S) = \left[\frac{CS}{LCS^2 + RCS + 1} \right] V(S) \qquad (1.46)$$

For a given voltage input, you can obtain the current output using the above equation.

1.6.2 Example 2: Spring, Mass and Damper System

Consider the system in Figure 1.18 which has both spring and viscous damping elements.

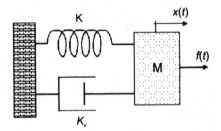

Figure 1.18: Mass, Spring, and Damper System

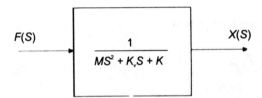

Figure 1.19: Block Diagram of the System in Figure 1.18

Let us select the values M, K_V and K as 1, 2 and 2 respectively. It will lead to the following transfer function:

$$X(S) = \left[\frac{1}{S^2 + 2S + 2} \right] F(S) \qquad (1.47)$$

Then for a given input force, you can get the output displacement against the time. For a unit input of the force you will obtain the following expression:

$$X(S) = \left[\frac{1}{S^2 + 2S + 2} \right] \frac{1}{S}$$

$$= \frac{1}{(S+a)(S+b)s}$$

$$= \frac{A}{S+a} + \frac{B}{S+b} + \frac{C}{S}$$

$$= \frac{A}{S+1+j} + \frac{B}{S+1-j} + \frac{C}{S}$$

Now you can compute A, B and C for the partial fractions and get the inverse Laplace transform. Once you have the inverse Laplace transform it is easy to visualize the time domain response as we discussed earlier.

1.6.3 Example 3: Electrical Network

Figure 1.20 shows an electrical circuit where you have all three types of basic elements. Branch currents and S-domain values are given in Figures 1.20 and 1.21 respectively.

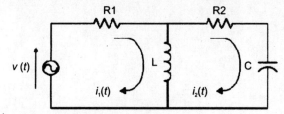

Figure 1.20: Electrical System

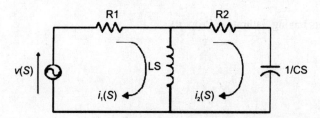

Figure 1.21: Transformed Network

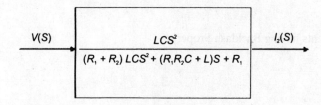

Figure 1.22: Block Diagram of Figure 1.20

Similarly, we can obtain the transfer function between the input $v(t)$ and the branch current as below:

$$I_2(S) = \frac{LCS^2}{[(R_1 + R_2)LCS^2 + (R_1 R_2 C + L)S + R_1]} V(S) \qquad (1.48)$$

1.7 NONLINEAR ELEMENTS

Sometimes, the systems consist of nonlinear elements, which are going to behave according to their inherent properties. These elements cannot be modeled under the above fundamental approaches. For an example, if you analyze a transistor, the characteristics curves are nonlinear. Then, you need a model to represent it and using that model, you may start a computer simulation. Figure 1.23 shows the nonlinear property which has the saturation property. Similarly, Figure 1.24 shows the backlash property.

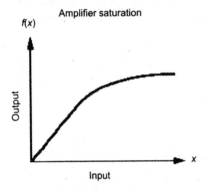

Figure 1.23: Nonlinear Elements having Saturation Property

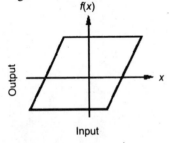

Figure 1.24: Nonlinear Elements having Backlash Property

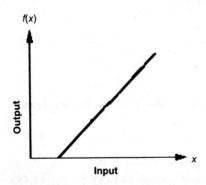

Figure 1.25: Elements having Dead Zone Property

Figure 1.26 shows a model of Coulomb friction developed by Lu Gre in order to model the friction in a rotating body. Angular velocity is in the *X*-axis and the friction is given in *Y*-axis. For this particular example, you need your own modeling. We can model nonlinear phenomena like dry friction (static and sliding friction) as they introduce discontinuous nonlinearities as below. This cannot be linearized locally.

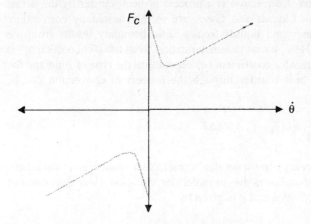

Figure 1.26: Nonlinear Elements having Dead Zone Property

1.8 THERMAL AND CHEMICAL SYSTEMS

1.8.1 Thermal Systems

Next, we will introduce basic heat transfer equations that are going to be useful in system modeling, especially when it comes to heat transfer problems. Whenever there is a temperature difference, there will be heat transform from one substance to another. For heat flow in this example, we consider only with conduction and convection. Figure 1.27 shows a model which is transferring heat from 1 to 2.

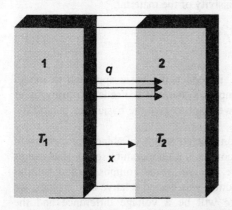

Figure 1.27: Modeling of Thermal Systems

We define the following parameters

q = heat flow rate [J/s], ΔT = temperature difference [K], h = heat transfer coefficient [W/m^{2}K], A = effective cross sectional area [m^2], and k [W/mK], = thermal conductivity.

Through the process of convection, heat transfer is due to the transport of bulk fluid through a media like air or water. Convection is a process of heat transfer by the actual movement of medium particles. Liquids and Gases are mainly heated by convection. Convection process through gases and liquids from a solid boundary results from the fluid motion along the surface. Here, a new parameter called "heat transfer coefficient" is introduced as above. The heat transfer coefficient (h) depends on the type of fluid and the fluid velocity. In Figure 1.27, heat transfer through the process of convection can be represented by

$$\frac{q}{A} = h(T_1 - T_2) = h\Delta T \tag{1.49}$$

Conduction heat transfer is energy transport due to molecular motion and interaction. Conduction heat transfer through solids is due to molecular vibration. Heat flow rate can be related to the thermal conductivity k and it is given by

$$\frac{q}{A} = k\frac{dT}{dx} = k\frac{T_1 - T_2}{x} \tag{1.50}$$

In general, radiation is energy that travels in waves which includes visible light, ultraviolet light, radio waves and other forms, including particles. Radiation heat transfer is energy transport due to emission of electromagnetic waves or photons from a surface or body. Moreover, this energy is radiated or transmitted in the form of rays or waves or particles. Note here that the radiation does not require a heat transfer medium, and even can occur in a vacuum. The heat transfer by radiation is proportional to the fourth power of the absolute material temperature. The proportionality constant is the Stefan-Boltzman constant σ equal to 5.67 x 10^{-8} [W/m^{2}K^4]. The radiation heat transfer also depends on the material properties represented by ε , the emissivity of the material.

$$\frac{q}{A} = \varepsilon \sigma T^4 \tag{1.51}$$

Above equations, (1.49), (1.50) and (1.51), introduce the basic approach to model thermal systems. Similarly, when you have complex systems it is needed to bring other related equations and model the system. Here, we want to give the basic idea behind the thermal systems.

However, there are elements, which are constructed using combined properties of electrical and thermal. For an example, thermocouple is a temperature sensor that makes use of electrical properties. Moreover, if there are two wires composed of dissimilar metals that are joined at both ends and one junction was heated relative to the other, we can see a resultant current. That means there will be a voltage difference and the relationship can be given as on next page:

$$\Delta V = \alpha \, \Delta T \tag{1.52}$$

Here, α is constant of proportionality [12]. Next example in Figure 1.28 will illustrate how to model a heat loss in a simple thermal modeling.

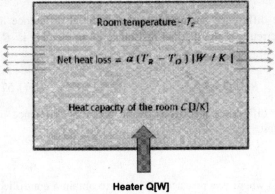

Figure 1.28: Modeling of Heat Loss

Figure 1.28 shows a room or a chamber, which has the heat capacity of C [J/K]. If the outside temperature is T_O and inside temperature of the room is T_R the term $\alpha(T_R - T_O)$ [W] will give the net heat loss due to exchange of air and heat conduction through the walls. Energy balance for the room requires the following relationship

$$\frac{d(CT)}{dt} = Q - \alpha(T_R - T_O) \tag{1.53}$$

Here, $\alpha[W/K]$ is a constant.

Up to now, we have stated some basics on thermodynamics and explained. However, when you need to find the specific equation for a particular application you have to find elementary equation or set of equation. Since these fundamentals associate with different applications, it is difficult to explain all. Let us take a simple example. The time-of-flight and the distance traveled by an electromagnetic wave can be related by

$$d = C\,t \tag{1.54}$$

Here, d is the distance traveled and t is the time of flight. C is the speed of the wave propagation and it depends on air properties.

$$C = \sqrt{\gamma R T} \tag{1.55}$$

γ is the ratio of specific heats and R is the gas constant. T denotes the temperature in Kelvin. Any modeling of ultrasonic sensors or ranging sensors, these equations play a key role.

In thermal modeling, certain elements act as thermal capacitors where they can absorb heat and keep. If the thermal capacitance of an element is C_t then the heat transfer rate Q can be expressed as below:

$$C_t \frac{dT}{dt} = Q \tag{1.56}$$

Here, T denotes the temperature difference analogous to the potential difference in capacitor, which is in an electrical circuit. If the thermal resistance of an element is R_t then the heat transfer rate Q can be represented as below:

$$RC_t \, Q = T \tag{1.57}$$

Here, T denotes the temperature difference analogous to the potential difference in resistor, which is in an electrical circuit.

1.8.2 Chemical Systems

Figure 1.29 shows a chemical system where you mix acid and base to obtain a controlled liquid in the tank [11]. Strong acid which has a pH value of -1 (Negative pH value is possible) is coming to the mixing tank. Strong base, which has a pH value of 15, is fed to the tank via a controllable value as shown in Figure 1.29. By mixing two liquids, the pH value in the tank is intended to keep at 7 or any desired value.

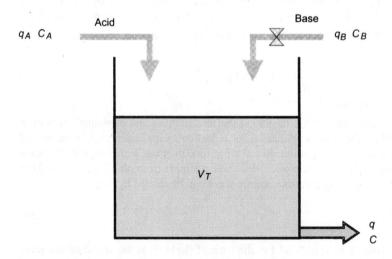

Figure 1.29: Mixing Tank

For an example, to keep the pH value at 7, you must balance the inflow of acid by adding base that is controlled by the value in Figure 1.29. To keep the liquid volume of the tank at constant, total inflow and the outflow should be equal. The system can be modeled by the following differential equation as on next page:

$$\frac{d(V_T C)}{dt} = q_A C_A + q_B C_B - qC \qquad (1.58)$$

Here, the flow rates of acid and base are taken as q_A [m³/s] and q_B [m³/s] respectively. The incoming acid mixer has C_A [mol/l] and the controlled base mixer has C_B [mol/l]. The tank has C [mol/l] outflow, which should be kept under control.

1.9. HYDRAULIC SYSTEMS

In designing complex system, there are hydraulic components and modeling of hydraulic systems plays a key role. It is necessary to study the basic terminology and governing principles on hydraulic systems. Liquids flow from higher energy points to points of lower energy until it reaches a stable point. Hydraulic concepts can be applied to both artificially constructed systems as well as to the natural systems. Average velocity V [m/s] can be defined as below (see Figure 1.30 for schematic view):

$$V = \frac{Q}{A} \qquad (1.59)$$

Here, Q is the flow rate in [m³/s] and A is the cross sectional area in [m²]. Figure 1.30 shows the velocity distribution through a circular pipe. Note that the flow through this circular pipe is assumed to be laminar and it can be explained as below.

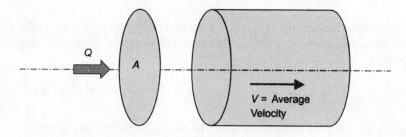

Figure 1.30: Flow through the Cross Sectional Area A.

Due to friction and other factors, nature of the flow of a hydraulic system can vary. There two types of flows, namely, laminar and turbulent. In a liquid flowing through straight piping at a low speed, the particles of the liquid move in straight lines parallel to the flow direction. Heat loss from friction is minimal. This kind of flow is called laminar flow. Laminar flow is characterized by smooth, predictable streamlines (the paths of single fluid particles as shown in Figure 1.31). On the other hand, in turbulent flow, the streamlines are unpredictable and irregular.

Pressure is force exerted against a specific area (force per unit area) expressed in Newtons per square meter. Pressure can cause an expansion, or resistance to compression, of a fluid that is being squeezed. A fluid is any liquid or gas (vapor) and force is anything that tends to produce or modify motion. Potential energy or head was the only way to express pressure as measurement. It was expressed as meters of water, so called a "Pressure Head". Scientifically, head is the vertical distance between two levels in a fluid. Kinetic energy of a liquid is the energy, which is due to its motion. When the speed is high the kinetic energy of that flow becomes high. When the flow goes through different channels or pipes, these parameters can be interrelated.

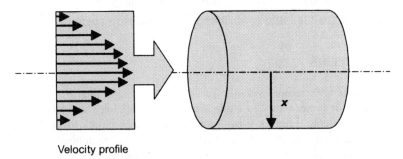

Velocity profile

Figure 1.31: Velocity Distributions: Magnitude and Direction (Not to Scale)

In order to carry out certain calculations, we have to decide whether the flow is laminar or turbulent. To classify flow as either turbulent or laminar, an index called the Reynolds number (Re) is used. It is computed as follows:

$$\text{Re} = \frac{4VR}{v} \tag{1.60}$$

Where, Re = Reynolds number (no units), V = average velocity (m/s) R = hydraulic radius (m), and v = kinematic viscosity (m^2/s). Hydraulic radius can be calculated from the following equation:

$$R = \frac{A}{Pw} \tag{1.61}$$

Note here that P_w is called the wetted perimeter (the portion of the channel in contact with the flowing fluid).

Potential energy is energy due to position and it is normally measured with respect to a datum. An object has potential energy in proportion to its vertical distance above the earth's surface or relative to a predefined datum. Friction is the resistance to relative motion between two bodies. When liquid flows in a hydraulic circuit, friction produces heat and it causes a head loss in the system. This causes some of the kinetic energy to be lost in the form of heat energy. Bernouilli's principle states that the static pressure of a moving liquid vary inversely with its velocity; that is, as velocity increases, static pressure decreases. Based on that, energy across any two points in a hydraulic system must be balanced. Energy at two different places can be expressed as below:

$$\frac{P_1}{\rho} + Z_1 + \frac{V_1^2}{2g} + H_G = \frac{P_2}{\rho} + Z_2 + \frac{V_2^2}{2g} + H_L \tag{1.62}$$

Here, P is the pressure of the point under consideration and ρ is the specific weight of the fluid. Z denotes the elevation with respect to a predefined datum and g represents gravitational acceleration. H_G is the head gain such as from a pump and H_L is the combined head loss. Energy loss in the fluid is due to the internal friction between fluid particles traveling at different velocities.

Example in Figure 1.32 illustrates how to apply the energy equation in order to find the velocity of the point 2. Here, the jet is open to the air and the pressure at point 2 is 0. There is no head gain and the velocity in the tank at point 1 is negligible

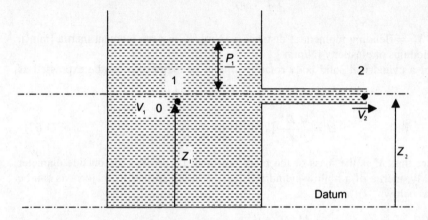

Figure 1.32: Illustration of Energy Balance

Energy equation of the system given in Figure 4.31 can be simplified as below:

$$\frac{P_1}{\rho} + Z_1 + \frac{0}{2g} + 0 = \frac{0}{\rho} + Z_2(=Z_1) + \frac{V_2^2}{2g} + H_L \qquad (1.63)$$

Under those assumptions, it will lead to the following equation:

$$V_2 = \sqrt{\frac{2gP_1}{\rho}} \qquad (1.64)$$

1.10 OTHER FORMULAS

Shear stress at outer surface of a twisted shaft (twisting moment or torque) can be expressed as below:

$$\tau = G\theta\frac{r}{L}$$

$$\theta = \frac{1000TL}{GJ} \qquad (1.65)$$

Here, τ = Shear stress [N/mm^2], θ = Angle of twist [rad], T = Applied torque [Nm], r = Radius of point at which shear stress is exerted [mm], G = Modulus of rigidity [N/mm^2], J = Polar moment of inertia [N/mm^4], and L = Length of the shaft under twist [mm].

The relationship between the deflection of a beam at distance x [mm] and stress distribution is given by:

$$\frac{d^2 y}{dx^2} = \frac{M}{EI} \tag{1.66}$$

Where, M = Bending moment at distance x [Nm], I = Area moment inertia [mm^4], and E = Modulus of elasticity [N/mm^2].

Inertia of a cylindrical solid body rotating around its major axis can be expressed as below:

$$J = \frac{M D^2}{8} [\text{kgm}^2] \tag{1.67}$$

Note here that M is the mass of the body [kg] and D denotes the outside diameter [m]. Similarly, inertia of a hollow-cylindrical body rotating around its major axis can be expressed as below:

$$J = \frac{M (D^2 + d^2)}{8} [\text{kgm}^2] \tag{1.68}$$

Here, d is the inside diameter of the hollow-cylindrical body [m].

Load torque requirement for a ballscrew drive can be calculated by the following equation:

$$T_L = \frac{F l}{2 \pi \eta} + T_c [Nm] \tag{1.69}$$

Here, F = Axial force required to move [N], η = Efficiency of the drive system, l = Lead of the ballscrew [m], and T_c = Friction torque [Nm]. For rack and pinion systems, you have a different formula [12].

REFERENCES

[1] C.L. Dym, "Principles of Mathematical Modeling," 2nd Edition, Elsevier Academic Press, Boston, 2004.

[2] T.L. Vincent and W.J. Grantham, "Nonlinear and Optimal Control Systems," Wiley and Sons, New York, NY, 1997.

[3] K. Watanabe and L. Udawatta, "Fuzzy-Chaos Hybrid Controllers for Nonlinear Dynamic Systems," Edited Book on Integration of Fuzzy Logic and Chaos Theory, 2006, pp. 481-506.

[4] R. Siegwart and I.R. Nourbakhsh, "Introduction to Autonomous Mobile Robot," 2005, Prentice Hall, New Delhi.

[5] Matlab Release 13, Version 6.5, "Help Manual and Toolboxes," The Mathworks Inc.

[6] J.B. Dabney and T.L. Harman, "Mastering Simulink 4", 2001, Prentice Hall, New Jersey.

[7] F. Daerden, "Conception and Realization of Pleated Pneumatic Artificial Muscles and Their use as Compliant Actuation Elements," Ph.D. Dissertation, Vrije Universiteit Brussel, July 1999.

[9] L. Ljung and T. Glad, "Modeling of Dynamic Systems," Prentice-Hall, Englewood Cliffs. NJ, 1994.

[9] T.D.C. Thanh and K.K. Ahn, "Intelligent Phase Plane Switching Control of Pneumatic Artificial Muscle Manipulators with Magneto Rheological Brake," Mechatronics ISSN 0957-4158 Vol. 16, pp. 85-95, 2006.

[10] S. Karunakuran *et. al.* "Mechatronics," 2005, Tata McGraw Hill, New Delhi, 11th Reprint.

[11] D.P. Kothari and I.J. Nagrath, "Basic Electrical Engineering," Tata McGraw Hill, New Delhi, 2nd edition, 2007.

[12] A. Preumont, "Mechatronics: Dynamics of Electromechanical and Piezoelectric Systems," Springer, Berlin, 2006.

[13] P.D. Cha, J.J. Rosenberg, and C.L. Dym, "Fundamentals of Modeling and Analyzing Engineering Systems," Cambridge University Press, Cambridge, 2000.

[14] C.M. Close, D.K. Frederick, and J.C. Newell, "Modeling and Analysis of Dynamic Systems," John Wiley, New York, 2002.

[15] F.P. Incropera and D.P. De Witt, "Fundamentals of Heat and Mass Transfer," Fifth edition, J. Wiley and Sons, New York, 2002.

Chapter 2

Creating Your Simulation Environment

The performance of a computer simulation environment is usually determined by hardware and software characteristics.

2.1 HARDWARE AND SOFTWARE

In a computer system, computer software consists of programs, which enable a computer system to perform specific tasks. Computer hardware is the physical part or solid state circuitry of a computer. This includes the digital circuitry with other electro-mechanical devices, distinguished from the computer software that executes within the hardware. If you want to build a new computer geared for video games, then you'll probably want to switch on to some of the latest new hardware, so you can really benefit all the new technology now featured in today's software. When it comes to software there are different software programs depending on the task or application. System software helps running the computer hardware and computer system as whole. It includes operating systems, device drivers, diagnostic tools, servers, windowing systems, utilities and other related tasks. Programming software usually provides tools to assist a programmer in writing computer programs and software using different programming languages in a more convenient way.

Typical applications include research and development, industrial applications, business, educational, medical, databases, and computer games. Software for computer simulations basically comes under research and developments. Software is loaded into the random access memory (RAM) and executed in the central processing unit (CPU). At the lowest level, software consists of a machine language specific to an individual processor. On the other hand, in application software, it is usually written in high-level programming languages. When it closes to high level, they are easier to use than machine language. Application software languages like C, C++, Pascal, Matlab, FORTRAN, and Mathematica allow end users to accomplish one specific task through high level commands. They can be employed for computer aided simulations while proving the facilities to hardware access. Matlab and Mathematica are specifically designed for engineering and scientific applications. In fact, this book will use Matlab as the programming language in illustrating design examples. Matlab is a powerful programming language that combines computation and visualization capability for realizing scientific and engineering simulations. To install Matlab software, you have to look into the computer hardware requirements for that particular version of Matlab release. In particular, Matlab can be employed for the tasks such as mathematical computations, algorithm developments, data acquisition, interfacing, system modeling, simulations and prototyping, data analysis, exploration, and visualization scientific and engineering graphics applications. Matlab is an interactive system whose basic data element is an array that does not require dimensioning. This allows you to solve many technical computing problems, especially those with matrix and vector formulations, in a fraction of the time it would have taken to write a program in a scalar non-interactive language such as C or FORTRAN. Matlab features a family of add-on application-specific solutions called toolboxes. Very important for most users of Matlab, toolboxes allow you to learn and apply specialized technology. Toolboxes are comprehensive collections of Matlab functions (M-files) that extend the Matlab environment to solve particular classes of problems [1]. Areas in which toolboxes are available include signal processing, control systems, neural networks, financial, fuzzy logic, wavelets, Simulink, and many others.

2.1.1 Hardware for Installing Matlab

Let us take Matlab version 6.5, release 13 requires one of the followings with a compatible operating system. For an example, Pentium, Pentium Pro, Pentium II, Pentium III, Pentium IV, Intel Xeon, AMD Athlon or Athlon XP based personal computer needs Microsoft Windows 98 (original and Second Edition), Windows Millennium Edition (ME), Windows NT 4.0 (with Service Pack 5 for Y2K compliancy or Service Pack 6a), Windows 2000, or Windows XP [1].

CD-ROM drive (for installation from CD), minimum 128 MB RAM (256 MB RAM recommended) is required. Disk space varies depending on the size of the partition and installation of online help files. The Math Works installer will inform you of the hard disk space requirement for your particular partition. For example, a partition with a 4K byte cluster size requires 120 MB for Matlab only and 260 MB for Matlab with online help files. 8-bit graphics adapter and display (for 256 simultaneous colors) is recommended. A 16, 24 or 32-bit OpenGL capable graphics adapter is strongly recommended. Other recommended items include Microsoft Windows supported graphics accelerator card, printer, and sound card Microsoft Word 8.0 (Office 97), Office 2000, or Office XP is required to run the Matlab Notebook. Note that Office 95 is no longer supported for release 13. One of the following is required to build your own MEX-files. Compaq Visual Fortran 5.0, 6.1, or 6.5 Microsoft Visual C/C++ version 5.0, 6.0, or 7.0 Borland C/C++ version 5.0 or 5.02 Borland C++ Builder version 3.0, 4.0, 5.0, or 6.0 WATCOM version 10.6 or 11 Lcc 2.4 (bundled with Matlab) Netscape Navigator 4.0 and above or Microsoft Internet Explorer 4.0 and above is required. Adobe Acrobat Reader is required to view and print the Matlab online documentation in PDF format.

If you are using Matlab version 7.0 then system requirements is as below (For an example, Student Version - Release 2007a):

For all platforms, DVD drive (for installation), 512 MB RAM or higher is required with 600 MB disk space. E-mail (required) and Internet access (recommended) need for product activation. For Microsoft Windows: PC with Intel / Pentium / Celeron / Core AMD or compatible processor, Windows Vista or Windows XP SP2. For Linux, PC with

Intel Pentium/Celeron/Core, AMD, or compatible processor, 32-bit Linux Kernel 2.4.x or 2.6.x; or glibc 2.3.2 or above 16-bit or higher graphics adaptor and display (24-bit recommended).

2.1.2 Features of Matlab Software

1. Development Environment: This is the set of tools and facilities that help you use Matlab functions and files. Many of these tools are graphical user interfaces. It includes the Matlab desktop and Command Window, a command history, an editor and debugger, and browsers for viewing help, the workspace, files, and the search path.

2. The Matlab Mathematical Function Library: This is a vast collection of computational algorithms ranging from elementary functions like sum, sine, cosine, and complex arithmetic to more sophisticated functions like matrix inverse, matrix eigenvalues, Bessel functions, and Fast Fourier Transforms (FFT).

3. The Matlab Language: This is a high-level matrix/array language with control flow statements, functions, data structures, input/output, and object-oriented programming features. It allows both "programming in the small" to rapidly create quick and dirty throw-away programs, and "programming in the large" to create complete large and complex application programs.

4. Graphics: Matlab has extensive facilities for displaying vectors and matrices as graphs, as well as annotating and printing these graphs. It includes high-level functions for two-dimensional and three-dimensional data visualization, image processing, animation, and presentation graphics. It also includes low-level functions that allow you to fully customize the appearance of graphics as well as to build complete graphical user interfaces on your Matlab applications.

5. The Matlab Application Program Interface (API): This is a library that allows you to write C and Fortran programs that interact with Matlab. It includes facilities for calling routines from Matlab (dynamic linking), calling Matlab as a computational engine, and for reading and writing MAT-files [1].

To start programming using Matlab, programmer has two basic options as follows:

- Command Window
- M-File Editor

When you run or start Matlab, the Matlab desktop or command window appears, containing tools (graphical user interfaces) for managing files, variables, and applications associated with Matlab. Command window can be visualized as shown in Figure 2.1 and M-File editor can be visualized as shown in Figure 2.2. On the command window, direct or instant programming can be run.

If you are handling large Matlab programs, you may need creating and editing M-files. In such situations, you have to use M-file editor. To create a new M-file in the Editor/Debugger, either click the new file button on the Matlab toolbar, or select File -> New -> M-file from the Matlab desktop. You can also create a new M-file using the context menu in the Current Directory browser--see Creating New Files. The Editor/Debugger opens, if it is not already open, with an untitled file in the Matlab current directory from which you can create an M-file. If the Editor/Debugger is open, create more new files by using the new file button on the toolbar, or select File -> New -> M-file. Here, you can write larger programs and save them for later usage or modifications.

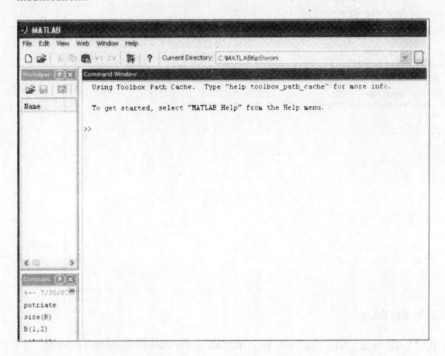

Figure 2.1: Command Window

To open an existing M-file in the Editor/Debugger, click the open button on the desktop or Editor/Debugger toolbar, or select File -> Open. The Open dialog box opens, listing all Matlab files. You can see different files by changing the selection for Files of type in the dialog box. Select the file and click Open. If you click the open icon from the desktop toolbar, the current directory files are shown (as shown in Figure 2.1), but if you open it from the Editor, the files in the directory for the current files are shown.

Here onwards, whenever we use the command window in executing any Matlab command, you have to use the enter key for executing that particular command or M-file once typed it. In this book, the entering key stroke is not shown most of the times. Following example will illustrate the above explanation clearly.

>> myfirstprogram (use enter key to execute myfirstprogram.m after typing the name)

Note here that your myfirstprogram.m (M-file) should be in the present working directory as shown in Figure 2.1. For instant, you can use DOS commands to change your directory from one to another. You can view the present directory with the command **pwd** as below:

>> pwd

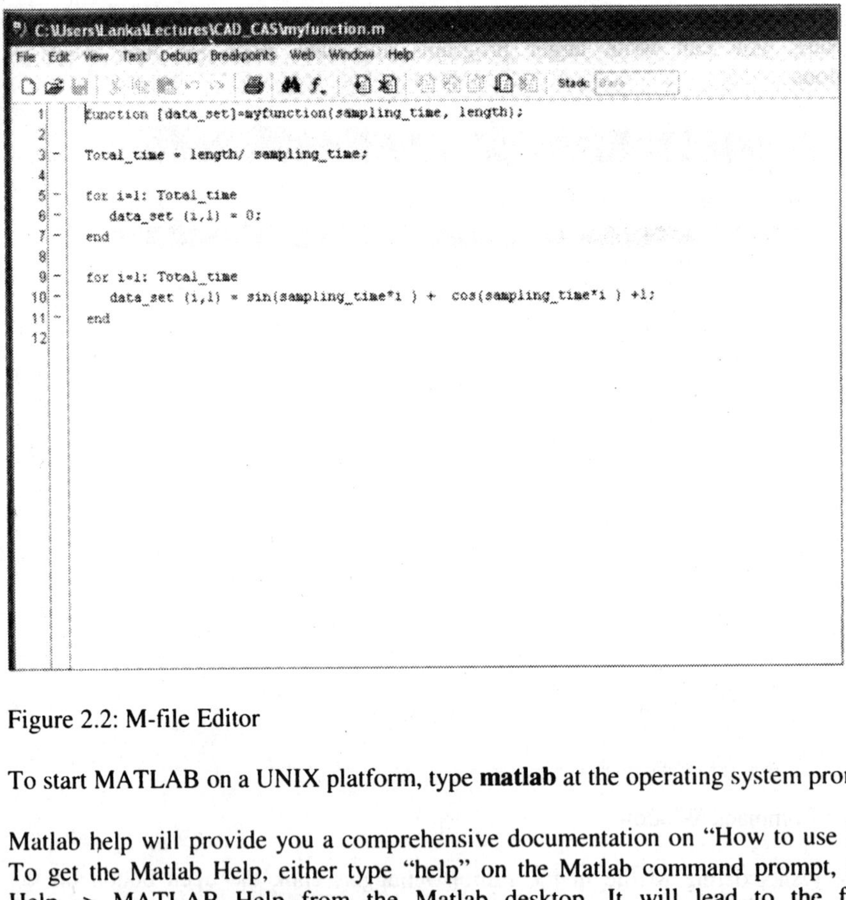

Figure 2.2: M-file Editor

To start MATLAB on a UNIX platform, type **matlab** at the operating system prompt.

Matlab help will provide you a comprehensive documentation on "How to use Matlab". To get the Matlab Help, either type "help" on the Matlab command prompt, or select Help -> MATLAB Help from the Matlab desktop. It will lead to the following instructions and you can then follow the steps:

1. Getting Started—Introduction to MATLAB.

2. Using MATLAB—user guides for all of MATLAB.

3. Programming Tips—tips on many aspects of programming with MATLAB.

4. Examples—major examples in the MATLAB documentation.

5. Release Notes—summary of new features, bug fixes, upgrade issues, etc.

2.2 MATLAB BASICS

Before starting computer simulations using Matlab, beginners have to be familiarized with basic Matlab commands in order to handle comprehensive computer simulations. This allows you to solve many technical computing problems, especially those with matrix and vector formulations leading to handle bulk data [2]-[4]. In most of the simulations, you are looking for bulk data for research outputs.

2.2.1 Getting Help

Type one of the following commands in the command window and use helping commands in Matlab:

1. **help** *topic* – provides help for the specified topic
2. **help** *command* – provides help for the specified command
3. **helpwin** – opens a separate help window for navigation
4. **lookfor** *keyword* – search all M-files for keyword

For an example, you can get the built in commands associated with matrix manipulations by

>> lookfor *matrices*

The output will be as follows:

DIAG Diagonal matrices and diagonals of a matrix.

GALLERY Higham test matrices.

ABCDCHK Checks dimensional consistency of A,B,C,D matrices.

MAT2CELL Break matrix up into a cell array of matrices.

airfoil.m: %% Graphical Representation of Sparse Matrices
buckydem.m: %% Graphs and Matrices
imagedemo.m: %% Images and Matrices
inverter.m: %% Inverses of Matrices
sparsity.m: %% Sparse Matrices

Cont…

2.2.2 Variables

Few points to be remembered on variable declarations in general can be given as below:

- Your variable must start with a letter.
- It may contain only letters, digits, and the underscore "_".
- Matlab is case sensitive, for an example, voltage and VOLTAGE are two different variables.
- Matlab only recognizes the first 31 characters in a variable name.

2.2.3 Assignment Statement

Variable = number;

Example:

>> A = 5;

Variable = expression;

>> A = 5 -7;

2.2.4 Special Variables

pi: π = 3.1415926 ......

eps: ε = 2.2204e-016, smallest value by which two numbers can differ

inf: ∞, infinity

NAN or nan: not-a-number

2.2.5 Commands Involving Variables

Once you defined the variable, it is essential to investigate the states of the variable whenever necessary. For an example, the defined variables up to now should be known and needed to clear some vectors.

who: lists the names of the defined variables

whos: lists the names and sizes of defined variables

clear: clears all variables

clear *name*: clears the variable *name*

clc: clears the command window

clf: clears the current figure and the graph window

2.2.6 Matrices

An *m* × *n* matrix is a rectangular or square array of elements with *m* rows and *n* columns. For an example, 3 × 6 matrix *A* can be defined as bellow:

$$A_{3\times6} = \begin{pmatrix} a & b & c & d & e & f \\ o & p & q & r & s & t \\ u & v & w & x & y & z \end{pmatrix}$$

In a Matlab programming environment, these values can be assigned to A as follows:

$$>> A = \begin{bmatrix} a & b & c & d & e & f & ; & o & p & q & r & s & t & ; & u & v & w & x & y & z \end{bmatrix}$$

Note here that the values of *a,b,c,...,* must be defined before assigning to *A* matrix. Moreover, following example will demonstrate the direct assignment for a matrix.

```
>> x = [1 2 3; 5 0 4; 3 2 -1]
    x =
    1    2    3
    5    0    4
    3    2   -1
```

zeros(M,N)

M x N matrix of zeros

Examples:

```
>> x = zeros(1,3)
x = 0    0    0
>> ones(M,N)
```

(M x N) matrix of ones

Example:

```
>> x = ones(1,3)

x = 1    1    1
```

rand(M,N)

(M x N) matrix of uniformly distributed random numbers on (0,1)

Example:

```
x = rand(1,3)

x =   0.1111  0.2223 0.3019
```

Get the details of the variables through *size* command (matrix dimension)
```
>> size(x);

ans =

    1    3
```

Number of rows in the matrix *x* is one and number of columns will be three.

2.2.7 Matrix Operations

Matrix is a two-dimensional rectangular array of real or complex numbers that represents a vector. The linear algebraic operations defined on matrices have found applications in a wide variety of technical fields, especially in science and engineering. This vector notation will be very useful when it comes to scientific simulations. In fact, it will allow you to carefully handle large amount of data without making mistakes. Any variable in the Matlab environment considers as a vector. Table 2.1 shows the typical Matlab operation for the variables *a* and *b*.

Table 2.1: Typical Matrix Operations and Matlab Syntax

Operation	Algebraic Form	Matlab Syntax
Addition	a + b	a + b
Subtraction	a − b	a − b
Multiplication	a x b	a .* b
Division	a ÷ b	a ./ b
Exponentiation	a^b	a .^ b

Table 2.2 shows the available command to create different matrices using Matlab once you define the matrix *A*. For an example, transpose of *A* is assigned to matrix *B*.

Table 2.2: Creating Different Matrix Formats

Operation	Syntax
Transpose	$B = A'$
Identity Matrix	eye(n) returns an (n x n) identity matrix eye(m,n) returns an (m x n) matrix with ones on the main diagonal and zeros elsewhere
Addition and Subtraction	$C = A + B$, $C = A - B$
Scalar Multiplication	$B = \alpha A$, where α is a scalar
Matrix Multiplication	$C = A * B$
Matrix Inverse	$B = inv(A)$, A must be a square matrix in this case
Matrix powers	$B = A * A$, A must be a square matrix
Determinant	$det(A)$, A must be a square matrix

Matlab provides different functions that create different kinds of matrices. The first example is creating a symmetric matrix using Pascal matrix. *Pascal*(n) is the Pascal matrix of order n: a symmetric positive definite matrix with integer entries, made up from Pascal's triangle. Its inverse has integer entries. Pascal(n,1) is the lower triangular Cholesky factor (up to signs of columns) of the Pascal matrix. It is involutary (is its own inverse). Pascal(n,2) is a rotated version of Pascal(n,1), with sign flipped if n is even, which is a cube root of the identity [5].

>> D = pascal(4)

D =

$$
\begin{array}{cccc}
1 & 1 & 1 & 1 \\
1 & 2 & 3 & 4 \\
1 & 3 & 6 & 10 \\
1 & 4 & 10 & 20
\end{array}
$$

This will give you a symmetric (3×3) matrix with certain properties. Magic(N) is an $(N \times N)$ matrix constructed from the integers 1 through N^2 with equal row, column, and diagonal sums. Produces valid magic squares for all $N > 0$ except $N = 2$.

>> E = magic(4)

E =

$$
\begin{array}{cccc}
16 & 2 & 3 & 13 \\
5 & 11 & 10 & 8 \\
9 & 7 & 6 & 12 \\
4 & 14 & 15 & 1
\end{array}
$$

Matrices can be partitioned into components matrices or row or column vectors. For an example, matrix A can be partitioned as bellow:

$$
A_{3\times6} = \begin{pmatrix} a & b & c & d & e & f \\ o & p & q & r & s & t \\ u & v & w & x & y & z \end{pmatrix} = \begin{pmatrix} a & b & c & d & \vdots & e & f \\ o & p & q & r & \vdots & s & t \\ \cdots & \cdots & \cdots & \cdots & \cdots & \cdots & \cdots \\ u & v & w & x & \vdots & y & z \end{pmatrix}
$$

Components of the partitioned matrix will be given by four matrices as follows:

$$
T = \begin{pmatrix} a & b & c & d \\ o & p & q & r \end{pmatrix}
$$

$$
U = \begin{pmatrix} e & f \\ s & t \end{pmatrix}
$$

$$
V = \begin{pmatrix} u & v & w & z \end{pmatrix}
$$

$$
W = \begin{pmatrix} y & z \end{pmatrix}
$$

where

$$
A_{3\times6} = \begin{pmatrix} T & U \\ V & W \end{pmatrix}.
$$

To demonstrate the above matrix partition, consider the following example. Matrix C can be considered as two partitions as bellow in the Matlab environment:

>> A=[1 2;3 4]

A =

   1   2
   3   4

>> B=[8;9]

B =

   1
   2

>> C=[A B]

C =

   1   2 8
   3   4 9

2.2.8 Matrix Properties

First, we define the elements of the matrix *A* with randomly generated numbers. Note here that the dimension of A is (4 x 4) and the randomly generated numbers are brought to rounded numbers through the *fix* function.

>> A=fix(10*rand(4))

A =

   4   8   8   8
   9   5   0   5
   4   2   6   7
   4   6   3   4

You can get the Eigen values of the matrix A as bellow:

>> eig(A)

ans =

   20.7402
   -4.9846
   3.4571
   -0.2126

You can see the Rank of the matrix A as below:

`>> rank(A)`

`ans =`

4

2.2.9 Programming: Flow Control Structures

Matlab has several flow control constructs as given below:
1. if
2. switch and case
3. for
4. while
5. continue
6. break

1. Loops
FOR loop

```
for variable = expression
    commands
end
```

WHILE loop

```
while expression
    commands
end
```

Example 1:
```
for t = 1: 50
    y(t) = sin (2*pi*t/10);
End
```

Example 2:
```
while EPS>1
    EPS=EPS/2;
end
```

2.2.10 Flow Control and Loops

Simple **if** statement: The **if** statement evaluates a logical expression and executes a group of statements when the expression is true.

```
if logical expression
    commands
end
```

Example: (Nested)

```
if d < 50
        count=count +1;
        disp(d);
        if b>d
                b=0;
        end
end
```

2.2.11 Elementary Functions

Table 2.3 shows typcal elementary function that we frequently use in the simulations. These functions provides you mathemetical subroutines for different types of calculations.

Table 2.3: Elementary Function for Simulations

Command	Meaning
abs(x)	Absolute value of the elements of x
angle(x)	Calculate the phase angle
sqrt(x)	Square root
real(x)	Real part of a complex number
imag(x)	Imaginary part of a complex number
conj(x)	Complex conjugate
round(x)	Round towards nearest integer
fix(x)	Round towards zero
floor(x)	Round towards minus infinity
ceil(x)	Round towards plus infinity
sign(x)	This the Signum function. sign(x) returns 1,0 or -1.
mod(x,y)	Modulus after division
rem(x,y)	Remainder after division
exp(x)	Exponential
log(x)	Natural logarithm
log10(x)	Common (base 10) logarithm
factor(x)	factor(x) returns a vector containing the prime factors of x
isprime(x)	True for prime numbers
factorial(x)	Factorial function

When you display numbers, it is necessary to visualize the desired accuracy of numerical values. In the command window you can define the number of digits required for a particular simulation. Format will be used to switch between different output display formats as follows:

>> format

Default. Same as SHORT.

>> format **short**

Scaled fixed point format with 5 digits.

>> format **long**

Scaled fixed point format with 15 digits.

>> format **short** *e*

Floating point format with 5 digits.

2.3 BASICS ON COMPUTER SIMULATIONS

2.3.1 Creating Data Files

In various simulations, it is essential to create data files for different requirements. Whether it is Matlab or C it is necessary to produce large amount of system data in order to carry out a good simulation, especially when you handle complex systems. You may need data files as inputs for feeding into the simulating systems. In some simulations, data files will come out as results through simulations. To create a data file named as "myfile.dat", it should follow the syntax given below:

>> fid=fopen('myfile.dat','w');

FID = fopen(Filename, Permission) opens the file Filename in the mode specified by Permission. Different permissions can be defined as below:

Table 2.4: Different Permissions for File Identifiers

Permission	Output
'r'	Read
'w'	Write (create if necessary)
'a'	Append (create if necessary)
'r+'	Read and write (do not create)
'w+'	Truncate or create for read and write
'a+'	Read and append (create if necessary)
'W'	Write without automatic flushing
'A'	Append without automatic flushing

Moreover, fid is a scalar Matlab integer, called "file identifier". You use the fid as the first argument to other file input/output routines. If *fopen* cannot open the file, it returns -1. Two file identifiers are automatically available and need not be opened. They are fid=1 (standard output) and fid=2 (standard error). Open a file or obtain information about open files following syntax should be used:

fid = fopen(filename)

fid = fopen(filename,permission)

[fid,message] = fopen(filename,permission,machineformat)

fids = fopen('all')

[filename,permission, machineormat] = fopen(fid)

2.3.2 Write Data on a File

The command *fprintf* writes formatted data to a predefined data file (opened with a file identifier). COUNT = fprintf(FID,FORMAT,A,...) formats the data in the real part of matrix A (and in any additional matrix arguments), under control of the specified FORMAT string, and writes it to the file associated with file identifier FID (see Table 2.5 for more details). See the following programming segment:

fprintf(fid,' %d %4.5f \n ',5,4.5);

Table 2.5: Formatted Data Outputs

Syntax	Formatted output
\n	produce linefeed
\r	produce carriage return
\t	produce horizontal tab
\b	produce backspace
\f	produce form feed characters
\\	Backslash
%%	Percent character
\" or "	Single quotation mark (two single quotes)

```
fid=fopen('sinewave.dat','w');
t=2;
x=0:0.1:t;
y=sin(x);
n=t/0.1 ;
for i=1:n
        fprintf(fid,' %d  %4.5f \n ',x(i),y(i));
end
fclose(fid);
```

Program 2.1: Write Generated Sine Wave Data on to a File

If you run the Program 2.1, you will get the date file named "sinewave.dat" in the current directory and the data stream as below:

```
0                0.00000
1.000000e-001  0.09983
2.000000e-001  0.19867
3.000000e-001  0.29552
4.000000e-001  0.38942
............................
............................
```

Table 2.6: Different Permissions for File Identifiers

Syntax	Output description
%c	Single character
%d	Decimal notation (signed)
%f	Fixed point notation
%e	Exponential notation (using a lowercase e as in 3.1415e+00)
%i	Decimal notation (signed)
%s	String of characters
%g	The more compact of %e or %f. Insignificant zeros do not print
%o	Octal notation (unsigned)

2.3.3 Loading a Data File

Load the desired data file into the memory. Note here that the data file should be in the current working directory.

>> load myfile.dat;

Copy that file into a z matrix

>> Z = myfile;

2.3.4 Deleting Rows and Columns

You can delete rows and columns from a matrix using just a pair of square brackets. Start with

>> z=[1 2 3;3 4 5;5 6 7]

z =

```
    1   2   3
    3   4   5
    5   6   7
```

>> X = Z;

Then, to delete the second column of X, use

>> X(:,2) = []

X =

```
    1   3
    3   5
    5   7
```

2.3.5 Long Command Lines

If a statement does not fit on one line, use three periods, ... , followed by return or enter to indicate that the statement continues on the next line. For example

```
>> s = 1 –1/2 + 1/3 –1/4 + 1/5 – 1/6 + 1/7 ...
    – 1/8 + 1/9 – 1/10 + 1/11 – 1/12;

s =

  0.6532
```

2.3.6 Vectorization

To effectively employ Matlab facilities, it is important to investigate the vectorization capability and include in your M-files. In fact, other programming languages might use FOR or WHILE loops, Matlab gives vectorization which is a speedy and effective measure in data handling. A simple example involves creating a table of sine values.

```
x = 0;
for k = 1:1000
        y(k) = sin(x);
        x = x + .01;
end
```

You will understand how easy if you use the Matlab vectorization facilities in order to get the same output from a different code. A vectorized version of the same code is

```
>> x = 0:.01:10;
>> y = sin(x);
```

For more complicated codes, vectorization options are not always so obvious.

2.3.7 Making Your Own Functions

Let us think about how the built-in-functions given in the Matlab work. For an example, built-in-function *diag* takes matrix *A* and gives matrix *B* as the output. It computes the diagonal of a given square matrix and brings the diagonal vector as the output. Figure 2.3 shows a typical input and output elements in a built-in-function. You can see following output when you execute the code

```
>> A=[16 5 9 4;3 10 6 15;2 11 7 14;13 8 12 1];

>> B=diag(A)

B =
   16
   10
    7
    1
```

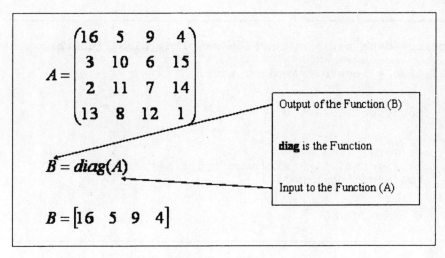

Figure 2.3: Input and Output Elements of a Built-in-functions

Functions in Matlab (like in any programming language) are M-files that accept input arguments and return output arguments. They operate on variables within their own workspace. In the above example, we explained how built-in-functions work. Here, we explain how to build your own function and call it whenever required. The function name will be "myfunction". It tries to create a data file for the following mathematical function $y(x)$:

$$y(x) = \sin(x) + \cos(x)$$

This function will compute the output $y(x)$ once you define the sampling time and time length that you want data to be generated. Sampling time and the length are the input arguments whereas data set will be your output from the function. It has two input arguments and one output argument as shown below:

function [data_set]=myfunction(sampling_time, length)

Then, coding of the inside of the program is done according to your requirement. You have to use the input arguments and generate the desired output.

Total_time = length/sampling_time;

for i=1: Total_time
   data_set (i,1) = 0;
end

Above code will create a matrix to initialize the array. Then, you can bring the generated data onto the file as below:

for i=1: Total_time
   data_set (i,1) = sin(sampling_time*i) + cos(sampling_time*i) +1;
end

Save this as a separate M-file in your current working directory. Whenever you want to calculate $y(x)$ function can be re-used without writing the whole code again.

```
function [data_set]= myfunction(sampling_time, length)

Total_time = length/ sampling_time;

for i=1: Total_time
      data_set (i,1) = 0;
end

for i=1: Total_time
      data_set (i,1) = sin(sampling_time*i ) +
      cos(sampling_time*i ) +1;
end
```

Program 2.2: Your Own Function

Note here that your own functions that are going to be created cannot have the built-in-function names already exit in Matlab.

>> D = myfunction(0.01, 24) ;

It is a common practice that programmers use descriptive function and variable names to make the code easier to understand. Especially, in function, if somebody is going to use them again your clear definition will lead to effective utilization. You may add comments whenever necessary as below:

```
%---------------------------------------------------------------
% This is a comment and it has no effect to the program
%---------------------------------------------------------------
```

Let us take one built-in-function in Matlab to illustrate the coding practices when you make the functions. This function gives you any power of a given number. C = power(A,B) is called for the syntax 'A .^ B' when A or B is an object. See the comments given in Program 2.3 and complete code is not given.

```
function B = power(A,p)

%POWER   Symbolic array power.
%    POWER(A,p) overloads symbolic A.^p.
%
%    Examples:
%        A = [x 10 y; alpha 2 5];
%        A .^ 2 returns [x^2 100 y^2; alpha^2 4 25].
%        A .^ x returns [x^x 10^x y^x; alpha^x 2^x 5^x].
```

(Contd.)

```
. . .
. . .

A = sym(A);
p = sym(p);

if all(size(p) == 1)
    % Scalar exponent
    B = A;
    for k = 1:prod(size(A))
        B(k) = maple(A(k),'^',p);
    end

elseif all(size(A) == 1)
    % Scalar base
    B = p;
    for k = 1:prod(size(p))
        B(k) = maple(A,'^',p(k));
    end

. . .
. . .

else
    error('Matrix dimensions must agree.')
end
```

Program 2.3: Sample Built-in-Matlab Function (Curtsey of MathWork Inc.)

2.4 MEMORY MANAGEMENT IN SIMULATIONS

If your simulation generates very large amounts of data it may lead to memory problems. For an example, consider a situation where you write data to the hard disk periodically. After saving that portion of the data, clear the variable from memory and continue with the data generation. Table 2.7 shows the given Matlab facilities in order to manage the memory during simulations. In C language, you have different techniques.

Table 2.7: Several Functions that are Useful in Managing Memory

Function	Functional Meaning
Clear	Remove variables from memory
Pack	Save existing variables to disk and then reload them contiguously.
Save	Selectively store variables to disk.
load	Reload a data file saved with the save function.
quit	Exit MATLAB and return all allocated memory to the system.

Since Matlab uses a heap method of memory management, extended Matlab sessions may cause memory to become fragmented. When memory is fragmented, there may be plenty of free space, but not enough contiguous memory to store a new large variable. If you get the Out of Memory message from Matlab, the pack function may be able to compress some of your data in memory, thus freeing up larger contiguous blocks [5]. To conserve memory when creating variables, avoid creating large temporary variables and clear temporary variables when they are no longer needed. When working with arrays of fixed size, pre-allocate them rather than having Matlab resize the array each time you enlarge it. Set variables equal to the empty matrix [5] to free memory, or clear the variables using the clear function. Reuse variables as much as possible. Since Matlab uses a heap method of memory management, extended Matlab sessions may cause memory to become fragmented.

If your Matlab application needs to store a large amount of data created through a simulation or for a simulation, and the definition of that data lends itself to being stored in either a structure of arrays or an array of structures, the former is preferable. A structure of arrays requires significantly less memory than an array of structures, and has a corresponding speed benefit [1].

for and *while* loops that incrementally increase, or grow, the size of a data structure each time through the loop can adversely affect memory usage and performance. On each iteration, MATLAB has to allocate more memory for the growing matrix and also move data in memory whenever it cannot allocate a contiguous block. This can also result in fragmentation or in used memory not being returned to the operating system. If you run out of memory often, you can allocate your larger matrices earlier in the Matlab session and also use these system-specific tips: UNIX: Ask your system manager to increase your swap space. Windows: Increase virtual memory using the Windows Control Panel. For UNIX systems, we recommend that your machine be configured with twice as much swap space as you have RAM. The UNIX command, pstat -s, lets you know how much swap space you have [1], [2].

2.5 CUSTOMIZED FUNCTIONS

Up to this section in Chapter 2, we discussed on general purpose command that might be useful any kind of simulations. However, Matlab provides customized or application oriented functions. If you want to know about the availability of a command which is going to be useful in your simulation you should use *lookfor* or *help* commands in searching the desired functions. Table 2.8 shows the given Matlab functions for special applications.

Table 2.8: Customized Functions for Special Applications

Function	Functional Meaning
bin2dec	Convert decimal integer to a binary string.
dec2bin	Convert decimal integer to a binary string
fwrite	Write binary data to file.
fread	Read binary data from file
dec2hex	Convert decimal integer to hexadecimal string.
dec2base(D,B)	Returns the representation of D as a string in base B.

Example 1

In the next example, we will introduce how to get the Discrete Fourier transform. Y = *fft*(X) returns the discrete Fourier transform (DFT) of vector X, computed with a fast Fourier transform (FFT) algorithm. See the following codes:

```
>> t = 0:0.001:0.6;
>> x = sin(2*pi*50*t)+sin(2*pi*120*t);
>> y = x + 2*randn(size(t));
```

(This will create *y* vector in order to have a data stream for FFT)

```
>> Y = fft(y,512);
```

(Original vector *y* is having nearly 600 points. We only take 512 point as it will be efficient to select 512. Converting to the frequency domain, the discrete Fourier transform of the noisy signal y is found by taking the 512-point fast Fourier transform (FFT))

```
>> Pyy = Y.* conj(Y) / 512;
```

The power spectrum, a measurement of the power at various frequencies, is Graph the first 257 points.

```
>> f = 1000*(0:256)/512;
>> plot(f,Pyy(1:257));
```

Figure 2.4 shows the power spectrum of the above signal.

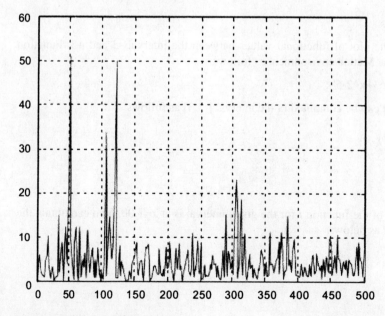

Figure 2.4: Power Spectrum

Let us define the *x* vector as below:

```
>> x = [4 3 7 -9 1 0 0 0]' ;
```

```
>> y = fft(x);
```

Note here that although the sequence x is real; y is complex and see the output y.

```
y =
6.0000
11.4853 - 2.7574i
-2.0000 -12.0000i
-5.4853 +11.2426i
18.0000
-5.4853 -11.2426i
-2.0000 +12.0000i
11.4853 + 2.7574i
```

We illustrated few special purpose commands and you will understand more on these when you step up to the next chapters.

Example 2

You can minimize a single variable function of on a fixed interval using a built in function called "fminbnd". Consider the following function:

$$f(x) = x^4 - 2x^3 + x^2 - 5$$

Figure 2.1 shows the plot of functional values between the interval -3 and +3. Function can be defined in the Matlab environment as follows:

f = inline('x.^4-2*x^3+x^2-5');

The minimum point can be computed in the interval [-3,3] as follows:

x = fminbnd(f, -3, 3)

x =
    1.0000

Minimum value of the function *f* for the given interval is at *x*=1.00. You can obtain the minimum value of *f* as below:

```
>> f(1.00)
```

ans =

-5

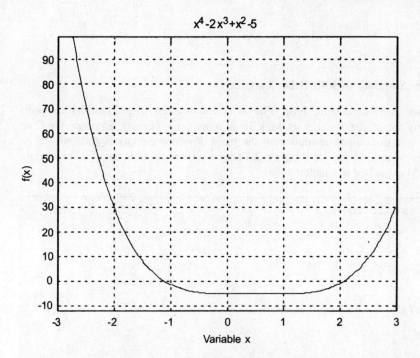

Figure 2.5: Functional value between the interval -3 and +3.

Note here that the function to be minimized must be continuous for the given interval. The command ***fminbnd*** may only give local solutions and it often exhibits slow convergence when the solution is on a boundary of the interval. Moreover, inline(Expression) constructs an inline function object from the Matlab expression contained in the string Expression. Following example creates a simple inline function to obtain the following:

Function:

$$F(t) = F = 3\sin(5t^3) + 6t$$

Code:

F = inline(' 3*sin(5*t.^3) + 6*t ')

You can convert the result to a string using the char function of the above define *F*.

>> char(F)

ans =

3*sin(5*t.^3) + 6*t

Following command returns the names of the input arguments of the INLINE object F as a cell array of strings.

>> argnames(F)

ans =

'ť'

2.6 Computer Simulations with Other Languages

Up to now, we introduced some basic Matlab codes in order to get familiarized with some essentials on simulations. Let us think about other programming language like C or C++. In fact, it is difficult to introduce all the basic developments associated with C or C++. However, sample C code in Program 2.4 shows how to create a data for the Lorenz Attractor (1.15) explained in Chapter 1.

```c
#include<stdio.h>
#include<math.h>
#include<stdlib.h>
#define   T   0.001

int main()
{
  int i;
  double x0,y0,z0,x1,y1,z1;
  FILE *fp = fopen("lor.dat","w");
  x0=y0=z0=1.0;
  for (i=0;i<5000;i++)
  {
    x1= x0 +T*(-10.0*(x0-y0));
        y1= y0 +T*(-x0*z0 + 28.0*x0 -y0);
        z1= z0 +T*(x0*y0 -8.0*z0/3.0);
        x0=x1;y0=y1;z0=z1;
        fprintf(fp,"%lf %lf\n",x1,z1);
  }
  fclose(fp);
  return 0;

}
```

Program 2.4: Creating Data with C

The programming language C is a general purpose language which was mainly developed to work with Unix systems and now you can see the Windows based versions as well [6]. C is relatively a low level language compared to Matlab and that is why authors recommend Matlab for complex simulations where you need not much expertise on programming. For an example, if you write a program to get the inverse of a given matrix in C or C++ it is necessary to write large program. On the other hand, if you use Matlab it is just two lines to obtain the answer. However, you can use library files or function written by different research institutes and organizations to reduce your programming time.

Now, we will create the same data file with Matlab that was obtained from Program 2.4 in order to analyze the dynamic system of the Lorenz Attractor. You can visualize the data file with a single command using Matlab whereas in C or C++ you have to do much work in obtaining the same graph. Figure 2.2 shows the output of the Program 2.5. Moreover, we will show the details of graphics and data visualization techniques in Chapter 3.

```
T=0.001;
x0=1.00;
y0=1.00;
z0=1.00;

fid=fopen('lor.dat','w');

for i=1: 50000
    x1= x0 +T*(-10.0*(x0-y0)) ;
    y1= y0 +T*(-x0*z0 + 28.0*x0 -y0);
    z1= z0 +T*(x0*y0 -8.0*z0/3.0);
    fprintf(fid,' %4.5f  %4.5f  \n ',x1,z1);
    x0=x1;y0=y1;z0=z1;
end
fclose(fid);
load lor.dat;
A=lor;
plot(A(:,1),A(:,2))
```

Program 2.5: Creating Same Data File with Matlab

Though Figure 2.2 shows a basic graph of the Lorenz Attractor Matlab provides a rich environment for drawing graphs or visualizing data. The data created by C or C++ can be visualized by using other software like Ngraph.

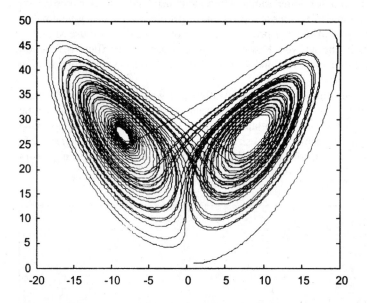

Figure 2.6: Output of Program 2.5.

REFERENCES

[1] Matlab Release 13, Version 6.5, "Help Manual and Toolboxes," The Mathworks Inc.

[2] J.B. Dabney and T.L. Harman, "Mastering Simulink 4", 2001, Prentice Hall, New Jersey.

[3] The Matlab Curriculum Series, "The Student Edition of Matlab – Version 4", 1995, Prentice Hall, New Jersey.

[4] G.C. Onwubolu, "Mechatronics: Principles and Applications," Elsevier Science, 2005.

[5] I. Danaila, P. Joly, S.M. Kaber, and M. Postel, "An Introduction to Scientific Computing: Twelve Computational Projects Solved with MATLAB" New York: Springer, 2007.

[6] B.W. Kernighan and D.M. Ritchie, "The C Programming Language," 2003, Prentice Hall, New Delhi, 2nd Edition.

If we use a 4 x n matrix whose i-th column is $z_i = [1 x_i x_i^2 y_i]$, it results that the x-coordinate of the i-th column is then x_i whereas the second line is y_i. The second line of the matrix, that is y_i, represents the x-coordinate of the i-th column, whereas the fourth line is y_i, represents the y-coordinate of the i-th column. If N = n then the resulting output y-vector has index 1-N.

Chapter 3

Data Visualization

Data visualization is the subject, which presents the world about your findings in an understandable language.

3.1 ELEMENTARY X-Y GRAPHS

After your simulations, you want to visualize your data in various forms in order to explore your results. These explorations will lead to fine-tune your results for a better design of your system under consideration [1]. In this chapter, we will investigate the facilities for data visualization, especially provided by Matlab.

3.1.1 Two-Dimensional Graphs

After a computer simulation, you want to see your output in various forms. One of the approaches might be to plot your data in various forms. Table 3.1 shows you some of the basic techniques for plotting data. Here, two dimensional plots are illustrated whereas some of the next sections will focus on three dimensional graphs and other techniques available in Matlab [2], [3].

Table 3.1: Elementary Functions for Plots

Command	Details
plot	Generate a linear plot of the values of x (horizontal axis) and y (vertical axis). If Y is complex, plot(Y) is equivalent to plot(real(Y),imag(Y)).
loglog	Generate a plot of the values of x and y (both logarithmic scale).
semilogx	Generate a plot of the values of x (logarithmic scale) and y (linear scale)
semilogy	Semi-log scale plot
polar	Polar coordinate plot
plotyy	Graphs with y tick labels on the left and right

The command *plot*(X,Y) plots vector Y versus vector X. If X or Y is a matrix, then the vector is plotted versus the rows or columns of the matrix, whichever line up. If X is a scalar and Y is a vector, length(Y) disconnected points are plotted. plot(Y) plots the columns of Y versus their index [5].

```
>> x = [1 2 3 4 5 6]; y = [1 -2 4 -0.5  2 5];
>> plot (x,y);
```

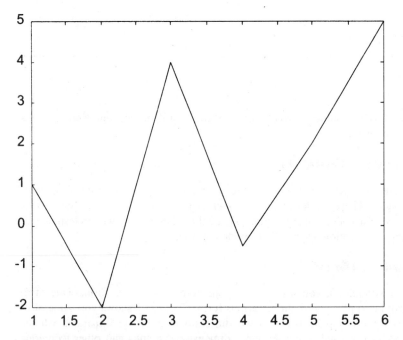

Figure 3.1: Basic 2-Dimentional Plot

This basic graph needs lots of formatting for better visualization and presentation. It is essential to include the title, axes labels, and other augmentations. Table 3.2 shows the supportive commands provided by Matlab to make the basic graph shown in Figure 3.1 more descriptive when the commands shown in Table 3.2 are applied. We will obtain more informative graph as shown in Figure 3.2.

For a better plot you have to pay much attention on the following things:

1. Line style
2. Line width
3. Color Marker type
4. Marker size
5. Marker face and edge coloring

Table 3.2: Supportive Commands for Plots

Command	Description
grid on	Add dashed grids lines at the tick marks. This will enhance the readability
grid off	Removes grid lines (default)
Grid	Toggles grid status (off to on or on to off)
title('text')	Labels top of plot with text
xlabel('text')	Labels horizontal (x) axis with text
ylabel('text')	Labels vertical (y) axis with text
text(x,y,'text')	Adds text to location (x,y) on the current axes, where (x,y) is in units from the current plot

```
>> title('My First Graph')
>> xlabel('Time [s]')
>> ylabel('Current [A]')
>> grid on
>> text(4,3,'Sampled Values are Taken')
```

Here, assume that you got this data from some experiment and want to visualize the variations of current [in A] against time [in s], from 1[s] to 6[s].

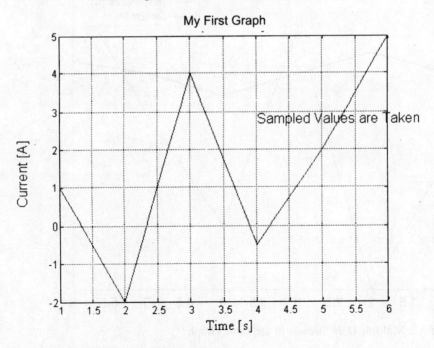

Figure 3.2: Enhanced Version of Figure 3.1

3.1.2 Multiple Plots and Curves

In certain situations, you are supposed to bring different data streams to the same graph, especially for comparison purposes. However, the same plot command can be employed in a different way.

```
>> x = [1 2 3 4 5 6]; y = [1 -2 4 -0.5 2 5];

> u = [1 2 3 4 5 6]; v = [3 3.5 3 2.5 3 3.3];

>> plot(x,y,u,v)
>> legend('Temperature [C]','Current [A]');
```

For an example, *plot*(x,y,'r-',x,y,'go') command plots the data twice, with a solid red line interpolating green circles at the data points. The plot command, if no color is specified, makes automatic use of the colors specified by the axes Color order property. The default Color order is listed in the Table 3.3 for color systems where the default is blue for one line, and for multiple lines, to cycle through the first six colors in the table. For monochrome systems, plot cycles over the axes LineStyleOrder property [5].

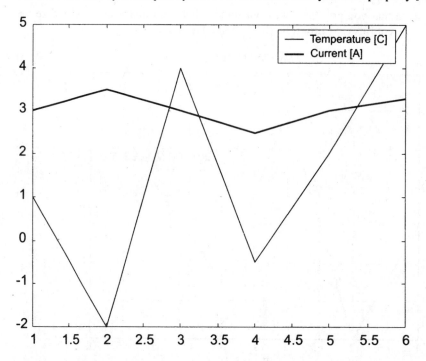

Figure 3.3: Multiple Data Streams in the Same Graph

At this point, we are not in a position to comment on the application where you need these commands. However, when you do different types of computer simulations you will automatically get used to apply these commands according to your situation.

Table 3.3: Symbols and Their Meanings

Symbol	Color	Symbol	Property	Symbol	Property
b	blue	.	point	-	solid
g	green	o	circle	:	dotted
r	red	x	x-mark	-.	dashdot
c	cyan	+	plus	--	dashed
m	magenta	*	star		
y	yellow	s	square		
k	black	d	diamond		
		v	triangle (down)		
		^	triangle (up)		
		<	triangle (left)		
		>	triangle (right)		
		p	pentagram		
		h	hexagram		

3.1.3 Polynomials

Consider the following polynomial

$$y = x^3 + 3x^2 + 3x + 1 \tag{3.1}$$

We define this polynomial function in Matlab as A = s ^ 3 + 3 * s ^ 2 + 3 * s + 1 for different analysis. If s is a vector or a matrix, use the array or element-by-element operation as A = s .^ 3 + 3 * s .^ 2 + 3 .* s + 1. Function polyval(a,s): evaluate a polynomial with coefficients in vector a for the values in s. You have to define the data range using the command linspace. Here, we define it from -5 to +5 and the use 100 computing points.

```
>> s = linspace(-5,5,100);
>> coeff = [1 3 3 1];
>> A = polyval(coeff,s);
>> plot(s,A)
>> xlabel('s')
>> ylabel('A(s)')
>> roots(coeff)

ans =

 -1.0000
 -1.0000 + 0.0000i
 -1.0000 - 0.0000i
```

Command *roots* returns the roots of the polynomial A in column vector form. Figure 3.4 shows the real root at s = 0.

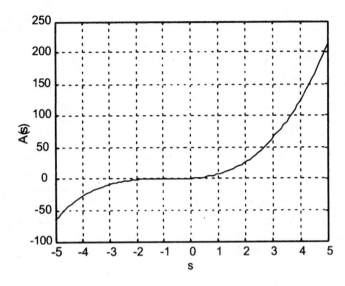

Figure 3.4: Roots of the Polynomial $y=f(x)$

3.1.4 Plotting Complex Numbers

Matlab will allow you to directly use the complex number notation and plot complex numbers in different ways.

```
>> z = 1 + 0.5j;
>> plot(z, '* ');
```

3.1.5 Axis Scaling

Table 3.4 shows the different scaling facilities provided by Matlab. In certain situations, you have to zoom out or zoom in a particular range and this can be done by scaling.

Table 3.4: Axis Scaling

Command	Description
axis([xmin xmax ymin ymax])	Define minimum and maximum values of the axes
axis square	Produce a square plot
axis equal	Equal scaling factors for both axes
axis normal	Turn off axis square, equal
axis (auto)	Return the axis to defaults

```
>> z = 1 + 0.5j;
>> plot(z, '* ');
>> axis([-1 3 -1 1])
```

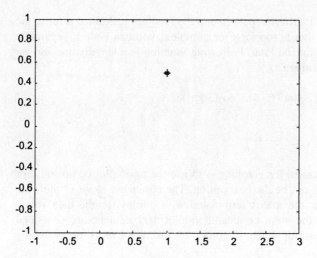

Figure 3.5: Complex Number with Scaled Axes

3.1.6 Polar Plots

Polar coordinate plots are very useful in certain applications where you define parametric functions. The basic command polar will plot any given polar coordinates where ***ezpolar*** can be employed to draw the parametric functions. Following codes will generate the polar plot in Figure 3.6.

>> polar(1, 3)

>> ezpolar('1+cos(t)')

ezpolar (' f(theta) ', [a,b]) plots f for a < theta < b.

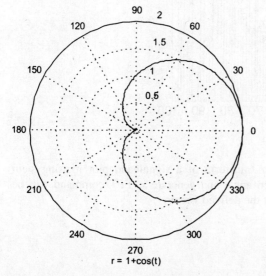

Figure 3.6: Polar Plot for the Parametric Function: r = 1+cos(t)

Following code will generate a different pattern and the function is defined prior to the plotting command. If your function is too large or complex, you can code it separetely and you may use the ezpolar command later. Following function is a lengthy one and we use ezpolar with a predefined parameter r.

```
>> r = '100/(100+(t-1/2*pi)^8)*(2-sin(7*t)-1/2*cos(30*t))';
>> ezpolar(r);
```

3.1.7 Discrete Sequence Plot

The most straightforward mechanism for graphing is to use the basic plot command. For different applications, this might not be the best option. The command *stem*(Y) plots the data sequence Y as stems from the x-axis terminated with circles for the data value. Figure 3.7 shows how to use the stem command to plot 100 data points generated randomly. This will be very useful when it comes to discrete events or switching applications.

```
>> x=rand(100,1);
>> stem(x);
```

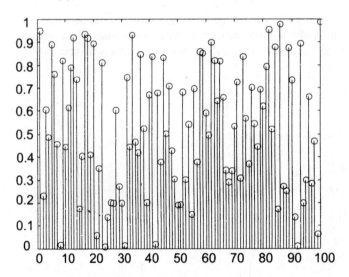

Figure 3.7: Plot Using *stem* Command

Following code will generate Fourier transform of a signal and plot it using stem command. Forst, it creates the vectorized angle and generate *x*. FFT command will be used to obtained the Fourier transform of the defined vector.

```
>> th=(0:127)/128*2*pi;
>> x=cos(th);
>> f=abs(fft(ones(5,1),128));
>> stem(x,f,'d','filled');
```

The command *stem*(...,'filled') produces a stem plot with filled markers. Figure 3.8 shows the output of the above code. At this point, you may not clearly understand the exact application. In fact, once you start computer simulations on different systems you find your own developments using these commands for the best visualization for that particular application. Similarly, the command *stairs* can be employed in a similar fashion to visualize data, especially with sampled data. Moreover, the command *hist* can be employed to plot histograms, especially when you deal with probabilistic approaches. The next sample code with Figure 3.9 illustrates how to plot a histogram.

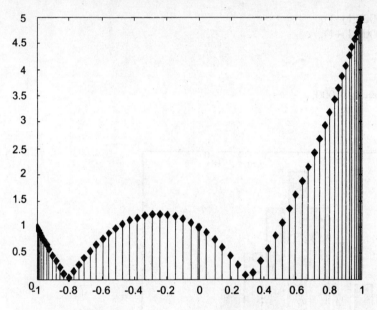

Figure 3.8: Plotting a Spectrum Using *stem* Command

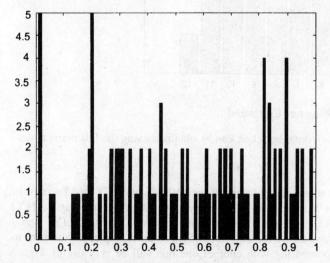

Figure 3.9: Plotting a Data Using *hist* Command

```
>> x=rand(100,1);
>> hist(x,100)
```

Probabilistic approaches are found in various scientific and engineering models. In some cases, these models finally come up with probability density functions. They need specific graphical representations and bar charts are one of the common visualizations in common practice. The following code illustrate how to generate random data for modeling. Figure 3.10 shows the bar chart generated using the command *bar*.

```
x1=floor(6*rand(10000,1)+1);
x2=floor(6*rand(10000,1)+1);
y=x1+x2;

for i =2:12
        z(i)=sum(y==i)/10000;
end
bar(z)
```

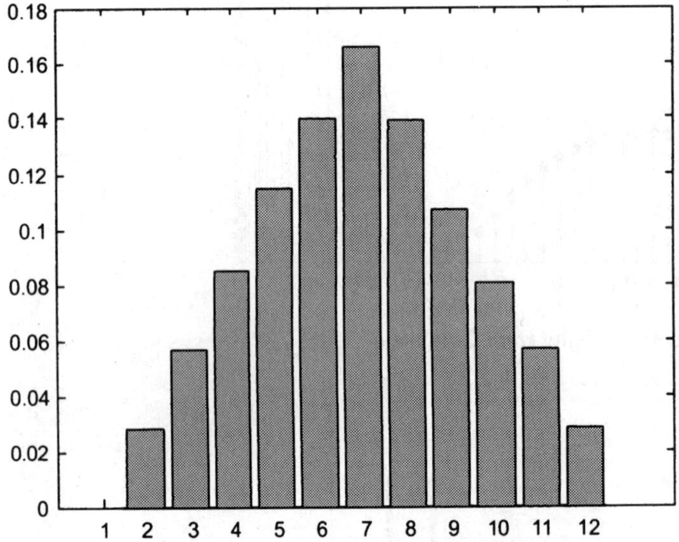

Figure 3.10: Plotting Data Using *bar* Command

For the same data set z, horizontal bar chart can be obtained using the following code:

```
>> barh(z*10)
```

The command *barh*(X,Y) draws the columns of the M-by-N matrix Y as M groups of N horizontal bars. The vector X must be monotonically increasing or decreasing. barh(Y) uses the default value of X=1: M. For vector inputs, barh(X,Y) or barh(Y) draws length(Y) bars. The colors are set by the colormap [5]. For an example, if you want to give an idea of a length in comparing with another one this will be very useful. Figure 3.11 shows the output to the above code for the same data set.

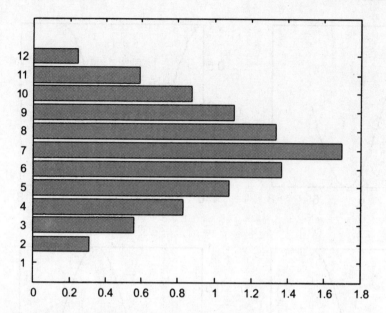

Figure 3.11: Plotting a Data Using ***barh*** Command

3.1.8 Multiple Graphs

Following codes will generate four data sets, which are having different properties. However, we need them to be visualized in the same place, not in the same single graph. Figure 3.12 shows the output for the following codes in order to visualize them in the same main graph but four different sub-plots.

```
>> t = 0:pi/100:2*pi;
>> y1=sin(t);
>> y2=sin(t+pi/2);
>> subplot(2,2,1)
>> plot(t,y1)

>> subplot(2,2,2)
>> plot(t,y2)

>> y3=cos(t);
>> y4=cos(t+pi/2);
>> subplot(2,2,3)
>> plot(t,y3)

>> subplot(2,2,4)
>> plot(t,y4)
>> ylabel('yy')
>> xlabel('xx')
```

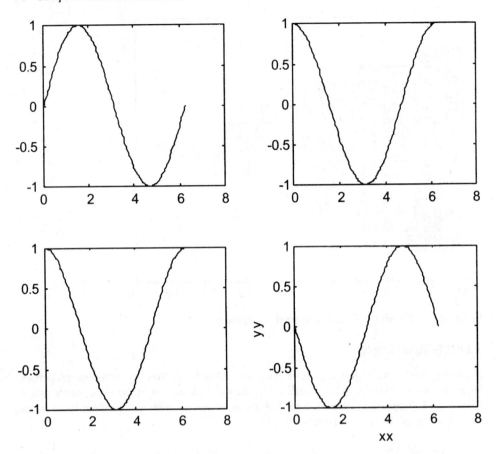

Figure 3.12: Plotting Data using *subplot* Command

3.2 ELEMENTARY X-Y-Z GRAPHS

3.2.1 Three-Dimensional Basic Plots

Up to this section, we discussed about two-dimensional plots. Matlab provides a rich environment for three-dimensional graphs with various options. The elementary command *plot3*(x,y,z), where x, y and z are three vectors of the same length, plots a line in 3-space through the points whose coordinates are the elements of x, y and z.

The command *plot3*(x1,y1,z1,s1,x2,y2,z2,s2,x3,y3,z3,s3,...) combines the plots defined by the (x,y,z,s) fourtuples, where the x's, y's and z's are vectors or matrices and the s's are strings. The above example shows the way of combining desired points for creating lines and gets the final object using the command *plot3* (see Figure 3.13).

```
p1x=[-1.5091 18.4858 8.4839 -1.5091 8.4882];
p1y=[2.7139   2.7184 20.0168 2.7139 8.4795];
p1z=[22.3235 23.2978 22.3233 22.3235 38.9072];

plot3(p1x,p1y,p1z,'b');

hold on;

p2x=[8.4839 8.4882  18.4858];
p2y=[20.0168 8.4795 2.7184];
p2z=[22.3233 38.9072 23.2978];

plot3(p2x,p2y,p2z,'r');
hold on;

xlabel('\fontsize{20} Variable x');
ylabel('\fontsize{20} Variable y');
zlabel('\fontsize{20} Variable z');

text(18.4858,2.7184,23.2978,' P_2');

view(-80,17.5)
grid on
```

Program 3.1: Three-dimensional Graphs using *Plot3*

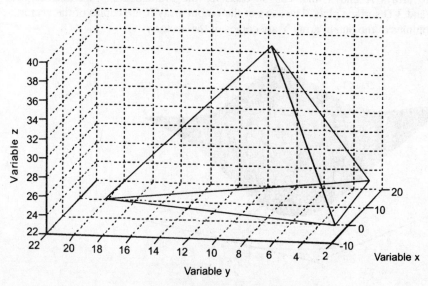

Figure 3.13: Three-dimensional Plots using *plot3* Command

3.2.2 Three-Dimensional Color Plots

The command ***mesh***(X,Y,Z,C) plots the colored parametric mesh defined by four matrix arguments. The viewpoint is specified by ***view***. The axis labels are determined by the range of X, Y and Z or by the current setting of axis. The color scaling is determined by the range of C, or by the current setting of ***caxis***. The scaled color values are used as indices into the current ***colormap***. Program 3.2 illustrates the codes for color plots using ***mesh*** command (see Figure 3.14 for the output).

```
x= -3: 0.05 :3;
y= -3: 0.05 :3;
 [X,Y]=meshgrid(x,y);

R=sqrt(X.^2+Y.^2);
Z=-sin(R)./R ;
mesh(X,Y,Z);
surfc(X,Y,Z);

xlabel('x1');
ylabel('x2');
zlabel('Function Value');
grid on;
```

Program 3.2: Three-dimensional Color Graphs using ***mesh***

Note here that [X,Y] = ***meshgrid***(x,y) transforms the domain specified by vectors x and y into arrays X and Y that can be used for the evaluation of functions of two variables and 3-D surface plots. The rows of the output array X are copies of the vector x and the columns of the output array Y are copies of the vector y.

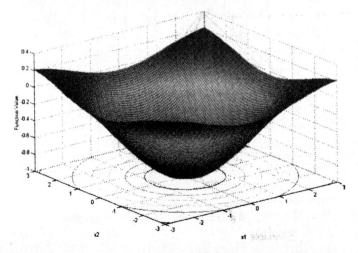

Figure 3.14: Three-dimensional Color Plots

3.2.3 Discrete Sequence Plot

The command stem3(Z) in Matlab plots the discrete surface Z as stems from the XY-plane terminated with circles for the data value (see Program 3.3 and Figure 3.15).

```
th=(0:127)/128*2*pi;

x=cos(th);
y=sin(th);

f=abs(fft(ones(5,1),128));

stem3(x,y,f','d','fill');

view([-65 30])
```

Program 3.3: Three-dimensional Graphs using *stem3*

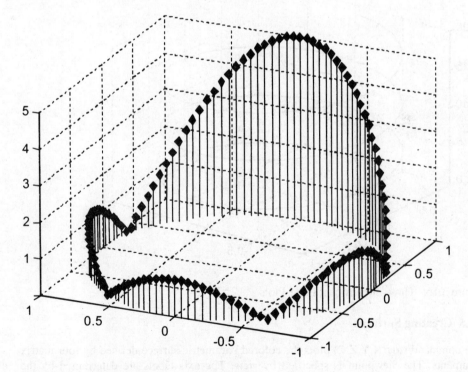

Figure 3.15: Three-dimensional Color Plots

3.2.4 Polar Plots

The command *ezplot3*(x,y,z) plots the spatial curve x = x(t), y = y(t), and z = z(t) over the default domain 0 < t < 2*pi. Following code will generate a three-dimensional parametric graph as shown in Figure 3.16.
>> ezplot3('sin(t)','cos(t)','t',[0,6*pi])

Note here that the axes labels will automatically generate as X, Y and Z as shown in Figure 3.16 though we do not name them separately.

The definition ezplot3(x,y,z,[tmin,tmax]) plots the curve x = x(t), y = y(t), and z = z(t) over tmin < t < tmax. See the following code for the syntax:

```
>> x=' t^3-8 ';
>> y=' exp(-t) ';
>> z=' cos(t) ';
>> ezplot3(x,y,z)
```

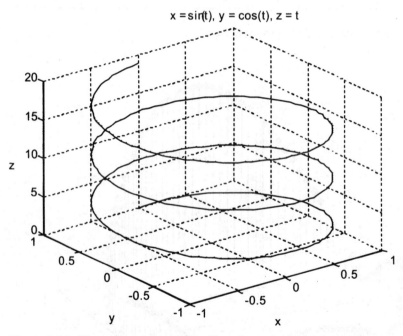

Figure 3.16: Three-dimensional Polar Plots

3.2.5 Creating Surfaces

The command *surf*(X,Y,Z,C) plots the colored parametric surface defined by four matrix arguments. The viewpoint is specified by *view*. The axis labels are determined by the range of X, Y and Z, or by the current setting of axis. The color scaling is determined by the range of C, or by the current setting of *caxis*. The scaled color values are used as indices into the current *colormap*. The shading model is set by *shading* Refer Program 3.4 and Figure 3.17).

```
k=5;
n=2^k -1;
theta=pi*(-n:2:n)/n;
phi=(pi/2)*(-n:2:n)/n;

X=[cos(phi)]'*[cos(theta)];
Y=[cos(phi)]'*[sin(theta)];
Z=[tan(phi)]'*ones(size(theta));

colormap([1 0 0;1 1 1]);
C=hadamard(2^k);

surf(X,Y,Z,C);
axis square;
```

Program 3.4: Three-dimensional Graphs using *surf*

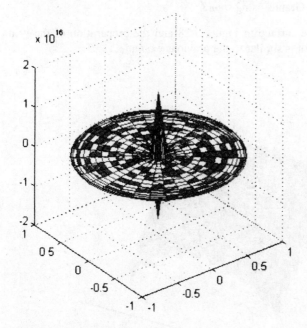

Figure 3.17: Three-dimensional Color Plots

```
>> t=0:pi/6:2*pi;
>> [x,y,z]=cylinder(1,30);
>> mesh(x,y,z)
>> t=0:pi/6:2*pi;
>> [x,y,z]=cylinder(t,30);
>> mesh(x,y,z)
```

```
>> t=0:pi/6:2*pi;
>> [x,y,z]=cylinder(cos(t), 30);
>> mesh(x,y,z)
```

```
x = -3:.05:3;
y = -3:.05:3;
[X,Y] = meshgrid(x,y);
Z=-X.*X - 2.0.*Y.*Y +cos(3.0.*pi.*X) +
03*cos(4.0.*pi.*Y) + 4;
contourf(X,Y,Z);
%mesh(X,Y,Z);
surfc(X,Y,Z);
xlabel('x1');
ylabel('x2');
zlabel('Function Value');
grid on;
```

Program 3.5: Three-dimensional Graphs using *stem3*

Program 3.5 will generate the surface in Figure 3.18 and the preparation of the grid data for the three-dimensional plot is similar to the previous example.

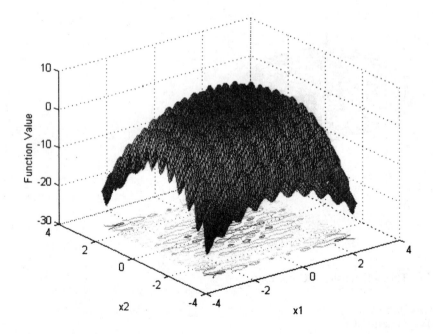

Figure 3.18: Three-dimensional Color Plots

In certain situations, it is necessary to get an idea about the functional values at different locations in a 3D graph. Color scale can be included with the following command (see Figure 3.19):

>> colorbar

```
x = -3:.05:3;
y = -3:.05:3;
[X,Y] = meshgrid(x,y);
Z=-X.*X - 2.0.*Y.*Y +cos(3.0.*pi.*X) +
03*cos(4.0.*pi.*Y) + 4;
surfl(X,Y,Z);
xlabel('x1');
ylabel('x2');
zlabel('Function Value');
shading interp
colormap(gray);
```

Program 3.6: Surface Plot with Colormap-based Lighting

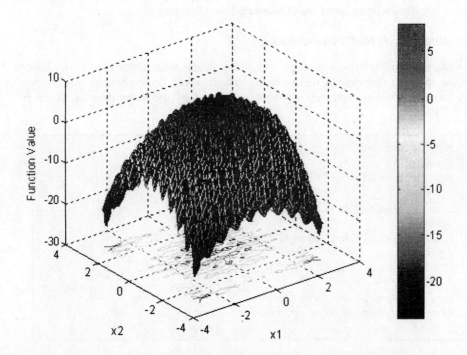

Figure 3.19: Three-dimensional Color Plots with Colored Functional Value

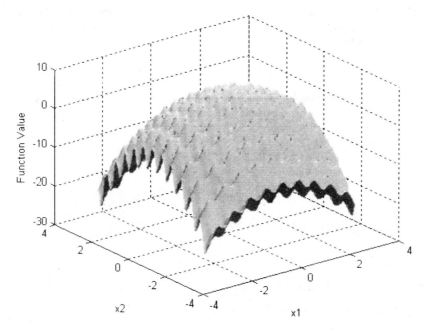

Figure 3.20: Three-dimensional with Colormap-based Lighting

3.2.6 Multiple Axes for Different Scaling

You can create multiple axes of display graphics objects with different scaling without changing the data that defines these objects (which would be required to display in a single axis). In this example, each *sphere* is defined by the same data as shown in Figure 3.19.

```
h(1) = axes('Position',[0 0 1 1]);
sphere
h(2) = axes('Position',[0 0 .4 .6]);
sphere
h(3) = axes('Position',[0 .5 .5 .5]);
sphere
h(4) = axes('Position',[.5 0 .4 .4]);
sphere
h(5) = axes('Position',[.5 .5 .5 .3]);
sphere
set(h,'Visible','off')
set(gcf,'Renderer','painters')
```

Program 3.7: Three-dimensional Graphs using *stem3*

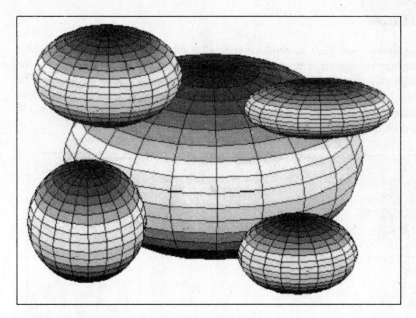

Figure 3.21: Three-dimensional Color Plots

3.2.7 Titles with Symbols

Program 3.8 illustrates possible generation of mathematical equations in the graph, especially with Greek fonts.

```
x=-2:.05:2;
y=-4:.1:4;
[X,Y]=meshgrid(x,y);
alpha=1;

Z=alpha*X.*exp(-X.^2-Y.^2);
contour(x,y,Z);
mesh(X,Y,Z);
surfc(X,Y,Z);

xlabel('x_1');
ylabel('x2');
zlabel('{\alpha}{x_1}{\ite}^{-({x_1}^2 +{x_2}^2 }) ');

grid on;
```

Program 3.8: Three-dimensional Surface

3.2.8 Special Graphs

In certain simulations, you have to produce special graphs. For an example, in sensor networks, Delaunay triangulation is an important graph. Given a set of data points, the Delaunay triangulation is a set of lines connecting each point to its natural neighbors. The Delaunay triangulation is related to the Voronoi diagram-- the circle circumscribed about a Delaunay triangle has its center at the vertex of a Voronoi polygon Refer Program 3.9, Figure 3.22 and Figure 3.23):

```
rand('state',0);
x = rand(1,50);
y = rand(1,50);
TRI = delaunay(x,y);
subplot(1,2,1),...
triplot(TRI,x,y)
axis([0 1 0 1]);
hold on;
plot(x,y,'or');
hold off
```

Program 3.9: Delaunay Triangulation

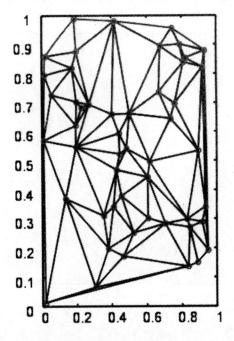

Figure 3.22: Delaunay triangulation

```
rand('state',0);
x = rand(1,50);
y = rand(1,50);
TRI = delaunay(x,y);
subplot(1,2,1),...
triplot(TRI,x,y)
axis([0 1 0 1]);
hold on;
plot(x,y,'or');
hold off

[vx, vy] = voronoi(x,y,TRI);
subplot(1,2,2),...
plot(x,y,'r+',vx,vy,'b-'),...
axis([0 1 0 1])
```

Program 3.10: Veronoi Polygon in 2D graph

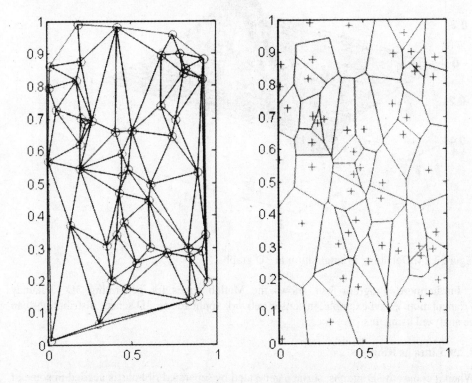

Figure 3.23: Delaunay triangulation and Veronoi Polygon in 2D graphs

```
x=-2:.5:2;
y=-4:.5:4;
[X,Y]=meshgrid(x,y);
alpha=1;

Z=alpha*X.*exp(-X.^2-Y.^2);
tri = delaunay(X,Y);
trisurf(tri,X,Y,Z)

grid on;
```

Program 3.11: Delaunay Triangulation in 3D graphs

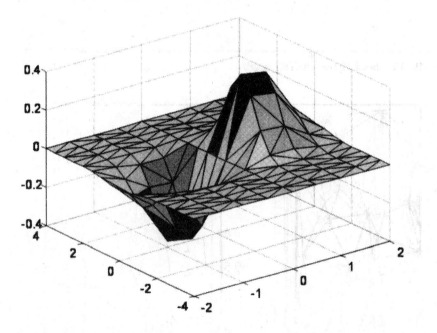

Figure 3.24: Delaunay Triangulation in 3D graphs

Furthermore, Program 3.11 shows the Matlab codes for generating 3D Delaunay Triangulation. As an example, in sensor network applications, 3D sensor distributions can be analyzed using this.

3.2.9 Lines as Ribbons

When it comes to 3D graphs, surface generated by separated ribbons is needed in some of the graphics applications. Program 3.10 shows an example for generating lines as ribbons. Moreover, Figure 3.25 shows the output of Program 3.10.

```
x=-2:0.5:2;
y=-4:.1:4;
[X,Y]=meshgrid(x,y);
alpha=1;
Z=alpha*X.*exp(-X.^2-Y.^2);
ribbon(Y,Z)
```

Program 3.12: Lines as Ribbons in 3-D

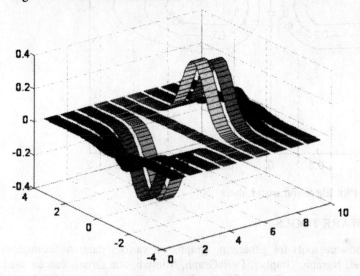

Figure 3.25: Lines as Ribbons in 3-D

3.2.10 Contour Plot

A contour plot is a graphical technique for representing a 3-dimensional surface by plotting constant z slices, called contours, on a 2-dimensional format. That is, given a value for z, lines are drawn for connecting the (x,y) coordinates where that z value occurs. Moreover, Figure 3.26 shows the output of Program 3.13 which draws contour lines of the function.

```
x=-2:0.5:2;
y=-4:0.1:4;
[X,Y]=meshgrid(x,y);
alpha=1;
Z=alpha*X.*exp(-X.^2-Y.^2);
[C,h] = contour(X,Y,Z);
clabel(C,h);
```

Program 3.13: Elevation with Labels

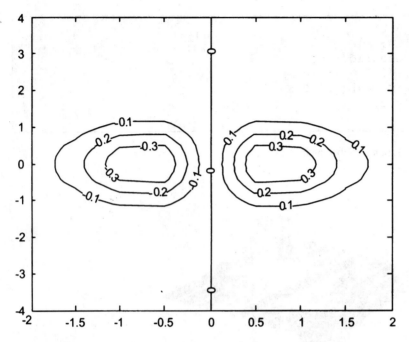

Figure 3.26: Contour Plot Elevation with Labels

3.3 OTHER SOFTWARE TOOLS

There are various software tools for generating graphs on various data. As examples, SmartDraw, MS Excel, Ngraph, Grapher, DeltaGraph, Minitab, and Oriana can be used for plotting various graphs depending on the application. Once you completed your simulation you are free to use one of these [5]-[8].

Ngraph is one of the programs creating scientific 2-dimensinal graphs for scientific researchers. Ngraph reads numerical data from a flexible text file, and plots it in the graph whereas Ngraph can create the graph suitable for presentations and for papers. Ngraph can be downloaded from the following web site:

http://www2e.biglobe.ne.jp/~isizaka/indexe.htm

Ngraph has the following features in general (courtesy of Ngraph):

- Easy to use due to graphical user interface.
- Easiness due to multi window interface.
- Plot with different styles of lines.
- Fitting by n-th polynomial or user defined math functions.
- Fitting with weight by any mathematical function.
- Data conversion by math expression.
- File output of converted data.
- Evaluation, mask, and movement of the plotted data.
- Linear plot, semi-log plot, log-log plot.
- Two or more graphs are created in a page.

- Linkage of the axis scale in multi graph.
- Appending the (saved) graph to the current graph.
- Saving graph with data attached.
- Zooming, trimming, undoing of the axis scale.
- Grid is added to the axis.
- Automatic setup of the axis scale.
- Detailed setup of gauging and numbering for axis.
- Legend by lines, curves, polygons, rectangles, ellipses, marks, texts.
- High functional text legend such as a display of date, file name, etc.
- Automatic legend creation.
- Legend by a parabola, gauss function, Lorentz function, and sin function.
- Automatic legend creation of fitting results.
- Fixed form processing by add-in scripts.
- Automatic processing by scripts.
- Export via clip board and meta file (Windows version).
- Compact PostScript file creation (suitable for electronic submission).
- Export via original simple graphics file.
- Perfect data compatibility between Windows and Unix.

Note here that Ngraph can be installed on Windows 95&98 / Windows NT/2000/XP (shareware) and Unix based systems (freeware, GNU General Public License).

REFERENCES

[1] W. Cleveland, "Visualizing Data," Hobart Press, 1993.

[2] Matlab Release 13, Version 6.5, "Help Manual and Toolboxes," The Mathworks Inc.

[3] J.B. Dabney and T.L. Harman, "Mastering Simulink 4," Prentice Hall, New Jersey, 2001.

[4] Draper and Smith, "Applied Regression Analysis," 2nd edition., 1981, John Wiley and Sons.

[5] E. Balagurusamy, "Object-Oriented Programming with C++," 2003, Tata McGraw-Hill, New Delhi.

[6] G. Rowe, An Introduction to Data Structures and Algorithms with Java, Prentice-Hall, 1997

[7] R. Sedgewick, "Algorithms," Addison-Wesley Series in Computer Science, 1988.

[8] S. Baase and A.Van Gelder, "Computer Algorithms—Introduction to Design & Analysis," Addison-Wesley, 2000.

Chapter 4

Examples of Different Systems

Understanding of basic concepts behind different systems will lay the foundation to system simulation.

4.1 Chaotic System 1: Lorenz Attractor

Under this chapter, we illustrate some of the examples, which show the behavior under their inherent properties and dynamics. Some systems are benchmark problems and you need to understand the scientific and engineering fundamentals behind them [1]. Let us take the first class of systems on chaos and normally described as chaotic system.

Edward Lorenz, the first experimenter in chaos theory was a meteorologist and described his model of weather prediction phenomena with a set of nonlinear differential equations in 1963. He was working on a problem of weather prediction, with a set of twelve equations to model and predict the weather [2]. Unfortunately, it did not predict the weather itself. However, his computer program did theoretically predict what the weather might be. From this set of equations, it is concluded that the system behavior sensitively depends on the initial condition or the place where it starts. At that time, there were only two kinds of orders previously known: a steady state, in which the variables never change, and periodic behavior, in which the system goes into a loop, repeating it indefinitely. Lorenz's equations were definitely in order and they always followed a spiral. They never settled down to a single point at steady state, however, they never repeated the same thing and they were not periodic either. In fact, this background will help you to imagine the importance of computer simulations in order to investigate a given problem. In fact this system is a nonlinear continuous system as shown below:

$$\dot{x}_1 = -\delta(x_1 - x_2) + u_1$$
$$\dot{x}_2 = -x_1 x_3 + r x_1 - x_2 \qquad (4.1)$$
$$\dot{x}_3 = x_1 x_2 - b x_3$$

Here, the terms δ, r, and b have the values 10, 28, and 8/3, respectively. When it graphs the above equations, the Lorenz attractor can be viewed as shown in Figure 4.1.

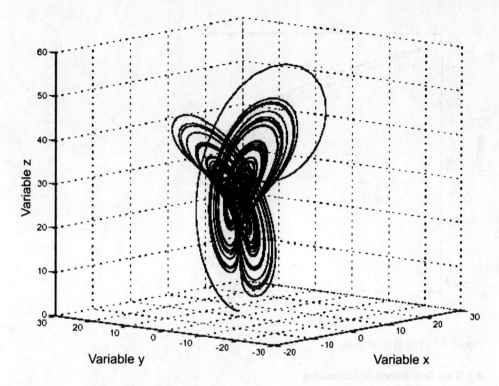

Figure 4.1: Three-dimensional Lorenz Attractor

4.2 Chaotic System 2: The Henon-Map

As described in the previous example and explained by astronomers, the word chaos denotes an abrupt change in some property of an object's orbit. Computers have always been known for their excellence capability at repetitive works; hence, the computer is our tool when simulating chaos. There is no doubt; one cannot really explore chaos without a digital computer. The first consumer product to exploit chaos theory was produced in 1993 by Goldstar Company in the form of a revolutionary washing machine. The washing machine is based on the principle that there are identifiable and predictable movements in nonlinear systems. The new washing machine was designed to produce cleaner and less tangled clothes. The key to the chaotic cleaning process can be found in a small pulsator that rises and falls randomly as the main pulsator rotates. In this example, the nonlinear discrete system, the Henon map, is presented to illustrate the dynamics. The nonlinear dynamic equation of the Henon map is given by

$$x_1(t+1) = -1.4x_1^2 + x_2 + 1$$
$$x_2(t+1) = 0.3x_1$$

$$(4.2)$$

For simplicity, uncontrolled Henon map, starting from (-0.3, 0.0) is given in Figure 4.2. Here, the points 1,2,3,4, and 5 denote the first consequent five points respectively.

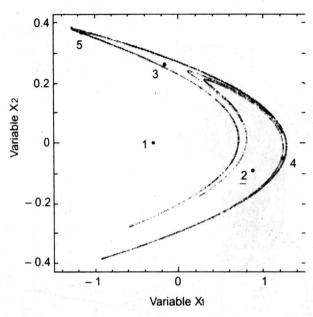

Figure 4.2: The Henon Map

4.3 Two-link Robot Manipulator

In this section, we try to give you an idea of robot dynamics rather than deriving dynamic equations. Webster's dictionary defines a robot as an automatic device that performs functions normally ascribed to humans or a machine in the form of a human. Moreover, robot is a re-programmable, multifunctional machine designed to manipulate materials, parts, tools, or specialized devices, through variable programmed motions for the performance of a variety of tasks. There are different types of robots with different functionalities. Two-link robot manipulator in Figure 4.3 is taken into consideration in order to illustrate the dynamics of the manipulator. Joint torque vector of the manipulator is given in the dynamic equation as below (see Figure 4.3 for the manipulator parameters):

$$\begin{bmatrix} \tau_1 \\ \tau_2 \end{bmatrix} = M \begin{bmatrix} \ddot{\theta}_1 \\ \ddot{\theta}_2 \end{bmatrix} + (\dot{\theta}_1 \dot{\theta}_2) B + C \begin{bmatrix} \dot{\theta}_1^{\,2} \\ \dot{\theta}_2^{\,2} \end{bmatrix} + F \begin{bmatrix} \dot{\theta}_1 \\ \dot{\theta}_2 \end{bmatrix} + G \tag{4.3}$$

Where,

$$M = \begin{bmatrix} m_2 l_2^{\,2} + 2m_2 l_1 l_2 c_2 + (m_1 + m_2) l_1^{\,2} & m_2 l_2^{\,2} + m_2 l_1 l_2 c_2 \\ m_2 l_2^{\,2} + m_2 l_1 l_2 c_2 & m_2 l_2^{\,2} \end{bmatrix} \tag{4.4}$$

Here, M is the inertia matrix, B denotes the Coriolis Component and C is the centrifugal force matrix.

$$B = \begin{bmatrix} -m_2 l_1 l_2 s_2 \\ 0 \end{bmatrix} \tag{4.5}$$

$$C = \begin{bmatrix} 0 & -m_2 l_1 l_2 s_2 \\ m_2 l_1 l_2 s_2 & 0 \end{bmatrix} \tag{4.6}$$

F is the friction matrix and G is the gravity component.

$$F = \begin{bmatrix} f_1 & 0 \\ 0 & f_2 \end{bmatrix} \tag{4.7}$$

$$G = \begin{bmatrix} m_2 l_2 g c_{12} + (m_1 + m_2) l_1 g c_1 \\ m_2 l_2 g c_{12} \end{bmatrix} \tag{4.8}$$

Note here that the manipulator dynamics represented in equation (4.3) is different from equation (1.1). In fact, this can be transformed to equation (1.1) after defining the states. This is the standard way of representing robot manipulator dynamics.

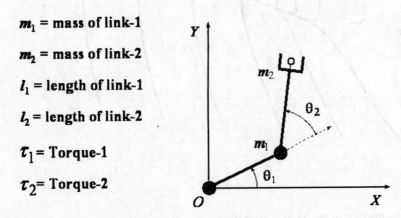

m_1 = **mass of link-1**

m_2 = **mass of link-2**

l_1 = **length of link-1**

l_2 = **length of link-2**

τ_1 = **Torque-1**

τ_2 = **Torque-2**

Figure 4.3: Two-link Robot Manipulator

In most of robotic applications, the common actuator technology is electrical systems with very limited use of hydraulics or pneumatics. By employing high accurate electric and mechanical actuators, robots are capable of dealing with nanometer precision in certain tasks, which need high accuracy. In this example, you have joint and torque vector consists of two inputs.

4.4 Nonlinear Systems: State Portrait

We will take the following nonlinear system in order to explain the concept of state portrait. A state portrait graphically depicts the behavior of nonlinear system in the vicinity of an equilibrium point or points (see Figure 4.4) [5],[6]. This system has an equilibrium point at (0,0).

$$\dot{x}_1 = -x_2$$
$$\dot{x}_2 = x_1 + x_1^3 - 3x_2 \tag{4.9}$$

State portrait is very important where you want to check the stability of the system. For an example, if you draw a plot of two variables as shown in Figure 4.4 you can see the behavior of the system at different values. These variables may be displacement, velocity or acceleration. In a thermodynamics application, it may be the temperature or the rate of change of the temperature.

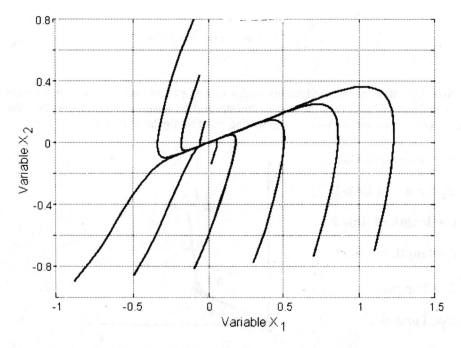

Figure 4.4: State Portrait of the Nonlinear System

4.5 Mechanical Systems: Two Mass-spring Cart System

The two mass-spring cart system in Figure 4.5 has four state variables and this is a linear system. To compute the system response we have to develop a model using Newton's laws of motion. Starting from the basic equations, we will derive the set of system equations to have the complete system dynamics. In this model, you have an input on the second mass. Applying $Ma=F$ on the first mass of the cart in the direction of x.

$$m_1\ddot{x}_1 = -D\dot{x}_1 + k(x_2 - x_1) \tag{4.10}$$

Applying $Ma = F$ on the second mass of the cart

$$m_2\ddot{x}_2 = k(x_1 - x_2) + u \tag{4.11}$$

Higher order derivative terms should be reduced to first order terms in order to develop a state space model with minimum number of variables. Therefore, we define another two variables as below:

$$\dot{x}_1 = x_3 \tag{4.12}$$

$$\dot{x}_2 = x_4 \tag{4.13}$$

If you combine the equations (4.10), (4.11), (4.12), and (4.13), it will lead to the state space model of the complete system.

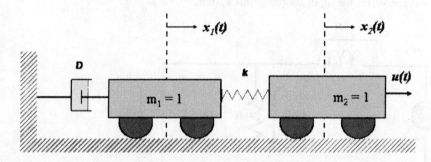

Figure 4.5: Two Mass-spring Cart System

With the above equations, following linear system can be obtained with four state variables.

$$\begin{bmatrix} \dot{x}_1 \\ \dot{x}_2 \\ \dot{x}_3 \\ \dot{x}_4 \end{bmatrix} = \begin{pmatrix} 0 & 0 & 1 & 0 \\ 0 & 0 & 0 & 1 \\ -k/m_1 & k/m_1 & -D/m_1 & 0 \\ k/m_2 & -k/m_2 & 0 & 0 \end{pmatrix} \begin{bmatrix} x_1 \\ x_2 \\ x_3 \\ x_4 \end{bmatrix} + \begin{bmatrix} 0 \\ 0 \\ 0 \\ 1/m_2 \end{bmatrix} u(t)$$

For the simplicity, following numerical values are assigned.

$k = D = 0.5$
$m_1 = m_2 = 1$

If we assign the values for different parameters as above, the following state space model can be obtained.

$$
\begin{bmatrix} \dot{x}_1 \\ \dot{x}_2 \\ \dot{x}_3 \\ \dot{x}_4 \end{bmatrix} = \begin{pmatrix} 0 & 0 & 1 & 0 \\ 0 & 0 & 0 & 1 \\ -0.5 & 0.5 & -0.5 & 0 \\ 0.5 & -0.5 & 0 & 0 \end{pmatrix} \begin{bmatrix} x_1 \\ x_2 \\ x_3 \\ x_4 \end{bmatrix} + \begin{bmatrix} 0 \\ 0 \\ 0 \\ 1 \end{bmatrix} u(t)
$$

When damper is included in the system, it will absorb the energy. In typical systems, you may include springs or viscous media for obtaining the desired damping. The motion of the system is affected by the magnitude of damping leading to under damped, critically damped or over damped conditions. You can perform basic matrix operations such as addition, multiplication, or concatenation on these linear models.

4.6 Electrical Systems: L-R-C Circuits

Figure 4.6 shows an LRC circuit in order to explain the system-modeling concept behind it. Supply voltage $V(t)$ is the input source to this system.

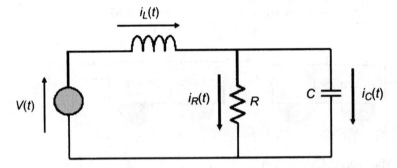

Figure 4.6: RLC Circuit

When we analyze the circuit in Figure 4.6, the current across the capacitor can be expressed as below (for further details refer Chapter 1):

$$
C \frac{dV_C(t)}{dt} = i_c \tag{4.14}
$$

The Voltage across the inductor can be obtained as

$$
L \frac{di_L(t)}{dt} = V_L \tag{4.15}
$$

From the first principles, the total voltage $V(t)$ can be expressed as

$$
V(t) = V_C + V_L \tag{4.16}
$$

Similarly, total current flow through the inductor is given by

$$
i_L = i_R + i_c \tag{4.17}
$$

This will lead to the following form,

$$\begin{bmatrix} \dot{V}_C \\ \dot{i}_L \end{bmatrix} = \begin{bmatrix} -1/RC & 1/C \\ -1/L & 0 \end{bmatrix} \begin{bmatrix} V_C \\ i_L \end{bmatrix} + \begin{bmatrix} 0 \\ 1/L \end{bmatrix} V(t)$$

$$i_R = \begin{bmatrix} 1/R & 0 \end{bmatrix} \begin{bmatrix} V_C \\ i_L \end{bmatrix}$$

(4.18)

Note here that this system of equations is in the general form of equation in Chapter 1.

4.7 Electro-Mechanical Systems: Magnetically Suspended Ball

Magnetically suspended ball system is an integrated system with some of the electrical and mechanical components. This example will illustrate the derivations related to linearization technique. Figure 4.7 shows the schematic diagram of the magnetically suspended ball with other elements. Using a voltage source, electromagnet is energized. Both Newton's laws of motion and Kirchhoff's circuit laws can be employed to derive the dynamics. The dynamic equations for the system in Figure 4.7 are as below:

$$M \frac{d^2h}{dt^2} = Mg - \frac{\alpha I^2}{h}$$

$$V = L\frac{dI}{dt} + IR$$

(4.19)

Where h is the vertical position of the ball, I is the current through the electromagnet, V is the applied voltage, M is the mass of the ball, g is gravity, L is the inductance, R is the resistance, and α is a coefficient that determines the magnetic force exerted on the ball. For simplicity, we will choose values M = 0.05 [Kg], α = 0.0001, L = 0.01 [H], R = 1 [Ohm], g = 9.81 [ms^{-2}].

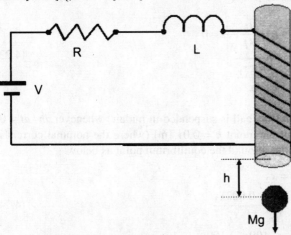

Figure 4.7: Magnetically Suspended Ball

Let the state vector $x = [x_1 \quad x_2 \quad x_3]^T$ in order to obtain A &B, where

$$x_1 = h$$
$$x_2 = \frac{dh}{dt} \tag{4.20}$$
$$x_3 = I$$

Let the input vector $u = [u_1 \quad u_2 \quad u_3]^T$, where

$$u_1 = 0$$
$$u_2 = 0 \tag{4.21}$$
$$u_3 = V$$

This will lead to the system of equations with state variables defined above

$$\dot{x}_1 = x_2$$
$$\dot{x}_2 = g - \frac{\alpha}{M} \frac{x_3^2}{x_1} \tag{4.22}$$
$$\dot{x}_3 = \frac{Rx_3}{L} + \frac{u_3}{L}$$

Now you have obtained the equations according to the following format:

$$\dot{x} = F(x) + G(u)$$

Equilibrium points of the above system for $x = [x_1 \quad x_2 \quad x_3]^T$ can be obtained as follows:

$$\dot{x} = 0$$

This will lead to the system equilibrium states

$$\dot{x}_2 = g - \frac{\alpha}{M} \frac{x_3^2}{x_1} = 0$$
$$x_3 = \sqrt{\frac{Mgx_1}{\alpha}} \tag{4.23}$$

The system is at its equilibrium (the ball is suspended in midair) whenever $dh/dt = 0$. It is linearized the equations about the point $h = 0.01$ [m] (where the nominal current is about 7 [Amp]) and get the equations around the equilibrium point as below:

$$\dot{x}_1 = x_2$$
$$\dot{x}_2 = g - \frac{0.002x_3}{x_1} \tag{4.24}$$
$$\dot{x}_3 = -100x_3 + 100u_3$$

For obtaining equation (4.24), we have to employ linearization equation (1.10) for a 3 dimensional case as below:

$$\frac{\partial F}{\partial x} = \begin{bmatrix} \dfrac{\partial F_1}{\partial x_1} & \dfrac{\partial F_1}{\partial x_2} & \dfrac{\partial F_1}{\partial x_3} \\ \dfrac{\partial F_2}{\partial x_1} & \dfrac{\partial F_2}{\partial x_2} & \dfrac{\partial F_2}{\partial x_3} \\ \dfrac{\partial F_3}{\partial x_1} & \dfrac{\partial F_3}{\partial x_2} & \dfrac{\partial F_3}{\partial x_3} \end{bmatrix}$$

$$\frac{\partial G}{\partial u} = \begin{bmatrix} \dfrac{\partial G_1}{\partial u_1} & \dfrac{\partial G_1}{\partial u_2} & \dfrac{\partial G_1}{\partial u_3} \\ \dfrac{\partial G_2}{\partial u_1} & \dfrac{\partial G_2}{\partial u_2} & \dfrac{\partial G_2}{\partial u_3} \\ \dfrac{\partial G_3}{\partial u_1} & \dfrac{\partial G_3}{\partial u_2} & \dfrac{\partial G_3}{\partial u_3} \end{bmatrix}.$$

This will lead to the following standard linear model of the equation as below:

$$A = \begin{bmatrix} 0 & 1 & 0 \\ 980 & 0 & -2.8 \\ 0 & 0 & -100 \end{bmatrix}; \quad B = \begin{bmatrix} 0 \\ 0 \\ 100 \end{bmatrix}; \quad C = \begin{bmatrix} 1 & 0 & 0 \end{bmatrix}. \tag{4.25}$$

One of the first things that you want to check with the state equations is finding the poles of the system. These are the values of the Eigen values of the A matrix:

$$\lambda = \begin{bmatrix} 31.2 & -31.2 & -100 \end{bmatrix}. \tag{4.26}$$

One pole is in the right-half plane, which means that the system is unstable in open loop configuration. On the above equations, you will work on simulations later. More details on the S-domain have been analyzed in Chapter 1 and analysis on this example will be discussed in Chapter 5.

4.8 Nonlinear Systems: Pendulum

Pendulum shown in Figure 4.8 is having a circular motion. Mass and the length of the string are given in Figure 4.8. Using Newton's second law of motion in the tangential direction,

$$ml\ddot{\theta} = -mg\sin\theta - kl\dot{\theta} \tag{4.27}$$

Define the states as $x_1 = \theta$ and $x_2 = \dot{\theta}$. This will lead to the dynamic system with its states as below:

$$\dot{x}_1 = x_2$$

$$\dot{x}_2 = -\frac{g}{l}\sin(x_1) - \frac{k}{m}x_2 \qquad (4.28)$$

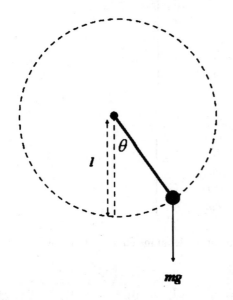

Figure 4.8: Pendulum

If we carefully observe this system of equations (4.28), some terms are having nonlinear properties. Therefore, this system cannot be treated with linear system theory directly. However, once this is linearized using set of equations (1.6)-(1.14), linear system theory can be employed. Matrix A_0 of equation (1.12) can be obtained as below:

$$A = \begin{pmatrix} \dfrac{\partial F_1}{\partial x_1} & \dfrac{\partial F_1}{\partial x_2} \\ \dfrac{\partial F_2}{\partial x_1} & \dfrac{\partial F_2}{\partial x_2} \end{pmatrix}$$

$$A_0 = \begin{pmatrix} 0 & 1 \\ -\dfrac{g}{l}\cos(x_1) & -\dfrac{k}{m} \end{pmatrix}$$

4.9 Pneumatic Artificial Muscles (PAM)

A pneumatic artificial muscle (PAM) is a contractile and linear motion engine operated by gas pressure. Its operation is based on a simple principle [7]-[9]. The actuator's core element is a flexible reinforced closed membrane attached at both ends to fittings along with mechanical power is transferred to a load. A PAM's energy source is gas, usually air that is either forced in to it or extracted out of it. PAM usually operated at an over pressure: generating and supplying compressed gas is easier to accomplish and, with ambient pressure mostly at about 100 kPa, a lot more energy can be conveyed by over pressure than by under pressure. They can be distinguished according to their operation such as pneumatic or hydraulic operations, over pressure or under pressure operations and according to their design such as stretching membrane or rearranging membrane, or type muscles (see Figure 4.9).

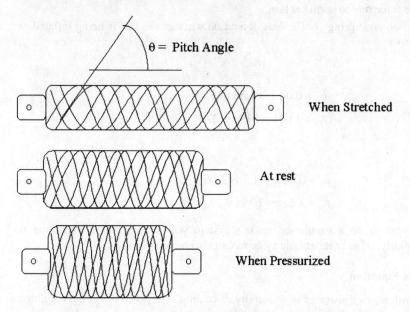

Figure 4.9: Pneumatic Muscle

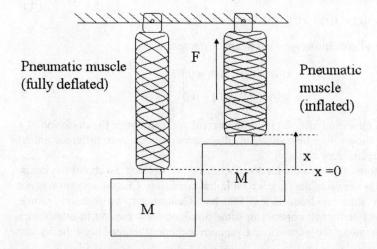

Figure 4.10: Pneumatic Muscle driving a mass

If we apply Newton's law of motion, the dynamic system can obtained as below (see Figure 4.10):

$$F + B(\dot{x})\dot{x} + K(x)x = -M\ddot{x} \tag{4.29}$$

Where, F = Force exerted on PM. $B(x)$ is the force exerted by the viscous friction and $K(x)$ gives the force due to spring action.

Viscous friction and spring coefficients defend on whether the PM is being inflated or deflated as follows.

At Inflation:

$$B_i = 0.04\ddot{x}^2 + 1.3\dot{x} + 12.6$$
$$K_i = 1.6x^2 + 10.9x + 27.1 \tag{4.30}$$

At Deflation:

$$B_i = 0.04\ddot{x}^2 + 1.3\dot{x} + 12.6$$
$$K_i = 1.6x^2 + 10.9x + 27.1 \tag{4.31}$$

When you plan to do a simulation on this system you can use these equations as explained. Similarly, other mechatronic systems can also be found in [10].

4.10 Duffing's Equation

This example will try to illustrate the sensitivity of chaotic systems to the initial condition here it starts. Consider the Duffing's equation given below:

$$\dot{x}(t) = y(t)$$
$$\dot{y}(t) = x(t) - x(t)^3 - 0.25y(t) + 0.3\cos t \tag{4.32}$$

Following two initial conditions are used to check the sensitivity.

$$x_0^1 \Rightarrow x(0) = 0.01,\ y(0) = 0.0$$
$$x_0^2 \Rightarrow x(0) = 0.0,\ y(0) = 0.0$$

Two points are so close and after 40 [s] time interval you can notice the deviation of x value. Figure 4.11 shows the behaviour of the system under two different initial conditions though they are very close.

Deterministic systems that exhibit random behavior are defined as chaotic systems. One feature of chaos is sensitive dependence on initial condition. Chaotic spectrum is not composed solely of discrete frequencies, but has Continuous, broad-band nature. Moreover, a chaotic system must contract in some directions and expand in others with the contraction outweighing the expansion. Lyapunov exponent under chaos theory can explain this.

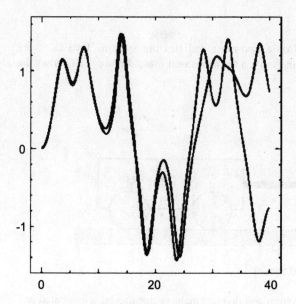

Figure 4.11: Two Initial Conditions

Figure 4.12 shows the phase trajectory for above two initial conditions; x_0^1 and x_0^2 .

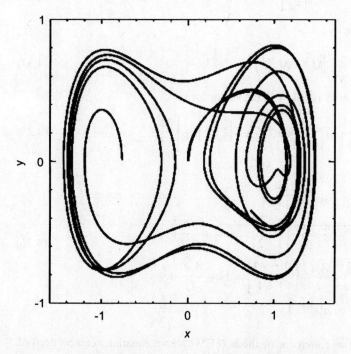

Figure 4.12: Phase Trajectory for above Two Initial Conditions

4.11 Two-Mass Flexible Rod

In this example, the plant consists of a two-mass rod flexible system. Two carts are connected via a flexible rod and input is given to the second mass. Figure 4.13 shows the schematic view of the system.

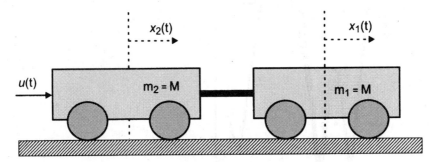

Figure 4.13: Two-Mass Flexible-Rod model

The input on mass 2 will drive the system and displacement vector cab be represented as

$$v = \begin{bmatrix} x_1 \\ x_2 \end{bmatrix}$$

(4.33)

Lump mass matrix is given by

$$\left[M^L + M^{rod} \right]$$

(4.34)

Total force can be represented as below in the vector form

$$\left[M^L + M^{rod} \right] \ddot{v} + \left[C^{rod} \right] \dot{v} + \left[K^{rod} \right] v = \begin{bmatrix} 0 \\ 1 \end{bmatrix} F$$

(4.35)

where

$$M^L = \begin{bmatrix} M & 0 \\ 0 & M \end{bmatrix}$$

$$M^{rod} = \frac{\rho A_r L_r}{6} \begin{bmatrix} 2 & 1 \\ 1 & 2 \end{bmatrix}; \quad (m_2 = \frac{\rho A_r L_r}{6})$$

(4.36)

$$K^{rod} = \frac{A_r \varepsilon_r}{l_r} \begin{bmatrix} 1 & -1 \\ -1 & 1 \end{bmatrix}; \quad (k = \frac{A_r \varepsilon_r}{l_r})$$

$$C^{rod} = \alpha \left[K^{rod} \right]$$

Note here that using finite element methods (FEM) above equations can be derived. Moreover, the symbols have their usual meaning.

The above model can be simplified as below:

$$\begin{bmatrix} M+2m_2 & m_2 \\ m_2 & M+2m_2 \end{bmatrix}\ddot{v} + \alpha \begin{bmatrix} 1 & -1 \\ -1 & 1 \end{bmatrix}\dot{v} + k \begin{bmatrix} 1 & -1 \\ -1 & 1 \end{bmatrix}v = \begin{bmatrix} 0 \\ 1 \end{bmatrix}F$$

(4.37)

Following values are selected in order to simplify the model

$$\begin{aligned} M &= 10 \\ m_2 &= 1 \\ k &= 1 \\ \alpha &= 0.1 \end{aligned}$$

(4.38)

This can be simplified as below:

$$[M_t]\begin{pmatrix} \ddot{x}_1 \\ \ddot{x}_2 \end{pmatrix} + [C_t]\begin{pmatrix} \dot{x}_1 \\ \dot{x}_2 \end{pmatrix} + [k_t]\begin{pmatrix} x_1 \\ x_2 \end{pmatrix} = [B_t]F$$

(4.39)

State space model can be given as below:

$$A = \begin{bmatrix} \begin{pmatrix} 0 & 0 \\ 0 & 0 \end{pmatrix} & \begin{pmatrix} 1 & 0 \\ 0 & 1 \end{pmatrix} \\ -M_t^{-1}K_t & -M_t^{-1}C_t \end{bmatrix}$$

$$B = \begin{bmatrix} 0 \\ 0 \\ M_t^{-1}B_t \end{bmatrix}$$

$$C = [0 \quad 1 \quad 0 \quad 0]$$

$$D = [0]$$

(4.40)

With the numerical values given in (1.52), above state space model can be further simplified as below:

$$A = \begin{bmatrix} 0 & 0 & 1 & 0 \\ 0 & 0 & 0 & 1 \\ -0.091 & 0.091 & -0.0091 & 0.0091 \\ 0.091 & -0.091 & 0.0091 & -0.0091 \end{bmatrix}$$

$$B = \begin{bmatrix} 0 \\ 0 \\ -0.007 \\ 0.0839 \end{bmatrix}$$

(4.41)

$$C = [0 \quad 1 \quad 0 \quad 0$$

4.12 Mobile Robot Model.

Mobile robot in Figure 4.14 is a typical test bed for experimenting different developments associated with mobile platforms [4], [11], [12]. Robot has the global reference frame G: $\{X, Y\}$ and the robot's local reference frame $\{X_R, Y_R\}$ as shown in Figure 4.15.

Figure 4.14: Mobile Robot

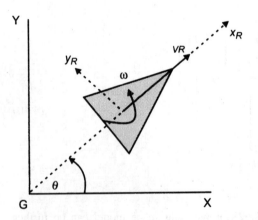

Figure 4.15: The Global Reference Frame and the Mobile Robot Local Reference Frame

Basic kinematics of the mobile robot can be represented by the equations given below:

$$\dot{x}_R = V_R$$
$$\dot{y}_R = 0 \qquad\qquad (4.42)$$
$$\dot{\theta}_R = \omega_R$$

$$\dot{x}_R = V_R \cos\theta_R$$
$$\dot{y}_R = V_R \sin\theta_R \qquad\qquad (4.43)$$
$$\dot{\theta}_R = \omega_R$$

REFERENCES

[1] P.D. Cha, J. J. Rosenberg, and C.L. Dym, "Fundamentals of Modeling and Analyzing Engineering Systems," Cambridge University Press, Cambridge, 2000.

[2] T.L. Vincent and W.J. Grantham, "Nonlinear and Optimal Control Systems," 1997, Wiley and Sons, New York, NY.

[3] K. Watanabe and L. Udawatta, "Fuzzy-Chaos Hybrid Controllers for Nonlinear Dynamic Systems," Edited Book on Integration of Fuzzy Logic and Chaos Theory, 2006, pp. 481–506.

[4] R. Siegwart and I.R. Nourbakhsh, "Introduction to Autonomous Mobile Robot," 2005, Prentice Hall, New Delhi.

[5] Matlab Release 13, Version 6.5, "Help Manual and Toolboxes," The Mathworks Inc.

[6] J.B. Dabney and T.L. Harman, "Mastering Simulink 4", 2001, Prentice Hall, New Jersey.

[7] F. Daerden, "Conception and Realization of Pleated Pneumatic Artificial Muscles and Their use as Compliant Actuation Elements," Ph.D. Dissertation, Vrije Universiteit Brussel, July 1999.

[8] D.G. Caldwell, G.A.M. Cerda, and M. Goodwin, "Control of Pneumatic Muscle Actuators," IEEE Control Systems Magazine, 1995, Vol. 15, pp. 40–48.

[9] T.D.C. Thanh and K.K. Ahn, "Intelligent Phase Plane Switching Control of Pneumatic Artificial Muscle Manipulators with Magneto Rheological Brake," Mechatronics ISSN 0957-4158 Vol. 16, pp. 85–95, 2006.

[10] S. Karunakuran *et.al.* "Mechatronics," 2005, Tata McGraw Hill, New Delhi, 11th Reprint.

[11] F. Han, T. Yamada, K. Watanabe, K. Kiguchi, and K. Izumi, "Construction of an Omnidirectional Mobile Robot Platform Based on Active Dual-Wheel Caster Mechanisms and Development of a Control Simulator," *Journal of Intelligent and Robotic Systems*, 2000, Vol. 29 no. 3, pp. 257–275.

[12] K. Izumi and K. Watanabe, "Fuzzy Behavior-Based Tracking Control for a Mobile Robot," in: Proc. of 2nd Asian Control Conference, Vol. 1, Seoul, Korea, 1997, pp. 685–688.

Chapter 5

Systems Identification and Modeling

To know something physical, it will first need to create a mathematical model, which represents that physical system.

5.1 SYSTEM IDENTIFICATION

5.1.1 Introduction

System identification process is the first step before switching on to system modeling. The system identification tries to estimate a model of a system based on observed input-output data. Matlab is also having a separate toolbox on system identification allowing you to a build mathematical model of a dynamic system based on measured data. Let us take this simple example. The current through a pure resistor obeys a certain rule when you apply a voltage across it. In fact, we already know this model as $V=rI$ and we have accepted it. Assume that you do not know this relationship and you are asked to identify this behavior. The first step may be to set up an experiment and get some data on this. Then you will try to analyze or plot the data in order to have a perception on it. Once you understand that the relationship is linear under certain assumptions, you will bring the well-known model; $V=rI$. Engineers and scientist have experimented on certain systems and modeled them in various ways. There are several ways to describe a system and to model. This section gives a brief introduction to a common approach in modeling. Let us take few examples in order to demonstrate the processes of system identification and modeling. Table 5.1 shows the population demography of Sri Lanka and Figure 5.1 shows the plot of that data.

Table 5.1: Population Demography in Sri Lanka

Year	Population [in Millions]	Year	Population [in Millions]
1992	16.63	1999	18.21
1993	16.85	2000	18.47
1994	17.09	2001	18.73
1995	17.28	2002	19.01
1996	17.49	2003	19.25
1997	17.70	2004	19.46
1998	17.94	2005	19.66

Next, we will try to obtain a model that will fit to the pattern of the population distribution and predict the future values (see Figure 5.2 and Program 5.1).

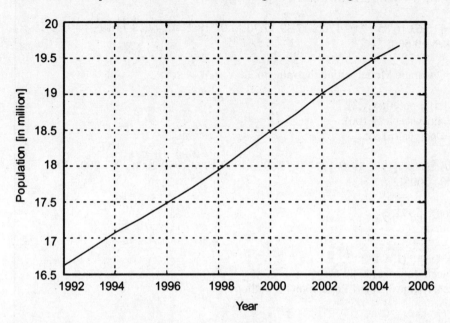

Figure 5.1: Population Demography in Sri Lanka

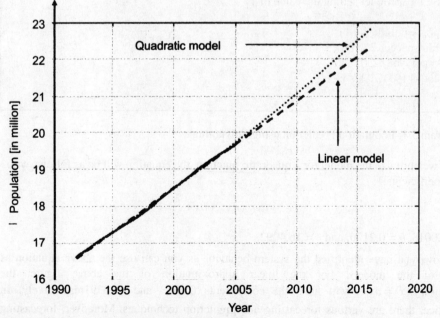

Figure 5.2: Population Demography Prediction

```
x =[1 2 3 4 5 6 7 8 9 10 11 12 13 14];

y =[16.63 16.85 17.09 17.28 17.49 17.70 17.94 18.21 18.47 18.73 19.01 19.25
19.46 19.66 ];

% Quadratic Model setting the value to 2

[p1,s] = polyfit(x,y,2);
s = linspace(1,25,100);
A = polyval(p1,s);

%Actual x=[1992 1993 1994 1995 1996 1997 1998 1999 2000 2001 2002 2003
2004 2005];

plot(x+1991,y)
hold on

plot(s+1991,A,'k-');
xlabel('\fontsize{16} Year');
ylabel('\fontsize{16} Population [in million]');

grid on;
hold on

% Linear Model setting the value to 1

[p2,s]=polyfit(x,y,1);
s=linspace(1,25,100);
A=polyval(p2,s);
plot(s+1991,A,'k--');
```

Program 5.1: Population Prediction using Polynomials

If we optimize the model for a quadratic function, the equation will be as follows with the coefficients:

$$f(x) = ax^2 + bx + c,$$

$a = 0.0018$, $b = 0.2120$, and $c = 16.4092$.

Now, you have identified the system behavior as you can use the above equation as one of the models. For the linear approximation of the above figure, the function $f(x) = ax + b$ will have the coefficients 0.2383 and 16.3391 respectively. In practice, there are various forecasting and prediction techniques. Moreover, forecasting software tools are available for different applications, which involve multivariable optimizations [1].

5.1.2 Steps of System Identification

In general, system identification process needs the following steps and according to the application, these steps might be changed [2]-[4]. However, when you plan to develop a model you are advised to go through all these steps and exercise.

1. Design of Experiments: In order to obtain good experimental data, you have to set up the experiment and have to make sure that the desired data streams are channeled. For an example, if you gather your data from an electrical circuit it might need to employ data loggers for storing data. In certain experiments, it is needed to fix sensors and through those sensors you will be able to gather data. Sometimes you have measuring equipment for different inputs and different outputs ports where you try to interface and collect data. Not only from this type of experiments, but also you collect data through valuable surveys. You make a questionnaire first according to the project objectives and prepare it where you finally obtain pieces of data in estimating the model parameters. Then you have to decide the sample size that you plan to distribute your questionnaire.

Whether you set up an experiment to collect data or planning to do a survey depends on your research methodology. Note here that in both cases you should plan to collect the desired data within a short period of time.

2. Selection of Model Structure: According to the data obtained, suitable model should be selected. To select the model, you need to have a prior knowledge or it may be trial and error. As a starting point, you may plot experimental data and get some idea on it. For an example, you may select a linear model initially and then try with a quadratic model. If these are going to fail you might try for higher order model.

3. Choice of Criterion to fit: A suitable cost function is chosen, which reflects how well the model fits the experimental data. You may use 80% of your experimental data for obtaining the model. Essentially by adjusting parameters within a given model, until its output coincides as well as possible with the measured output parameters should be tuned. Next, examine the data and polish it so as to remove trends and outliers, Then select useful portions of the original data, and apply filtering to enhance important frequency ranges.

4. Parameter Estimation: An optimization problem is solved to obtain the numerical values of the model parameters. This model may be a very simple model like a linear model approximated according to your model selection or a complex multi-layer neural network model. In both cases, what you have to do is to find the model parameters of that particular model. In the linear model you have to find the two coefficients whereas your neural network might need 100 parameters to run it.

5. Model Validation: The last step is the model validation where you try to justify your model obtained. Most important thing is that you keep some data away from the initial data set gathered through the experiment. These data are used to validate your model and reserved amount may be 20% of the total data.

In the above population demography example, two models were taken into account and optimum coefficients were selected. Finding the coefficient under different algorithms are suggested when you carry out a research type project. In the validation process, data after 2005 can be used to validate your model.

5.1.3 System Identification in Matlab

One of the approaches of system identification is to use the time series properties and associated theories in order to model a system. In mathematical modeling of a time series, it is based on the assumption that each value of the series depends only on a weighted sum of the previous values of the same series plus noise. Auto-regressive (AR) model is equivalent to assuming that the time signal can be modeled as a summation of sinusoids. In some applications, there is memory or feedback and therefore the system can generate internal dynamics with available past data. A number of techniques exist for computing AR or auto regressive exogenous (ARX) coefficients. The main two categories are least squares and Burg method. Within each of these there are a few variants, the most common least squares method is based upon the Yule-Walker equations. In general, if $y(k)$ is the k-th value of the time series, the AR model of order N is given by:

$$y(k) = \sum_{i=1}^{N} a_i y(k-i) + n(k),$$

where $n(k)$ is the noise term.

In practice, your system has not only an output but also an input to generate that output. Matlab provides a toolbox for system identification and let us try to get some idea on basic developments. There are different types of system identification algorithms in Matlab and ARX model is one of the common models. The input $u(t)$ and output $y(t)$ relationship can be mathematically defined as follows:

$$A(q)y(t) = B(q)u(t-nk) + e(t)$$
$$na : A(q) = 1 + a_1 q^{-1} + a_2 q^{-2} + \cdots + + a_{na} q^{-na} \tag{5.1}$$
$$nb : B(q) = b_1 + b_2 q^{-1} + b_3 q^{-2} + \cdots + + b_{nb} q^{-nb+1}$$

Here, A and B denote the coefficients of the inputs and outputs at different delays in the ARX model. The dimensions na and nb can be related to the Matlab ARX model as below:

```
m = arx(data,orders)
m = arx(data,'na',na,'nb',nb,'nk',nk)
m= arx(data,orders,'Property1',Value1,...,'PropertyN',ValueN)
```

When it comes to real world problems, it can be noticed that in certain measurements via experiments samples are missing. The reasons might be sensor failures, data acquisition failures and problems in the data loggers or memory. In these situations, you have to create missing data under certain assumptions or under available algorithms for data corrections. As we will demonstrate in the next example, subtracting of the mean levels from the input and output sequences before the estimation is a common practice. With the following command it can be done easily with Matlab:

```
>> Processed_Data = detrend(Data);
```

In this example, first, we will generate some artificial data as coded in the following lines:

```
>> t=1:1:200;
>> u=sin(t);
>> t1=rand(200);
>> y=cos(t+t1(:,1)');
```

The input signal to the system is *u* and the output is denoted by *y*. Figure 5.3 shows the input and output data produced by the above code.

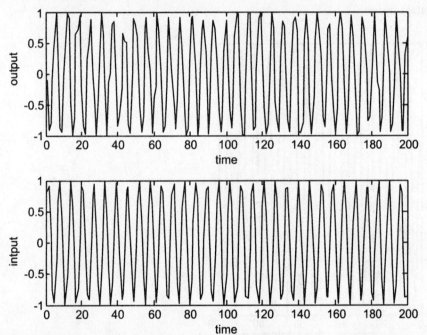

Figure 5.3: Input and Output Data for the Simulation

With the following codes we do some preprocessing on the selected data.

```
>> data =[y', u'];
>> datad = detrend(data,0);
>> datae = datad([1:100],:);
>> datav = datad([101:200],:);
```

From the above program code, we select a certain portion of the data for vectorization. In your own simulation, according to the data created, you may design your own methodology for obtaining desired results. Moreover, whether you are going to use an auto-regressive model, auto regressive exogenous model or any other technique depends on the input-output relationship. Furthermore, in the system identification toolbox in Matlab has different techniques such as polynomial black-box models, structured state-space models with free parameters, multivariable ARX models, state-space models with coupled parameters and so on. Now, we will define the ARX model parameters and Figure 5.4 shows the measured output and the 1-step ahead predicted model output through the following codes.

```
>> na = 1;
>> nb = 3;
>> nk = 1;

>> arxmodel= arx(datae, [na nb nk]);
>> compare(datav, arxmodel,1);
>> resid(datav, arxmodel);
>> present(arxmodel);
```

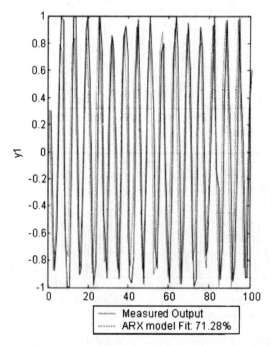

Figure 5.4: Measured Output and 1-step Ahead Predicted Model Output

This example demonstrated a single-input-single-output (SISO) system and you can also apply these techniques to a multi-input-multi-output (MIMO) system.

5.2 SYSTEM MODELING

5.2.1 Systems Control Approaches

Today, many engineering applications employ control techniques in order to get the best possible operation while optimizing certain parameters of the system. For an example, we may try to minimize the energy consumption of a particular system if it is an energy intensive process. The control system toolbox builds on the foundations of Matlab to provide functions designed for control engineering. The control system toolbox is a collection of algorithms, written mostly as M-files, that implements common control system design, analysis, and modeling techniques. Convenient graphical user interfaces (GUIs) simplify typical control engineering tasks. The basic modeling to obtain A and B matrices in Figure 5.5 has explained in Chapter 1. Furthermore, we introduce a feedback loop (as shown in Figure 5.5) in order to optimize or condition the control input *U* after getting back the states of the state variables *X*. If you want to observe the states you may use an observer *Y*.

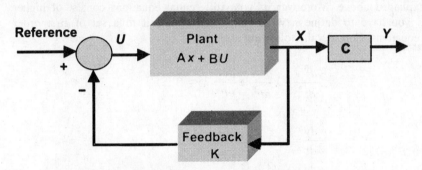

Figure 5.5: Schematic Diagram of a Typical Control System

The reference value will set the desired input to the plant and feedback gain matrix *K* will improve the system performance. In fact, you may find some systems that operate without having a feedback loop. The systems having no feedback are called as open loop control. To obtain the system parameters of the plant (like *A, B, C,* and *D*) in Figure 5.5, you should follow the steps explained in Chapter 1.

Control is the operation mode of a control system which includes two subsystems: controlling (a controller), and controlled (a system to be controlled). Here, in Figure 5.5, you have both components in the plant. The controller may change the state of the controlled system in any way, including the destruction of the system. However, the designer should make sure to minimize the destruction, in other words, to reduce or curb undesired performances. Feedback loop provides the present states of the plant in order to decide the best possible action through the controller. To get the signals, you have to employ a good sensory system.

When you have the feedback loop, the new system can be represented as bellow:

$$\dot{X} = (A - BK)X + Bu$$
$$Y = CX$$

$$(5.2)$$

This approach is based on a dynamical model where you consider forces and/or torques that cause the dynamic system. There is another approach where consider the mechanisms of motion. This mathematical model refers to all geometric and/or time-based properties of motion and this referred kinematics of a system [5]. Moreover, when it comes to robotics you will find direct kinematics and inverse kinematics. To control a robot manipulator you need both direct and inverse kinematic models. When you try to derive a dynamic model for a given system you will try to obtain a relationship considering forces and/or torques in applying fundamental laws. These mathematical equations are generally referred as system dynamics or equations of motion. However, you will try to employ fundamental physics behind these scenarios. For an example, in robotics, Lagrange-Euler (LE) or Newton-Euler (NE) method can be applied to derive the dynamics. In an electrical circuit you may apply fundamentals on electricity theory. In general dynamics, Newton laws of motion can play a big role. In a heat transfer application, thermodynamics laws and other theories can be applied. However, if you end up with a set of differential equations (in continuous time systems) or difference equations (in discrete time systems) and these can be useful in building a state space model as explained above. Moreover, if your differential equations consist of higher order terms you have to define new variables and reduce it to a set of first order differential equations. Consider the following example.

$$\frac{d^3 y}{dt^3} + 3\frac{d^2 y}{dt^2} + \frac{dy}{dt} - 2y = 0$$

$$y = x_1$$

$$\frac{dy}{dt} = x_2$$

$$\frac{dx_2}{dt} = \frac{d^2 y}{dt^2} = x_3$$

$$\dot{x}_3 + 3x_3 + x_2 - 2x_1 = 0$$

With the above definitions of new variables, you will end up with the following model in the form $\dot{x} = Ax + Bu$:

$$\dot{x}_1 = x_2$$
$$\dot{x}_2 = x_3$$
$$\dot{x}_3 = -3x_3 - x_2 + 2x_1$$

If these equations were nonlinear, as we discussed in Chapter 1 you would try to linearize your model around a selected point. In previous chapters, authors were discussing some of the fundamental issues where you frequently apply in various engineering and scientific problems. The next example will illustrate the procedure in order to have a state model as above.

5.2.2 DC Motor Controller

Direct Current (DC) motors are available in various applications in the world ranging from conventional DC motors to sophisticated servo grades. The DC motor can be modeled as shown in Figure 5.6 and it been connected to a load.

Assume that for the above system is having the following parameters as shown in Table 5.2. In the simulations, you can change the values and get different responses for different values. If we analyze the system, you will end up with set of differential equations.

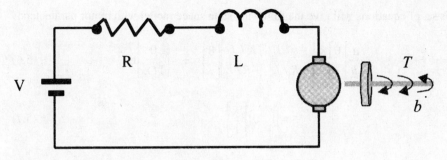

Figure 5.6: Modeling of DC Motor with a Load

Table 5.2: DC Motor Parameters

Parameter	Value
Moment of inertia of the rotor (J)	0.01 kg.m^2/s^2
Damping ratio of the mechanical system (b)	0.1 Nm
Electromotive force constant (K_e)	0.01 Nm/A
Armature constant (K_t)	0.01 Nm/A
Electric resistance (R)	1Ω.
Electric inductance (L)	0.5 H

The parameters of the DC motor should be first identified. There are standard tests to perform in order to identify the system parameters. For an example, in electrical machines, you can carry out no load test and full-load test for determining certain parameters. As explain in the previous section, system identification is the first step before coming to system modeling in example.

The torque produce by the DC motor (T) is given by the following equation in terms of motor current (i) and the electromotive force constant (Motor constant).

$$T = K_e i \tag{5.3}$$

The torque generated in the motor shaft gives the rotary motion, leading to the angular displacement (θ) of the system

$$J \ddot{\theta} + b \dot{\theta} = K_e i \tag{5.4}$$

Forces created by the damping (constant *b)* and the moment of inertia (value *J)* are in the opposite direction of the torque.

The supply voltage will not directly appear across the system as the back electro-motive force (constant in the armature, K_t) is in opposite direction leading to the following:

$$L \frac{di}{dt} + R.i = v - K_t.\dot{\theta} \tag{5.5}$$

This set of equations will give the following state space model with motor parameters:

$$\frac{d}{dt}\begin{bmatrix}\dot{\theta}\\i\end{bmatrix}=\begin{bmatrix}-b/J & K/J\\-K/L & -R/L\end{bmatrix}\begin{bmatrix}\dot{\theta}\\i\end{bmatrix}+\begin{bmatrix}0\\1/L\end{bmatrix}v \tag{5.6}$$

$$\div=\begin{bmatrix}1 & 0\end{bmatrix}\begin{bmatrix}\dot{\theta}\\i\end{bmatrix} \tag{5.7}$$

Now, we have just completed the system modeling part to some extend. Note here that you define the state variables as the angular velocity and the current. If we check the eigen values of A, you will get the followings ($K = K_t = K_e$):

>> eig(A)

ans =

-9.9975
-2.0025

If we take the values $K = K_t = K_e$, then Program 5.2 will produce the output in Figure 5.7. Moreover, the command *ss2tf* (state space to transfer function) will give you the numerator and the denominator of the system. You can execute this as below:

>> [num,den]=ss2tf(A, B, C, D)

num =

    0   0 0.2000

den =

1.0000 3.0000 2.0020

These values will be very useful in order to analyze the system further. You may get the poles of the system through the roots of the denominators as below:

>> roots (den)
ans =

-1.9980
-1.0020

The transfer function $G(s)$ of the system can be derived as shown in the following form:

$$G(s)=\frac{0.2}{(s^2+3s+2)}$$

In the general form, it should be as follows:

$$G(s) = \frac{\omega_n^2}{s^2 + 2\zeta\omega_n s + \omega_n^2} \tag{5.8}$$

With this, the desired parameters can be computed. For an example, the settling time is given by

$$T_s = \frac{4}{\zeta\omega_n} \tag{5.9}$$

If you properly select the two values of the above equation, the settling time can be obtained according to your requirement. The two parameters can be changed in such a way you keep the poles of the system in the left half-plan.

```
J=0.01;
b=0.1;
K=0.01;
R=1;
L=0.5;
A=[-b/J  K/J ; -K/L   -R/L];
B=[0 ;1/L];
C=[1  0];
D=0;
step(A,B,C,D);
```

Program 5.2: Getting the Step Response

The command *step* will give the step response of linear time invariant (LTI) models. The time range and number of points are chosen automatically. For multi-input models, independent step commands are applied to each input channel. Figure 5.7 shows the output response.

If you want to have different state space model for the same system, you can define few systems as below:

```
>> sys1 = ss(A1,B1,C1,D1)
>> sys2 = ss(A2,B2,C2,D2)
```

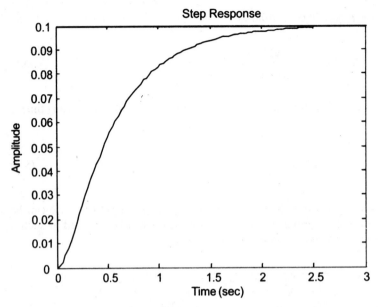

Figure 5.7: Output Response of the System

Next, we set the inertia parameter J to $0.1[kg.m^2/s^2]$ and see the response. Figure 5.8 shows the response of the system for two different inertia values. Note that the dashed line gives the new response of the system. This can be directly obtained as follows:

```
>> Step(sys1,'k',sys2,'--k');
```

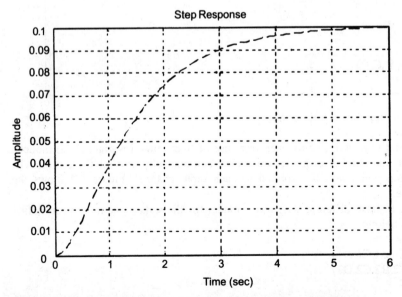

Figure 5.8: Output Response of the System for different *J* Values

For an example, select the two values of the general transfer function at $\zeta = 0.3826$ ($\zeta > 0$) and $\omega_n = 5.2271$. The transfer function will be as follows:

$$G(s) = \frac{27.323}{s^2 + 3.3767s + 27.323}$$

```
>> P= [ 1 3.3767 27.323];
>> roots(P)
```

ans =

```
-1.6883 + 4.9470i
-1.6883 - 4.9470i
```

Then you select the new transfer function with the feed back loop gains and the above poles, setting the values as follow:

```
>> p1 = -1.6883 + 4.9470i;
>> p2 = -1.6883 - 4.9470i;
>> K = place(A,B,[p1 p2]);
```

You can obtain the gain matrix at K = [46.7686 -4.3117] of the system shown in Figure 5.5. Let us get the step response of the system executing the following and see the output of the system shown in Figure 5.9.

```
>> step(A-B*K,B,C,D,1)
```

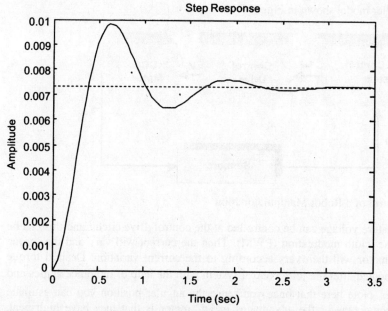

Figure 5.9: Output Response of the System with the Feedback Loop

Similarly, you can obtain the state space model from the new transfer function. You may use the command *tf2ss* (transfer function to state space model). See the following code and the output

```
>> num=[0 0 100];
>> den=[1 5 30];
>> [A,B,C,D] = tf2ss(num,den)

A =

   -5  -30
    1    0
B =

    1
    0
C =

    0  100
D =

    0
```

In different electrical systems, particularly in actuators, you will find DC motors, induction motors, synchronous motors, stepper motors, and other types of motors. DC motors are very popular in servo applications; especially in robotics applications [5]. AC motors are difficult to control and stepper motors are available for low power applications. The DC motor model explained above can be further improved with the following controller model shown in Figure 5.10.

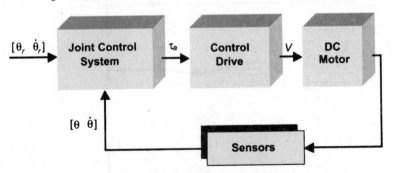

Figure 5.10: Control of a Robot Manipulator Joint

Here, the armature voltage can be controlled at the control drive circuit and this can be achieved by pulse width modulation (PWM). Then the current will vary and the torque produce by the motor will then vary according to the current variation. Desired torque (τ_a) can be computed after the joint control system with the help of reference angles and angular velocities. Note here that once you sense the angular position you can estimate the angular velocity. One of the advantages in DC motor is that they have high peak torque for quick accelerations.

In practice, you can see the DC motors with gear trains in order to obtain different speeds and these motors are permanent magnet (PM) type in which the stator magnetic flux remains constant at different armature currents. Hence, this will provide a linear speed-torque relationship where the control laws are built and executed [6]. Sometimes, you can see a tacho generator, which is directly built into the rotor and it will sense the speed. In certain situations, optical encoders are employed to estimate the position, i.e., angular position.

5.2.3 Further Analysis on Magnetically Suspended Ball

The magnetically suspended ball in Figure 1.8 is further analyzed in order to observe the behavior. Program 5.3 shows the codes used in order to investigate the behavior without giving any external inputs. First, we analyze it using the command *lsim*.

```
% Define the state matrices
A=[0 1 0;980 0 -2.8;0 0 -100];
B=[0;0;100];
C=[1 0 0];

% Check the stability
Poles=eig(A);

%Initial Conditions
x0=[0.005 0 0];
t=0:0.01:2;

% Input Vector
u=0*t;

% Run Simulation
[y,x]=lsim(A,B,C,0,u,t,x0);
h=x(:,2);

% Graphing
plot(t,h)
xlabel('Time [s]');
ylabel('Position [m]');
```

Program 5.3: Getting the Step Response

One of the poles is in the right-half plane, which means that the system is unstable in the open-loop mode. If you observe the position, the value after 1.5 seconds will be closing to infinity (see Figure 5.11). If we get back to the gain scheduling concept shown in Figure 5.5, the characteristic polynomial for this closed-loop system is the determinant of $(sI-(A-BK))$. Since the matrices A and $B*K$ are both 3 by 3 matrices, there will be 3 poles for the system. By using full-state feedback, we can place the poles anywhere we want. We could use the Matlab function place to find the control matrix, K, which will give the desired poles. At present, three poles are as below:

>> Poles=eig(A)

Poles =
   31.3050
  -31.3050
 -100.0000

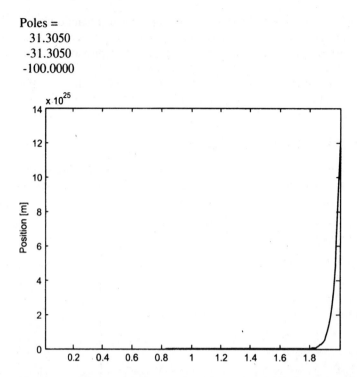

Figure 5.11: Output Response of the System in the Open-loop Mode

```
A=[0 1 0;980 0 -2.8;0 0 -100];
B=[0;0;100];
C=[1 0 0];
Poles=eig(A);
x0=[0.005 0 0];
t=0:0.01:2;
u=0*t;

p1 = -10 + 10i;
p2 = -10 - 10i;
p3 = -50;

K = place(A,B,[p1 p2 p3]);

[y,x]=lsim(A-B*K,B,C,0,u,t,x0);
h=x(:,2);
plot(t,h)
xlabel('Time [s]');
ylabel('Position [m]');

Grid on
```

Program 5.4: Gain Scheduling at Desired Poles

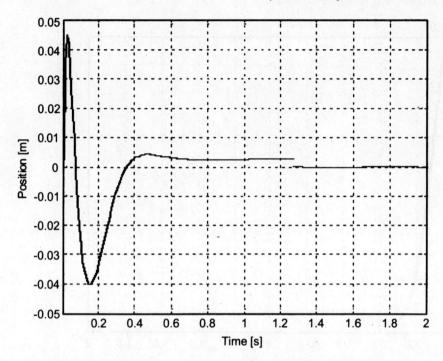

Figure 5.12: Output Response of the System in the Closed-loop Mode

If you want to introduce a reference input *u* and see the output following code can be used. The system output is shown in Figure 5.12.

```
>> t = 0:0.001:2;
>> u = 0.005*ones(size(t));
>> y = lsim(A-B*K,B,C,0,u,t) ;
>> plot(t,y)
>> xlabel('Time [s]');
>> ylabel('Position [m]');
>> grid on
```

It is noted that the three different approaches give three different results while optimizing the output. According to the requirement, you will design the system and select the parameters such a way that it meets your ultimate requirement. Note here that we have selected the control system input as defined above and apply a step input. We have to choose a small value for the step so that we remain in the region where our linearization is valid around a small region.

```
>> t = 0:0.001:2;
>> u = 1.5*ones(size(t));
>> x0=[0.5 0 0];
>> y = lsim(A-B*K,B,C,0,u,t) ;
```

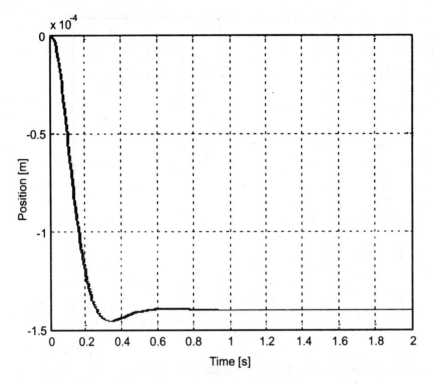

Figure 5.13: Output Response of the System with a Reference Input

```
>> plot(t,y)
>> xlabel('Time [s]');
>> ylabel('Position [m]');
>> grid on
```

The next program will illustrate you to handle multiple outputs and get the phase portrait. Program 5.5 shows the inclusion of the command *deal* in order to get three data streams for the three variables. You will copy from state values x to $Y1$, $Y2$, and $Y3$. Figure 5.14 and Figure 5.15 shows the phase portrait and the behavior of three states variables respectively. You may plot the three variables as below;

```
>> plot(t,Y1(:,1),'--k',t,Y1(:,2),'-k',t,Y1(:,3))
```

In fact, you may change the initial conditions, different input values, gain matrices or poles and observe the behavior of the system. If you get into this type of different simulations, you will understand the concept behind "computer aided simulations" at this stage. Whether it is a mechanical or electrical system this code of practice should be repeated when you are doing a research project.

```
A=[0 1 0;980 0 -2.8;0 0 -100];
B=[0;0;100];
C=[1 0 0];
Poles=eig(A);
x0=[0.005 0 0];

t=0:0.001:2;
u=0*t;

p1 = -10 + 10i;
p2 = -10 - 10i;
p3 = -50;

K = place(A,B,[p1 p2 p3]);

[y,x]=lsim(A-B*K,B,C,0,u,t,x0);

[Y1,Y2,Y3] = deal(x);

% Phase portrait
plot(Y1(:,1),Y1(:,2))

xlabel(' \fontsize{16} Variable x_1 [m]');
ylabel(' \fontsize{16} Variable x_2 [m/s]');

Grid on
```

Program 5.5: Accessing Multi-Variable Data

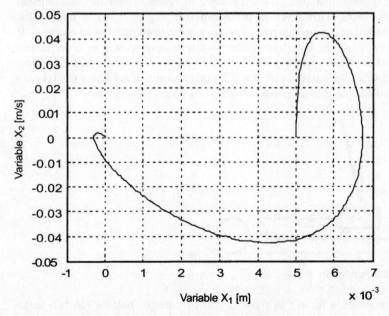

Figure 5.14: Phase Portrait of the System Variables

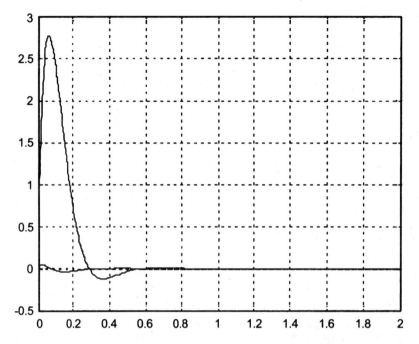

Figure 5.15: Behavior of Three State Variables

5.2.4 Inverted Pendulum

There are certain systems that use as test benches in order to test the fundamental developments as concepts. This inverted pendulum (see Figure 5.16) is one of the systems that can be used as test bed for testing your own development. For an example, if you develop a fuzzy reasoning based controller as a new development in order to test your control algorithm you can use this test bed as platform. A controller should reflect the relationship between two variables θ and f. In other words, if we know the relation between θ and f, we can use it to write control rules or a control algorithm.

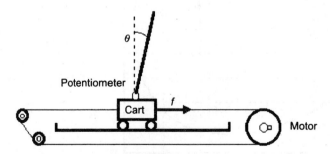

Figure 5.16: Inverted Pendulum

A servomotor produces a force f to move a cart in order to balance the two stage inverted pendulum (see Figure 5.17) on the cart, *i.e.*, to keep θ_1 and θ_2 to be zero. θ_1 is the angle of the first stage pendulum from the vertical direction, while θ_2 is the angle of the second stage pendulum from the vertical direction. These two angles are measured with two potentiometers. You can analyze both systems with your knowledge at this stage.

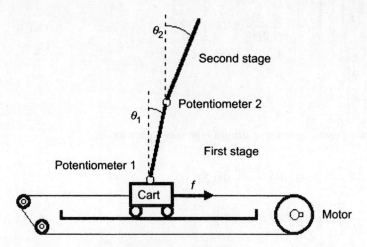

Figure 5.17: Two Stage Inverted Pendulum

We will try to model the cart-pendulum system in order to illustrate the modeling concept. This system is little bit different from the systems what we explained above. Figure 5.18 shows the parameters of the inverted pendulum. Masses of the cart and pendulum are mc and mp respectively. The position x and angle θ will be controlled by the input u. Let us try to model this as below:

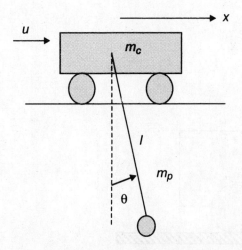

Figure 5.18: Modeling of Cart-Pendulum System

$$\begin{bmatrix} \dot{x} \\ \dot{\theta} \\ \ddot{x} \\ \ddot{\theta} \end{bmatrix} = \begin{bmatrix} 0 & 0 & 1 & 0 \\ 0 & 0 & 0 & 1 \\ 0 & 0 & 0 & 0 \\ 0 & 0 & 0 & 0 \end{bmatrix} \begin{bmatrix} x \\ \theta \\ \dot{x} \\ \dot{\theta} \end{bmatrix} + \begin{bmatrix} 0 \\ 0 \\ f_1 \\ f_2 \end{bmatrix} + \begin{bmatrix} 0 \\ 0 \\ \dfrac{1}{M} \\ \dfrac{-3}{2lM}\cos(\theta) \end{bmatrix} u \tag{5.10}$$

$$y = \begin{bmatrix} 1 & 0 & 0 & 0 \\ 0 & 1 & 0 & 0 \end{bmatrix} \begin{bmatrix} x \\ \theta \\ \dot{x} \\ \dot{\theta} \end{bmatrix}$$

We define the following terms in order to simplify the state space model.

$$f_1(\theta,\dot{\theta}) = \frac{1}{M}\left(\frac{m_p l}{2}\dot{\theta}^2 \sin(\theta) + \frac{3m_p g}{8}\sin(2\theta) \right)$$

$$f_2(\theta,\dot{\theta}) = \frac{-3}{2l}\left(g\sin(\theta) + f_1(\theta,\dot{\theta})\cos(\theta) \right) \tag{5.11}$$

$$M = m_c + m_p\left(1 - \frac{3}{4}\cos^2(\theta) \right)$$

Figure 5.19 shows a cart with an inverted pendulum that moving on a platform. Displacement is measured from the direction of X and two masses are shown in the diagram. Here, mass of the cart is m_c and the mass of the pendulum is m_p. Total system is controlled by the force U and pendulum is balanced.

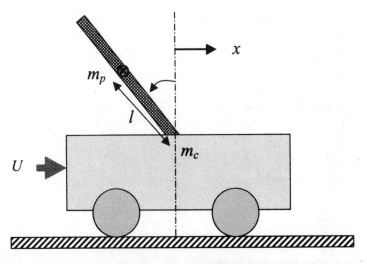

Figure 5.19: Modeling of Cart-Inverted Pendulum System

If we take two masses separately, Figure 5.20 and Figure 5.21 show the forces acting on them. Consider the pendulum in Figure 5.20 with the forces and try to apply Newton's second law of motion in the direction of x.

$$H = m_p \ddot{x} + m_p l \ddot{\theta} \cos\theta - m_p l \dot{\theta}^2 \sin\theta,\qquad(5.12)$$

Now, consider the cart in Figure 5.19 with the forces. Again, we apply Newton's second law of motion in the direction of x.

$$U - b\dot{x} - H = m_c \ddot{x},\qquad(5.13)$$

Equations (5.12) and (5.13) will lead to the following equation

$$U = (m_c + m_p)\ddot{x} + b\dot{x} + m_p l \ddot{\theta} \cos\theta - m_p l \dot{\theta}^2 \sin\theta,\qquad(5.14)$$

Note here that the friction between the cart and the floor (Fl) in Figure 5.21 is assumed to be zero.

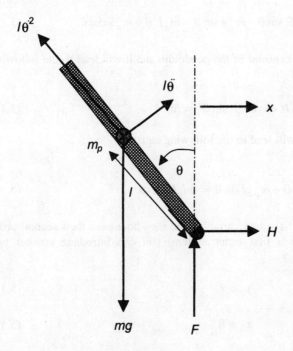

Figure 5.20: Forces on Pendulum

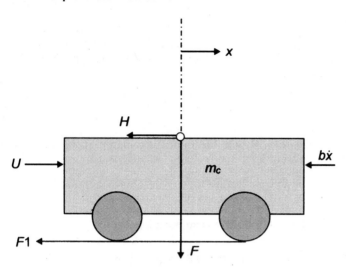

Figure 5.21: Forces on Cart

Summation of all forces perpendicular to the pendulum can be given as follows:

$$H \cos\theta + F \sin\theta - m_p g \sin\theta = m_p l^2 \ddot{\theta} + m_p \ddot{x} \cos\theta \tag{5.15}$$

Moment is taken around the centroid of the pendulum and it will lead to the following equation:

$$- H \cos\theta - F \sin\theta - = I\ddot{\theta} \tag{5.16}$$

Equations (5.12) and (5.13) will lead to the following equation

$$(I + m_p l^2)\ddot{\theta} + m_p gl \sin\theta = -m_p l\ddot{x} \cos\theta \tag{5.17}$$

Equations (5.14) and (5.17) have two variables and they both have their second order derivatives. To reduce this to a first order system, you can introduce another two variables as below:

$$x_1 = x \tag{5.18}$$

$$x_2 = \theta \tag{5.19}$$

$$x_3 = \dot{x} \tag{5.20}$$

$$x_4 = \dot{\theta} \tag{5.21}$$

With the above equations, you will end up with the following form:

$$\dot{x} = f(x) + g(u) \tag{5.22}$$

Here,

$$x = \begin{bmatrix} \dot{x}_1 \\ \dot{x}_2 \\ \dot{x}_3 \\ \dot{x}_4 \end{bmatrix} \tag{5.23}$$

Note here that the equation (5.22) is a nonlinear and you have to linearize around a selected point in order to treat under linear systems theory. Most important thing is that now you have a model to analyze or simulate the cart-inverted pendulum system. For an example, linear control theory can be applied to the system once it is approximated to a linear model.

5.2.5 Pneumatic Muscle Arm

In most of robotic applications, the common actuator technology is electrical systems with very limited use of hydraulics or pneumatics. However, electrical systems suffer from relatively low power/weight ratio and power/volume ratio. Electromagnetic motors dc motors, ac motors, stepper motors, linear motors, which are widely used in robotics at present fail on the requirements of weight and direct transmission. Weight is the major drawback of electric motors in this application. Electric motors have power to weight ratios in the order of magnitude of 100 W/kg, although peak values are higher, and their torque to weight ratios range more or less within 1-10Nm/kg [7]-[10]. Mean while hydraulic system suffer from relatively less reliability and expensiveness. Hydraulic actuators have a very good power to weight ratio, 2000W/kg on average and high torques at low speeds, but their energy source can leak due to the high operating pressures, typically 20Mpa. They can be directly connected to the robot joints, however. Compliance is not inherent to this type of actuators; in fact, it can be introduced by means of servo valve control. The most common pneumatic actuators are cylinders. These have power to weight ratios of 400W/kg. Pneumatic cylinders have been used for many years and are well adapted to simple repetitive tasks requiring only a very limited amount of system control. Here, we are going to model one such system (see Figure 5.22).

The system in Figure 5.22 shows a pneumatic muscle arm and let us assume pneumatic muscle inflate x[m] from it is initial position. According to equation (1.43), muscle will create a force on point Q. Point R is a friction less joint. By considering the moment around point R, the system equation can be derived as follows:

$$[F + B(x)x + K(x)x](a \sin \alpha) - MgL \sin \theta = I(\ddot{\theta}) \tag{5.24}$$

Where, I is moment of inertia and other symbols are given in Figure 5.22. With the help of sine and cosine laws, equation (5.24) can be simplified as follows:

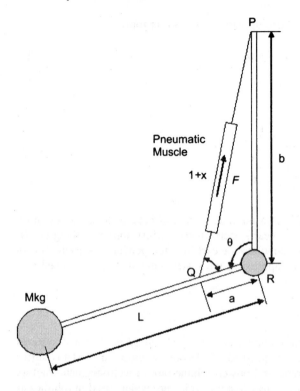

Figure 5.22: Pneumatic Muscle Arm

$$\frac{\sin \alpha}{b} = \frac{\sin \theta}{l+x} \qquad (5.25)$$

$$a \sin \alpha = \frac{ab \sin \theta}{l+x} \qquad (5.26)$$

$$[F + B(x)x + K(x)x]\{\frac{ab \sin \theta}{l+x}\} - MgL \sin \theta = I(\ddot{\theta}) \qquad (5.27)$$

In order to include angle θ as a variable with the muscle inflation, it is required to have angular acceleration $\ddot{\theta}$, with the help of cosine law, it can obtain relationship between a, b, $(l+x)$ and angle θ :

$$\cos \theta = \frac{(a^2 + b^2 - (l+x)^2)}{2ab} \qquad (5.28)$$

By differentiating θ with respective to time, the angular velocity and acceleration can be expressed as follows:

$$(-\sin\theta)\dot{\theta} = \frac{-(l+x)\dot{x}}{ab}$$

$$\dot{\theta} = \frac{(l+x)\dot{x}}{ab\sin\theta} \tag{5.29}$$

$$\ddot{\theta} = \frac{\{ab\sin^2\theta[(l+x)\ddot{x}+\dot{x}^2]-(l+x)^2\dot{x}^2\cos\theta\}}{a^2b^2\sin^3\theta} \tag{5.30}$$

REFERENCES

[1] A. Kharab and R.B. Guenther, "An Introduction to Numerical Methods, A MatLab Approach," Chapmann & Hall/CRC, Second Edition, Singapore, 2006.

[2] D. Graupe, "Identification of Systems," Second Edition, Krieger Publ. Co., Malabar, FL, 1979.

[3] L. Ljung, "System Identification - Theory for the User," 2nd Edition, PTR Prentice Hall, Upper Saddle River, N.J., 1999.

[4] J. Juang, "Applied System Identification," Prentice Hall, Upper Saddle River, N.J., 1994.

[5] R.K. Mittal and I.J. Nagrath, "Robotics and Control," Tata McGraw-Hill Publishing, New Delhi, 2004.

[6] S. Karunakuran *et. al.* "Mechatronics," Tata McGraw Hill, New Delhi, 11th Reprint, 2005.

[7] P. Beyl, B. Vanderborght, R.V. Ham, M.V. Damme, R. Versluys, D. Lefeber "Compliant actuation in New Robotic Applications," Proceedings of the 7th National Congress on Theoretical and Applied Mechanics (NCTAM06), Belgium, May 2006.

[8] F. Daerden, D. Lefeber, B. Verrelst, R.V. Ham, "Pleated pneumatic artificial muscles," compliant robotic actuators 2001 IEEE/RSJ International Conference on Intelligent Robots and Systems, Maui, Hawaii October-November 2001, pp. 1958-1963.

[9] F. Daerden and D. Lefeber, "The Concept and Design of Pleated Pneumatic Artificial muscles," *International Journal of Fluid Power*, 2001.

[10] M. Wisse and J.V. Frankenhuyzen, "Design and Construction of Mike; 2D Autonomous Biped Based on Passive Dynamic Walking," International Symposium on Adaptive Motion of Animals and Machines, 2003.

Chapter 6

System Integration

An integration environment provides you to bring different components to model, simulate, and analyze dynamic systems.

6.1 INTEGRATION OF COMPONENTS

A good integration environment provides the facilities to investigate the behavior of a wide range of real-world dynamic systems such as mechanical systems, electrical circuits, chemical and process engineering systems, and many other different systems. These systems consist of different components, which have different properties. For an example, if we take a resistor it will obey Ohm's law. However, not all the resistors in the world will obey this law due to different inherent properties. In fact, if we analyze the internal properties properly, we will be able to model them and come to certain conclusions after experimenting. Once you come up with a model for this component then you can bring this to an environment, where you integrate different things together with this one. Behavior of each element should be clearly modeled. This principle applies even if you have different sub-system and going to integrate to a single system. One of the examples is to take a car engine shown in Figure 6.1.

Figure 6.1: Car Engine with Integrated Components

In this system, you have different systems like mechanical systems, electrical systems, electronic components, chemical systems and other items. However, finally, you have a model to simulate the whole unit and we need to see the behavior of the system as a single unit under different conditions. Before manufacturing this car engine with other accessories, it is necessary to see the dynamic behavior. For this, the first step would be to model this integrated system in a simulation environment. Then you will be able to see the dynamic behavior after activating the system.

There are different approaches for system integration. One of the approaches to system integration is mechatronic design approach. Mechatronics is synergistic integration of mechanical engineering, electronics and intelligent computer control in design and manufacture of products and processes [1]. Figure 6.2 shows a schematic view of the mechatronic design (MD) approach to develop any product or system under this concept.

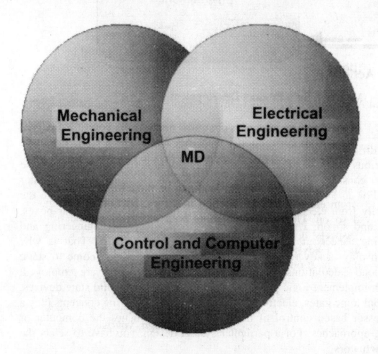

Figure 6.2: Mechatronic Design (MD) Approach

The definition emphasizes synergetic characteristics of component integration in mechatronic objects. Integrated mechatronic components are always chosen at the designing stage. David Alciatore and Michael Histand define this conceptual approach as "rapidly developing, interdisciplinary field of engineering dealing with the design of products whose function relies on the integration of mechanical and electronic components coordinated by control architecture". Mechatronics concepts blend mechanical and electrical components under well established technologies in producing smart consumer products and engineering systems involving both mechanical and electrical functions such as cameras, camcorders, washing machines, hard disk drives, robots, teller machines, and so on [10]-[15].

This mechatronic product or system design can be anything with hardware/software) that percepts information from its environment through sensors and acting upon that environment through actuators (see Figure 6.3). Some products have been enriched by solid state semiconductor devices. Japanese who introduced this mechatronics approach are having numerous developments.

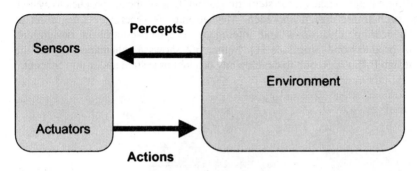

Figure 6.3: Conceptual Approach for a Product Development

One of the examples of mechatronic system is computer numerically controlled (CNC) machines which are different from conventional machines tools. These CNC machines generally employ various types of mechatronic elements. When you integrate all these elements you have to consider all mechanical, electrical and electronic, and computer engineering aspects. For an example, the thermal load can be modeled according to the heat sources, especially from electric motors, friction in drives, friction in gear boxes, machine processing, and so on. Unless you combine both electrical engineering and mechanical engineering aspects it is impossible to have better model. That is why mechatronic approach plays a key role in this CNC designs. When you come to static loads and dynamic load calculations mechanical engineering concepts are employed. Digital systems which implement logic gates are also needed through solid state devices. For these combinatorial logic gates, electronics and computer engineering concepts play a key role. Microprocessor based control of the overall system touches the computer or electrical engineering approaches. For a particular system design, you have to select the sensing devices and actuators.

A combination of hardware and software elements will form a mechatronic system with desired sensors and actuators as shown in Figure 6.3. In the product development level, embedded systems are designed to run on its own without human intervention, and may be required to respond to events in real time at high level. In addition to this integration, most of the times you need certain optimizations in order to improve the overall performance of the systems. Optimization techniques iteratively improve the quality of solutions until an optimal, or at least feasible, solution is found.

6.2 MATLAB SIMULINK

Simulink is a software package in Matlab that enables you to model, simulate, and analyze systems whose outputs change over time. Such systems are often referred as dynamic systems and we have already discussed on this during the last few Chapters. Simulink can be used to explore the behavior of a wide range of real-world dynamic systems, including electrical circuits, shock absorbers, braking systems, and many other electrical, mechanical, and thermodynamic systems [1]. You can go to the Simulink environment by opening the Simulink library browser as shown in Figure 6.4 in the Matlab main window.

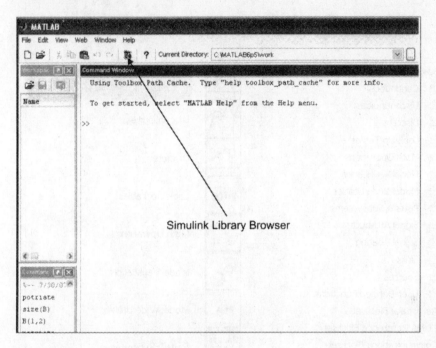

Figure 6.4: Simulink Library Browser

Once you open the Simulink library browser, you will be in the Simulink environment as shown in Figure 6.5. It will allow you to bring different individual components and connect them as you wish. In Figure 6.5, you will see different systems and components like continuous systems, discrete systems, ports, sub-systems, lookup tables, sources and other components. Not only the components in the Simulink library but also there are other block sets like control system toolbox, CDMA block set, fuzzy logic toolbox, system Identification tool box etc [4]-[5].

In Figure 6.5, on your right hand side, you will see different components under each toolbox or block set. Then you can go to those sub-classes and you will handle individual components under that particular model. The next step is to create a new model selecting **Model** in the **New** submenu from the Simulink library browser's **File** menu. Then you will see a new window coming up as shown in Figure 6.6. Now you are in a position to build a new model in the Simulink environment. To create a model you will copy different blocks in the library browser. For an example, if you want to bring a sine wave source, you will follow the following steps:

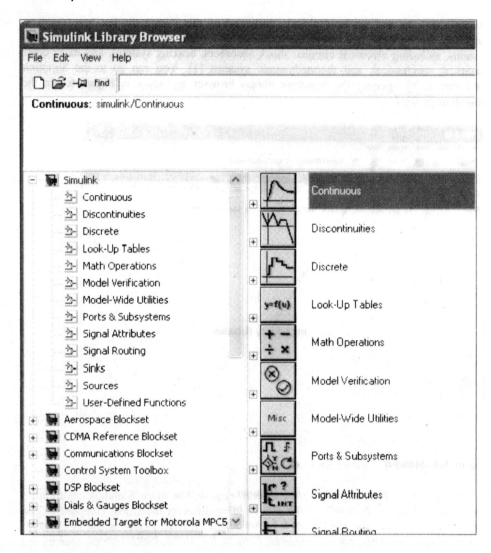

Figure 6.5: Simulink Environment

1. Go to the Simulink library and select **sources**
2. Copy the **Sine Wave** and paste it on the development environment

Note here that without copying and pasting you can drag the element and drop it in the new model. Once you bring the necessary components, you will connect them as you wish (see Figure 6.7).

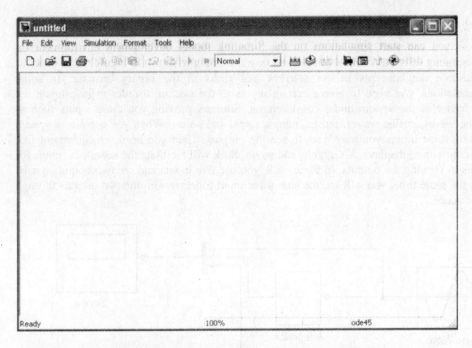

Figure 6.6: Simulink Model Development Environment

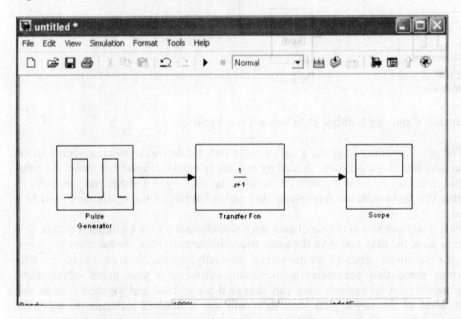

Figure 6.7: Blocks are in Simulink Mode! Development Environment

6.3 BASIC SIMULATIONS

Now you can start simulations on the Simulink model development environment by integrating different components. Let us take the example shown in Figure 6.8 in order to illustrate the concepts behind **sources** and **sinks** in the library browser. In some simulations, you need to give a certain inputs to the system in order to investigate the behavior of the system under consideration. **Sources** provide you these inputs such as sine waves, cosine waves, pulses, ramps, steps, and so on. When you activate a system using these inputs you may want to see the outputs. Then you need the equipment like oscilloscopes, displays, XY-graphs and so on. **Sink** will facilitate the necessary things for this in viewing the outputs. In Figure 6.8, you use two inputs and see two output signals. In the same time, you will see the sine wave input together with the two outputs through the scope.

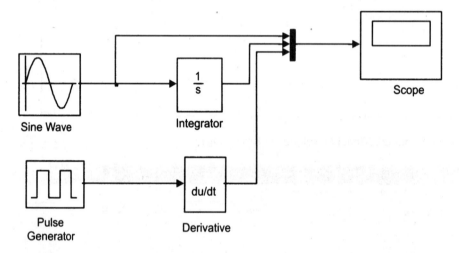

Figure 6.8: Capturing Multiple Data Streams and Viewing

The pulse generator is giving a square pulse into the derivative block as shown in the figure and sine wave generator is feeding into the integrator. Figure 6.9 shows the three outputs that can be seen through the scope. The sine wave through the integrator is another sine wave with a certain phase shift and derivative of the square wave will be a pulse.

First, you have to run the simulation once you connect all the elements. For this, you have to press the **play** button in the menu (start simulation). Now, double click the scope and see the output appeared on the screen. Secondly, set the simulation parameters by choosing **simulation parameter** in the simulation menu in your model development environment. For an example, you can change the start time and the stop time as you wish. Most of the times, your simulation will use a standard technique to solve the ordinary differential equations (ODE) developed by some group of people (sometimes with their names). If you know the exact algorithm to be used in that particular simulation, you can change it according to your requirement. Otherwise, the default algorithm will handle it. Thirdly, you may set the mechanical parameters by choosing mechanical environment parameter in the simulation menu in your same model development environment. Here you may change the settings of different parameters in the inputs.

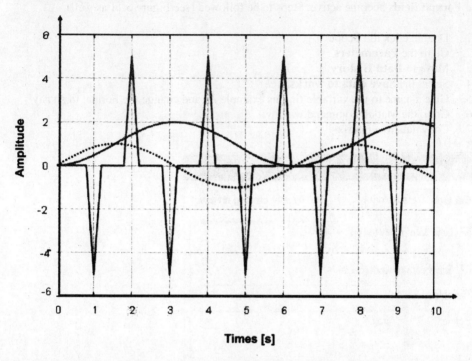

Figure 6.9: Output of the System Implemented in Figure 6.8

6.4 DATA CAPTURING

In certain situations, it is necessary to save your data after the simulation. For an example, take the scope in Figure 6.10 and assume that you want to save the displayed data. You can automatically save the data collected by the **Scope** at the end of the simulation by selecting the **Save data** to workspace check box.

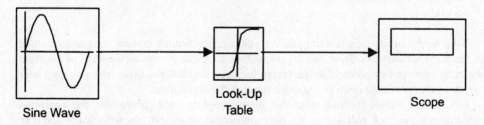

Figure 6.10: Nonlinear Function

In the parameter menu in the scope, you have two sub categories, namely; general and data history.

If you select **data history** and click on **save data to workspace**, the **Variable name** and **Format fields** become active. Steps to be followed (see Figure 6.11 as well):

1. Double click the Scope
2. Go to the **Parameters**
3. Move to **Data History**
4. Select the **Save data to workspace**
5. Give a name to the variable (in this example A) and change the Format to **Array**
6. Go to the Matlab command window
7. Copy data to a matrix

Figure 6.11: Scope Parameters

When you are in the command window, you will get the data array directly as below:

```
>> plot(A(:,1),A(:,2))
>> grid on;
```

Note here that the axis labeling, titling, scaling, positioning can be done as explained in the previous chapters. Here, we do not include all these points, as we want to illustrate the main concept behind the data capturing for your simulations, especially you may later use this streams of data once you acquire through the simulation.

Figure 6.12 shows the output of the above program code. Moreover, the nonlinear element in Figure 6.8 will distort the pure sinusoidal wave and you will clearly see it in the output.

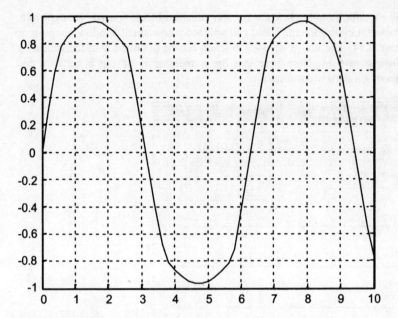

Figure 6.12: Output of the System Implemented in Figure 6.8

6.5 ANALYSIS IN THE S-DOMAIN

Some engineering problems cannot be analyzed in the time domain whereas we have to move into the S-domain. Here, we explain how to use this model development environment in Simulink in order to accommodate S-domain analysis. In the same model development environment, you can bring S-domain blocks from the **continuous** block-set in the Simulink library browser. Figure 6.13 shows a typical feedback system, which can be created in this model development environment.

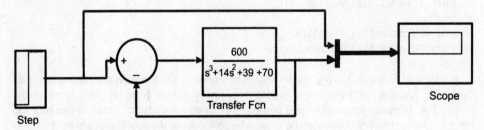

Figure 6.13: System Modeling in S-domain

Once you brought the transfer function block, you can create models of any order. For an example, let us take the block in Figure 6.11. It is in the following form:

$$\frac{600}{S^3 + 14S^2 + 39S + 70}$$

To create this element, double click the transfer function block that you brought in to the model development environment. Then, you will see a new small window popping up as shown in Figure 6.14. The above transfer function can be obtained with the following setting shown in Figure 6.14. Note here that the numerator is having a constant and denominator is having a third order function.

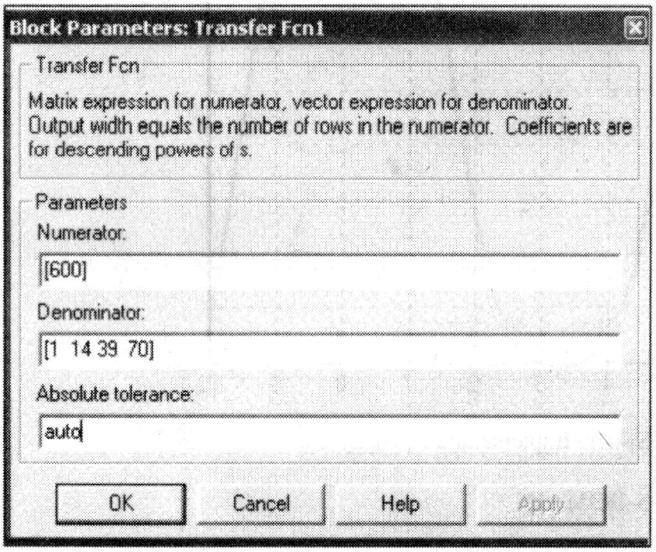

Figure 6.14: Block Parameter Settings for Transfer Functions

Once again, you can select data history in the scope parameters and click on save data to the workspace. Assigning a variable name and changing the **Format** field to **array**, you can import the data to the command window in order to execute the following code:

```
>> plot(A(:,1),A(:,2),'k',A(:,1),A(:,3));
>> grid on
>> xlabel('\fontsize{16} Time [s]');
>> ylabel('\fontsize{16} Amplitude');
```

It will lead to the following results shown in Figure 6.15. You can see the input signal (unit step function) and the output signal (oscillatory output decaying with time) in the graph. For different parameters, you can run this simulation several times optimizing the output. The oscillatory nature can be ceased by introducing the feedback gain as shown in Figure 6.16. However, the overshoot is not reduced even with the new system parameter settings.

Moreover, the transfer function in Figure 6.13 is derived from a dynamic system after transforming the time domain model into the S-domain. If you simulate the model in the time domain, still you can see the results. In fact, this model development environment is one of the approaches that you can follow in analyzing dynamic systems.

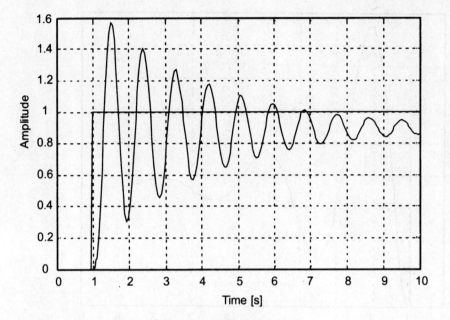

Figure 6.15: Output of the System Shown in Figure 6.13

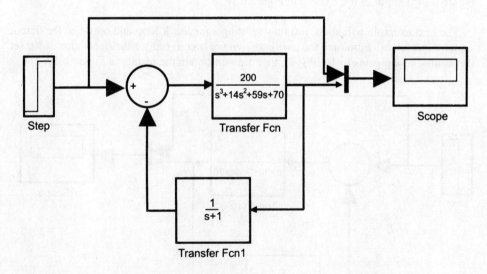

Figure 6.16: Modified System Having a Feedback Loop

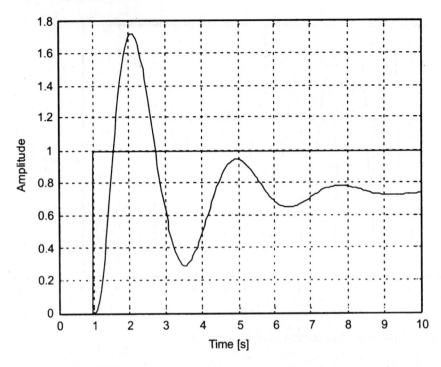

Figure 6.17: Output of the System in Figure 6.16

The next example will show you how to bring a feedback loop and optimize the output signal, especially to eliminate the oscillatory nature and to reduce the overshoot. If we set the feedback loop gains to 1/(20S+7), then we will obtain the results in Figure 6.17.

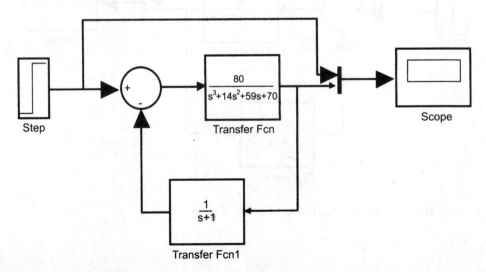

Figure 6.18: Modified System Having a Feedback Loop Gain at 1/(20S+7)

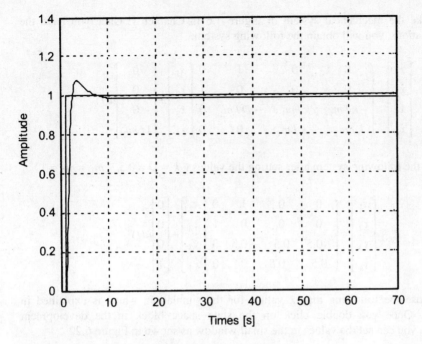

Figure 6.19: Output of the System in Figure 6.18

6.6 STATE SPACE MODELS

In Chapter 1, we explained the basic concept behind the state space approach in order to model a dynamic system. Whether it is linear or nonlinear, for the both cases, the modeling techniques were explained. You can bring your system parameters in to the model development environment as shown in Figure 6.20.

In Simulink, it uses this notation: *A* must be an $n \times n$ matrix, where *n* is the number of states. *B* must be an $n \times m$ matrix, where *m* is the number of inputs. *C* must be an $r \times n$ matrix, where *r* is the number of outputs. *D* must be an $r \times m$ matrix.

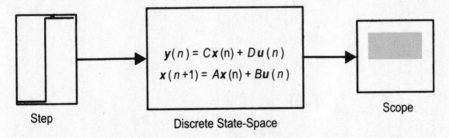

Figure 6.20: State Space Modeling in the Model Development Environment

The block accepts one input and generates one output. The number of columns in the *B* and *D* matrices determines the input vector width. The numbers of rows in the C and D matrices determine the output vector width (see Figure 6.21).

Let us take the mechanical system in Figure 1.6 in Chapter 1. Once you have the dynamic equations, you will obtain the following system:

$$
\begin{bmatrix} \dot{x}_1 \\ \dot{x}_2 \\ \dot{x}_3 \\ \dot{x}_4 \end{bmatrix} = \begin{pmatrix} 0 & 0 & 1 & 0 \\ 0 & 0 & 0 & 1 \\ -k/m_1 & k/m_1 & -D/m_1 & 0 \\ k/m_2 & -k/m_2 & 0 & 0 \end{pmatrix} \begin{bmatrix} x_1 \\ x_2 \\ x_3 \\ x_4 \end{bmatrix} + \begin{bmatrix} 0 \\ 0 \\ 0 \\ 1/m_2 \end{bmatrix} u(t)
$$

You will get the following system after setting the values ($k = D = 0.5$, $m_1 = m_2 = 1$)

$$
\begin{bmatrix} \dot{x}_1 \\ \dot{x}_2 \\ \dot{x}_3 \\ \dot{x}_4 \end{bmatrix} = \begin{pmatrix} 0 & 0 & 1 & 0 \\ 0 & 0 & 0 & 1 \\ -0.5 & 0.5 & -0.5 & 0 \\ 0.5 & -0.5 & 0 & 0 \end{pmatrix} \begin{bmatrix} x_1 \\ x_2 \\ x_3 \\ x_4 \end{bmatrix} + \begin{bmatrix} 0 \\ 0 \\ 0 \\ 1 \end{bmatrix} u(t)
$$

We will use the following matrix values for the simulation, which is explained in Figure 6.20. Once you double click on the state space block in the development environment, you can set the values in the small window as shown in Figure 6.22.

$$
A = \begin{bmatrix} 0 & 0 & 1 & 0 \\ 0 & 0 & 0 & 1 \\ -0.5 & 0.5 & -0.5 & 0 \\ 0.5 & -0.5 & 0 & 0 \end{bmatrix}
$$

$$
B = \begin{bmatrix} 0 \\ 0 \\ 1 \\ 0 \end{bmatrix}
$$

$$
C = \begin{bmatrix} 1 & 0 & 0 & 0 \end{bmatrix}
$$

$$
D = \begin{bmatrix} 1 \end{bmatrix}
$$

The step block (see Figure 6.20) provides a step between two definable levels at a specified time. If the simulation time is less than the step time parameter value, the block's output is the initial value.

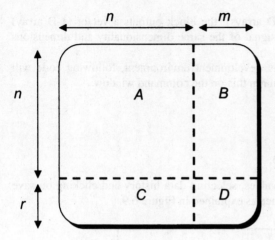

Figure 6.21: Dimensions of the State Space Matrices

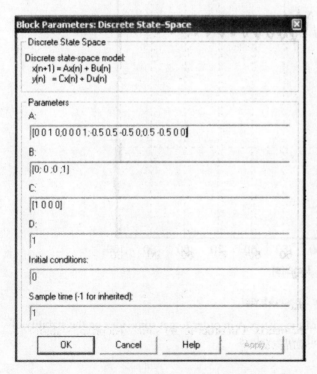

Figure 6.22: Block Parameters for State Space Matrices

For simulation time greater than or equal to the Step time, the output is the Final value parameter value. The block's numeric parameters must be of the same dimensions after scalar expansion. If the interpret vector parameters as 1-D option is off, the block outputs a signal of the same dimensions and dimensionality as the parameters. If the Interpret vector parameters as 1-D option is on and the numeric parameters are row or column vectors (i.e., single row or column 2-D arrays), the block outputs a vector (1-D array) signal; otherwise, the block outputs a signal of the same dimensionality and dimensions as the parameters [1].

Once you run the simulation on the development environment, following code will generate the output in Figure 6.23 if you run this on the command window.

```
>> plot(A(:,1),A(:,2));
>> grid on
>> xlabel('\fontsize{16} Time [s]');
>> ylabel('\fontsize{16} Variable x_1 ');
```

Note here that you have to set the values, selecting data history and clicking on save data in the scope parameters to workspace as explained in Figure 6.9.

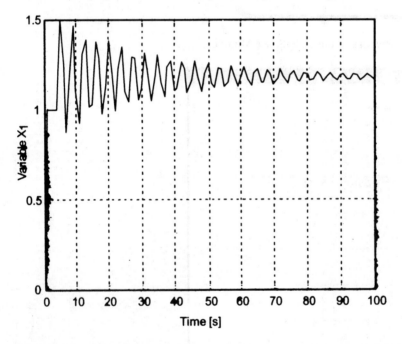

Figure 6.23: Output of the State Space Model

Let us see the Eigen values of the matrix A in order to get some idea on the stability of the system. We will have the following values:

```
>> eig(A)

ans =

 -0.1167 + 0.9613i
 -0.1167 - 0.9613i
  0.0000
 -0.2666
```

If all the eigen values are negative then the system is stable. This is not an exact way of analyzing the stability. But you can get some idea whether the system is going to be a stable one or not.

Furthermore, you can obtain the same results if you run the following codes (Program 6.1) in the normal command window. The sampling time is *dt* and the total time span is 600 [s]. To store data, file identifier will open the data5.dat file with following initial conditions.

$$\mathbf{x}_0 = \begin{bmatrix} 0.2 \\ 0 \\ 0 \\ 0 \end{bmatrix}$$

The command ***fprintf*** will write on *data5.dat* file and the matrix A is the system matrix. Then, you have to generate all data points with a repetitive loop where it uses a *For-End* loop. Once you closed the data file you will plot the variable values obtained.

```
t0 = 0.0;
dt=0.01;
total_time = 600;
n=total_time/dt;

fid = fopen('data5.dat','w');

x10 = 0.2;    x20 = 0.0;   x30 = 0.0; x40 = 0.0;
t=t0;

fprintf(fid,'%6.2f %6.2f %6.2f %6.2f %6.2f \n',t,x10,x20,x30,x40);

a11  =   0;     a12  =   0;      a13 = 1 ;     a14=0;
a21  =   0;     a22  =   0;      a23 = 0;      a24=1;
a31  =  -0.5;   a32  =  0.5;     a33 = -0.5;   a34=0;
a41  =   0.5;   a42  =  -0.5;    a43 =0 ;      a44=0;

A=[a11 a12 a13 a14; a21 a22 a23 a24; a31 a32 a33 a34; a41
a42 a43 a44];

for i=1:n
    x1 = a11*x10*dt + a12*x20*dt + a13*x30*dt +
a14*x40*dt + x10;
    x2 = a21*x10*dt + a22*x20*dt + a23*x30*dt +
a24*x40*dt + x20;
    x3 = a31*x10*dt + a32*x20*dt + a33*x30*dt +
a34*x40*dt + x30;
    x4 = a41*x10*dt + a42*x20*dt + a43*x30*dt +
a44*x40*dt + x40;
```

(Contd.)

```
    fprintf(fid,'%6.2f %6.2f %6.2f %6.2f %6.2f
\n',t,x1,x2,x3,x4);
    x10 = x1;      x20 = x2;      x30 = x3;      x40 = x4;
    t = t + dt;
end
```

Program 6:1 Simulating the State State Space Model

In the next example, we will discuss the principle of quantization in Matlab Simulink. The Quantizer block passes its input signal through a stair-step function so that many neighboring points on the input axis are mapped to one point on the output axis. The effect is to quantize a smooth signal into a stair-step output. The output is computed using the round-to-nearest method, which produces an output that is symmetric about zero [1].

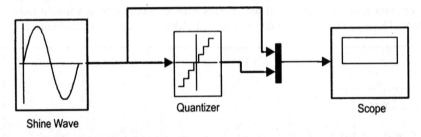

Shine Wave   Quantizer   Scope

Figure 6.24: Quantization of Sine Wave

Similarly, once you get the output value to the scope you can bring data to the command window and plot it as you wish. Figure 6.26 shows the output of the scope.

>> plot(A(:,1),A(:,2),A(:,1),A(:,3));
>> hold on
>> axis([0 10 -1.1 1.1])
>> grid on

Note that you can change the quantization interval as shown in Figure 6.25. The output is quantized in this interval around. The Matlab default value of this quantization interval is 0.5.

Block Parameters: Quantizer

Quantizer
Discretize input at given interval.

Parameters
Quantization interval:
0.5
☐ Treat as gain when linearizing

| OK | Cancel | Help | Apply |

Figure 6.25: Block Parameters of the Quantizer

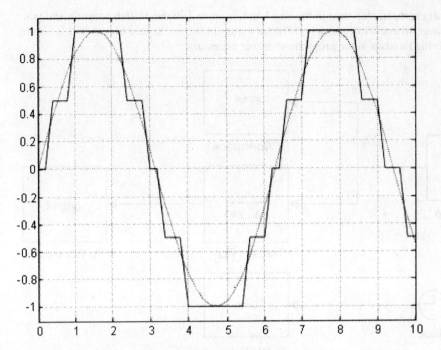

Figure 6.26: Output of the Quantized Sine Wave

The next example will illustrate to run a Simulink program through a Matlab program. Here, you build your own Simulink blocks separately, while you develop your Matlab codes supporting to your Simulink program giving a name. You run your Matlab program and you call your Simulink one whenever necessary. Here, we give the name "workspace" as the Simulink program and call it with ***sim*** command (see Program 6.2).

```
% Transfer function values
k=1.5;
Tau=5;

%Step Input
step_time=1;
initial_value=0;
final_value=1;

% Run Simulink Block
sim workspace

plot(time,input,'k',time,output,'k--');
axis([-1 40 0 1.6]);
grid on;
```

Program 6.2: Matlab codes to run the Simulink Blocks in Figure 6.25

For an example, step time in the step block is set to 1 in the Matlab program and you may change whenever necessary. Different names in the workspace blocks will facilitate you to bring the data in the program wherever necessary.

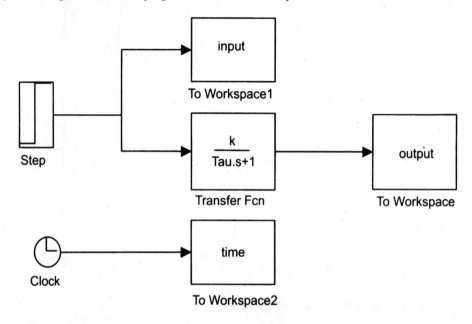

Figure 6.27: Simulink Blocks to Run the Program 6.2 (File Name = workspace.mdl)

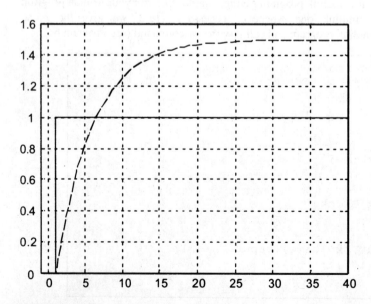

Figure 6.28: Output of the System in Figure 6.25

6.7 INTEGRATION OF LOGICAL BLOCKS

When you want to integrate digital systems into other systems it is necessary to use logic gates in Simulink. Logic gates control the output in a digital system based input conditions. A gate is a logic circuit where you have solid state devices or semiconductors in general where it gives a single output to multi-input system. In the Simulink environment, you can bring your logic blocks with the other elements in a system. Logical operations like AND, OR, NAND, NOR, XOR, and NOT can be realized and combinational logic of these are also realizable. Consider the truth table in Table 6.1.

Table 6.1: Truth Table for the Logical Expression $(ab) + (bc)$

a	b	c	output
0	0	0	0
0	0	1	0
0	1	0	0
0	1	1	1
1	0	0	0
1	0	1	0
1	1	0	1
1	1	1	1

Figure 6.29 shows the Simulink block diagram for the truth table in Table 6.1 with two different implementations. For the combinatorial logic block in Figure 6.29 you can give the outputs sequence for a standard truth table. For an example, the output in Table 6.1 can be realized with the vector of [0; 0; 0 ;1; 0 ; 0; 1;1]. For an example, if you give 1, 0, and 0 as inputs to a, b, and c respectively, output will be 0. Two displays use two different approaches which will give the same results.

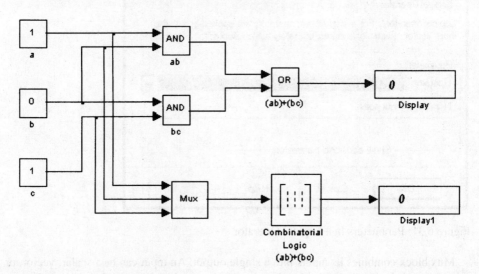

Figure 6.29: Combination of Logics

Complex logical structures with multi inputs are possible to feed into the combinatorial logic block in Simulink. In Figure 6.29, block parameters of combinatorial logic can be fed into the Simulink block as shown in Figure 6.30. Though a Mux the values are fed into the combinatorial logic.

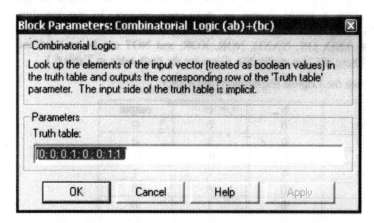

Figure 6.30: Parameters in a Truth Table for a Combinatorial Logic

In Figure 6.31, setting of parameters to a logical operator is shown. Here, you set it to an OR gate with two inputs. Two inputs are coming through two AND gates where the two logics (ab and bc) are realized using three inputs (a, b, and c).

Block Parameters: (ab)+(bc)

Logical Operator

Logical operators. For a single input, operators are applied across the input vector. For multiple inputs, operators are applied across the inputs.

Parameters

Operator: OR

Number of input ports:

2

☐ ------------- Show additional parameters -------------

| OK | Cancel | Help | Apply |

Figure 6.31: Parameters in a Logical Operator

Mux block combines its inputs into a single output. An input can be a scalar, vector, or matrix signal. In Figure 6.29, Mux has three inputs and you set display option to none.

Depending on its inputs, the output of a Mux block is a vector or a composite signal, i.e., a signal containing both matrix and vector elements are possible [5].

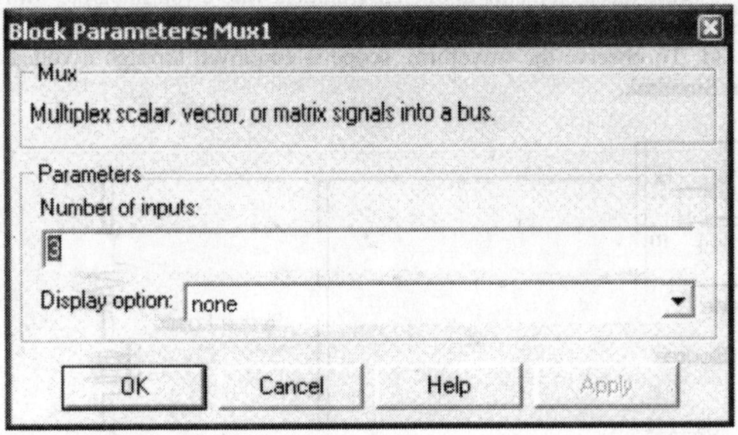

Figure 6.32: Parameters in a Mux

Three inputs, a, b, and c, are fed into the digital system via three constant block sets as shown in Figure 6.29. Here, you use Boolean values as the data type (see Figure 6.33). The Constant block generates a real or complex constant value and you can generate a scalar, vector, or matrix output of the Constant value parameter [5].

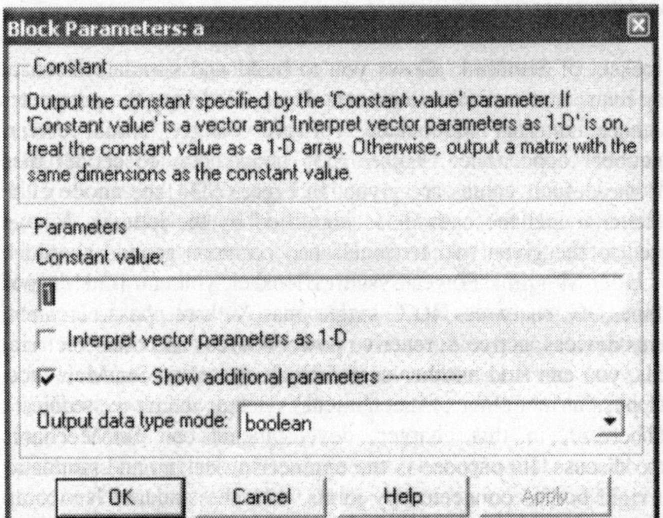

Figure 6.33: Parameters in a Constant

6.8 INTEGRATION OF ELECTRICAL ELEMENTS

In the previous chapters, basic circuit simulations with RLC circuits were discussed. However, you need to bring these elements to one environment where you integrate with other elements in a complex system. Here, RL load is supplied through a power diode as shown in Figure 6.34. To observe the waveform, scope is employed through a voltage measuring device in Simulink.

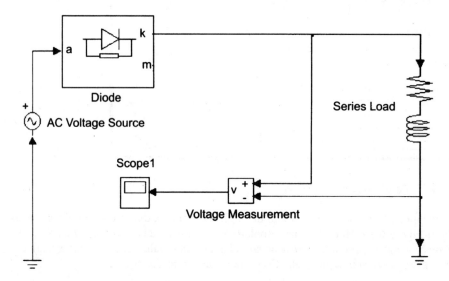

Figure 6.34: Parameters in a Constant

The Power System Blockset of Simulink allows you to build and simulate electrical circuit elements containing linear and nonlinear elements. Here, diode has the parameters like diode internal resistance, internal inductance, forward voltage, initial current, snubber resistance and snubber capacitance. Figure 6.35 shows how to set all these parameters in a diode and the default values are given. In Figure 6.34, the anode of the diode is denoted by the letter *a* and the cathode is identified by the letter *k*. Voltage source should be connected to the given two terminals and common ground should be used whenever necessary. Under Simulink Power System Blockset, you can find various devices such as AC machines, DC machines, RLC single phase & three phase elements, solid state power electronics devices, active & reactive power sources and other electrical equipment. Apart from this, you can find another useful block-set called SimMechanics. SimMechanics is a part of physical modeling of mechanical systems which we studied in the previous chapters. Therefore, in this chapter, developments on SimMechanics techniques are not going to discuss. Its purpose is the engineering design and simulation of mechanical systems of rigid bodies connected by joints, with the standard Newtonian dynamics of forces and torques [5]. Not only the electrical circuit elements but also you can bring analytical tools into the Simulink environment. For an example, Fourier block performs a Fourier analysis of the input signal over a running window of one cycle of the fundamental frequency of the signal where you can use this in a system itself.

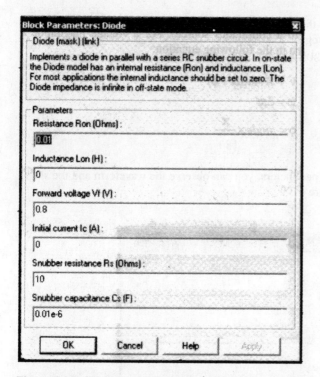

Figure 6.35: Changing the diode Parameters

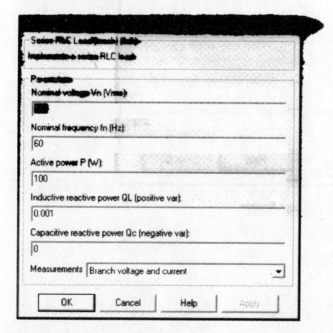

Figure 6.36: Changing the RLC values

Figure 6.37 shows how to set the voltage source parameters and the sample period can be set (default is 0 corresponding to a continuous source). For a voltage magnitude *A* (peak), the other parameters are given in the following equation:

$$V = A\sin(\omega t + \phi)$$
$$\omega = 2\pi f$$
$$\phi = angle \times \frac{\pi}{180}$$

Once you set all these above parameters, you can observe the waveform and the shape of the waveform is given in Figure 6.38.

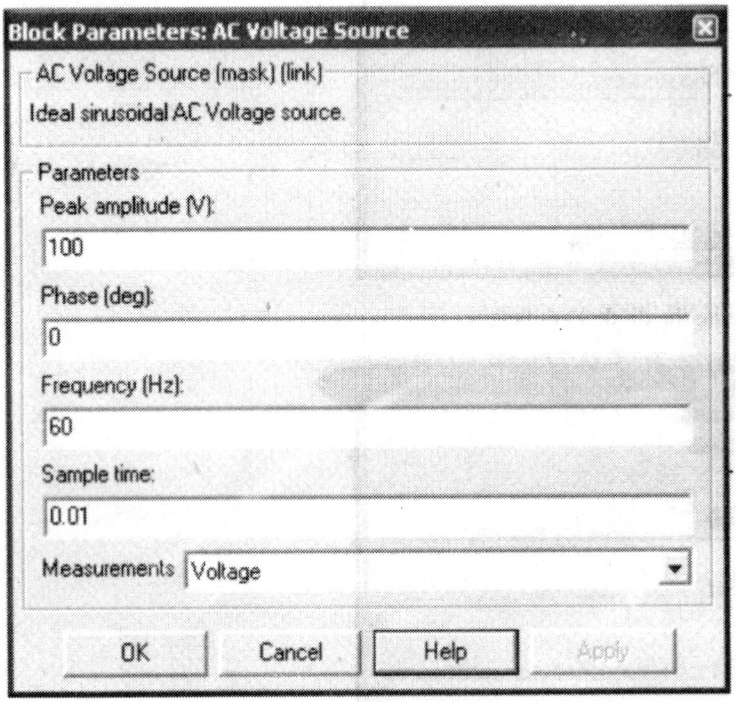

Figure 6.37: Parameters of the Voltage Source

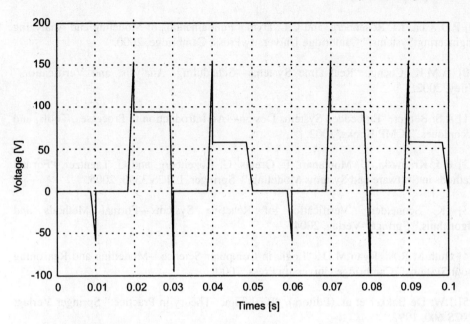

Figure 6.38: Output Voltage across the RL Element

REFERENCES

[1] C.W. De Silva, "Mechatronics: An Integrated Approach," Taylor-Francis, CRC Press, Boca Raton, FL, 2004.

[2] C.W. De Silva, "Sensors and Actuators: Control System Instrumentation," CRC Press, Boca Raton, FL, 2007.

[3] S. Karunakuran *et.al.* "Mechatronics," Tata McGraw Hill, New Delhi, 11th Reprint, 2005.

[4] J.B. Dabney and T.L. Harman, "Mastering Simulink 4", New Jersey, Prentice Hall, 2001.

[5] Matlab Release 13, Version 6.5, "Help Manual and Toolboxes," The Mathworks Inc., 2002.

[6] Rajagopalan, V., "Computer-Aided Analysis of Power Electronic Systems," Marcel Dekker, Inc., New York, 1987.

[7] Mohan, N., T.M. Undeland, and W.P. Robbins, "Power Electronics: Converters, Applications, and Design," John Wiley & Sons, Inc., New York, 1995.

[8] A. Preumont, "Mechatronics: Dynamics of Electromechanical and Piezoelectric Systems," Springer, Berlin, 2006.

[9] P.D. Cha, J.J. Rosenberg, and C.L. Dym, "Fundamentals of Modeling and Analyzing Engineering Systems," Cambridge University Press, Cambridge, 2000.

[10] A.M.K. Cheng, "Real-Time Systems—Scheduling, Analysis, and Verification," Wiley, 2002.

[11] A.S. Berger, "Embedded Systems Design—An Introduction to Processes, Tools, and Techniques," CMP Books, 2002.

[12] H.J. Kreowski, U. Montanari, F. Orejas, G. Rozenberg, and G. Taentzer, "Formal Methods in Software and Systems Modeling," Springer, LNCS 3393, 2005.

[13] K. Schneider, "Verification of Reactive Systems—Formal Methods and Algorithms," Springer-Verlag, 2004.

[14] Huth M.R.A., Ryan M.D., "Logic in Computer Science—Modelling and Reasoning about Systems," Cambridge University Press, 2000.

[15] J.W. De Bakker et al. (Editors), "Real-Time: Theory in Practice," Springer-Verlag, LNCS 600, 1992.

Chapter 7

Advanced Simulations

Knowledge on basic research lays the foundation for the advanced technological developments and beyond.

7.1 INTRODUCTION

Practically, system modeling for computer simulations abstracts a mathematical model under certain assumptions. This is basically due to the difficulty of including all the constraints and difficulty of including all the parameters found in the real system under investigation. This has become a common practice of mathematical modeling of many physical systems. Generally, modeling procedure of a given system is based on mathematical models, which attempt to predict the behavior of systems from set of parameters. Selected parameters in a model may be less than the actual system parameters and this will lead to have a simplified version of the actual system. Before going into a complex model or an advanced simulation directly, you will have a simplified model and simulate that one first. Later you can switch on to a complex model including the rest of the parameters or remaining constrains which were not taken into account.

Computer simulation uses simulation software packages to simulate the mathematical models in science and engineering applications as we discussed already in the previous chapters. Most simulation software tools, which are customized for a particular task, are capable of simulating and analyzing parameters of that selected system. For an example, if you consider the power systems computer aided design (PS-CAD) software, you can handle power system related simulations. As far as power system simulations are concerned, Matlab will not provide that type of customized solutions compared to PS-CAD.

Consider the function shown in the equation (7.1) as an example for the analysis. Computer aided simulations can be used to analyze mathematical functions and models directly. You may begin from the basics, representing variable variations to some advanced problems like optimization. Figure 7.1 illustrates the function variation simulated using Matlab.

$$f(x, y) = x^4 + y^2 \tag{7.1}$$

In addition to implementation of basic operations and algorithms, simulations are helpful in designing and simulating artificial intelligence concepts like fuzzy logic (FL), neural networks (NN) and genetic algorithms (GA). This chapter covers an advanced simulation, which illustrates a technique in optimizing a multi-dimensional problem using genetic algorithms.

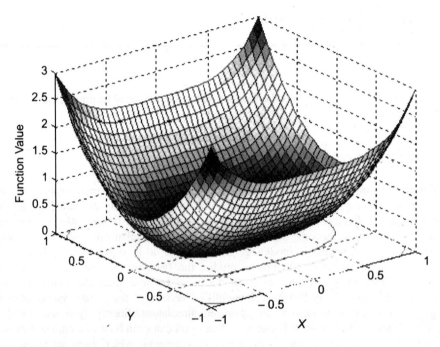

Figure 7.1: Function Values at Different X-Y Coordinates

7.2 GENETIC ALGORITHMS

J. Holland introduced the genetic algorithms (GAs) in 1960s and subsequently it has been made widely popular by David Goldberg. The original GA and its many variants, collectively known as Genetic Algorithms, are computational procedures that mimic the natural process of evolution. The theories of evolution and natural selection were first introduced by Darwin to explain his observations of plants and animals in the natural world. Darwin observed that, as variations are introduced into a population with each new generation, the less fit individuals tend to die off in the competition for food, and then survival of the fittest principle is emerged [1].

7.2.1 Biological Analogy

In the context of GA, the biological terms are used in analogy with the real biology. According to the biology, all living organisms consist of cells, and each cell contains the same set of one or more chromosomes (strings of DNA) that serve as a "blueprint" for the organism. A chromosome can be conceptually divided into genes (functional blocks of DNA), each of which encodes a particular protein. Very roughly, one can think of a gene as encoding a triat, such as eye color. The different possible settings for a triat are called as allels. Each gene is located at a particular locus on the chromosome. Many organisms have multiple chromosomes in each cell. The complete set of genetic materials (all chromosomes) is called the organism's genome. The term genotype refers to the particular set of genes contained in the genome. The organism's physical and mental characteristics, such as eye color, height, brain size are called as phenotype. In genetic Algorithms, the term chromosome typically refers to a candidate solution to a problem, often encoded as a bit string. The "genes" are either bits or short block of adjacent bits that encode a particular element of a candidate solution. An allel in a bit string is either '1' or '0' [2], [3].

7.2.2 Algorithm

The genetic algorithms are good at taking a larger, potentially huge, search spaces and navigating them looking for an optimal combination of things and solutions. A more striking difference between genetic algorithms and most of the traditional optimization methods is that, GA uses a population of points at one time in contrast to the single point approach by traditional optimization methods. All individuals in a population evolve simultaneously without central coordination [4]. The major steps of a genetic algorithm are:

(1) Create Initial population/Genotype (i.e. create initial set of solutions to the selected problem)
(2) Phenotypic decoding and objective function calculation
(3) Ranking and selection
(4) Apply genetic operators like crossover, mutation to create offspring
(5) Evaluate the objective function
(6) Repeat the above procedure until stopping criteria

The typical series of operations carried out for implementing a GA is listed and the overview of the GA is illustrated in the Figure 7.2. First, initialization is done by seeding the population with random values. The objective function or fitness function is the one of the most important parts in a GA. It should represent the parameter to be optimized. The fitness value is proportional to the performance measurement of the function being optimized. It is this fitness that guides the search of the problem space. Then the evolution from one generation to the next one involves three steps: Fitness evaluation, Selection and Reproduction. The current population is evaluated using the fitness evaluation function and then ranked based on their fitness values. The GA stochastically selects parents from the current population with a bias where the better chromosomes are more likely to be selected. This is accomplished using a selection probability that is determined by the fitness value or the ranking of a chromosome. Third, GA produces "children" or "Off springs" from the selected "parents" using the main genetic operators: crossover and mutation. This cycle of objective function evaluation, selection and reproduction, terminates when an acceptable solution is found, when a convergence criterion is met, or when a predetermined limit on the number of generations is reached.

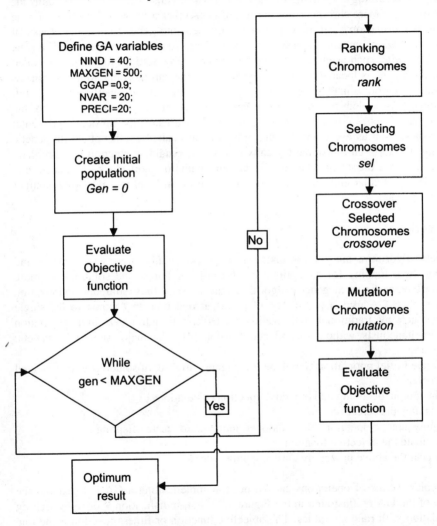

Figure 7.2: Main Steps of a Genetic Algorithm

7.2.3 Binary Encoding

In a binary implementation of genetic algorithms, a binary string represents a chromosome. There are other many ways of representing individual genes. Holland worked mainly with bits, but we can use arrays, trees, lists, or any other object. Two binary coded chromosomes are illustrated in Figure 7.3. Chromosome consists of several genes and these genes represent the variables of a real world problem.

Chromosome1:   100011111010100000111110000011
Chromosome2:   111110101011100011110111010100

Figure 7.3: Sample Chromosomes

In order to use the GA to solve the optimization problem, unknown variables X_is are first coded in some string structures and those variables are called as decision variables. The length of the string is usually determined according to the desired accuracy. The decision variable may have both upper and lower limits as:

$$X_i^L \le X_i \le X_i^U \tag{7.2}$$

However, n-bit string can represent integers from 0 to $2^n - 1$, which add up to 2^n integers. Assume that X_i is coded as a substring S_i of length n_i. The decoded value and the corresponding variable can be calculated as in the equation (7.3).

$$X_i = X_i^L + \frac{\left(X_i^U - X_i^L\right)}{\left(2^{n_i} - 1\right)} \times \left(\sum_{k=0}^{k=n_i-1} 2^k S_k\right) \tag{7.3}$$

7.2.4 Selection

Various selection schemes have been used; roulette wheel selection, stochastic universal selection, tournament selection and Boltzmann selection. The commonly used selection operator is the proportionate operator where a string is selected from the mating pool with a probability proportional to fitness. Thus, the ith string in the population is selected with a probability proportional to F_i, where F_i is the fitness value for mating. The sum of the probabilities of each string being selected for the mating pool must be one. The probability of the ith selected string is;

$$p_i = \frac{F_i}{\sum_{j=1}^{n} F_j} \tag{7.4}$$

Where, n is the population size. As illustrated in the Figure 7.4 (a), Roulette wheel selection is a proportionate selection scheme in which the slots of a roulette wheel are sized according to the fitness of each individual in the population.

An individual is selected by spinning the roulette wheel and noting the position of the marker. The probability of selecting an individual is therefore proportional to its fitness. As illustrated in the figure 7.4 (b), stochastic universal selection is a less noisy version of roulette wheel in which, N equidistance markers are placed around the roulette wheel, where N is the number of individuals in the population. N individuals selected in a single spin of the roulette wheel, and the number of copies of each individual selected is equal to the number of marker inside the corresponding slot.

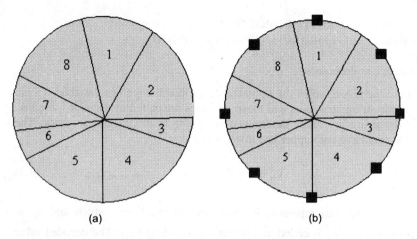

(a) (b)

Figure 7.4: (a): Roulette Wheel Selection, and (b) Stochastic Universal Selection

7.2.5 Genetic Operators

The most frequently used genetic operators are crossover and mutation. The crossover operator is applied to the mating pool with the hope that it would create a better string. The aim of the crossover operator is to search the parameter space. In addition, search is to be made in a way that the information stored in the parent string is maximally preserved because the parent strings are instances of good strings selected during reproduction. The crossover operator is a recombination operator which precedes three steps. First, the reproduction operator selects at random a pair of two individual strings for mating, then the cross site is selected at random along the string length and the position values are· swapped between the two strings following the cross site [5]. According to the crossover site selection and the number of crossover sites, there are three methods; single point crossover, two-point cross over and multipoint crossover. In a single point crossover, a cross site is selected randomly along the length of the mated strings. The bits, next to the cross site are exchanged as shown in Figure 7.5.

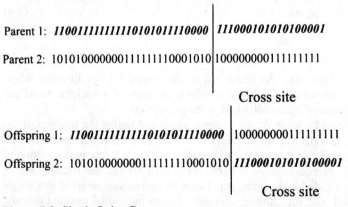

Parent 1: *11001111111110101011110000* 111000101010100001

Parent 2: 10101000000011111111110001010 100000000111111111

Cross site

Offspring 1: *11001111111110101011110000* 100000000111111111

Offspring 2: 10101000000011111111110001010 *111000101010100001*

Cross site

Figure 7.5: Single Point Crossover

In a two point crossover operator, two random cross sites are selected and the contents bracketed are swapped between two parents. This phenomenon is illustrated in the Figure 7.6.

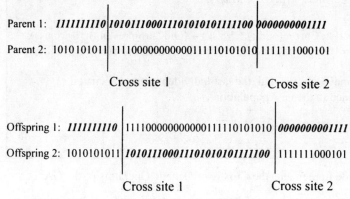

Parent 1: ***111111110*** | 1010111000111010101011111100 | 0000000001111

Parent 2: 1010101011 | 111100000000000111110101010 | 1111111000101

Cross site 1   Cross site 2

Offspring 1: ***111111110*** | 111100000000000111110101010 | ***0000000001111***

Offspring 2: 1010101011 | ***1010111000111010101011111100*** | 1111111000101

Cross site 1   Cross site 2

Figure 7.6: Two Point Crossover

An overall probability is assigned to the crossover process. This is the probability that determines crossover process for given two parents. This probability is often in the range of 0.65--0.80. Program 7.1 describes Matlab code for the crossover operation.

```
% This function performs crossover between pairs of individuals
% OldChrom : Parent Chromosome
% Rate : Crossover rate (0<Rate< 1)

function NewChrom = crossover(OldChrom, Rate);

  NewChrom = [ ];

  % Identify the population size
  [Nind,Lind] = size(OldChrom);

  Xops = floor(Nind/2);
  DoCross = rand(Xops,1) < Rate;
  odd = 1:2:Nind-1;
  even = 2:2:Nind;

  % Compute the effective length of each chromosome pair
  Mask = 1 1 (OldChrom(odd, :) ~= OldChrom(even, :));
  Mask = cumsum(Mask')';

  % Compute cross sites for each pair of individuals
  xsites(:, 1) = Mask(:, Lind);

  xsites(:,2) = rem(xsites + ceil((Mask(:, Lind)-1) .* rand(Xops, 1))...
          .* DoCross - 1 , Mask(:, Lind) )+1;
```

```
% Express cross sites in terms of a 0-1 mask
Mask = (xsites(:,ones(1,Lind)) < Mask) == ...
                (xsites(:,2*ones(1,Lind)) < Mask);

% Perform crossover
NewChrom(odd,:) = (OldChrom(odd,:).* Mask) + (OldChrom(even,:).*(~Mask));
NewChrom(even,:) = (OldChrom(odd,:).*(~Mask)) + (OldChrom(even,:).*Mask);


% If the number of individuals is odd, the last individual cannot be mated
% but must be included in the new population
if rem(Nind,2),
    NewChrom(Nind,:)=OldChrom(Nind,:);
end
```

Program 7.1: Matlab Code Implements the Crossover Genetic Operators of the GA.

As new individuals are generated, each character is mutated with a given probability. In a binary coded GA, mutation may be done by flipping a randomly selected bit. While in a non-binary coded GA, mutation involves randomly generating a new character in the specified position. The mutation produces incremental random changes in the offspring produced by crossover operator as in the Figure 7.7.

Before: 11100001111010101111110011
After: 11101001111010101101110011

Figure 7.7: Mutation Process

In GA, mutation serves as the crucial role of replacing the gene values lost from the population during the selection process. They can be tried in a new context, or be provided with new gene values that were not present in the initial population. Thus, mutation makes the entire search space reachable, despite the finite population size. The mutation probability P_m is defined as the probability of mutating each gene. It controls the rate at which new gene values are introduced into the population. If it is too low, many gene values that would have been useful are never tried. If it is too high, too much random perturbation will occur, and offspring will lose their resemblance to the parents. The ability of the algorithm to learn from the history of the search will therefore be lost. Finally, the probability of mutation can vary widely according to the application and the preference of the person who is exercising the GA. However, the values of between 0.001 and 0.01 are not unusual. Program 7.2 describes a Matlab code, which implements mutation operation. The mutation probability is assigned as 0.01.

7.2.6 Example 1

Find the minimum value of the following function given in equation (7.5) and variable values using Genetic Algorithms.

$$f(x, y) = x^2 + 2y^2 + \cos(3\pi x) + 3\cos(4\pi x) + 4 \tag{7.5}$$

where, $0 \le x \le 1$ and $-1 \le y \le 1$

```
% Mutates each element with given probability and returns the resulting population.
function NewChrom = mutation(OldChrom)

% get population size
[Nind, Lind] = size(OldChrom) ;
Pm = 0.01; % Mutation rate

% create mutation mask matrix
BaseM = 2*(ones(Nind,Lind));

% perform mutation on chromosome structure
NewChrom = rem(OldChrom+(rand(Nind,Lind)<Pm),BaseM);
```

Program 7.2: Matlab Code Implements the Mutation Genetic Operator of the GA.

First, it is possible to analyze the function behavior. Program 7.3 and Program 7.4 illustrates the Matlab code, which describe the function variations.

```
x=-1:.05:1;
y=-1:.05:1;
[X,Y]=meshgrid(x,y);
Z=X.*X+2*Y.*Y+cos(3*pi*X)+3*cos(4*pi*X)+4;
contour(X,Y,Z);
xlabel('X');
ylabel('Y');
figure,surfc(X,Y,Z);
xlabel('X');
ylabel('Y');
Zlabel('Function Value');
figure,mesh(X,Y,Z);
xlabel('X');
ylabel('Y');
Zlabel('Function Value');
grid on;
```

Program 7.3: Matlab Code which Implements Function Behavior

First, we have to define the main parameter such as number of individuals in a population, generation gap, precision of representation, Number of variables and maximum number of generations for the stopping criteria as in Program 7.4.

```
NIND = 40;       % Number of individuals per populations
MAXGEN = 100;    % maximum Number of generations
GGAP = .90;      % Generation gap, how many new individuals are created
NVAR = 2;        % Generation gap, how many new individuals are created
PRECI = 20;      % Precision of binary representation
```

Program 7.4: Matlab Code, which Defines the GA

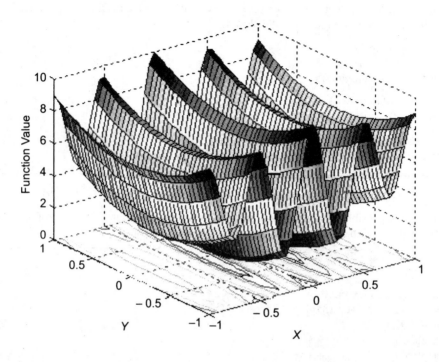

Figure 7.8: Values of the Function (7.5)

Then the initial population is created using random method. Program 7.5 illustrates Matlab codes that create a binary population.

```
% Creates the binary population
% Nind : Number of individuals
% Lind : Length of an individual (NVAR * PRECI)

function [Chrom] = createbp(Nind, Lind)

Chrom = floor(rand(Nind,Lind).* 2) ;
```

Program 7.5: Matlab Code which Create a Binary Population

The objective function also can be implemented as a separate file and it illustrated in Program 7.6. Binary encoded chromosomes should converted to decimal and then feed to the function to calculate the fitness values.

```
function ObjVal = objfun (Chrom);

    %Select Varibles To Seperate matrices
    x1=Chrom(:,1);
    x2=Chrom(:,2);

    % Evaluating objective function

    ObjVal=x1.*x1+2*x2.*x2+cos(3*pi*x1)+3*cos(4*pi*x1)+4;
```

Program 7.6: Matlab code which Implements the Objective Function.

Then, first generation of population is used to generate the next generation. It should follow a ranking and a selection steps. Ranking can be done in linear or non linear manner. Selection of parent chromosomes are achieved using one of the available methods like Roulette wheel selection, stochastic universal selection, tournament selection and Boltzmann selection. Program 7.7 and Program 7.8 illustrate the Matlab implementations of stochastic universal selection and Roulette wheel selection respectively.

```
% Input parameters:
%    FitnV    - Column vector containing the fitness values of the
%                 individuals in the population.
%    Ns       - number of individuals to be selected
%
% Output parameters:
%    NewChrIx  - column vector containing the indexes of the selected
%                 individuals relative to the original population and shuffled.

function NewChrIx = sus(FitnV,Ns);

% Identify the population size (Nind)
    [Nind,ans] = size(FitnV);

% Perform stochastic universal sampling
    cumfit = cumsum(FitnV);
    trials = cumfit(Nind) / Ns * (rand + (0:Ns-1)');
    Mf = cumfit(:, ones(1, Ns));
    Mt = trials(:, ones(1, Nind))';
    [NewChrIx, ans] = find(Mt < Mf & [ zeros(1, Ns); Mf(1:Nind-1, :) ] <= Mt);

% Shuffle new population
    [ans, shuf] = sort(rand(Ns, 1));
    NewChrIx = NewChrIx(shuf);
```

Program 7.7: Matlab code Implements the Stochastic Universal Selection.

```
%       This function selects a given number of individuals Nsel from a
%       population. FitnV is a column vector containing the fitness
%       values of the individuals in the population.

function NewChrIx = rws(FitnV,Ns);

% Identify the population size (Nind)
[Nind,ans] = size(FitnV);

% Perform Stochastic Sampling with Replacement
cumfit  = cumsum(FitnV);
trials = cumfit(Nind) .* rand(Ns, 1);
Mf = cumfit(:, ones(1, Ns));
Mt = trials(:, ones(1, Nind))';
[NewChrIx, ans] = find(Mt < Mf & ...
            [ zeros(1, Ns); Mf(1:Nind-1, :) ] <= Mt);
```

Program 7.8: Matlab code Implements the Roulette Wheel Selection

Next, application of genetic operators can be done using the code discussed in previous sections. User can combine all the supported functions and build their own GA to optimize a particular function. The following Figure 7.9 describes the variation of best fitness values with the generation number. This will give the minimum of functional value as 0.3202 at (0.2614, 0.0000). But it is convenient to use built in functions than writing a GA from basics. The use of built functions is discussed in section 4.

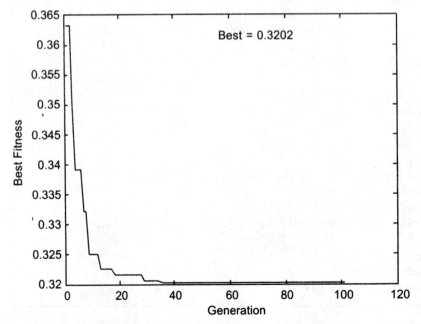

Figure 7.9: Best fitness Variation with Generation Number.

7.3 GENETIC ALGORITHM BASED CABLE SELECTION

7.3.1 Background

This example presents a new genetic algorithm based approach for cable type selection in micro hydro distribution systems. The method leads to a choice of selecting optimal cable size by considering standard voltage regulations and current carrying capacities. The objective function includes voltage drops and current carrying capacities of each selected distribution sections. The main constraints are the consumer point voltage drop should maintain below 15% from the nominal voltage of the systems and the load current should be less than the current rating of the selected cable. The genetic algorithm computes improved generations of chromosomes and candidate cable sizes until the solution is obtained. A suitable case study involving two potential sites, adopted from upper Walawe Ganga basin and Kalu Ganga basin located in Sabaragamuwa province of Sri Lanka, is presented as illustrative example. Micro hydro is a valuable source of energy for rural industries and village electrification schemes. It has been a traditional method of grain processing throughout the world. Micro hydro now offers similar potential to most developing countries such as Sri Lanka [6],[7]. Usually loads are remote from the best power house site and a distribution system is needed. The sizing of the cables is very important. The main design criteria to consider are; the maximum allowable voltage regulation from no-load to full load, the current carrying capacity, the maximum economic power loss and safety for people living and working near the lines. Overhead lines are used more often, by using air as the cable insulation; the cable is less expensive [8],[9]. The Distribution cost is also vital. Then it requires an optimization technique to select cable sizes to utilize properly. Reference [10] proposed a fuzzy mutated genetic algorithm for radial distribution system reconfigurations. Distribution system design is a multi-objective problem. In recent years, it has been recognized that GA is particularly well suited for multi-objective optimization problems since they can simultaneously evolve an entire set of multi-objective solutions [11],[12]. Genetic algorithm based optimization approaches were common in recent past. Research in [13] proposed a genetic algorithm solution to the hydrothermal coordination problem. The objective of the hydrothermal coordination is to determine the optimal operation schedule of thermal units and hydro plants that minimizes the total thermal production cost over a predefined short-term period. GA used in optimal selection, placement and sizing procedure in power systems. A new approach to shunt capacitor placement in distribution systems having customers with different load patterns was presented in [14].

7.3.2 Cable Selection

The micro hydro power plants use an off grid distribution system to supply the electricity to consumers. The cable sizes can be designed by considering the load currents and the standard allowable voltage limits. The current carrying capacity of the cable should be higher than the load current. The voltage drop at the end locations should follow the standard voltage regulations. The distribution line impedance (Z) can be calculated as follows [8]:

$$Z = \sqrt{X_L^2 + R^2} \qquad (7.6)$$

Where, R is the cable resistance (Ω) and X_L is reactance due to inductive effect. The cable reactance can be calculated using [7], [8] and [9].

$$X_L = 2\pi fL \tag{7.8}$$

$$d = \sqrt{d_1 d_2 d_3} \tag{7.9}$$

$$L = A\left(5 + 46\log_{10}\left(\frac{d}{r}\right)\right)*10^{-8} \tag{7.10}$$

Where L is the inductance of the cable, d is the effective conductor spacing, d1, d2, d3 are the distance between conductors, r is the overall radius of the conductor and A is the effective line length. The voltage drop can be calculated as follows:

$$V_{drop} = I_{load} Z \tag{7.11}$$

First, cable size can be selected looking at the load current. Secondly the selected cable can be checked for the voltage drop. It has to select the next larger cable if that is not satisfactory. The same procedure is carried out for all the identified distribution sections.

7.3.3 Genetic Algorithm Based Cable Selection

One of the most interesting aspects of GA is that they do not require any prior knowledge, space limitations, or special properties of the function to be optimized such as smoothness, convexity, unimodality, or existence of derivatives. They only require the evaluation of the so called "fitness function" to assign a quality value to every solution. Another interesting feature of GA is that they are inherently parallel. Instead of using a single point and local gradient information, they evolve a population of candidate solutions where each individual represents a specific solution not related to other solutions. Therefore, their application to large-scale optimization problems can be easily implemented on parallel machines resulting in a significant reduction of the required computation time. Genetic algorithms are generally considered as offline optimization algorithms due to the large amount of the computation time required to converge to an optimal solution. However, their performance can be significantly improved when a suitable combination of the basic genetic operators, with other problem-specific operators is employed. Assuming a randomly generated initial population, genetic evolution proceeds by means of three basic genetic operators: selection, crossover, and mutation. The major steps of Genetic Algorithm are as below [4]:

- Create Initial population/Genotype (i.e., create initial set of solutions to the selected problem)
- Phenotypic decoding and objective function calculation
- Ranking and selection
- Apply genetic operators like Crossover, Mutation to create offspring
- Evaluate the objective function
- Repeat the above procedure until stopping criteria (Maximum number of generations)

The implementation of a GA to find a solution for an optimization problem begins with the selection of the decision variables and their encoding scheme, which are crucial for the overall efficiency of the algorithm. The parameter set must be selected in such a way that the resulting model fully describes the physical system and the encoding method must guarantee the effective transfer of information between chromosome strings. In this system, cable types of all the selected distribution line sections are considered as decision variables. The chromosome can be build by combining all the decision variables. The encoding scheme can be represented as follows:

$$\boxed{S_1[1..n] \quad | \quad S_2[1..n] \quad | \quad \dots \quad | \quad S_{PQ}[1..n] \quad | \quad \dots \quad | \quad S_T[1..n]}$$

Figure 7.10: Chromosome structure

The overview of the distribution system is illustrated in Figure 7.11. Where $S_{PQ}[1..n]$ is the cable size of the selected cable type. When GAs are applied for the solution of an optimization problem, the "Objective function" (OF) that assigns a quality value to every member of the population must be defined. This quality value is used as a comparative measure of each solution against other members of the population and its formulation is a key problem for the application of GA to practical optimization problems. The OF is formulated by considering the total distribution as a collection of virtual radial lines. Each line starts from the generator and stops at a far end. Consider a distribution system with N virtual radial lines.

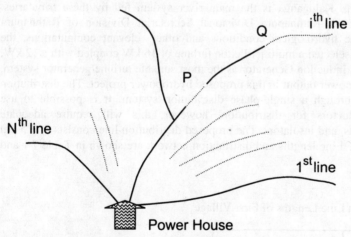

Figure 7.11: Distribution System

The objective function f can be designed by considering the allowable voltage drop and the current carrying capacities.

$$\textbf{IF } [(\,C_{PQ} > L_{PQ}\,), \text{for all PQ] } \textbf{AND } \left[\left(r_s V_{Nom} - \sum_{\substack{for \ \forall \ PQ \\ in \ i^{th} \ line}} V_{PQ} \right) > 0 \right] \textbf{ THEN}$$

$$f = \sum_{\substack{for \ \forall \ PQ}} \left(C_{PQ} - L_{PQ} \right)^2 + \sum_{i=1}^{N} \left(r_s V_{Nom} - \sum_{\substack{for \ \forall \ PQ \\ in \ i^{th} \ line}} V_{PQ} \right) \qquad (7.12)$$

ELSE

$$f = \sum_{\substack{for \ \forall \ PQ}} \left(C_{PQ} - L_{PQ} \right)^2 + \sum_{i=1}^{N} \left(r_s V_{Nom} - \sum_{\substack{for \ \forall \ PQ \\ in \ i^{th} \ line}} V_{PQ} \right) + P$$

END

Where, l_{PQ} is the length of the PQ distribution line. It carries a L_{PQ} load current through the distribution line section and generates V_{PQ} voltage drop across the section. N is the number of apparent radial lines and V_{Nom} is the nominal voltage of the distribution system. The selected cable has Current carrying capacity of C_{PQ}. r_s is the allowable standard voltage regulation. Our method applied to two potential sites, adopted from upper Walawe Ganga basin and Kalu Ganga basin located in Sabaragamuwa province of Sri Lanka. The first village hydro site is situated on Pandi-Oya, which is a tributary of Bambarakotuwa Ganga. Kaluganga is the main river system fed by these tributaries. Village is located in the Rathnapura Divisional Secretariat Division of Rathnapura District. Based on the hydrological conditions and other relevant computations, the technical experts have selected a multi jet Pelton turbine of 16 kW coupled with a 12 kW, 50 Hz, 400V, 3 phase, Induction Generator as the most suitable turbine/generator system, to obtain the required power output in this proposed hydropower project. The distribution of power would be through a single-phase distribution system. It is possible to use bare aluminum conductors for distribution, however, this will require adequate clearances, strong posts, and insulators. The proposed distribution line consists of 3.5 km single-phase lines. The Line lengths and distribution network are shown in Table 7.1 and Figure 7.12.

Table 7.1: Distribution Line Lengths of First Village

Line Section	Length (m)
AB	611
BC	593
AD	249
DE	611
DF	786

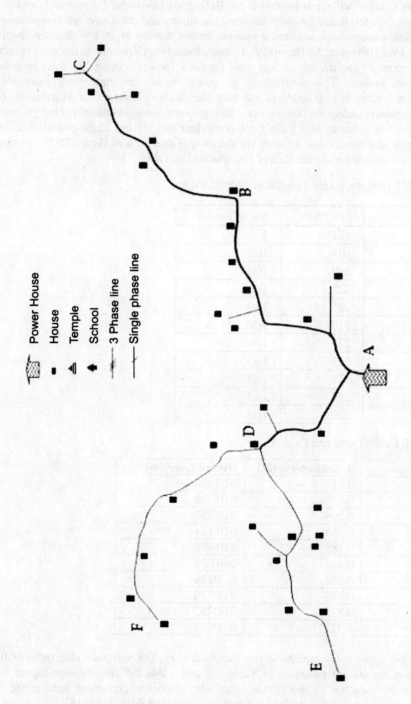

Figure 7.12: Distribution Network of First Village

The second proposed village hydro site is situated on Uman-Oya which is a tributary of Walawe Ganga. Village is located in the Balangoda Divisional Secretariat Division of Rathnapura District. Based on the hydrology conditions and other relevant computations, the technical experts have selected a multijet Pelton turbine of 26 kW directly coupled with a 18 kW, 1000-rpm, 50 Hz, 400V, 3 phase, Induction Generator as the most suitable turbine/generator system to obtain the required power output in this proposed hydropower project. The distribution of power would be through a three-phase distribution system. It is possible to use bare aluminum conductors for distribution, but this will require adequate clearances, strong posts, and insulators. The proposed distribution line consists of 0.5 km three-phase line and 3.8 km single-phase lines. The Line lengths and distribution network are shown in Table 7.2 and Figure 7.13. Ten cable types are investigated and their ratings are tabulated in Table 7.3.

Table 7.2: Distribution Line Lengths of Second Village

Line Section	Length (m)	No. of phases
AB	422	3
BC	105	1(a)
CD	599	1(a)
CE	322	1(a)
BF	105	1(a)
BG	317	1(b)
GH	225	1(b)
BI	573	1(c)
IJ	479	1(c)
IK	243	1(c)
IL	120	1(c)

Table 7.3: Cable Types and Cable Data

Cable type	Resistance/km (Ω)	Overall radius(m)
7/4.90	0.217	0.01470
7/4.39	0.270	0.01316
7/4.17	0.299	0.01250
7/3.78	0.365	0.01134
7/3.66	0.389	0.01092
7/3.4	0.451	0.01020
7/2.79	0.669	0.00836
7/2.59	0.777	0.00776
7/2.44	0.875	0.00732
7/2.06	1.227	0.00618

We have applied this method to two potential sites. The selected cable types of first village and second are tabulated in Table 7.4 and Table 7.5 respectively. Figure 7.14 illustrates the variation of best fitness value with respect to generation number for this example. There are various applications on GA in different fields [15]-[18].

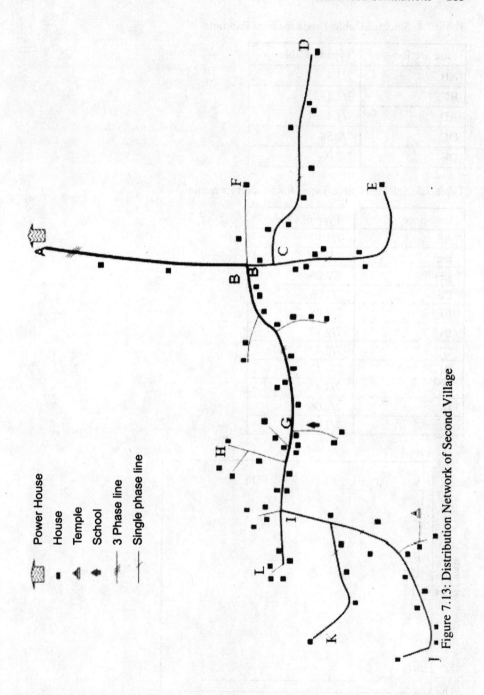

Figure 7.13: Distribution Network of Second Village

Legend:
- Power House
- House
- Temple
- School
- 3 Phase line
- Single phase line

Table 7.4: Selected Cable Types for First Example

Line Section	Type of Cable
AB	7/3.4
BC	7/2.44
AD	7/3.4
DE	7/2.59
DF	7/2.06

Table 7.5: Selected Cable Types for Second Example

Line Section	Type of Cable
AB	7/4.17
BC	7/3.4
CD	7/2.06
CE	7/2.06
BF	7/2.06
BG	7/4.17
GH	7/3.4
BI	7/4.17
IJ	7/3.4
IK	7/2.06
IL	7/2.06

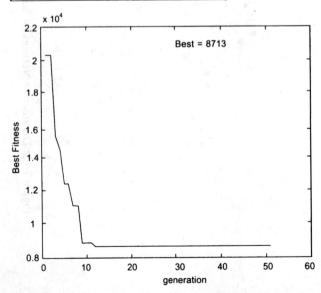

Figure 7.14: Variation of Best Fitness Values with Generation for First Example

7.4 ADVANCED IMPLEMENTATION TOOLS

The genetic algorithm is a method for solving optimization problems that is based on natural selection. Now, MatLab is enriched with built in commands to implement genetic algorithms and it also consists of functions to visualize the optimization process. It is very convenient to use built in functions than building our own algorithms. There are two ways to build a genetic algorithm with the Genetic Algorithm Toolbox: calling the in-built functions in command line and using the in-built graphical user interface. Consider the following function as an example for a minimization problem. The function variation respect to two selected inputs is illustrated in Figure 7.15.

$$f(x) = \sum_{i=1}^{20} x_i^2 \qquad\qquad (7.13)$$

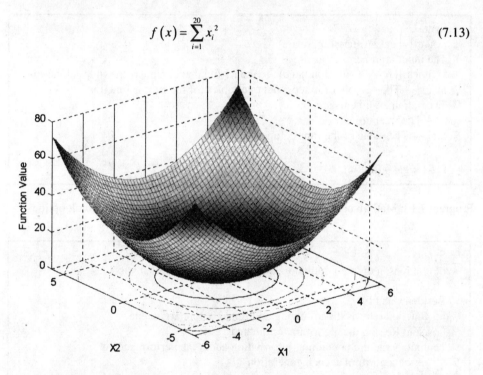

Figure 7.15: Variation of the Function (7.13)

7.4.1 Calling Built in Function in Command Line

First, you must prepare an M-file that computes the function which you want to optimize. The M-file should accept a vector, which consists of independent variables for the objective function, and return a scalar. Program 7.9 illustrates the MatLab code to implement the function of the above example. Then, call the genetic algorithm function "ga" as illustrated in the Program 7.10. The more information about the performance of the genetic algorithm can be obtained by adding additional output arguments as shown in Program 7.11. The GA parameters can also be change by using the function "gaoptimset". The Program 7.12 illustrates the algorithm with changed stop criterion.

```
function z = firstfun(x)
z = 0;
%Calculate the function
for i = 1:20
    z = z + x(i)^2;
end
```

Program 7.9: MatLab code Implements the objective function of function (7.13).

```
% Syntax
% [x fval] = ga(@fitnessfun, nvars)
% The input arguments to ga are
% @fitnessfun — A function handle to the M-file that computes the fitness function.
% nvars — The number of independent variables for the fitness function.
% The output arguments are
% x — The final point
% fval — The value of the fitness function at x

[x fval] = ga(@firstfun, 20)
```

Program 7.10: MatLab code implements the genetic algorithm with the default options.

```
% Syntax
% [x fval reason output population scores] = ga(@fitnessfcn, nvars)
%
% Besides x and fval,
%this function returns the following additional output arguments:
%    reason: Reason the algorithm terminated
%    output: Structure containing information about the performance of
%         the algorithm at each generation
%    population: Final population
%    scores: Final scores

[x fval reason output population scores] = ga(@firstfun, 20)
```

Program 7.11: Code implements the genetic algorithm with additional output arguments

Its number of generations and another stop criterion called "Stall generations" have changed. Likewise, other main parameters also possible to set as required. The program 7.13 implements a genetic algorithm by changing the selected set of parameters. The number of generations are changed to 2000. Two point crossover method is used with 0.7 rate. The 'PlotFcns' option is used to visualize the variation of best fitness values and mean fitness values with the generation number as shown in the Figure 7.16.

```
%Start with default options
options = gaoptimset;
%%Modify some parameters
options = gaoptimset(options,'Generations' ,1000);
options = gaoptimset(options,'StallGenLimit' ,1000);
 [x fval reason] = ga(@firstfun, 20, options)
```

Program 7.12: Code implements the genetic algorithm with changed stop criterion.

```
%%Fitness function
fitnessFunction = @firstfun;
%%Number of Variables
nvars = 20;
%Bounds
LB = [];
UB = [];
%Start with default options
options = gaoptimset;
%%Modify some parameters
options = gaoptimset(options,'CrossoverFraction' ,0.7);
options = gaoptimset(options,'Generations' ,2000);
options = gaoptimset(options,'StallGenLimit' ,2000);
options = gaoptimset(options,'SelectionFcn' ,@selectionroulette);
options = gaoptimset(options,'CrossoverFcn' ,@crossovertwopoint);
options = gaoptimset(options,'MutationFcn' ,{ @mutationgaussian 1  1  });
options = gaoptimset(options,'Display' ,'off');
options = gaoptimset(options,'PlotFcns' ,{ @gaplotbestf });
%%Run GA
[X,FVAL] = ga(fitnessFunction,nvars,[],[],[],[],LB,UB,[],options)
```

Program 7.13: MatLab code implements a genetic algorithm with changed parameters.

The following options can be used to visualize the additional parameters as shown in the Program 7.14.

```
...
% Plots the best function value in each generation versus iteration number.
options = gaoptimset(options,'PlotFcns' ,{ @gaplotbestf });
% Plots the average distance between individuals at each generation
options = gaoptimset(options,'PlotFcns' ,{ @gaplotdistance });
%  Plots the vector entries of the individual with the best fitness function value in
options = gaoptimset(options,'PlotFcns' ,{ @gaplotbestindiv });
% Plots the genealogy of individuals
options = gaoptimset(options,'PlotFcns' ,{ @gaplotgenealogy });
%  Plots the minimum, maximum, and mean fitness function values in each generation
options = gaoptimset(options,'PlotFcns' ,{ @gaplotrange });
```

Program 7.14: MatLab code implements additional visualization tools.

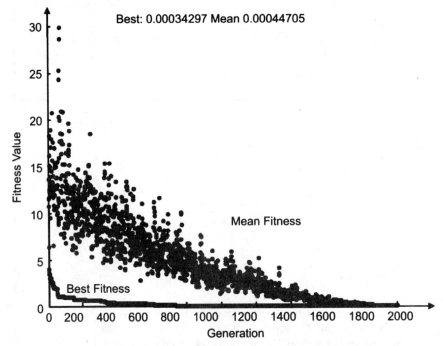

Figure 7.16: Variation of best fitness and mean fitness for the function (7.13).

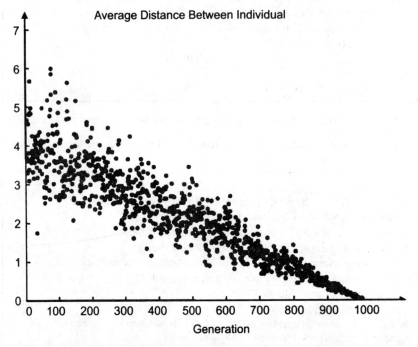

Figure 7.17: Variation of distance between individuals for the function (7.13).

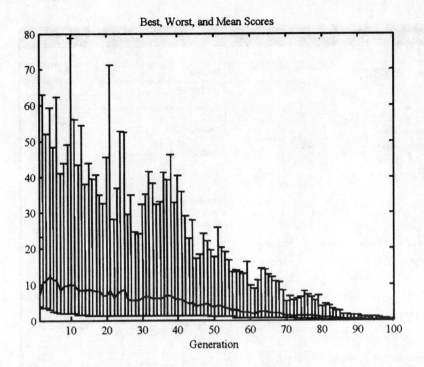

Figure 7.18: Variation of the minimum, maximum, and mean fitness function values in each generation.

The Figure 7.17 illustrates the variation of average distance between individuals. The variation of the minimum, maximum, and mean fitness function values in each generation are shown in the Figure 7.18.

7.4.2 Using the Genetic Algorithm Tool

The Genetic Algorithm Tool is the built in graphical user interface to run genetic algorithms in MatLab. This tool enables you to use a genetic algorithm without working at the command line. You can enter "gatool" to open the Genetic Algorithm Tool at the MATLAB command prompt. The following Figure 7.19 shows the graphical user interface. First, enter the objective function in "Fitness function" section and in the form @firstfun, where firstfun.m is an M-file that computes the fitness function. Then, enter the number of variables, which is the length of the input vector to the fitness function. Next, press "start" to optimize the given function with default genetic algorithm parameters.

You can customize the genetic algorithm by changing the stopping criterion, population, selection, reproduction, mutation, crossover, and other parameters according to the problem. Maximization problems can be solved by converting to a minimization problem.

Figure 7.19: Graphical user interface of the Genetic Algorithm Toolbox.

7.5 ADDITIONAL EXAMPLES

This section illustrates some additional test functions and they can be used to familiar with the simulations using genetic algorithms.

7.5.1 Rastrigin's Function

Let's consider the Rastrigin's function as defined by equation 7.14.

$$f(x) = 10n + \sum_{i=1}^{n} \left(x_i^2 - 10\cos(2\pi x_i) \right) \tag{7.14}$$

The following Figure 7.20 illustrates the function variations when n is 2. The cosine term produces the regularly distributed set of local minima.

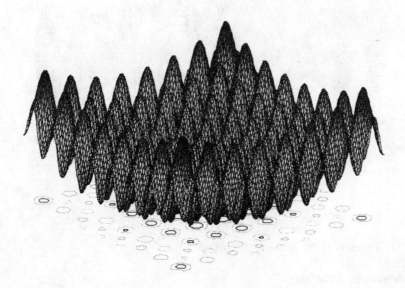

Figure 7.20: Variation of the Rastrigin's function

The global minimum of the Rastrigin's function is;

$$f(x) = 0, \text{ when } x(i) = 0, \forall i = 1:n$$

7.5.2 Schwefel's Function

Let's consider the Schwefel's function as defined by the Equation 7.15.

$$f(x) = \sum_{i=1}^{10} \left(-x_i \sin\left(\sqrt{|x_i|} \right) \right) \ , \quad -400 \leq x_i \leq 400 \tag{7.15}$$

The following Figure 7.21 illustrates the function variations with two selected input variables.

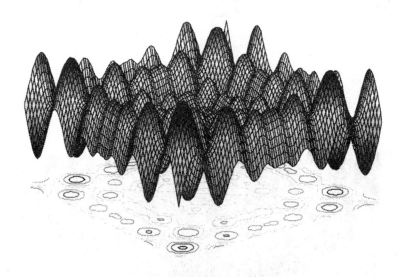

Figure 7.21: Variation of the Schwefel's function

7.5.3 Griewangk's Function

Let's consider the Griewangk's function as defined by the equation 7.16.

$$f(x) = \sum_{i=1}^{n} \frac{x_i^2}{4000} - \prod_{i=1}^{n} \cos\left(\frac{x_i}{\sqrt{i}} \right) + 1 , \quad -500 \leq x_i \leq 500 \tag{7.16}$$

The following Figure 7.22 and Figure 7.23 illustrate the function variations with two selected input variables. The global minimum of the Griewangk's function is;

$$f(x) = 0, \text{ when } x(i) = 0, \forall i = 1:n$$

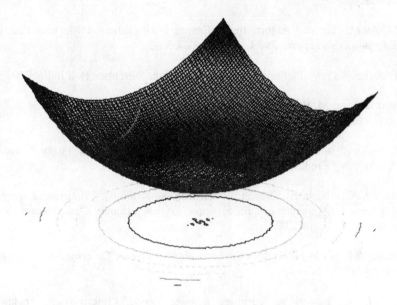

Figure 7.22: Major variation of the Griewangk's function

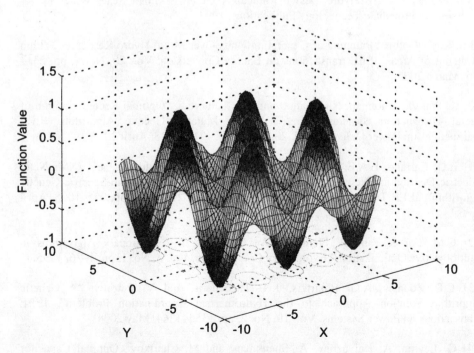

Figure 7.23: Minor variation of the Griewangk's function

REFERENCES

[1] D.E. Golberg, "Genetic Algorithms in Search Optimization & Machine Learning," Pearson Education (Singapore) Pvt. Ltd., India, 2003.

[2] M. Mitchell, "An Introduction to Genetic Algorithms," Prentice Hall India, 2002.

[3] I. Mazumder and M. Rudnick, "Genetic Algorithms for VLSI Design, Layout & Test Automation," Pearson Education (Singapore) Pvt. Ltd. India, 2003, ch1.

[4] S. Rajasekaran and A. Vijayalakshmi Pai, "Neural Networks, Fuzzy Logic, and Genetic Algorithms," Prentice-Hall, New Delhi, 2003.

[5] A. Czarn, C. MacNish, K. Vijayan, B. Turlach and R. Gupta, "Statistical Exploratory Analysis of Genetic Algorithms, " IEEE Trans. on Evolutionary Computation, Vol. 8, No. 4, pp. 405–421, August 2004.

[6] N. Smith, "Motors as Generators for Micro Hydro Power," Intermediate Technology Publications, 1995.

[7] A. Williams, "Pumps as Turbines a User Guide," Intermediate Technology Publications, 1995.

[8] A Harvey, "Micro Hydro Design Manual A Guide to Small Scale Water Power Schemes," Intermediate Technology Publications, 1993.

[9] S. Roy, "Optimal Planning of Generating Units Over Micro-Hydro Resources Within a Catchment Area," IEEE transactions on Energy Conversion, Vol. 20, No. 1, pp. 231–236, March 2005.

[10] K. Prasad, R. Ranjan, N.C. Sahoo and A. Chaturvedi, "Optimal Reconfiguration of Radial Distribution Systems Using a Fuzzy Mutated Genetic Algorithm, IEEE Transactions on Power Delivery, Vol. 20, No. 2, pp. 1211–1213, April 2005.

[11] E.G. Carrano, L.A.E. Soares, R.H.C. Takahashi, R.R. Saldanha, and O.M. Neto, "Electric Distribution Network Multiobjective Design Using a Problem-Specific Genetic Algorithm", IEEE Transactions on Power Delivery, Vol. 21, No. 2, pp. 995–1005, April 2006.

[12] C.M. Fonseca and P. Fleming, "An Overview of Evolutionary Algorithms in Multiobjective Optimization," Evolutinary Computation, Vol. 3, No. 1, pp. 1–16, 1995.

[13] C.E. Zoumas, A.G. Bakirtzis, J.B. Theocharis, and V. Petridis, "A Genetic Algorithm Solution Approach to the Hydrothermal Coordination Problem", IEEE Transactions on Power Systems, Vol. 19, No. 2, pp. 1356–1364, May 2004.

[14] G. Levitin, A. Kalyuzhny, A. Shenkman, and M. Chertkov "Optimal Capacitor Allocation in Distribution Systems Using a Genetic Algorithm and a Fast Energy Loss

Computation Technique", IEEE Transactions on Power Delivery, Vol. 15, No. 2, pp. 623–628, April 2000.

[15] K. Watanabe, L. Udawatta and K. Izumi, "A Solution of Fuzzy Regulator Problems via Evolutionary Computations," in Procs. of SICE'99, Morioka, Japan, 1999, pp. 835-836.

[16] C.T. Lin, C.P. Jou, "Controlling of Chaos by GA—Based Reinforcement Learning Neural Network," in IEEE Trans. on Neural Networks, Vol. 10, No. 4 pp. 846-859, 1999.

[17] S. Limanond and J. Si, "Neural-Network Based Control Design: An LMI Approach," in IEEE Trans. on Neural Networks, Vol. 9, No. 6, pp. 1422-1429, 1998.

[18] S. Koziel and Z. Michalewicz, "Evolutionary Algorithms, Homomorphous Mapping, and Constrained Parameter Optimization," Evolutionary Computation, Vol. 7, No. 1, pp. 20-43, 1999.

Chapter 8

Modeling of Complex Systems

As complexity rises, precise statements lose meaning and meaningful statements lose precision. – Prof. Lotfi Zadeh

8.1 COMPLEX SYSTEMS

A complex system can be defined as a system composed of different individual components or individual entities. As a single entity, this complex system exhibits one or more properties not obvious from the properties of the individual components. Systems discussed up to now were able to model using fundamental approaches like Newton's three laws of motion or Kirchhoff's circuit laws. Moreover, these systems are linear or can be approximated to linear ones. Traditional methods of analyzing dynamical systems rely on linear models or approximated linear models. These multi-input-multi-output systems show complex nonlinear behavior. Sometimes, these systems are coupled or linked to natural scenarios like weather, which shows deterministic random behaviors. Not only the natural systems but also the systems like robot manipulators which were designed and created by humans show nonlinear dynamics. Some of the examples taken into account in previous chapters were also nonlinear with complex dynamics. As examples, you can observe the system properties and dynamics of inverted pendulums, chaos examples, and two-link robot arm. However, these can be modeled up to a certain extend and scientists have already developed some tools in analyzing and treating. When you combine this type of systems with different systems it will lead to make complex systems. As examples, if you want to model and analyze voice recognition systems, molecule concentrations for artificial noses, intelligent security systems, landmine detections, stock market prediction and so on it will be understood that systems show complex and nonlinear nature. In real-world problems, you will find uncertainties that cannot be eliminated.

Soft computing techniques have experienced major advances in modeling complex systems. Neural networks, evolutionary computational algorithms, fuzzy logic based reasoning, dynamic programming, probabilistic modeling, and other techniques are employed in order to handle nonlinear systems. Artificial Neural Networks (ANN) or Neural Networks (NN) are simplified models of biological brains or nervous systems. In fact, approaches like neural networks are one of the techniques, which can be used to analyze and model nonlinear complex systems. Fuzzy logic or fuzzy reasoning is another powerful technique and it uses natural reasoning in modeling systems. In fuzzy logic, knowledge is encoded into the antecedent and consequent parts of fuzzy logic system. The mathematical concepts behind fuzzy reasoning are very simple and it deals with imprecise data or incomplete data. It is possible to create a fuzzy model to match any set of input-output data. This process is made particularly easy by adaptive techniques like ANFIS (Adaptive Neuro-Fuzzy Inference Systems), which are available in the Matlab Fuzzy Logic Toolbox. Nevertheless, you have to optimize these systems under constraints and it may contain large number of variables. Evolutionary algorithms or evolutionary computational techniques give you a new way to perform optimization without actually solving equations in the traditional sense. Optimization iteratively improves the quality of solutions until an optimal, or at least feasible, solution is found.

Next, we would like to introduce some basic developments associated with neural networks. We want to train a multi-layer feed-forward network by gradient descent to approximate an unknown function, based on some training data consisting of pairs (x, t). The vector x represents a pattern of input to the network, and the vector t the corresponding target (desired output). Figure 8.1 shows a sample neural network with three inputs and two outputs. It has one hidden layer with five nodes. The next challenge ill be the question how to determine the number of hidden layers. If gradient descent fails to find a satisfactory solution, grow the network by adding a hidden unit. You can further increase the hidden units or hidden layers in order to increase the power of the network.

Inside each node you have an activation function which is going to produce an output according to the input value to the node. Between two given nodes, you have a weight and therefore each input has an associated weight w. This value can be modified so as to model synaptic learning.

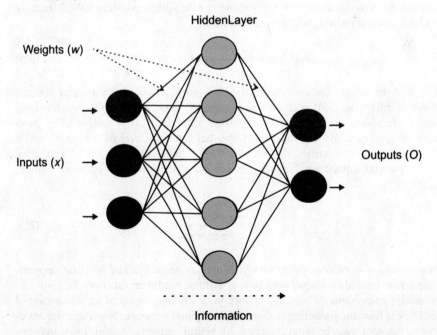

Figure 8.1: Basic Neural Network Concept

Back-propagation algorithm is used to train hidden units, leading to a new wave of neural network research and applications. Output O can be related to the error function as below:

$$E(w) = \frac{1}{2} \sum_{d \in D} (t_d - O_d)^2 \qquad (8.1)$$

In a neural network training process, from different weights, optimum weight set is computed. Therefore, variables of the optimization function would be weights. Error function can be minimized with respect to the weights of the network as follows:

$$\frac{\partial E}{\partial w_i} = \frac{\partial}{\partial w_i} \left(\frac{1}{2} \sum_d (t_d - O_d)^2 \right) \qquad (8.2)$$

This will lead to the following equation

$$\frac{\partial E}{\partial w_i} = \sum_d (t_d - O_d)(-x_{i,d}) \qquad (8.3)$$

Weights can be now updated with the following rule with a constant called learning rate (η), which determines weight change at each step.

$$\Delta w_i (k+1) = \Delta w_i + \eta (t - O) x_i \qquad (8.4)$$

This is called the weight update-rule for the back-propagation algorithm and you can use a desired learning rate. Almost all types of neural nets use an activation function. This function translates the activation of a node into the node's output. The most commonly used type of activation function is one that limits the size of the output and it is called hard-limiter. It squashes the activation. For an example, sigmoid activation function is a popular squashing function. Following equation gives you the sigmoid activation function,

$$f(x) = \frac{1}{1 + \exp(-x)} \qquad (8.5)$$

As above, using a nonlinear function which acts as an activation function approximates a linear threshold allows a network to approximate nonlinear functions or nonlinear dynamics of the total system. A Neural Network basically maps a set of inputs to a set of outputs and this is how the modeling is done using a neural network. Nonlinear dynamics of a complex system can be approximated to neural network model by using this conceptual approach.

Program 8.1 illustrates how to start a simple training process using a neural network. *P* and *T* denote two vectors. Two given vectors (input and output) can be used to configure a network with ***newff***.

```
P = [0 1 2 3 4 5 6 7 8 9 10];
T = [0 1 2 3 4 3 2 1 2 3 4];

net = newff([0 10],[5 1],{'tansig' 'purelin'});

Y = sim(net,P);

plot(P,T,P,Y,'o')

net = train(net,P,T);

Y = sim(net,P);
plot(P,T,P,Y,'o')
```

Program 8.1: Training of a Simple Neural Network

In the initial configuration, first you have to provide the maximum and minimum values of the input vector. The first layer has five 'tansig' neurons and the output layer has one 'purelin' neuron. Figure 8.2 and Figure 8.2 show the results of the two programs given.

```
P = [0 1 2 3 4 5 6 7 8 9 10];
T = [0 1 2 3 4 3 2 1 2 3 4; 0 1 2 3 1 3 2 1 2 3 1];

net = newff([0 10],[15 15 2],{'tansig' 'purelin'
'purelin'});

Y = sim(net,P);

plot(P,T,P,Y,'o')

net = train(net,P,T);

Y = sim(net,P);

plot(P,T(2,:),P,Y(2,:),'o');figure;
plot(P,T(1,:),P,Y(1,:),'o')
```

Program 8.2: Training of a Simple Neural Network

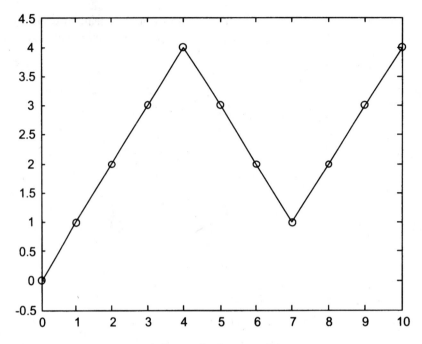

Figure 8.2: Neural Network Output for Program 8.1

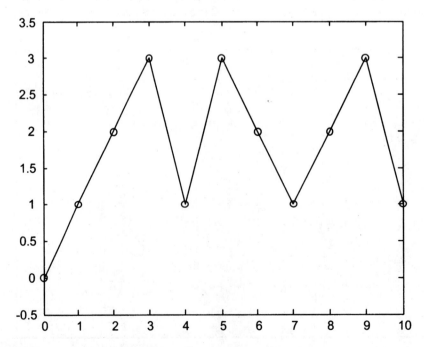

Figure 8.3: Neural Network Output for Program 8.2

Here a two-layer feed-forward network is created. The network's input ranges from [0 to 10]. The first layer has five TANSIG neurons, the second layer has one PURELIN neuron. The TRAINLM network training function is to be used.

Matlab command SIM simulate a Simulink model and it will simulate your Simulink model using all simulation parameter dialog settings including Workspace I/O options. The SIM command also takes the following parameters. By default time, state, and output are saved to the specified left hand side arguments unless OPTIONS overrides this. If there are no left hand side arguments, then the simulation parameters dialog Workspace I/O settings are used to specify what data to log.

However, in training a neural network, there are many different ANN models but each model can be precisely specified by the following eight major aspects:

1. A set of processing units
2. A state of activation for each unit
3. An out put function for each unit
4. A pattern of connectivity among units or topology of the network.
5. A propagation rule, or combining function, to propagate the activities of the units through the network.
6. An activation rule to update the activities of each unit by using the current activation value and the inputs received from other units.
7. An external environment that provides information to the network and/or interacts with it.
8. A learning rule to modify the pattern of connectivity by using information provided by the external environment.

The objective of this section is to explain how to create the network, train the network to get the desired output and to simulate the network. The steps involved in this process are:

1. Assemble the training data.
2. Create the network
3. Train the network
4. Simulate the network.

There are other two important factors which determines the architecture of the network (i.e. number of hidden layers and number of neurons in each layer) Because Networks are sensitive to the number of hidden layers and number of neurons in each layer. Too few neurons can lead to under fitting. Too many neurons can contribute to over fitting. Therefore, in this analysis several experiments have been carried out by varying the no of hidden layers and number of neurons and their performances has been compared to select the best architecture. Feed-forward topology of the Matlab neural network tool box has been used to implement the network. The learning rate has been fixed to its default value 0.01 initially. Later, the effect of the learning rate also has been discussed.

8.2 CASE STUDY

Let us take the following example. Laxapana hydropower complex (one of the main hydropower complexes in Sri Lanka) is a cascaded system that operates under three levels as shown in Figure 8.4. The main two branches of the cascade system start at the upper most reservoirs of Castlereigh (Reservoir 1) and Moussakele (Reservoir 2), which deliver water to the Wimalasurendra (PH 1) and Canyon (PH 2) power houses respectively; the first level of the cascaded system. The water discharge through Wimalasurendra and Canyon machines are being collected at Norton (pond 1) and Canyon (pond 2) ponds and are released for electricity generation to the second level of the cascaded system; Old Laxapana (PH 3) and New Laxapana (PH 4) power houses respectively. The above two main branches join at Laxapana forming Laxapana (pond 3) pond where the discharge of Old and New Laxapana power houses are being collected and fed to the Polpitiya power house (PH 5), which is the lower most power house and the third level of the cascaded system [51]. The total installed capacity of power generating scheme is 335 MW. Moreover, Table 8.1 gives the power generation capacities of each station.

Table 8.1: Details on Laxapana Cascaded Hydropower Generating System

Power House	Capacity [MW]	No. of Generator units	Turbine Type	Flow Requirement [m³/MW]
PH1	50	2	Francies	20
PH2	60	2	Francies	23
PH3	50	5	Pelton	10
PH4	100	2	Pelton	8
PH5	75	2	Francies	16

The power generating system comprises of five power stations at three levels. This system consists of thirteen generating units with different capacities and different characteristics (Pelton and Francies type turbines). The only function of this scheme is to generate electric power, making use of the hydro potential available at the upper-most two main reservoirs. The electric power generation of this system is characterized by several factors such as reservoir and pond levels, rainfalls to different reservoir areas, machine availabilities and turbine characteristics. There is a deficit between the electricity demand and generation. At present, the balance is provided by thermal generation and the cost of generation of thermal is very much higher than hydro generation. Hence, getting the maximum share from hydro, which reduces thermal power purchasing, would be a great saving to the national economy.

The objective is to model the system in order to get the maximum usage of the stored hydro potential to generate electricity. Here, two models have been developed. First model is to schedule the generator loads and the second model is to predict the water levels of three ponds for a short duration, once the generator loads are fixed and other parameters are known. At present, there is no any sort of methodology used for scheduling generator loads and balancing/monitoring pond water levels at all, rather than using rule of thumb methods developed according to the experience. As this is a cascaded system operating under three levels and due to complexity of the other parameters, which affects to the characteristics of the system, a well-defined methodology is required for generator load scheduling and balancing/monitoring pond water level. Rainfall is an uncertain and random factor one which influences to the characteristics of the system and hence to the operation of the system. At the same time due to the multi-dimensional nonlinear (see Table 8.1) nature of the system, a suitable modeling technique should be selected to model the system.

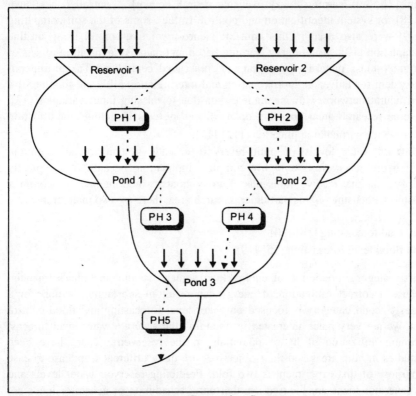

Figure 8.4: Cascaded Hydropower Generating System

   Utilization of maximum available hydro potential in a hydropower system is a key issue. The optimum utilization would result in the least possible total loss of water for the storage capacity obtained, especially in the rainy seasons. This problem is more critical and utter important when the total system consists of cascade multi-reservoirs (see Figure 8.1) for power generation. Scheduling of generator loads according to the water levels of reservoirs and machine availability is an optimization process. Modeling the variation of reservoir water levels due to the variation of generator loads and rainfall, which is an uncertain and a random factor [1]-[3]. Because at present there is no any well defined methodology used to schedule the generator loads and balancing according to the pond water level variations, especially when it comes to multi-reservoir systems, rather than using rule of thumb methods based on the past experience. This is basically due to the inherent non-linear and discontinuous features [4].

During the last decade, there have been various studies on nonlinear dynamic system identification and control via neural networks [5]. In particular, neural networks have been successfully applied to problems in pattern classification, function approximation, optimization, and pattern matching and associative memories [6]. Introducing a technique for forcing the calibration of a financial model to produce valid parameters for the Japanese Yen swaps market and U.S. Dollar yield market using consistency hints is presented in [7]. Self-learning fuzzy wavelet neural networks controller has been designed in [8] for system identification and control. In fact, some of the soft computing techniques [9] were also used in this context: Neuro-predictive control using on-line controller adaptation [10], evolutionary learning based automatic systemization of sets of features for multi-class pattern recognition [11], cascaded centralized Takagi-Sugeno-Kang fuzzy system for universal approximation and interpretation [12], and training of a feed-forward neural network with incomplete data due to missing input variables [13]. Moreover, some research areas focusing on nonlinear systems modeling, classification and identification for particular applications [12]-[17].

Forecasting of water levels of multi-reservoir cascade system for an optimum utilization of hydro reservoir is a highly complex application, because it is typically dealing with systems that receive thousands of noisy inputs, which interact in a complex nonlinear fashion. Focusing on this particular research area, there are two main branches:

- Electricity load forecasting [18]-[20]
- Water and flood level forecasting [15]-[19]

In the first category, prediction of energy load demand is vital in today's financial system because a correct estimation of energy can result in substantial savings for a power system. Second category is focused on water level forecasting and flood control [15]. In fact, we are very much interested in obtaining the accurate water level forecast for an optimum utilization of hydro potentials in the reservoirs. There have been numerous studies in both areas and their objectives are quite different from case to case [22]. The purpose of this experiment is two fold: Predicting reservoir water levels and scheduling generator loads are focused. Furthermore, scheduling of generator loads are carried out by considering the data of water levels of reservoirs and the machine availability. Modeling of reservoir levels is analyzed by taking the variation of water levels due to the power generation and rainfall. Due to the nonlinear inherent properties of the total problem, both of the system modeling were done by using two feed-forward neural networks.

8.3 NEURAL NETWORK MODEL

Neural networks have found profound success in the area of pattern understanding and identification. An artificial network consists of a pool of simple processing units, which communicate by sending signals to each other over a large number of weighted connections. Figure 8.5 shows the basic arrangement, which consist of one input layer, one hidden layer and one output layer.

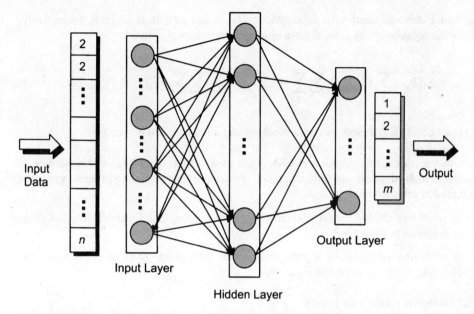

Figure 8.5: Basic Neural Network Concept

It is important to investigate the scheduling of generator loads and modeling the variation of reservoir water levels. In both cases, water level variations of two main reservoirs (Reservoir 1 and Reservoir 2) were not taken into consideration. This is due to the large capacity of the two main reservoirs. However, during the rainy season, with the highest rainfall, the water levels of main reservoirs rise and tend to spill. Therefore, the variation of the water levels in the two main reservoirs can be considered as constant or the variation as negligible.

8.3.1 General Framework for ANN model

A multi-layer feed-forward network consists of input layer, out put layer and several hidden layers. The input layer passes their output to the first hidden layer or (with skip layer connection) to directly to output layer. Each of the hidden layer units takes a weighted sum of its inputs, add a constant (the bias) and calculates a fixed function Φ_h of the result. This is then passed to the hidden units in the next layer or to the out put unit(s). The fixed function is given by,

$$f(z) = \exp(z) / \left[1 + \exp(-z) \right] \tag{8.1}$$

The output units apply a threshold function Φ_0 to the weighted sum of their inputs plus their bias. If the input is p_i and outputs is a_k for one hidden layer,

$$a_k = \Phi_0 \left[b_k + \sum_i^k W_{ik} P_k + \sum_j^k W_{jk} \Phi_h (b_i + \sum_i^j W_{ij} P_i) \right] \tag{8.2}$$

i, j, and k denotes number of input, hidden layer and output layer units respectively. Following equation gives general form of a multi layer neural network.

$$a_i = \phi_0 \left[b_k + \sum_j w_{ij}^{(1)} P_j + \sum_j \sum_k W_{ijk}^{(2)} P_j P_k + \sum_j \sum_k \sum_l W_{ijkl}^{(3)} P_j P_k P_l + \ldots + \right] \qquad (8.3)$$

(8.1),(8.2), and (8.3) denote the layer numbers and others are usual notations.

In this research, this problem is considered as a system identification problem, with non-linear multi-dimensional inputs/outputs. To simplify the modeling process, system is decomposed into two models;

1. For predicting the individual generator loads for existing pond water levels and other inputs as shown in Figure 8.6.

2. For predicting the variation of pond water levels for a given set of generator loads and other existing inputs as shown in Figure 8.7.

8.3.2 Modeling Generator Loads

This section describes the development of the neural network model for selecting the appropriate input data, method of selecting network architecture and training the network.

Figure 8.6 shows the inputs/outputs selected for developing the model 1 for scheduling the generator loads.

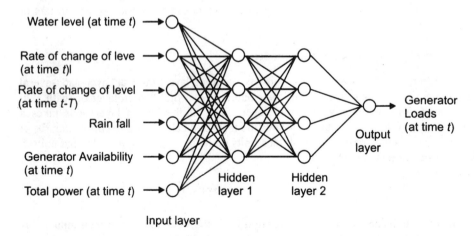

Figure 8.6: General Architecture of the Model 1

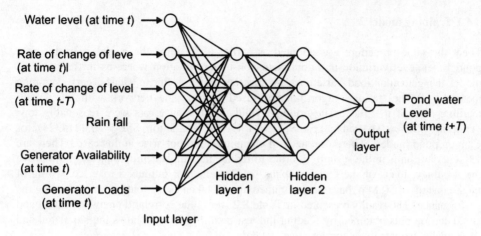

Figure 8.7: Inputs/Outputs for Water Level Predicting Model 2

8.4 DATA AND SYSTEM TRAINING

There are other two important factors which determines the architecture of the network (i.e. number of hidden layers and number of neurons in each layer) Networks are sensitive to the number of hidden layers and number of neurons in each layer. Too few neurons can lead to under fitting .Too many neurons can contribute to over fitting.

Therefore, in this analysis several experiments were carried out by varying the number of hidden layers and number of neurons in each layer in order to compare their performances and to select the best architecture. Feed-forward topology of the Matlab neural network toolbox was used to implement the network. Initially the learning rate was fixed as 0.01 to its default value. Later, the effect of the learning rate is discussed.

Number of hidden layers and the number of neuron in each layer was determined by trial and error. Initially, on training the networks the learning rate *(η)* was set to *0.01*. Early stopping method was used to stop the training and 'trainbr' algorithm was used as the training algorithm. A data set consisting of 1000 records were selected for training the NN. The best NN architecture was determined from results shown in Figure 8.8. The lowest training, validation and testing errors obtained are (i.e. Training error = 2.67, Testing error=1.4, Validation error = 2.01 SSE) According to the results '30-26-20-13' gives the best performance for $\eta=0.01$ which is the default Learning rate of Matlab NN tool box.

Learning rate plays a vital role in back propagation training, The weight updating characteristics is given by the 'delta rule' as given below by the equation,

$$\Delta W_i = -\eta(a_i - t_i)P_{ki} \tag{8.4}$$

where η is the learning rate , a_i and t_i are the actual and target values correspond to the kth component of the ith training vector. Δw_{ij} is the change in the weight to the corresponds simulated output a_i.

Fig 8.9 shows the results obtained by training the '30-26-20-13' model for different learning rates. When the η = 0.18, SSE reaches a minimum giving the best performance.

8.4.1 Training model 2

Then, the same procedure was adopted as earlier for training the model 2. In this case pond water level variation is a continued non-linear variation where as in the previous model the generator load variations are discrete and non-linear. Hence, early stopping method with the 'trainer' algorithm was used to train the network with the default learning rate, of $\eta = 0.01$. The training, validation testing errors were reasonably low. (Training SSE $= 0.610544$, Test SSE $= 1.49636$, Validation SSE $= 0.0814324$) for Canyon pond model. Therefore, need of changing η did not arise in this case. There are 13 generator units in the system. In order to reduce the number of outputs and to improve the accuracy, loads of the Old Laxapana (PH3) generator outputs 5 to 9, consisting of total capacity of 50 MW have been summed up and taken as one output for evaluating the performance. The results presented in Table 8.2 shows the correlation between actual and simulated outputs obtained by feeding the test data. Figure 8.1 shows the simulated and the actual generator loads for the same test data.

8.4.2 Model 2 Performance

A set of test data was fed into each of the pond models and performance was evaluated. The regression analysis results in Table 8.2 shows the correlation between actual water level variation and the simulated variation. Figure 8.8 and Figure 8.9 show the neural network architecture performances when we do their training. Similarly, actual and simulated water level variations of Canyon, Laxapana and Norton ponds and their corresponding regression analysis graphs are shown in Figure 8.11 to Figure 8.17.

Table 8.2: Correlation Coefficients

Generator No	Correlation Coefficient (R)
1	0.988
2	0.991
3	0.990
4	0.994
5	0.806
6	0.910
7	0.815
8	0.836
9	0.879

Note here that the neural network based simulations cannot be directly applied unless you have a proper knowledge on neural network theory. In fact, these results and modeling concepts might be useful for somebody who is going to carry out simulations on neural networks.

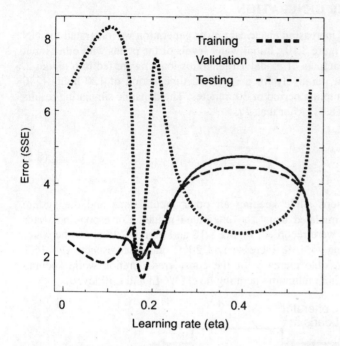

Figure 8.8: NN Architecture vs. Performance

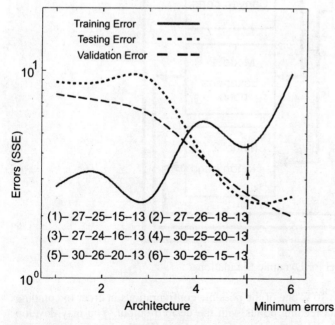

Figure 8.9: NN Architecture vs. Performance

8.5 MAXIMIZING POWER GENERATION

To examine the feasibility of increasing electrical power generation we integrated the NN model 1 and 2 as shown in Figure 8.10. Initial water levels of the ponds with other input fed into the model 1. Then, outputs of model 1 (generator loads) were fed into model 2. This process was carried out iteratively for a specified time period of 120 hours (240 number of records) with a sampling period of 30 minutes. The dynamic simulating results obtained are shown in Figure 8.11. After that, *Pt*,

$$P_t = \sum_{k=1}^{13} L_k \quad , \tag{8.5}$$

was increased by several steps while keeping all other inputs same and the system behavior was dynamically simulated using the integrated model. Corresponding water level variations of the ponds were recorded. Figure 8.18 and Figure 8.19 show the water level variations corresponding to 16% increase and 20 % increase respectively. 16% increase is the maximum possible increase for the considered duration while keeping pond water levels stable. (within minimum operating level (*MOL*) and spill level).

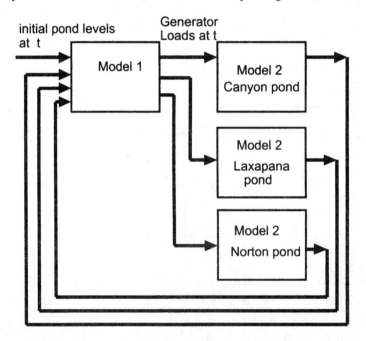

Figure 8.10: Integrated Model for Dynamic Simulation

This modeling in Figure 8.10 is one of the possible configurations in order to combine two neural networks and data feeding points with the desired output. You may develop other network configurations as you wish depending on the application.

A set of test data was fed into each of the pond models and performance was evaluated. The regression analysis results in Table 3 shows the correlation between actual water level variation and the simulated variation. Actual and simulated water level variations of Canyon Laxapana and Norton ponds and their corresponding regression analysis graphs are shown in Figure 8.11 to Figure 8.16 respectively.

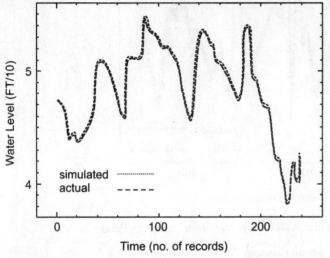

Figure 8.11: Simulated vs. Actual Water Level Variation

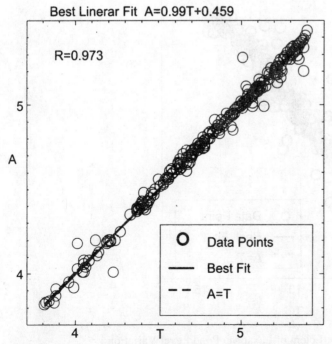

Figure 8.12: Correlation Coefficient for Canyon Pond Level Variation

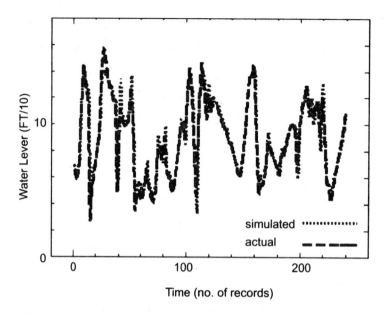

Figure 8.13: Simulate vs. Actual Water Level Variation Laxapana Pond

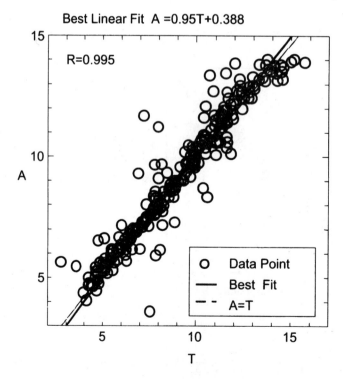

Figure 8.14: Correlation Coefficient of Laxapana Pond Level Variation

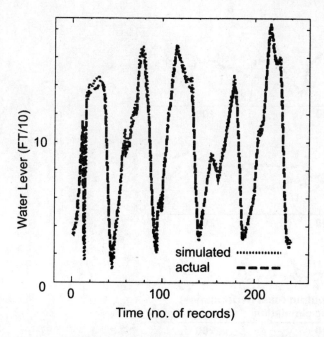

Figure 8.15: Simulated vs. Actual Water Level Variation of Norton Pond

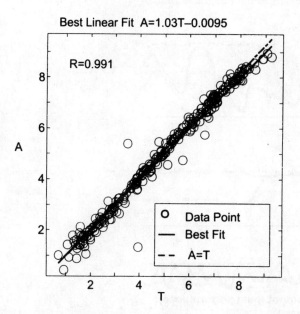

Figure 8.16: Correlation Coefficient for Norton Pond Level Variation

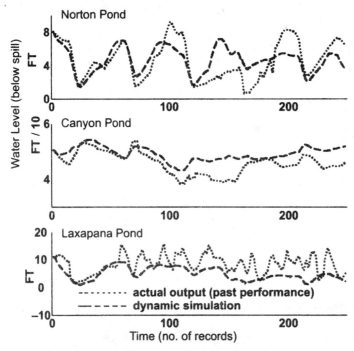

Figure 8.17: Dynamic Simulation Results of the Integrated Model

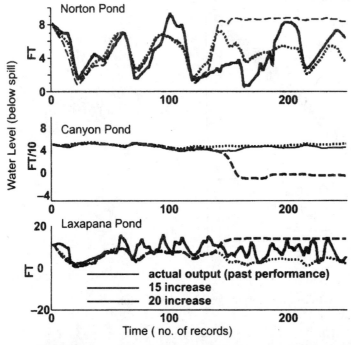

Figure 8.18: Water Level variation due to 20 % Generation Increase

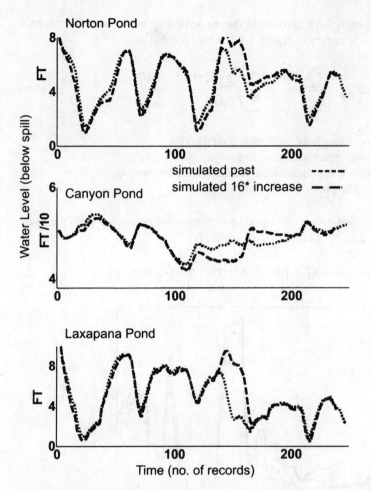

Figure 8.19: Water level Variation due to 16% Generation Increase.

8.6 POWER AND ENERGY CALCULATIONS

It can be seen from Figure 8. 18 that when the value of *Pt* (i.e. total load is increased by 20%) Canyon pond level reaches to the spill level and becomes unstable. So that water level of Canyon pond has become the limiting factor for power generation during this period. Hence, the maximum feasible generation increase is by 16% while keeping the ponds stable. It is shown in Figure 8.16. When the total Load *Pt* is increased by a fraction, all individual generator loads contributes to that increase. Hence, for a known load pattern we can find out best possible loading schedule for individual generator units, which would help operate the system economically.

The percentage excess energy ΔE, generated due to 16% increase is given by the area between lowest and middle curves in Figure 8. 17, which is equal to,

$$\Delta E_{max} = \frac{[\sum P^{max}(t)T - \sum P^{0}(t)T] \times 100}{\sum P^{0}(t)T} \qquad (8.6)$$

where, P^{max} - power generated with maximum increase,
$\quad\quad\quad P^{0}$ - power generated according to past performances
$\quad\quad\quad \Delta E_{Ma}$ - excess energy generated due to increased generation
$\quad\quad\quad T$ - Sampling period (*30* minutes)

Obtaining the normal and power corresponding to increased generation from the excel sheet , $890 \times 0.5 \times 50$ and $767 \times 0.5 \times 50$ respectively .

Percentage energy increases, $\Delta E = [(890-767)/767] \times 100 = 16.0\ \%$

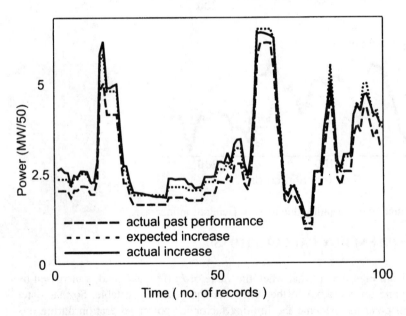

Figure 8.20: Energy curves due to increased generation

From the above result it can be noted that, when the value of P_t is increased, the actual generated energy also increases by the same percentage. In this case the maximum possible increase is 16 %.

Amount of excess energy generated is given by,

$$\Delta E_{max} = \sum P^{max}(t)T - \sum P^{0}(t) \qquad (8.7)$$

Substituting the values from the excel data sheet for the 120 hour period considered,

$$\Delta E_{Max} = 890 - 767 = 123 \times 0.5 \times 50 \text{ [MWhrs]}$$
$$= 3075 \text{ [MWhrs]}$$

Now, if we consider the average value of a thermal unit cost, using the typical values given in the Table 8.3 obtained from utility, which depend on various thermal and hydro unit commitment constraints. Similarly, unit cost of a hydro unit also varies in a wide range depending on the water value variation over the time under different conditions as shown in Table 8.3 (arrow mark denotes whether the storage capacity is on the increase or decrease). Hence, depending on the relative values of thermal and hydro unit costs the economic benefit varies. Consider the situation in the second raw of Table 8.3, where the water levels are in the rise and the storage capacities of Castlereigh and Moussakele are 94% and 96% respectively.

Table 8.3: Water Values

Duration in 2005	Castlereigh		Moussakele		Avg Water value u/kWh
	Value u/kWh	% Storage	Value u/kWh	% Storage	
Jun	11.20	22 ↑	10.01	23.8 ↑	10.60
Nov	7.72	94 ↑	7.15	96 ↑	7.44
Dec	11.80	95 ↓	11.58	92 ↓	11.59

Then, assuming a average thermal unit cost of u 12.00 considering the typical values given in Table 4, the energy saving would be,

$$= (3075 \times 1000) \text{ kWHrs} \times (12.00 - 7.44) \text{ u/kWHr}$$
$$= 140,220 \text{ u\$/120 hrs}$$

Saving, $= 28,044$ u\$/day (for the period considered)

8.7 REMARKS

8.7.1 Economical Benefits

The problem considered here is a multi-dimensional system. Some of the inputs to the system are random and uncertain factors and hence cannot be mathematically formulated using conventional methods as explanatory theories are lacking for the input output relationship. This investigation has been carried out based on the historical data or past examples; considering the behavior of the system under different conditions. Due to the advancement of information technology and improvement of computational and data processing power have made this type of approach possible. In this study two neural network models were developed.

Then, above two models were integrated to dynamically simulate the pond level variation with different generator load patterns for a pre-defined period. From the above analysis maximum feasible power generation at any given set of inputs or a state was calculated. According to the results of the calculation it was found that, 16% increase in power generation could be achieved while keeping the ponds stable under the same input conditions for the period considered. When evaluating the economical benefit, the relative unit costs of thermal and hydro have to be considered, which depend on unit commitment constraints and water value respectively. This model optimizes the usage of water by generating the maximum possible electrical power, while keeping the water levels of the three ponds stable. During a period where the upper main two reservoirs are spilling or about to spill, extracting the maximum possible usage of water by generating the highest possible electrical power would be an obvious economical benefit irrespective of the thermal unit cost or the prevailing water value. In other situations the economical benefit depends on the relative prevailing water value and the thermal unit cost which involves with the unit commitment constraints. Typical values have been used in the above calculation. According to that in a situation where the reservoir levels are at 95% the saving is US 28,044 /day. When the water levels increase further and as the water value goes down the economical benefit due to increased generation would be higher.

8.7.2 Soft Computing Approaches

Soft computing approaches can be employed in various situations like system identifications, system modeling, optimizations under different constraints, system validations and systems control applications. The following explanation gives an idea about soft computing approaches for this type of applications explained by Prof. Lotfi Zadeh who introduced fuzzy reasoning concept.

"Soft computing differs from conventional (hard) computing in that, unlike hard computing, it is tolerant of imprecision, uncertainty and partial truth. In effect, the role model for soft computing is the human mind. The guiding principle of soft computing is: Exploit the tolerance for imprecision, uncertainty and partial truth to achieve tractability, robustness and low solution cost. The basic ideas underlying soft computing in its current incarnation have links to many earlier influences, among them my 1965 paper on fuzzy sets; the 1973 paper on the analysis of complex systems and decision processes; and the 1979 report (1981 paper) on possibility theory and soft data analysis".

The inclusion of neural network theory in soft computing came at a later point. At this juncture, the principal constituents of soft computing (SC) are fuzzy logic (FL), neural network theory (NN) and probabilistic reasoning (PR), with the latter subsuming belief networks, genetic algorithms, chaos theory and parts of learning theory. Rather; it is a partnership in which each of the partners contributes a distinct methodology for addressing problems in its domain. In this perspective, the principal contributions of FL, NN and PR are complementary rather than competitive.

REFERENCES

[1] S. Gunasekara, L. Udawatta, and S. Witharana "Neural Network Based Optimum Model for Cascaded Hydro Power Generating System," Proc. of the 2nd International Conference on Information and Automation ICIA'06, Colombo, Sri Lanka, 2006, pp. 51-56.

[2] J.W. Nicklow, "Discrete-Time Optimal Control for Water Resources Engineering and Management," *Journal of Water International*, Vol. 25, No. 1, pp. 89-85, 2000.

[53] A.F. Atiya, S.M. El-Shoura, S.I. Shaheen, and M.S. El-Sherif, "A Comparison between Neural-Network Forecasting Techniques Case Study: River Flow Forecasting," IEEE Trans. on Neural Networks, Vol. 10, No. 2, pp. 402-409, 1999.

[4] R.W. Brockett, "Pattern Generation and the Control of Nonlinear Systems," IEEE Trans. on Automatic Control, Vol. 48, No. 10, pp. 1199-1711, 2003.

[5] L.C. Kiong, M. Rajeswari, and M.V.C. Raob, "Nonlinear Dynamic System Identification and Control via Constructivism Inspired Neural Network," *Journal of Applied Soft Computing*, Vol. 3, pp. 237-257, 2003.

[6] R. Parekh, J. Yang and V. Honavar, "Constructive Neural-Network Learning Algorithms for Pattern Classification," IEEE Trans. on Neural Networks, Vol. 11, No. 2, pp. 346-451, 2000.

[7] Y.S. Abu-Mostafa, "Financial Model Calibration Using Consistency Hints," IEEE Trans. on Neural Networks, Vol. 12, no. 4, pp. 791-808, 2001.

[8] S. Srivastava, M. Singha, M. Hanmandlub, and A.N. Jha, "New Fuzzy Wavelet Neural Networks for System Identification and Control," *Journal of Applied Soft Computing*, Vol. 6, pp. 1-17, 2005.

[9] S. Mitra and Y. Hayashi, "Neuro-Fuzzy Rule Generation: Survey in Soft Computing Framework," IEEE Trans. on Neural Networks, Vol. 11, No. 3, pp. 748-768, 2000.

[10] A.G. Parlos, S. Parthasarathy, and A.F. Atiya, "Neuro-Predictive Process Control Using On-Line Controller Adaptation," IEEE Trans. on Control Systems Technology, Vol. 9, No. 5, pp. 741-755, 2001.

[11] M.A. Zmudaa, M.M. Rizki, and L.A. Tamburino, "Hybrid Evolutionary Learning for Synthesizing Multi-class Pattern Recognition Systems," *Journal of Applied Soft Computing*, Vol. 2, pp. 269-282, 2003.

[12] S. Wang, F.L. Chungb, S. HongBina, and H. Dewen, "Cascaded Centralized TSK Fuzzy System: Universal Approximator and High Interpretation," *Journal of Applied Soft Computing*, Vol. 5, pp. 131-145, 2005.

[13] R.K. Brouwer and W. Pedrycz, "Training a Feed-forward Network with Incomplete Data Due to Missing Input Variables," *Journal of Applied Soft Computing*, Vol. 3, pp. 23-36, 2003.

[14] S.V. Dudul, "Prediction of a Lorenz Chaotic Attractor Using Two-layer Perceptron Neural Network," *Journal of Applied Soft Computing*, Vol. 3, pp. 333-355, 2005.

[15] L.I. Kuncheva and J.C. Bezdek, "Presupervised and Postsupervised Prototype Classifier Design," IEEE Trans. on Neural Networks, Vol. 10, No. 5, pp. 1142-1152, 1999.

[16] O. Montiel, O. Castillo, P. Melin, and R. Sepulveda, "The Evolutionary Learning Rule for System Identification," *Journal of Applied Soft Computing*, Vol. 3, pp. 342-352, 2003.

[17] S. Alvisi, G. Mascellani, M. Franchini, and A. Bardossy, "Water Level Forecasting Through Fuzzy Logic and Artificial Neural Network Approaches," *Journal of Hydrology and Earth System Sciences*, Vol. 10, pp. 1-17, 2006.

[18] T. Rashid, B.Q. Huang, M.T. Kechadi, and B. Gleeson, "Auto Regressive Recurrent Neural Network Approach for Electricity Load Forecasting," *Journal of Computational Intelligence*, Vol. 3, No. 1, pp. 36-43, 2006.

[19] I. Drezga and S. Rahman, "Short-term Load Forecasting with Local ANN Predictors," IEEE Trans. on Power Systems, vol. 14, no. 3, pp. 402--409, 1999.

[20] S. Russell and P. Norvig, "Artificial Intelligence-A Modern Approach," 2nd Edition. Printice-Hall, India, 2003

[21] K.Y. Lee and J.H. Park, "Short-term Load Forecasting Using an Artificial Neural Network," IEEE Trans. on Power Systems, Vol. 7, No. 1, pp. 124-132, 1992.

[22] D.T. Cox, P. Tissot and P. Michaud, "Water Level Observations and Short-term Predictions Including Meteorological Events for the Entrance of Galveston Bay, Texas," *Journal of Waterway, Port, Coastal, and Ocean Engineering*, Vol. 128, No. 1, pp. 21-29, 2002.

Chapter 9

Selecting the Right Software Tool

For a given simulation, unless you select the right software tool, results of the simulation will not drive you in the right research direction.

9.1 SCIENTIFIC SOFTWARE TOOLS AND MATLAB TOOLBOXES

From the right beginning, researcher should plan for better simulation and have to use the most appropriate software tool. Depending on the system to be simulated or designed, software tools will be selected. Different types of computer simulations need different types of software tools or programming environments. As it has been explained Matlab is one of the best scientific and engineering software tools, which provide you a rich environment for scientific computations. However, there are other scientific and engineering software packages like Mathematica (symbols are the basic named objects in Mathematica), Minitab (by OMNITAB, a high-level spreadsheet for statistical analysis), PSCAD (Power Systems Computer-Aided Design), EWB (Electronic Workbench), OrCAD (Oregon CAD), FORTRAN (FORmula TRANslation language), PSS/E (Power System Simulator for Engineering), Pro/ENGINEER (integrated 3D CAD/CAM/CAE solution for mechanical engineering and designs), AutoCAD (CAD software application for 2D and 3D design and drafting, developed and sold by Autodesk), and so on.

Moreover, FORTRAN is a scientific programming language whereas LISP is used for symbolic computations. For business data processing applications you can use a language like COBOL. BASIC is simple computer language for beginners and there are various versions of BASIC like PICBASIC (BASIC for Programmable Interface Controllers). C is a systems programming language as it can use for machine level instructions. Nevertheless, PROLOG is also used for symbolic computation like LISP. Ada is used for the applications where you use real-time distributed systems and Smalltalk is language where it uses a graphical user interface for object oriented programming. C++ is an extension of C and it supports the concept of object oriented programming. Software tool JAVA is used and supported for web programming.

There are several software tools which can be used for engineering and scientific drawing based computer simulations. You can model a given system and visualize them in these environments. However, these can also be employed to get the basic drawings done though they are not simulations. In computer simulations, for different parameters variations you can optimize your systems using these packages like ProEngineer, SolidWorks or AutoCAD. In ProEngineer, you can design components and get it manufactured at a CNC machine based on the initial development. Moreover, ProEngineer started introducing the concept of parametric, feature-based solid modeling. Furthermore, SolidWorks software is a 3D computer-aided design program that was developed mechanical engineering drawings and designs. Though these are mostly used for engineering and scientific drawing purposes you can use for simulating systems under different parametric variations. OrCAD is a software tool used primarily for electronic designs and automations. This software is used mainly to create electronic prints for manufacturing of printed circuit boards. In general, this is useful for electronic design engineers and electronic technicians to manufacture electronic schematics and diagrams

Mathematica is software, which has design for scientific and engineering research works. It has the libraries of elementary and special mathematical functions with 2D and 3D data and visualization tools. Especially, matrix and data manipulation facilities with symbols, solutions for systems of equations, ODEs, PDEs, recurrence relations, and integrals can be handled. Moreover, multivariate statistics libraries are provided for statistical analysis and constrained/unconstrained optimizations can be also carried out. It has also programming language supporting procedural, functional and object oriented constructs, a toolkit for adding user interfaces to calculations and applications. Import and export filters for data, images, video, sound, CAD, GIS, document and biomedical formats can also be accommodated. It also provides a database containing economic, scientific, mathematical, and other information in a format that is easy to access within Mathematica.

However, programming languages like C, C++, PASCAL, FORTRAN, BASIC, VISUAL BASIC, JAVA, Python, Delphi, and assembly language can be used in general purpose computer simulation. For an example, Python is a general purpose computing technique and also a very high-level programming language. On the other hand, you may also need very low level languages like assembly or PICBASIC in certain applications where you cannot use high level languages.

In recent past, many image processing and computer vision software packages have also been developed. For an example, in an image processing based simulation, you may select either Inage Processing Toolbox of Matlab or OpenCV (open source computer vision library). In Matlab, if you want to employ some of the Matlab algorithms already exist in the general Matlab or in other toolboxes, together with Image Processing Toolbox. With this integration, it is possible to reduce your development time of the simulation. However, if you use OpenCV as the programming tool, you can write your own C codes if they are not available in a standard library. This has the following features and options as explain in [1]:

- Image processing and analysis.
- Object structural analysis.
- Motion analysis and object tracking.
- Object and face recognition.
- Camera calibration and 3D reconstruction.
- Stereo, 3D tracking and statistically boosted classifiers.
- User interface and video acquisition support.

Matlab provides a set of toolboxes, a collection of M-files built for solving particular classes of problems. These toolboxes are to help users in modeling and simulating different systems. In fact, any users can create their own toolboxes by introducing new developments. Some examples for these toolboxes are virtual reality, communications, mapping and financial, fuzzy logic, control system, data acquisition, image processing, etc. Table 9.1 shows few selected toolboxes in Matlab in order to provide customized solutions to engineering and scientific groups. Matlab has been widely recognized by the universities and research institutes as a high-performance language for technical computations and simulations. Basically, it integrates computational techniques, visualization facilities, and basic programming in an environment as we explained in the previous chapters.

In Matlab, you will find numerical solutions for nonlinear equations, finite difference methods, interpolations, forecasting problems, and solutions for simultaneous linear algebraic equations. Moreover, ordinary differential equations (ODE) and partial differential equations (PDE) can also be solved using Matlab in your computer simulations. Linear programming, nonlinear programming and integer programming problems can be solved.

Table 9.1: Examples of Matlab Toolboxes (Curtsey of Matlab)

Toolbox	Applications and Details
Communications Toolbox	Random signal production, error analysis including eye diagrams and scatter plots, source coding, including scalar quantization, differential pulse code modulation, and companders, error-control coding, including convolutional and linear block coding, analog and digital modulation/ demodulation, filtering of data using special filters, computations in Galois fields
Control System Toolbox	Transfer functions, zero-pole-gain or state-space forms, both classical and modern control techniques, continuous-time and discrete-time, conversions between various model representations, time responses, frequency responses, root loci and graphing.
Neural Network Toolbox	Analysis and modeling of complex and nonlinear problems, pattern recognition and nonlinear system identification and control,
Fuzzy Logic Toolbox	Fuzzy logic and fuzzy reasoning, steps of fuzzy inference system design, fuzzy clustering, adaptive neuro-fuzzy learning, and compre-hensive model of the entire dynamic system
Genetic Algorithm and Direct Search Toolbox	Large scale optimization problems, simulated annealing, and direct searching techniques for multi-dimensional large optimization problems

(Contd.)

Toolbox	Applications and Details
Filter Design Toolbox	Advanced filter design techniques that support designing, simulating, and analyzing fixed-point and custom floating-point filters for a wide range
Optimization Toolbox	Unconstrained nonlinear minimization, constrained nonlinear minimization including goal attainment problems, mini-max problems, and semi-infinite minimization problems, quadratic and linear programmming, nonlinear least squares and curve-fitting, nonlinear system of equation solving, constrained linear least squares, sparse and structured large-scale problems
Statistics Toolbox	Probability distributions, linear and nonlinear models, principal components analysis, design of experiments, statistical process control, and descriptive statistics.
Virtual Reality Toolbox	The virtual reality toolbox allows you to connect a virtual world, defined with VRML, to Simulink and Matlab. Understanding the features of the Virtual Reality Toolbox and some basic VRML concepts will help you to use this product more effectively.
Image Processing Toolbox	Spatial image transformations, morphological operations, neighborhood and block operations, linear filtering and filter design, transforms Image analysis and enhancement, image registration, Deblurring and region of interest operations
Financial Time Series Toolbox	The toolbox contains a financial time series object constructor and several methods that operate on and analyze the object. Financial engineers working with time series data, such as equity prices or daily interest fluctuations, can use this toolbox for more intuitive data management than by using regular vectors or matrices.
Data Acquisition Toolbox	A framework for bringing live, measured data into Matlab using PC-compatible, plug-in data acquisition hardware Support for analog input (AI), analog output (AO), and digital I/O (DIO) subsystems including simultaneous analog I/O conversions and support for these popular hardware vendors/devices:
Partial Differential Equation (PDE) Toolbox	Define a PDE problem, e.g., defining 2-D regions, boundary conditions, and PDE coefficients. Numerically solve the PDE problem, e.g., generate unstructured meshes, discretize the equations, produce an approximation to the solution, and visualizations of results.

In addition to these, there are several software tools, which are developed particularly for computer simulations. As an example, Flexsim (flexible simulation) software provides to build and simulate your model with the aid of object oriented approach. Following abstract shows the conceptual approach of Flexsim as described by William B. Nordgren, Flexsim Software Products, Inc. in a conference proceedings [2]. "Flexsim is an object-oriented software environment used to develop, model, simulate, visualize, and monitor dynamic-flow process activities and systems. Flexsim is a complete suite of development tools to develop and compile simulation applications. There are 3 levels of use within the Flexsim environment: (1) The Flexsim Compiler, (2) The Flexsim Developer, and (3) Flexsim Application products. The Flexsim environment is completely integrated with the C++ compiler and uses flexscript (a C++ library that is precompiled) or C++ directly. All animation is OpenGL and boasts incredible virtual reality animation. Animation can be shown in tree view, 2D, 3D, and virtual reality. All views can be shown concurrently during the model development or run phase. Flexsim has been used to model manufacturing, warehousing, material handling processes, semiconductor manufacturing, marine container terminal processes, and shared access storage network (SANS) simulation." In Fexsim, you can bring models or components according to a hierarchical structures and facilitating the designer to organize objects logically. You can apply this concept to model large complex systems. Flexsim allows the scientist and engineers to make full use of the Microsoft Visual C++ object oriented and hierarchical features. This Flexsim is commercially available software. However, you can find limited number of software tools which available as open source as given in Table 9.2.

Table 9.2: Open Source Tools

Name of the Software	Applications and Details
ASCEND	This is a flexible modeling environment for solving hard engineering and science problems.
COIN	Computational Infrastructure for Operations Research (COIN) - free open-source operations research code
NS2	An open source network simulator (NS), discrete event simulator targeted at networking research.
OPEN DESIRE	Open Source Dynamic-system Simulation (OPEN DESIRE). This is a modeling/simulation language for dynamic systems and neural networks. It supports up to 20,000 differential equations or matrix/vector operations.
PDQ	PDQ (Pretty Damn Quick) an open-source computer modeling package, PDQ uses queue-theoretic paradigms to represent computer systems.
SimPy	SimPy (Simulation in Python) an open-source discrete-event simulation package based on Python. It is an object-oriented, process-based discrete-event simulation languag. Modeling and simulation of epidemics, traffic simulation, air space surveillance planning, industrial engineering, performance modeling, industrial process optimization, workflow studies and etc.

Table 9.3 shows some of the computer simulation software tools which are available commercially.

Table 9.3: Commercially Available Software for Simulations

Name of the Software	Applications and Details
ACSL	ACSL is a modeling, execution, and analysis environment for continuous dynamic systems and processes.
AIMMS	Decision support and advanced planning applications to optimize strategic operations
AMESim	AMESim (Advanced Modeling Environment for Simulations) Dynamic modeling system which is applying the Bond Graph techniques
AnyLogic	Dynamic simulation tool that brings together system dynamics, process-centric, and agent based approaches within one modeling language and one model development environment..
Arena	simulation and automation software developed by Rockwell Automation.
Delsi 2.0	- Discrete-event simulation components for .NET 2.0 Extend Simulation Tools
Dymola	Dymola (Dynamic Modeling Laboratory) is for modeling and simulating systems.
FACSIMILE	Discrete-event simulation/emulation library, models complex steady state and time dependent processes. It is especially suitable for solving chemical reactions with diffusion and/or advection.
Flexsim	Flexsim (flexible simulation) Build and simulate the model with the aid of object oriented approach
Mathematica	General scientific and engineering research works
Matlab	General scientific and engineering research works with large number of customized toolboxes
NetSim	- Network simulator for Academics and Research
PSIM	PSIM (Powersim) is for product development in power supplies, motor drives, and power conversion and control systems.
Poses++	Poses++ can model and simulate any arbitrary system which is based on a discrete and discontinuous behavior
Simigon	Simigon is used for system modeling, simulation and training solutions
VisSim	Visual block diagram language for modeling and simulation of complex nonlinear dynamic systems.
VisualSim	Modeling and simulation software for embedded systems, large complex systems, ICs, processors, FPGA, real-time software and network systems. VisualSim is a graphical modeling and simulation environment.

9.2 IMAGE PROCESSING BASED APPLICATION

9.2.1 Introduction

Computer vision is a new and rapidly growing field, currently focusing on building intelligent systems. When it comes to active vision, it processes active image data captured by a vision system and draws intelligent or logical conclusions through a feedback system. Much accurate timely information could be obtained without human involvements. In practice, this would also save time, avoid the occurrence of any disturbances and enhance the security. As an example, in a multi storey building, required information of a particular floor that is used for common, seating could be displayed at other floors. In a parking, registration numbers and the entering time of the vehicles could be recorded. Camera system would be used to obtain a view of that particular environment and the desired data is transmitted to the location where the data is processed in order to display the useful information. Finally, all these disciplines are needed for building advanced intelligent systems [3]. Image processing plays a great role in this research field [4] backed by artificial intelligent techniques [5] in order to build these intelligent vision systems. Combining visual model acquisition and agent control system was presented for visual space robot task specification, planning and control [6]. In [7], an evolutionary based approach was described to develop an active vision system for dynamic feature selection with simple neural control system.

In practice, you will have different practical problems due to the dynamic environmental conditions. The system could detect and indicate the variations of illumination level in the environment. When the illumination level goes down below a certain level, it uses an enhancement algorithm to produce correct results. If the illumination level drops exceedingly causing enhancement algorithm to fail, it holds the rest of the processing part until it gets an image frame with a working illumination level [8]-[14].

Mainly the system can be used in intelligent building applications. In a multi storey building, required information of a particular floor, which is used for common seating, could be displayed at other floors. For an example, in a library displaying seating availability in each floor would assist those who search for a seat. In a building with several restaurants, displaying of seat availability in each restaurant would help to select a place with a fewer crowd. Parking space availability of a huge building complex could be displayed at the entrance to the car park.

This case study will illustrate you the possibility of utilizing the Matlab toolboxes in a selected application. In particular, the ability to use image processing toolbox for vision based application developments. However, there are various techniques for image processing based applications and you can employ these techniques whenever necessary [15]-[22].

9.2.2 System Development

In this example, the system first detects objects or humans on the seats using a wide-angle image and analyzes them for conclusions. Image data is continuously transmitting from the environment and analyzing for vacant seats using image-processing techniques. Reasoning based conclusions are drawn for the users entering into the environment for optimum seat searching. The recognition algorithm with image processing tools will be used in order to analyze video images. The simulation results can be used to have a better experimental setup or to check the feasibility of the system. In Figure 9.1, active image acquisition is done by a camera system and video streams will be transmitted to a image processing system through a receiver. Current situation of the seating will be displayed in the display as shown in Figure 9.1.

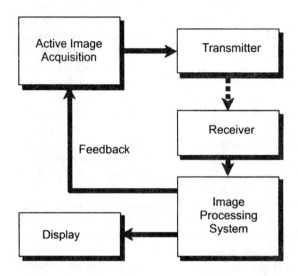

Figure 9.1: Intelligent Vision System Architecture

In this illustration, we use a cinema theater hall, which should be arranged in such a way that a clearly distinguishable mark should be stuck on each chair and seat locations should be unchanged after setting up the system. Once the system is set up, seat locations should be unchanged and if seat locations are going to be changed the system should be set up again before using the system. If it is going to change, simple recognition mechanism can be employed in order to apply this technique. The video camera should be fixed at a correct elevation to get the plan view of the theater hall. Install and configure the transmitter receiver camera system. Focus the camera, adjust the position and correct the lighting level if required by previewing the video stream. The system used for the experiment is similar to the system in Figure 9.2. Follow the set of instructions that comes with image acquisition device.

Without employing a feedback system, we can still provide some useful conclusions as explained above. In this system, we will take the cinema theatre example as the case study. Setup typically involves:

- Installing the frame grabber board in your computer
- Installing any software drivers required by the device
- Connecting a camera to a connector on the frame grabber board
- Verifying that the camera is working properly by running the application software that came with the camera and viewing a live video stream

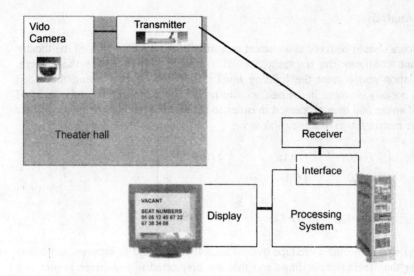

Figure 9.2: System Architecture for the Experiment

The device ID is a number that the adaptor assigns to uniquely identify each image acquisition device with which it can communicate. The video format specifies the image resolution (width and height) and other aspects of the video stream. However, before starting, you might want to see a preview of the video stream to make sure that the image is satisfactory. For example, you might want to change the position of the camera, change the lighting, correct the focus, or make some other change to your image acquisition setup. The system has detected objects or humans on the seats using a wide-angle image and analyzed them for conclusions. Image data was continuously transmitting from the environment and analyzing for vacant seats using image-processing techniques. The reasoning based conclusions were drawn for the users entering into the environment for optimum seat searching. The system can be further developed and generalized for other applications. In a multi storey building, required information of a particular floor that is used for common seating could be displayed at other floors. In a vehicle park, the registration number and the entering time of the vehicles could be recorded.

We develop this algorithm to setup the system explained in above section:
1. Read the color image frame acquired from image acquisition device
2. Convert color image to an intensity image
3. Resize intensity image so that the image matrix could be viewed
4. Suppress light structures connected to image border
5. Convert clear border image to a binary image
6. Create sub matrices
7. Process and determine whether the seats are vacant or not
8. Display the results

Note here that once the system is set up, seat locations should be unchanged and if seat locations are going to be changed, the system should be set up again before using the system.

9.2.3 Image Analysis

The video camera should be fixed at a correct elevation to get the plan view of the theater hall. Install and configure the transmitter-receiver camera system. Focus the camera, adjust the position and correct the lighting level if required by previewing the video stream. When nobody is seated in the hall, a color image frame is acquired and converted to an intensity image and then processed in order to set up the system as below. Consider intensity image matrix $f(x, y)$ of dimension $m \times n$

$$
f = \begin{bmatrix}
f(0,0) & f(0,1) & \cdots & f(0,n-1) \\
f(1,0) & f(1,1) & \cdots & \\
\vdots & \vdots & \vdots & \vdots \\
f(m-1,0) & f(m-1,1) & \cdots & f(m-1,n-1)
\end{bmatrix}
\tag{9.1}
$$

Here, $f(x, y)$ was subjected to reduce overall intensity level and to suppress structures that are lighter than their surroundings and that are connected to the image border and converted to a binary matrix A.

Three distinguishable marks are pasted on each seat as shown in Figure 9.3. Two reasoning methods are introduced by the analysis of images in the spatial domain. In the RGB color model, each color appears in its primary spectral components of red, green, and blue. Images represented in this model consist of three components images, one for each primary color. Consider 24-bit color image in which each of the red, green, and blue is an 8-bit image. The color image is subjected to the spatial transformation, which uses the nearest-neighbor interpolation to reduce the size of image. This transformation maps pixel locations in an input image to new locations in an output image in order to resize the image according to the given size or a given proportion. The need of this transformation is to reduce the processing time. However, reducing the size with a higher proportion factor may cause loosing important information of the image. Therefore, the resizing factor should be correctly decided. The analysis is mainly focused on finding certain locations (seat locations) in the image. Therefore, all the images that are to be analyzed should be of same size.

9.2.4　First Reasoning Criterion

Figure 9.3 shows the resulting images according to the basic steps used in the algorithms explained in the latter sections. The color image is processed so that the marks pasted on seats appear in the resulting binary image. The reasoning based conclusion is drawn by analyzing binary image matrix to determine whether the mark appears in the incoming image frame, and then to decide whether the seat is vacant or not on the following manner. The acquired color image is converted to an intensity image. This is done by transforming RGB color space into NTSC color space and then eliminating the hue and saturation components while retaining the luminance and then converting it back to RGB color space.

Morphological reconstruction [3], [16] method based on dilations is applied to reduce light structures connected to the image border using 4-connected neighborhood. A pixel p at coordinates (x, y) of intensity image matrix $f(x, y)$ has four horizontal vertical neighbors whose coordinates are given by

$$(x+1, y), (x-1, y), (x, y+1), (x, y-1) : (x, y) \quad \in \Re \quad (9.2)$$

Mask image is the input intensity image f(x,y). Marker image is zero everywhere except along the border, where it equals the mask image. Morphological processing starts at the peaks in the marker image. It spreads throughout the rest of the image based on the connectivity of the pixels. Dilation of the marker image is repeated until the contour of the marker image fits under the mask image. Then the resulting intensity image is converted to a binary image, based on a luminance threshold. The output binary image B has values of 0 (black) for all pixels in the input image with luminance less than threshold level and 1 (white) for all the other pixels. Threshold level is a normalized intensity value that lies in the range [0, 1].

For an example, Figure 9.3 shows intermediate processing stages when a color image frame is transformed to a binary image using above procedure. It should be noted that in this example, only one mark is used on a seat and the color of the mark (white) is clearly distinguishable compared to the seat color (red).

Then consider a mark location as shown in Figure 9.3 and analyze the binary image array. It can be noted that all the elements relevant to the mark location have value 1 and the neighboring elements outside the boundary have value zero.

Step 1 Original image

Step 2 Intensity image

Step 3 Clear border image

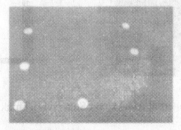

Step 4 Isolating image

Figure 9.3: Image Processing Steps

As shown in Figure 9.4 when the seat is occupied by a person all three marks will be covered and when there is an object placed on the chair such as a bag may not cover all three marks. Use of remarkable color mark with a fine thick edge as shown in Figure 9.5 and suitable lighting conditions enhanced the system. Use of three marks on the seat instead of one mark enhanced the reliability as shown in Figure 9.4.

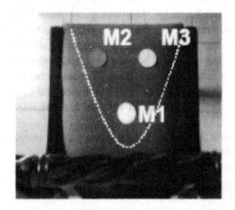

Figure 9.4: Use of Marks on Seats

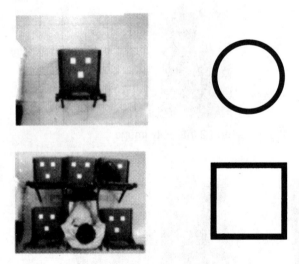

Figure 9.5: Different Marks on Seats with Thick Edge

It is necessary to create sub matrices A_k for $k = 1, 2, 3, ..., S$ so that considerable number of elements covering mark locations on each seat location k come in to the matrix A_k.

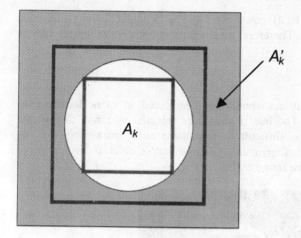

Figure 9.6: Definition of Matrices

Where $k = 1, 2, - - - - S$ and k is the Seat number. The S is the total number of seats detected by the camera. Sub matrix A'_k should be selected from matrix B such that its centre element or elements should align with the centre element relevant to the mark on seat k and dimension of A'_k should be as large as possible subjected to the criteria that all the elements should cover the mark area and also some more space around the mark. Then the dimensions of A'_k should be $(M+P, N+P)$ and $P = 1$ or 2 or 3 etc. with each other. Then the following reasoning criterion could be used to determine whether the seat is vacant or not.

$$\text{IF } \sum_{i=1}^{M}\sum_{j=1}^{N} a_{ij} = MN \text{ AND } \sum_{i=1}^{M+P}\sum_{j=1}^{N+P} a'_{ij} \neq (M+P)(N+P) \qquad (9.3)$$

THEN Seat is vacant (The Mark is visible in the binary image)

ELSE Seat is occupied (The Mark is visible in the binary image)

9.2.5 Second Reasoning Criterion

Another approach which uses RGB color space for obtaining the states of seats will be explained here. Three marks are used on seat to differentiate states when a mark is covered by a small object. In this reasoning criterion each component image is individually processed and the analysis determines whether the correct color is there in the mark locations of the incoming color image frames.

Let us take three component image matrices.

R – Red component image matrix
G – Green component image matrix
B – Blue component image matrix

In the full color image, each RGB color pixel has a depth of 24-bits and each component image is an 8-bit image. Therefore, pixel values in component images vary in the range of 0 to 255.

Determination of Mark Locations

As shown in Figure 9.7 sub matrices should be considered in mark locations of components images R, G, and B. The matrix should be selected in a way that all the elements lie inside the mark. It is difficult to find these color marks locations by analyzing color image matrix. By using intensity image matrix or clear border image matrix, those mark locations could be found easily.

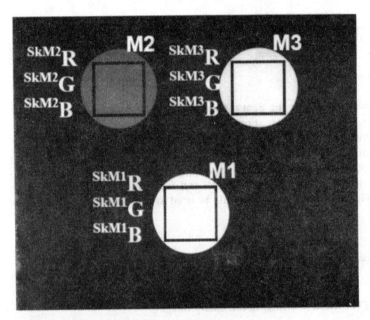

Figure 9.7: Component Image Matrices

SkM/R – Red component image matrix for mark number l of seat number k
SkMlG – Green component image matrix for mark number l of seat number k
SkMlB – Blue component image matrix for mark number l of seat number k

Analysis for Mark2

If the average pixel values of each matrices (SkM1R, SkM1G, SkM1B) are in the specified range, the relevant mark color is there in the considering location of the incoming image frame.

Reasoning criteria is give below:

$$\mathbf{IF} \qquad \left[\left(\sum_{i=1}^{M}\sum_{j=1}^{N}{}^{SkM2}r_{ij}\right)/MN\right] \in [v1, v2]$$

$$\text{AND} \quad \left[\left(\sum_{i=1}^{M} \sum_{j=1}^{N} {}^{SkM\,2} g_{ij} \right) \Big/ MN \right] \in [v3, v4] \tag{9.4}$$

$$\text{AND} \quad \left[\left(\sum_{i=1}^{M} \sum_{j=1}^{N} {}^{SkM\,2} b_{ij} \right) \Big/ MN \right] \in [v5, v6]$$

THEN Mark 2 is visible in the color image

ELSE Mark 2 is not visible in the color image

The values v1, v2, v3, v4, v5, and v6 are constant values calculated when setting up the system.

Where

$$v1 = \left[\left(\sum_{i=1}^{M} \sum_{j=1}^{N} {}^{SkM\,2} r_{ij} \right) \Big/ MN \right] - d1$$

$$v2 = \left[\left(\sum_{i=1}^{M} \sum_{j=1}^{N} {}^{SkM\,2} r_{ij} \right) \Big/ MN \right] + d2$$

$$v3 = \left[\left(\sum_{i=1}^{M} \sum_{j=1}^{N} {}^{SkM\,2} g_{ij} \right) \Big/ MN \right] - d3$$

$$v4 = \left[\left(\sum_{i=1}^{M} \sum_{j=1}^{N} {}^{SkM\,2} g_{ij} \right) \Big/ MN \right] + d4 \tag{9.5}$$

$$v5 = \left[\left(\sum_{i=1}^{M} \sum_{j=1}^{N} {}^{SkM\,2} b_{ij} \right) \Big/ MN \right] - d5$$

$$v6 = \left[\left(\sum_{i=1}^{M} \sum_{j=1}^{N} {}^{SkM\,2} b_{ij} \right) \Big/ MN \right] + d6$$

The values of d1, d2, d3, d4, d5, and d6 are decided according to the allowable lighting level variations. Similar analysis is there for other marks.

9.2.6 How to Use Criteria

The first criterion is applied for the mark 1(white color mark) and the second criterion is applied for the other two marks. The first criterion checks whether the mark appears with its shape whereas the second criterion checks only the relevant color in the location. Therefore mark 1 can be given a higher weight in determining a vacant seat.

9.2.7 Detection of Illumination Level Variation

Illumination level could vary due to several factors such as weather condition change, effect of outside illumination change, day and night conditions etc. Variation in illumination and surface reflectance can also give rise to differences as noise. If illumination level goes below certain level erroneous results would be shown. To overcome this white reference [14], [15] option is introduced. A particular white color reference mark is placed in the hall at the seating level to get white reference value.

1. White Reference

White reference value (W) is the average intensity value of a matrix considered at the reference mark location of the incoming image frame.

$$W = \left[\left(\sum_{i=1}^{M} \sum_{j=1}^{N} w_{ij} \right) / MN \right] \tag{9.6}$$

(a) White Reference value (W1)

W1 is the minimum white reference value that the normal program provides accurate results and if white reference value falls below W1, the program automatically enhances the intensity image to produce correct results.

(b) White Reference value (W0)

If white reference value goes below W0, the enhancement algorithm will also fail. Then the program will indicate it and hold the rest of the processing part until it gets an image frame with a working illumination level.

9.2.8 Image Enhancement

The first reasoning criterion can be used more effectively with the enhancement algorithm even in poor illumination conditions. Image enhancement is achieved by mapping the values in intensity image to new values such that 1% of data is saturated at low and high intensities. This increases the contrast of the output image and the data values fill the entire intensity range [0, 255]. Enhanced intensity image is used to suppress light structures connected to image border and then converted to a binary image.

1. Effect of Enhancement

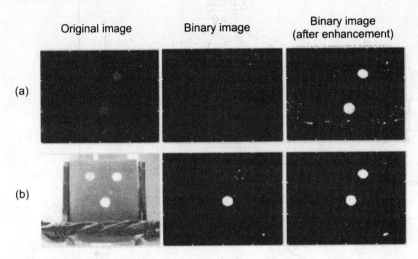

Figure 9.8: Effect of Enhancement

Figure 9.8 shows the effect of enhancement. In Figure 9.8 (a) original image has very poor illumination level. In the binary image mark 1(white) is not visible. But mark 1 is visible after the enhancement. In Figure 9.8 (b) original image has very good illumination level. In the binary image the mark is visible. It could be noted that after enhancement even mark 3 (yellow) is also visible in the binary image.

9.3 SETTING UP THE SYSTEM

Seat arrangement, camera positioning and focusing, and obtaining correct illumination level are the very basics to be considered before running setup programs. Once the system is set up seat locations should be unchanged. The size of the mark pasted on seats can be made small, but the camera should be able to detect the mark and in the image matrix there should be considerable amount of elements in the mark location for the analysis.

The number of seats that can be detected by the camera mainly depends on the height to the camera from the floor level, effective height (h) of a person when seated, and distances between seats, along the length of the hall ($x1$) and along the width of the hall ($x2$). Figure 9.9 depicts the effective distances, the length ($d1$) and the width ($d2$) which can be monitored by the camera when the camera is fixed at a height of H. Figure 9.9 (b) is the end elevation of Figure 9.9 (a) when viewed in right direction. The effective area that can be monitored by the camera is given by

Effective Area = $d1 d2$

Three programs are provided for setting up the system. All programs should be run when nobody is seated in the hall.

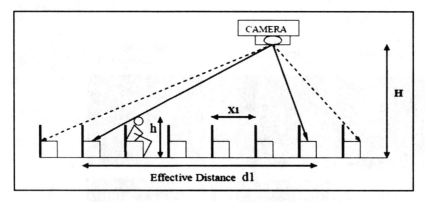

(a) Effective length

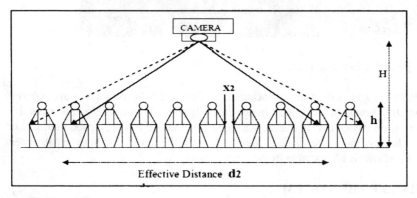

(b) Effective width

Figure 9.9: Sample Hall Arrangement

9.3.1 Setup Program 1

The purpose of this program is to feed mark locations in to the main program and to two other setup programs. It acquires an image frame, processes and displays the acquired image frame, the clear border image and the binary image. By viewing binary image array the locations of marks could be identify. As described in the first criterion sub matrices Ak and Ák should be selected for each white color mark location. A matrix should be created at the white reference mark location too.

   Row and column values of first and last elements of matrices created at mark locations should be fed in to the main program and to two other setup programs. Since the locations of white marks are known the locations of other two color marks could be easily identified with the use of clearborder image. It could be noted that row and column values of first and last elements are same for components matrices (e.g.: S1M2R, S1M2G, S1M2B). The smaller the matrix created better the processing speed and the larger the matrix lesser the processing speed.

9.3.2 Setup Program 2

This acquires image frame and calculates values v1 to v6 described in the second criterion. Setup program 2 automatically makes the calculated values v1 to v6 available to the main program.

To compensate for the minor lighting level variations, values d1, d2, d3, d4, d5, and d6 should be decided and fed in to the main program. It is necessary to run setup program 2 several times under different timeframes and the same lighting conditions and table the average pixel values calculated by setup program 2. The values for d1, d2, d3, d4, d5 and d6 should be decided so that v1, v3, v5 get their minimum value and v2, v4, v6 get their maximum value.

9.3.3 White Reference Program

By running White Reference program several times while gradually decreasing the illumination level, values W1 and W0 could be found and fed in to the main program.

9.4 IMAGE ACQUISITION AND PROCESSING

The Image Acquisition rate depends on the processor speed, the complexity of the processing algorithm, and the frame rate. Installing image acquisition device typically involves

- Installing the frame grabber board in the computer.
- Installing any software drivers required by the device
- Running the application software that came with the camera and viewing a live video stream.

It is needed to get several pieces of information such as adapter name, device ID, and video format that is needed to uniquely identify the image acquisition device to be accessed. An adaptor is the software that is used to communicate with an image acquisition device via its device driver. The device ID is a number that the adaptor assigns to uniquely identify each image acquisition device with which it can communicate. The video format specifies the image resolution and other aspects of the video stream. Video input object creates a connection with an image acquisition device. The characteristics of the image or other aspects of the acquisition process can be modified by setting the values of image acquisition object properties. It is important to move frames from the memory buffer into the workspace in a timely manner. If not, it can quickly exhaust all the memory available on the system.

The created graphical user interface is capable of acquiring images from eight acquisition devices while running the main program. The important points of acquisition and processing algorithms are given below.

9.4.1 Acquisition Algorithm

1. Create infinite loop to do the following execution
    1. Create video input object
    2. Get single frame to the workspace
    3. Delete and clear the video input object

4. Introduce delay timer
5. Start the timer
6. Wait for a suitable time gap
7. Run the image processing program
2. End the loop

9.4.2 Image processing (main) Algorithm

1. Read the color image frame acquired
2. Resize the color image
3. Convert the color image to an intensity image
4. Calculate the white reference value (W) and if it is below W0 then go to step 1. If W value is less than W1 then increase contrast of the intensity image.
5. Suppress light structures connected to image border and convert to a binary image
6. Create matrices required for first criterion(Ak and Ák) for k = 1,2,.....S
7. Check the first criterion
8. Create matrices required for second reasoning criterion and calculate average pixel values of created matrices
   S1M2R, S1M2G ,S1M2B
   S1M3R, S1M3G ,S1M3B
   S2M2R, S2M2G ,S2M2B
   S2M3R, S2M3G ,S2M3B,......
9. Determine states of seats using first and second criteria
   Display the result

Program 9.1, Program 9.2 and 9.3 show some of the Matlab codes used in the main algorithm explained above.

```
I = imread('vacant.jpg');
I0 = imread('Nvacant.jpg');
I1 = imread('object.jpg');

Iframe= imread('b7.jpg');
Ig = rgb2gray(Iframe);

S1M1I(1:16,1:16)=Ig(195:210,275:290);
WR = sum(sum(S1M1I,1),2)/numel(S1M1I);

if WR >= WR0
    J = imadjust(Ig)
else J = Ig
end

Ib = imclearborder(J, 4);
IB=im2bw(Ib);
figure, imshow(Iframe ,'notruesize'),
title('original image');
```

```
figure, imshow(IB,'notruesize'), title('binary
image');

S1M1(1:16,1:16)=IB(195:210,275:290);
S1M1L(1:26,1:26)=IB(190:215,270:295);
S1M2K1=Iframe (:,:,1);
S1M2K2=Iframe (:,:,2);
S1M2K3=Iframe (:,:,3);
S1M3K1=Iframe (:,:,1);
S1M3K2=Iframe (:,:,2);
S1M3K3=Iframe (:,:,3);

S1M2N1(1:16,1:16)=S1M2K1(195:210,348:363);
S1M2N2(1:16,1:16)=S1M2K2(195:210,348:363);
S1M2N3(1:16,1:16)=S1M2K3(195:210,348:363);
S1M3N1(1:16,1:16)=S1M3K1(260:275,310:325);
S1M3N2(1:16,1:16)=S1M3K2(260:275,310:325);
S1M3N3(1:16,1:16)=S1M3K3(260:275,310:325);
S1M2R = sum(sum(S1M2N1,1),2)/numel(S1M2N1);
S1M2G = sum(sum(S1M2N2,1),2)/numel(S1M2N2);
S1M2B = sum(sum(S1M2N3,1),2)/numel(S1M2N3);
S1M3R = sum(sum(S1M3N1,1),2)/numel(S1M3N1);
S1M3G = sum(sum(S1M3N2,1),2)/numel(S1M3N2);
S1M3B = sum(sum(S1M3N3,1),2)/numel(S1M3N3);

VS1M1=0
VS1M2=0
VS1M3=0
```

Program 9.1: Sample Matlab Codes for Image Reading

```
clear all. close all, clc

frame= imread('b1.jpg');
Iframe = imresize(frame,[300 400],'nearest');
Ig = rgb2gray(Iframe);
Ib = imclearborder(Ig, 4);
IB=im2bw(Ib);

S1M1I(1:16,1:16)=Ig(195:210,275:290);
WR0 = sum(sum(S1M1I,1),2)/numel(S1M1I);
```

Contd.

```
S1M1(1:16,1:16)=IB(195:210,275:290);
S1M1L(1:26,1:26)=IB(190:215,270:295);

S1M2K1=Iframe (:,:,1);
S1M2K2=Iframe (:,:,2);
S1M2K3=Iframe (:,:,3);
S1M3K1=Iframe (:,:,1);
S1M3K2=Iframe (:,:,2);
S1M3K3=Iframe (:,:,3);

S1M2N1(1:16,1:16)=S1M2K1(195:210,348:363);
S1M2N2(1:16,1:16)=S1M2K2(195:210,348:363);
S1M2N3(1:16,1:16)=S1M2K3(195:210,348:363);
S1M3N1(1:16,1:16)=S1M3K1(260:275,310:325);
S1M3N2(1:16,1:16)=S1M3K2(260:275,310:325);
S1M3N3(1:16,1:16)=S1M3K3(260:275,310:325);
S1M2R = sum(sum(S1M2N1,1),2)/numel(S1M2N1);
S1M2G = sum(sum(S1M2N2,1),2)/numel(S1M2N2);
S1M2B = sum(sum(S1M2N3,1),2)/numel(S1M2N3);
S1M3R = sum(sum(S1M3N1,1),2)/numel(S1M3N1);
S1M3G = sum(sum(S1M3N2,1),2)/numel(S1M3N2);
S1M3B = sum(sum(S1M3N3,1),2)/numel(S1M3N3);

v1  = S1M2R + 4
v2  = S1M2R - 4
v3  = S1M2G + 4
v4  = S1M2G - 4
v5  = S1M2B + 4
v6  = S1M2B - 4
v7  = S1M3R + 4
v8  = S1M3R - 4
v9  = S1M3G + 4
v10 = S1M3G - 4
v11 = S1M3B + 4
v12 = S1M3B - 4
```

Program 9.2: Sample Matlab Codes for the Main Algorithm

```
if (nnz(S1M1) == numel(S1M1)& nnz(S1M1L) ~=
numel(S1M1L))
    VS1M1=1
end

if (v1 < S1M2R & S1M2R < v2 & v3 < S1M2G & S1M2G <
v4 & v5 < S1M2B & S1M2B < v6)
    VS1M2=1
end

if (v7 < S1M3R & S1M3R < v8 & v9 < S1M3G & S1M3G <
v10 & 250 < v11 & S1M3B < v12)
    VS1M3=1
end

VV=    VS1M1+VS1M2+VS1M3

if VV== 3
    figure,subplot(3,3,1); subimage(I),title('vacant
No 1')
elseif VV== 1|2
    figure,subplot(3,3,1);
subimage(I1),title('Attention 1')
```

9.5 EXPERIMENTAL RESULTS

9.5.1 Intensity Variation

The following set of pictures (see Figure.9.10) taken at different illumination levels are analyzed to find intensity levels of mark areas. Illumination level reduces from picture p1 to picture p15.

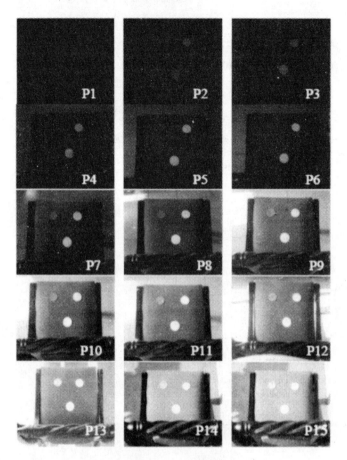

Figure 9.10: Illumination Level Variation

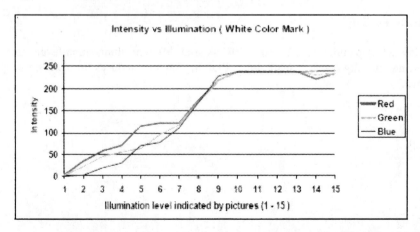

Figure 9.11: Variation in Color Components with Illumination Level for White Color Mark

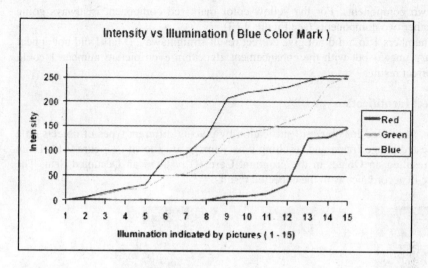

Figure 9.12: Variation in Color Components with Illumination Level for Blue Color Mark

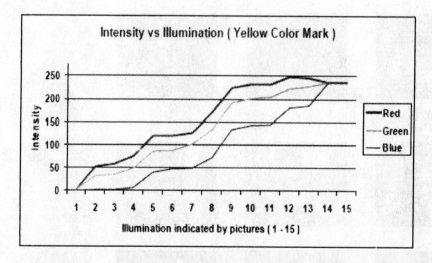

Figure 9.13: Variation in Color Components with Illumination Level for Yellow Color Mark

For the white color mark, all three components coincide during the illumination level indicated from 7 to 13 (see Figure 9.11).

It can be seen from pictures, 7 to 13 that the colors of marks are clearly visible. In pictures 13, 14, and 15, yellow color mark is visible like white in color due to reflection. There is a considerable gap between color components from 7 to 13 for blue color mark (see Figure 9.12). It can be noticed that the blue color component is always going above the other two components. For the yellow color mark red component is always going above the other two components (see Figure 9.13).

Picture numbers 1 to 5 did not give correct result straightaway, (Mark1 did not appear in the binary image) but with the enhancement algorithm even picture number 1 could produce correct result.

9.5.2 Object Identification

The system was tested for object identification by placing different types of objects on a seat. The tested image frame and resulting binary image are shown in Figure 9.14. From (a) to (e) resulted an Object in the program. Case (f) resulted an Occupied Seat. The results were in accordance with the expected results.

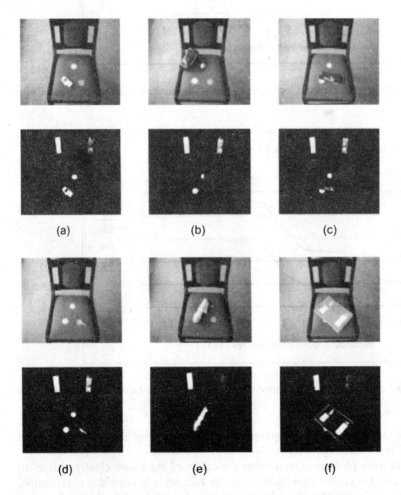

Figure 9.14: Object Identification – Result

REFERENCES

[1] Q. Yua, H. Chenga,W. Chengb and X. Zhoub, "Ch OpenCV for interactive open architecture computer vision," *Journal of Advances in Engineering Software,* Vol. 35, 2004 pp. 527–536.

[2] William B. Nordgren, "Flexible simulation (Flexsim) software: Flexsim simulation environment," Proceedings of the 35th conference on Winter simulation: driving innovation New Orleans, Louisiana, pp. 197-200, 2003

[3] R.C. Gonzalez and R.E. Woods, "Digital Image Processing," Boston, MA, Addison-Wesley Longman Publishing Inc., 1992.

[4] P. Peursum, S. Venkatesh, and G.A.W. West, "Using Interaction Signatures to Find and Label Chairs and Floors," IEEE Trans. Pervasive Computing, Vol. 3, No. 4, pp. 58–65, 2004.

[5] Y. Amit, D. Geman and X. Fan, "A Coarse-to-Fine Strategy for Multiclass Shape Detection," IEEE Trans. Pattern Analysis and Machine Intelligence, Vol. 26, No. 12, 2004.

[6] J. Jiang, M.G. Liu, and C.H. Hou, "Texture-Based Image Indexing in the Process of Lossless Data Compression," in IEE Proc. of Image Signal Process., Vol. 150, No. 3, pp. 198-204, 2003.

[7] J. Kim, and T. Chen, "Combining Static and Dynamic Features Using Neural Networks and Edge Fusion for Video Object," in IEE Proc. of Image Signal Processing, Vol. 150, No. 3, pp. 160-167, June 2003.

[8] M. Bertozzi, A. Broggi, P. Grisleri, A. Tibaldi, and M. Del Rose, "A tool for vision based pedestrian detection performance evaluation," in Proc. of the IEEE Intelligent Vehicles Symposium, University of Parma, Parma, Italy, pp. 784-789, June 14-17, 2004.

[9] A. Broggi, M. Bertozzi, A. Fascioli, and M. Sechill, "Shape-based Pedestrian Detection," in Proc. of the IEEE Intelligent Vehicles Symposium, Dearbon (MI), USA, pp. 215-220, October 3-5, 2000.

[10] A. Bensrhair, M. Bertozzi, A. Broggi, P. Mich´e, S. Mousset, and G. Toulminet, "A Cooperative Approach to Vision-based Vehicle Detection," in Proc. of the IEEE Intelligent Transportation Systems Conference, Oakland (CA), USA, pp. 209-214, August 25-29, 2001.

[11] T.M. Jochem, "Vision Based Tactical Driving," Master Thesis, Carnegie Mellon University, Pittsburgh, January 1996.

[12] A. Broggi, "Parallel and Local Feature Extraction: A Real Time Approach to Road Boundary Detection," IEEE Trans. Image Processing, Vol. 4, No. 2, pp. 217-223, February 1995.

[13] M. Bertozzi, A Broggi, M. Cellario, A. Fascioli, P. Lombardi and M. Porta, "Artificial Vision in Road Vehicles," in proceedings of the IEEE artificial vision in road vehicles, Vol. 90, No. 7, pp. 1258-1271, July 2002.

[14] NCR-iTRAN 8000 & 180e/300e Item Processing Transport Course Participants Guide, Course Nos.19245,20264, NCR Corporation, USA, September 2004, pp. 6.3–6.10, 6A.27-6A.39.

[15] NCR-iTRAN 180e/300e Item Processing Transport On-Site Repair Information, NCR Corporation, USA, B004-0000-0430, 02.00.00, September 2004, pp. 6.11–6.25 (CD ROM).

[16] P. Soille, "Morphological Image Analysis: Principles and Applications," Springer, pp. 164-165, 1999.

[17] N. Baba, L Jain, R. Howlett, "Knowledge Based Intelligent Information Engineering Systems and Allied technologies," pp. 663-668, 2001.

[18] X.D. Jiang, "Image Detail Preserving Filter for Impulsive Noise Attenuation," in IEE Proc. of Image Signal Process., Vol. 150, No. 3, pp. 179-185, June 2003.

[19] K.D. Rao, M.N.S. Swamy and E.I. Plotkin, "Adaptive Filtering Approaches for Color Image and Restoration," in IEE Proc. of Image Signal Process., Vol. 150, No. 3, pp. 179-185, June 2003.

[20] S.M. Hsu and H.K. Burke, "Multisensor Fusion with Hyperspectral Imaging Data: Detection and Classification," *Lincoln Laboratory Journal*, Vol. 14, No. 1, pp. 145-159, 2003.

[21] V. Blanz and T. Vetter, "Face Recognition Based on Fitting a 3D Morphable Model," IEEE Transactions on Pattern Analysis and Machine Intelligence, Vol. 5, No. 9, pp. 1-12, 2003.

[22] J.S. Lee, "Digital image enhancement and noise Filtering by use of local statistics," IEEE Transactions on Pattern Analysis and Machine Intelligence, Vol. 2:165-168, 1980.

Chapter 10

Exercises

10.1 MATRICES

Q1.

In a computer simulation program, matrix A is defined as below:

$$A = \begin{bmatrix} 1 & 2x & 3x & 4x & 5x \\ 2x & x^2 & 1 & 1 & 1 \\ 3x & 1 & x^2 & 1 & 1 \\ 4x & 1 & 1 & x^2 & 1 \\ 5x & 1 & 1 & 1 & x \end{bmatrix};$$

Where x is an integer variable (Example $x = 45$). Calculate the followings:

(a) $A(A + A^T)$

(b) Determinant of A

(c) A^{-1}

(c) $\begin{pmatrix} A & A+1 \\ A+1 & 2A \end{pmatrix}$

(d) Rank of matrix A

(e) Eigen values of A

(f) A^3

Q2.

Solve the system of equations $AX + b = 0$ for all z_i $(i = 1,..,5)$, where

$$X = \begin{pmatrix} z_1 \\ z_2 \\ z_3 \\ z_4 \\ z_5 \end{pmatrix}, \quad b = \begin{pmatrix} 1 \\ 1 \\ 1 \\ 1 \\ 1 \end{pmatrix}$$

(Matrix A has the value of $A = \begin{bmatrix} 1 & 20 & 30 & -10 & 5 \\ 2 & 29 & 1 & 1 & 1 \\ 13 & 1 & 5 & 1 & 1 \\ 4 & 1 & 1 & 25 & 1 \\ 15 & 1 & 1 & 1 & -6 \end{bmatrix}$)

Q3.

Calculate the Hilbert Matrix H with the dimensions (5×5)

Q4.

(a) Determine the value of Y using above H.

$$Y = \begin{pmatrix} 1 & 2 & 2 & 2 & 2 \\ 0 & 1 & 2 & 2 & 2 \\ 0 & 0 & 1 & 2 & 2 \\ 0 & 0 & 0 & 1 & 2 \\ 0 & 0 & 0 & 0 & 1 \end{pmatrix} + H^5 + H^4 + H^3 + H^2 + H$$

(b) What are the outputs on the Matlab command prompt of the followings, after running Q4 (a)?

(i) Y(5,4)

(ii) Y(8,9)

Q5.

Determine the QR decomposition of A such that $A = QR$, where Q is an orthogonal matrix $(QQ^T = I)$, and R is an upper triangular matrix. Use value of A in **Q 1**.

Q6.

Define a matrix which has the dimension of A and all elements are having random values between 50 and 100.

Q7.

Matrix *A* is defined as follows:

$$A = \begin{bmatrix} 1 & 2 & 3 & 4 & 5 \\ -1 & -2 & -3 & -4 & -5 \\ 100 & 200 & 300 & 400 & 500 \end{bmatrix}$$

How do you obtain the matrix B from Matrix A by using a single Matlab instruction?

$$B = \begin{bmatrix} 5 & -5 & 500 \\ 4 & -4 & 400 \\ 3 & -3 & 300 \\ 2 & -2 & 200 \\ 1 & -1 & 100 \end{bmatrix}$$

Q8.

Matrices *P*, *Q* and *R* are defined as follows:

$$P = \begin{bmatrix} 1 & 3 & 3 & 4 & 2 \\ 1 & 2 & 3 & 4 & 5 \\ 10 & 2 & -3 & 4 & -5 \end{bmatrix} \quad ; \quad Q = \begin{bmatrix} 1 & 1 & 0 & 1 & 0 \\ 0 & 1 & 0 & 1 & 1 \\ 1 & 1 & 0 & 0 & 1 \end{bmatrix} \quad ; \quad R = \begin{bmatrix} -1 \\ 2 \\ 5 \end{bmatrix}$$

If the above matrices are associated with the following dynamic system, define the new state variables in order to have first order system.

$$P \begin{bmatrix} \ddot{x}_1 \\ \ddot{x}_2 \\ \ddot{x}_3 \\ \ddot{x}_4 \\ \ddot{x}_5 \end{bmatrix} + Q \begin{bmatrix} \dot{x}_1 \\ \dot{x}_2 \\ \dot{x}_3 \\ \dot{x}_4 \\ \dot{x}_5 \end{bmatrix} + \begin{bmatrix} x_1 + x_2 \\ x_3 \\ x_5 + x_4 \end{bmatrix} = R$$

Q9.

Matrix *A* is defined as follows:

$$A = \begin{bmatrix} 1 & 2 & 3 & 4 & 5 \\ -1 & -2 & -3 & -4 & 5 \\ -10 & 20 & 30 & 40 & 50 \end{bmatrix}$$

How do you obtain the singular value decomposition from Matrix A by using a single Matlab instruction?

Show that the following matrices can be obtained under the standard notation.

$$U = \begin{bmatrix} -0.0960 & 0.0403 & -0.9946 \\ 0.0055 & -0.9991 & -0.0411 \\ -0.9954 & -0.0094 & 0.0957 \end{bmatrix}$$

$$S = \begin{bmatrix} 74.5069 & 0 & 0 & 0 & 0 \\ 0 & 7.4107 & 0 & 0 & 0 \\ 0 & 0 & 01.9506 & 0 & 0 \end{bmatrix}$$

$$V = \begin{bmatrix} 0.1322 & 0.1530 & -0.9793 & -0.0000 & -0.0000 \\ -0.2699 & 0.2551 & 0.0034 & -0.4252 & 0.8254 \\ -0.4049 & 0.3826 & 0.0051 & -0.6091 & -0.5645 \\ -0.5398 & 0.5102 & 0.0068 & 0.6694 & 0.0107 \\ -0.6740 & -0.7105 & -0.2020 & -0.0000 & 0.0000 \end{bmatrix}$$

Q10.

Matrices A and B are defined as follows:

$$A = \begin{bmatrix} 1 & 1 & 3 & 4 & 5 \\ 1 & -2 & 3 & 4 & 5 \\ 1 & 4 & -1 & 9 & 7 \end{bmatrix} \quad ; \quad B = \begin{bmatrix} 1 & 1 & 3 \\ 1 & -2 & 3 \\ 1 & 4 & -1 \end{bmatrix}$$

Using Matlab, what the results that you expect if you compute A^{-3} and B^{-3}?

10.2. GRAPHICS

Q1.

Plot the following three graphs with the Bessel function which is available in Matlab.

(a) Y_1=bessel(1,x);
Y_2=bessel(2,x);
Y_3=bessel(3,x);

Where $x = \begin{vmatrix} 0 & 0.2 & 0.4 & ... & t \end{vmatrix}^T$ and *t* represents a two digit number.

(b) Name X and Y axis

(c) Title your graph and show the scale properly

Q2.

Following MATLAB codes (Program Q2) will produce a 3D graph as shown in Figure Q2. Explain all the coding instructions (Program Q2) in your own worlds.

```
k=5;
n=2^k -1;
theta=pi*(-n:2:n)/n;
phi=(pi/2)*(-n:2:n)/n;
X=[cos(phi)]'*[cos(theta)];
Y=[cos(phi)]'*[sin(theta)];
Z=[sin(phi)]'*ones(size(theta));
colormap([0 0 0;1 1 1]);
C=hadamard(2^k);
surf(X,Y,Z,C);
axis square;
```

Program Q2

Note that you will obtain a graphics object as shown in Figure Q2

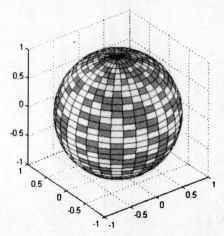

Figure Q2

Q3.

Plot the curve using **polar(sin(x),cos(x),'r')**, where *x* represents the following vector. Title the graph with proper a name and you may select the value *t*.

$$x = \begin{vmatrix} 0 & 0.8 & 1.4 & ... & t \end{vmatrix}^T$$

Q4.

What is the output of the following program and explain the functional outcomes of the steps.

```
th=(0:127)/128*2*pi;

x=cos(th)+th;y=sin(th);

f=abs(fft(ones(5,1),128));

stem3(x,y,f', 'r','d','fill');

view([-65 30])
```

Program Q4

Q5.

What are the outputs of the following two programs and compare the results obtained in two programs if they are different?

```
% PROGRAM 1 of Q5

x=0:0.2:10;
y=0:0.2:10;

[X,Y]=meshgrid(x,y);
Z=2*sin(sqrt(X.^2 + Y.^2));

contour(x,y,Z);

mesh(X,Y,Z);

surfc(X,Y,Z);

xlabel('x1');
ylabel('x2');

zlabel('Function Value');
grid on;

% PROGRAM 2 of Q5

g = 0:0.2:10;
[x,y] = meshgrid(g);
z = 2*sin(sqrt(x.^2 + y.^2));
mesh(z);
```

Program Q5

Q6.

What are the steps that you need to generate the following output (see Figure Q6)?

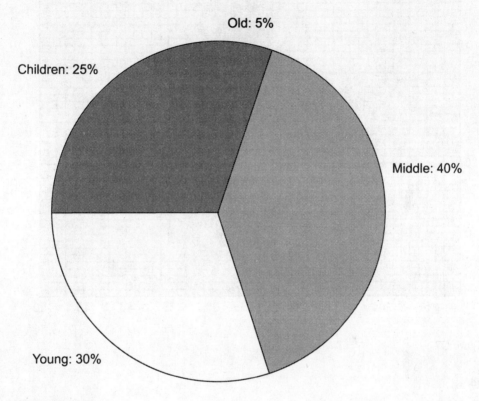

Figure Q6

Q7.

Following Matlab code generates the graph in Figure Q7. Explain the algorithm used to generate this graph.

```
>> [X,Y,Z] = peaks(50);
>> pcolor(Z);
```

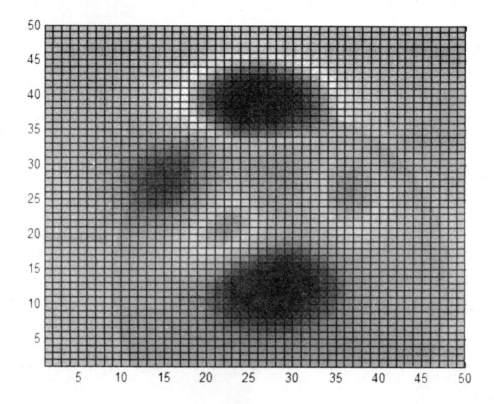

Figure Q7

Q8.

QUIVER plots velocity vectors as arrows with components (u, v) at the points (x, y). What are the additional codes that you need to generate the following output (see Figure Q8)? You may use the codes in Program Q8.

```
[X,Y,Z] = peaks(-2:0.25:2);

[U,V] = gradient(Z, 0.25);

contour(X,Y,Z,10);
```

Program Q8

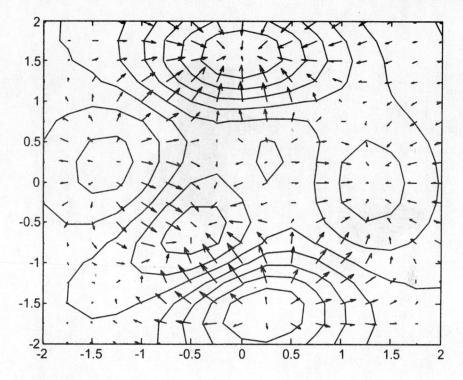

Figure Q8

Q9.

Following Matlab code generates the graph in Figure Q9. Explain the algorithm used to generate this graph.

```
A=[1 2 3 4 5 ;4 5 11 2 15;0 2 12 3 6];

bar3(A)

xlabel('row'),ylabel('column'),zlabel('entries')

set(gca,'Xtick',[1:9])

colormap hsv
```

Program Q9

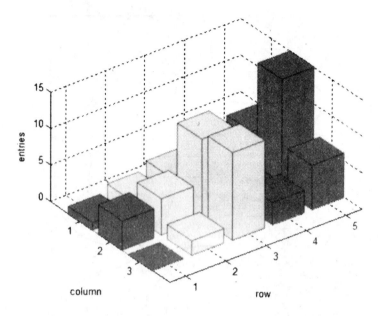

Figure Q9

Q10.

What is the output of the following program and explain the functional outcomes of the steps.

```
subplot(2,3,1)
x = -3:0.3:3; y = -3:0.3:3;
[X,Y]=meshgrid(x,y);
[theat,R] = cart2pol(X,Y); Z = sinc(R);
contourf(peaks(30), 10); colorbar
grid on
title('Function = Peaks: (CONTOURF & COLORBAR)')


subplot(2,3,2)
plot3(X,Y,Z);grid on; axis([-3 3 -3 3 -1 1]);
title('Function = Sinc - (PLOT3)')
```

(Contd.)

```
subplot(2,3,3)
waterfall(membrane(1));
title('L-shaped Membrane - (WATERFALL)')


subplot(2,3,4)
contour3(peaks(30), 25);
title('Function = Peaks - (CONTOUR3)')


subplot(2,3,5)
mesh(X,Y,Z)
axis([-3 3 -3 3 -1 1])
title('Function = Sinc - (MESH)')


subplot(2,3,6)
surf(membrane(1))
title('L-shaped Membrane - (SURF)')
```

Program Q10

10.3 ANALYTICAL SOLUTIONS

Q1.

Find all the possible solutions to the following equation using a computer aided graphical method.

$$Ax^3 \sin x + x^2 + A = 0$$

Where A is an integer number which has two digits.

Q2.

Evaluate the value of the following integration

$$\int_{-2.5}^{2.5} \cos^2(10x)\exp(-x^2)dx$$

How will you improve the accuracy, if you use any numerical computation?

Q3.

Write a program to create a data file to plot $f(x)$, where

$$f(x) = \cos^2(10x)\exp(-x^2)$$

The file name should reflect your name/index number and the format should be as follows: (Data range: From x= -5 to x= +5, you may select a desired sampling interval)

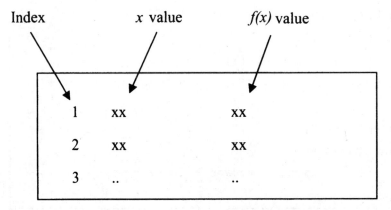

Index x value $f(x)$ value

1	xx	xx
2	xx	xx
3	..	..

Using the above created data file, plot $f(x)$, taking the range from x = -3 to x = +3

Q4.

Explain the flow control structures provided by Matlab in order to address logical and iterative problems.

Q5.

Following differential equation represents the motion of a forced spring system.

$$\frac{d^2 y}{dt^2} + 25y = \cos 4t$$
$$y(0) = 0; \quad y'(0) = 0$$

(a) Show that the response is in the shape of Figure Q5(a).

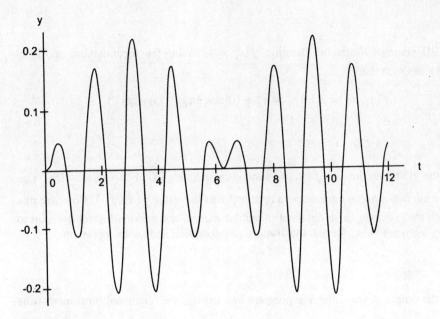

Figure Q5(a)

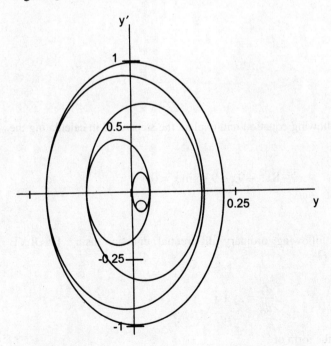

Figure Q5(b)

(b) What is the importance of plotting the graph $\dot{y}$ vs y in real engineering applications?

Q6.

Plot the 3D graph of *Rastrigin's* function $f(x_1, x_2)$, having few local maxima and local minima values such that

$$f(x_1, x_2) = 20 + x_1^2 + x_2^2 + 10(\cos 2\pi x_1 + \cos 2\pi x_2)$$
$$-1 \leq x_1 \leq 1$$
$$-1 \leq x_2 \leq 1$$

Find the global minima of $f(x_1, x_2)$ and corresponding (x_1, x_2) values. (Hint: You may generate two random numbers at a time and find the value $f(x_1, x_2)$. Compare that value with the previous value obtained in similar manner and make a logical decision to get a more accurate value. Repeat this for a large population and get the optimum.

Q7.

What is the output of the following program and explain the functional outcomes of the steps.

```
r = zeros(1,32);
for n = 3:32
    r(n) = rank(magic(n));
end
bar(r);
```

Q8.

Find the real roots of the following equation and explain the steps used in calculating the roots.

$$x^4 + x^3 - 8x^2 - 9x - 9 - \sin x = 0$$

Q9.

Find the solution to the following ordinary differential equation using DSOLVE command in Matlab.

$$\frac{dy}{dx} = xy + x$$

Prove that the solution is in the form of

$$y = -1 + C \exp(x^2 / 2),$$

Here, C is a constant.

Q10.

Find the solution to the following ordinary differential equation using DSOLVE command in Matlab.

$$\frac{d^2 y}{dx^2} + 10\frac{dy}{dx} + y = \sin x$$

Hint: You may use the following Matlab codes.

```
>> eqn1 = 'D2y + 10*Dy + y = sin(x)';
>> inits1 = 'y(0)=0, Dy(0)=1';
>> y=dsolve(eqn1,inits1,'x')
```

10.4 TRANSFORMATIONS

Q1.

Find the Laplace transform of the followings using LAPLACE command in Matlab.

1. $f(t) = t^2 + \sin t$
2. $g(t) = f(t) + \cos t + u(t)$
3. $h(t) = g(t) + \delta(t)$

Hint: you may use the following codes in obtaining the solution.

```
>> syms t;
>> laplace(t^2 +sin(t))
```

Q2.

Find the inverse Laplace transform of the followings using ILAPLACE command in Matlab.

1. $F(s) = \dfrac{1}{(s+1)}$

2. $G(s) = F(s) + \dfrac{(3s-5)}{(s-1)}$

3. $H(s) = G(s) + \dfrac{(s+1)}{(s^2 + 2s + 2)}$

Hint: you may use the following codes in obtaining the solution.

```
>> syms s;
>> ilaplace(1/(s+1))
```

Q3.

How do you define several functions separately and obtain the inverse Laplace transform in a single command line?

Hint: You may use the following command

```
>> syms F S;
```

Q4.

Find the output of the following Matlab codes in Program Q4

```
syms F S;

syms G S;

F=2/(s*(s-5));

G=4/(s*(s+5));

ilaplace(F+G)
```

Program Q4

Q5.

Obtain the inverse Laplace transform of the following function using partial fractions of $F(s)$.

$$F(s) = \frac{(4s^2 + 4s + 4)}{s^2(s + 3s + 2)}$$

Hint: You may use the following program codes in obtaining the answer to Q5.

```
num=[0 0 4 4 4];
den=[1 3 2 0 0];
[r,p,k]=residue(n,d)
```

Program Q5

$$\left(F(s) = \frac{-3}{s+2} + \frac{4}{s+1} - \frac{1}{s} + \frac{2}{s^2} \right)$$

Q6.

Obtain the Fourier transform of the following function using the following Matlab codes.
Explain the steps used.

```
n = [0:149];

x1 = cos(2*pi*n/10)+ exp(-2*pi*n/10);

N = 2048;

X = abs(fft(x1,N));

X = fftshift(X);

F = [-N/2:N/2-1]/N;

plot(F,X),

xlabel('Frequency / f s')
```

Program Q6

Q7.

Obtain the Fourier transform of the following function using the following Matlab codes.

```
n = [0:29];

x1 = sin(2*pi*n/10); % 3 periods of the sine wave

x2 = [x1 x1]; % 6 periods of the sine wave

x3 = [x1 x1 x1]; % 9 periods of the sine wave

N = 2048;
```

(Contd.)

```
X1 = abs(fft(x1,N));

X2 = abs(fft(x2,N));

X3 = abs(fft(x3,N));

F = [0:N-1]/N;

subplot(3,1,1)

plot(F,X1),title('3 periods'),axis([0 1 0 50])

subplot(3,1,2)

plot(F,X2),title('6 periods'),axis([0 1 0 50])

subplot(3,1,3)

plot(F,X3),title('9 periods'),axis([0 1 0 50])
```

Program Q7

Explain the reasons to have different amplitudes under these three functions.

Q8.

In a simulation you need to calculate the parameters of a Fourier transform. Obtain the Fourier transform and associated graphs using the following Matlab codes.

```
fs = 10000;
% sampling rate

t = 0:1/fs:0.1;
% sampling instants

x = sin(2*pi*1500*t) + sin(2*pi*4000*t);
% two sinusoids

% perform 1000-point transform

y = fft(x,1000);
% y contains 1000 complex amplitudes

y = y(1:500);
% just look at first half
```

(Contd.)

```
m = abs(y);
% m = magnitude of sinusoids

p = unwrap(angle(y));
% p = phase of sinusoids, unwrap()

% copes with 360 degree jumps
% plot spectrum 0..fs/2

f = (0:499)*fs/1000;
% calculate Hertz values

subplot(2,1,1), plot(f,m);
 % plot magnitudes

ylabel('Abs. Magnitude'), grid on;

subplot(2,1,2), plot(f,p*180/pi);
% plot phase in degrees

ylabel('Phase [Degrees]'), grid on;
xlabel('Frequency [Hertz]');
```

Program Q8

Q9.

Obtain the Fourier transform of the following data for the function F using Matlab.

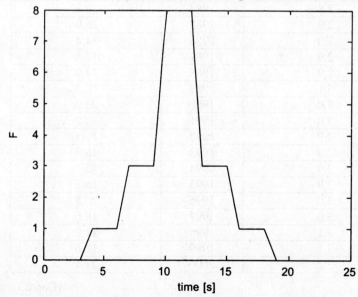

```
>> F=[0 0 0 1 1 1 3 3 3 8 8 8 3 3 3 1 1 1 0 0 0];
>> plot(F)
>> ylabel('F')
>> xlabel('time [s]')
```

Q10.

Taking examples, explain the other transformation facilities provided by Matlab in order to carry out simulations.

10.5 MODELING AND FORECASTING

Q1.

Crude oil is a fossil fuel or non-renewable source and it was made naturally from decaying plants and animals living in ancient seas millions of years ago. Table Q1 shows approximated crude oil prices in a certain market from year 1946 to 2008. Develop a model to predict the crude oil prices for the next 10 year period.

Table Q1: Crude Oil Prices in US $.

Year	Crude Oil Price (US $)	Year	Crude Oil Price (US $)
1946	1.6	1978	15.0
1947	2.2	1979	25.1
1948	2.8	1980	37.4
1949	2.8	1981	35.8
1950	2.8	1982	31.8
1951	2.8	1983	29.1
1952	2.8	1984	28.8
1953	2.9	1985	26.9
1954	3.0	1986	14.4
1955	2.9	1987	17.8
1956	2.9	1988	14.9
1957	3.1	1989	18.3
1958	3.0	1990	23.2
1959	3.0	1991	20.2
1960	2.9	1992	19.3
1961	2.9	1993	16.8
1962	2.9	1994	15.7
1963	2.9	1995	16.8
1964	3.0	1996	20.5
1965	3.0	1997	18.6
1966	3.1	1998	11.9
1967	3.1	1999	16.6
1968	3.2	2000	27.4

(Contd.)

Year	Crude Oil Price (US $)	Year	Crude Oil Price (US $)
1969	3.3	2001	23.0
1970	3.4	2002	22.8
1971	3.6	2003	27.7
1972	3.6	2004	37.7
1973	4.8	2005	50.0
1974	9.4	2006	58.3
1975	12.2	2007	64.2
1976	13.1	2008	120
1977	14.4	2009	–

Q2.

Table Q1 shows the approximated world population from year 1950 to 2007. Using a neural network, develop a model to predict the world population in year 2010. When you develop your model you may use certain percentage of this data for validation purposes.

Table Q1: World Population.

Year	Population	Year	Population
1950	2,555,948,654	1979	4,371,180,108
1951	2,593,708,555	1980	4,446,260,631
1952	2,635,742,254	1981	4,521,666,800
1953	2,681,052,111	1982	4,600,856,834
1954	2,728,990,073	1983	4,681,966,411
1955	2,780,413,010	1984	4,761,766,338
1956	2,833,343,848	1985	4,842,981,705
1957	2,889,141,358	1986	4,926,041,825
1958	2,945,617,330	1987	5,011,979,781
1959	2,997,920,881	1988	5,098,520,091
1960	3,039,962,148	1989	5,185,002,390
1961	3,080,693,027	1990	5,272,635,763
1962	3,136,636,618	1991	5,356,364,188
1963	3,206,104,053	1992	5,439,616,354
1964	3,277,169,635	1993	5,520,491,240
1965	3,346,090,254	1994	5,600,321,230
1966	3,416,212,203	1995	5,680,970,858
1967	3,485,843,329	1996	5,760,822,316
1968	3,557,577,129	1997	5,839,712,012
1969	3,632,093,337	1998	5,917,751,492
1970	3,707,183,055	1999	5,994,573,609
1971	3,784,506,549	2000	6,070,587,733
1972	3,860,549,542	2001	6,146,294,339
1973	3,936,068,571	2002	6,221,194,426
1974	4,010,484,962	2003	6,295,971,218

(Contd.)

Year	Population	Year	Population
1975	4,082,959,684	2004	6,371,333,715
1976	4,153,925,718	2005	6,447,427,283
1977	4,225,464,920	2006	6,523,764,154
1978	4,296,918,082	2007	6,600,411,051

Q3.

Ho do you use Matlab System Identification Toolbox for obtaining a solution to the problem in Q2.

Q4.

Obtain system identification model for the following function which is generated by a cosine input using the following Matlab codes. How do you improve the program Q4?

```
t=1:1:200;

u=cos(t);
t1=rand(200);

y=cos(t+t1(:,1)') + 100*exp(-t);

data =[y', u'];

datad = detrend(data,0);

datae = datad([1:100],:);

datav = datad([101:200],:)

% ARX model

na = 1;
nb = 3;
nk = 1;

arxmodel= arx(datae, [na nb nk]);

compare(datav, arxmodel,1);
figure;
```

(Contd.)

```
resid(datav, arxmodel);

present(arxmodel);

ssmodel =
n4sid(datae,3,'Focus','Simulation');
figure;

compare(datav, ssmodel);
figure;

resid(datav, ssmodel);
present(ssmodel);
```

Program Q4

Q5.

Table Q5 shows the truth table for the combinational logic output for a four input system. Show that the output is equivalent to $Y = \overline{(AB + CD)}$. Using Matlab Simulink, implement the expression $Y = \overline{(AB + CD)}$ in the both forms Logical Operator Blocks and a Combinatorial Logic Block.

A	B	C	D	Y
0	0	0	0	1
0	0	0	1	1
0	0	1	0	1
0	0	1	1	0
0	1	0	0	1
0	1	0	1	1
0	1	1	0	1
0	1	1	1	0
1	0	0	0	1
1	0	0	1	1
1	0	1	0	1
1	0	1	1	0
1	1	0	0	0
1	1	0	1	0
1	1	1	0	0
1	1	1	1	0

Q6.

Consider the following nonlinear system.

$$\dot{x}_1 = -x_2$$
$$\dot{x}_2 = x_1 + x_2^3 - 3x_2$$

1. Linearize the above system around an equilibrium point.
2. Comment on the stability of the unforced system.
3. Design a controller to a unit input which brings the close loop stability.

Q7.

In the following system of equations, θ and ϕ are variables whereas τ is the input to the system. Here, m, l, g, and I_m are constants. Define the state variables and obtain a state space model after linearizing around a selected point.

$$\ddot{\theta} = \frac{(l\dot{\phi}^2 \cos\theta - g)\sin\theta}{l}$$
$$\ddot{\phi} = \frac{(\tau - 2ml^2\dot{\phi}\dot{\theta}\sin\theta\cos\theta)}{I_m + ml^2\sin^2\theta}$$

Q8.

Consider the system shown in Figure Q8. The mass m is connected to the point O with the aid of a sting having a length of l. The axis of rotation is OZ and mass is hinged at O.

The input to the rotating body is the horizontal force H which is generated by the fan run by a simple CD motor. In order to keep θ at a constant angle, find the angular velocity (ω) of the rotating body. Obtain a model which represents the states of the system and the input. Note here that the friction and aerodynamic drag forces may be neglected.

Q9.

Discuss the advantages and disadvantages of different software tools available for system identification and modeling.

Q10.

Discuss the advantages and disadvantages between open source and commercially available software tools for computer simulations in general.

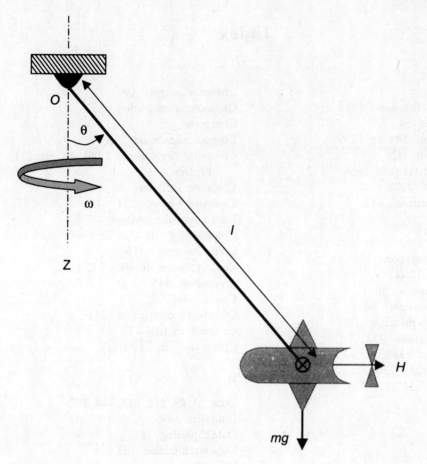

Figure Q8

Index